**IN ST JAMES'S ⬚
AS THE INH⬚
THEIR SUPPER⬚
HEARD A TER⬚
THE PERETTI FLAT.**

Men paused over their perusal of the evening paper to listen; women hovered over boiling pans of pasta, ears straining to hear what was said. Even the children, who usually played noisy games of hide-and-seek on the landings and stairwells, now stood in silent groups, somehow sensing the depth of anger emanating from number 104. They could hear the raised voice of Tony Peretti and the deeper tones of his father; but what had halted everyone in their tracks was the third voice in the argument, for it was Marionetta – quiet little Marionetta with the scarred face, who hardly looked anyone in the eye nowadays, and kept herself to herself – and here she was, yelling like a fishwife for everyone to hear! ...

ABOUT THE AUTHOR

Among other things, Lilie Ferrari was a waitress in the South of France and a teacher in California before gaining a Master's degree in French literature, writing a thesis about Flaubert and suicide. She then went on to more cheerful work at the British Film Institute, where she worked in the Television Unit, taking particular interest in popular dramas and soap operas. From there she went to the BBC, script-editing *Eastenders*. Currently a full-time scriptwriter for television, she lives in Essex with her partner. She has one son and is a reluctant grandmother. Her first novel, *Fortunata*, inspired by the history of her own immigrant family, is also published by Signet.

LILIE FERRARI

ANGELFACE

A SIGNET BOOK

SIGNET

Published by the Penguin Group
Penguin Books Ltd, 27 Wrights Lane, London W8 5TZ, England
Penguin Books USA Inc., 375 Hudson Street, New York, New York 10014, USA
Penguin Books Australia Ltd, Ringwood, Victoria, Australia
Penguin Books Canada Ltd, 10 Alcorn Avenue, Toronto, Ontario, Canada M4V 3B2
Penguin Books (NZ) Ltd, 182–190 Wairau Road, Auckland 10, New Zealand

Penguin Books Ltd, Registered Offices: Harmondsworth, Middlesex, England

First published by Michael Joseph 1994
Published in Signet 1995
1 3 5 7 9 10 8 6 4 2

'Smoke Gets in Your Eyes' copyright © reproduced by kind permission of Polygram
Music Publishing Ltd, 347–353 Chiswick High Road, London W4 4HS.
'Embraceable You', 'Sentimental Journey', 'Accentuate the Positive'
copyright © Warner Chappell Music Ltd, London W1Y 3FA.
Reproduced by permission of International Music Publications Ltd

Printed in England by Clays Ltd, St Ives plc

This book is dedicated to all Italians who have worked or played in Soho, and in particular to my father, Stan Ferrari, my aunt and uncle, Olive and Bruno Besagni, and to Elena Salvoni and Romano Viazzani, with thanks for generously sharing their memories with me.

Author's note

Saint Martha has traditionally been regarded as the patron both of housewives and of servants, because she had charge of her brother's house, and because she waited on Jesus. In 1963 the Pope also declared her to be the patron saint of Italian hoteliers, their staff, waiters and waitresses.

CHAPTER ONE

1947

A pigeon, pecking hopefully on the pavement, turned its head sideways, its tiny eye gleaming, and watched the girl in the window.

'Marionetta! Wake up, girl! Three teas and two ham sandwiches over by the window!'

Francesca Peretti, frail and bad-tempered, was glowering at her daughter from her perch at the sink piled with dirty dishes. The café was full to overflowing, and people clamoured for attention at the counter.

Marionetta, who had been leaning in the doorway gazing wistfully out at the crowds hurrying by, returned to earth with a jolt. The old man at the corner table watched her, his face thoughtful as he stirred his tea.

'Sorry, Mamma,' she said, penitent, turning back into the steamy interior of the Imperial Café. The last thing she wanted to do was upset her mother, so pale and ill. Pushing back an unruly curl of black hair, she hastened to the counter where her father Tomasso was frantically buttering a mountain of sliced white bread.

'Two spam, three cheese and tomato!' he yelled, too preoccupied with the orders to reprimand his daydreaming daughter; but his wife was still frowning at the sink, her damp, reddened hands on her hips.

'More customers than we've had all summer, and she's

staring out of the window!' Francesca muttered, cross. 'And where's Antonio, for heaven's sake?'

Her younger son Mario, arriving at the counter with a trayload of dirty teacups, grinned at her.

'Don't you dare,' she said, smiling in spite of herself, 'Don't you dare sing at me . . .'

But it was too late. Mario had his arm round his mother's bony shoulders, his cheek next to hers. 'You've got to accent-uate the positive,' he crooned. 'Elim-inate the negative . . .' Customers turned and listened, as they always did when Mario sang, and Marionetta paused by the window table, proud, listening too.

'He ought to be on the radio,' someone at the table said.

'That voice – like an angel,' Marionetta heard one of the regulars remark. She turned to him wryly as Mario's voice soared. 'Latch on to the affirmative, don't mess with Mr In-between . . .'

'He may sound like an angel,' she said, mopping the table briskly, 'pity he doesn't behave like one!' But she stopped to listen again. The old man in the corner smiled to himself. What a picture she made, slender in her black waitress's dress, standing there listening to her brother sing. She reminded him of another girl, another time, another place . . .

Mario finished his song with a flourish and a mock bow, and was applauded by his admirers at the counter and hugged by his relenting mother. At sixteen, Marionetta mused, he still had the baby-faced charm of a boy rather than the aquiline, manly good looks of his older brother, the missing Antonio.

As if on cue, the tall figure of Antonio appeared from behind her and whisked away the cloth she was using to wipe the tables.

'Tony!' she protested. 'I was –'

2

'Sssh!' He was already scrubbing away at a table his sister had just cleaned, much to the bemusement of the family of four seated around it, trying to eat their fruit cake in peace. 'Mamma won't notice I've been away . . .'

And sure enough, Francesca chose that moment to look up from her sink of steaming crockery and saw Antonio industriously cleaning. 'There you are!' she called. 'Good boy, Antonio, you can finish early.'

'Mamma!' Marionetta was indignant. 'I've been here since six this morning . . .'

'And so you should be.' Her mother's voice was brisk, brooking no argument. 'Your place is here, learning the work. Antonio's a man, he has other business.'

Antonio smirked at his sister. Angrily, she snatched the cloth from his hands and turned to another table, as Antonio sauntered to the counter and disappeared out into the back of the café to collect his coat.

'More tea, Nonno?' she asked. She was standing at the table in the corner, where the old man sat smoking a cigarette and coughing. He scowled at his grand-daughter, in an effort to hide the flood of affection that he had been feeling for her, and the mixed emotions he had experienced when he remembered that other girl, who looked so much like Marionetta, but who had long since gone.

'Filthy English drink,' he said, spluttering in between gulps at his cigarette. 'Coffee – proper coffee.'

Marionetta looked down at him, despairing. 'Nonno, you know I can't. Mamma has forbidden coffee. She says it'll kill you.'

The old man coughed some more. 'I'm seventy-one,' he said. 'Time to die.'

'Nonsense!' Marionetta swept his cup away. 'I'll get you more tea.'

Up at the counter, her father, his mountain of sandwiches

3

almost complete, glanced over at the old man in the corner, irritated. 'Why does he have to come here today of all days?' The question, although directed at Marionetta, did not require an answer. 'Our busiest day and he takes up a whole table.'

'It's still his café, Papa,' Marionetta reminded her father gently, 'and he wanted to be part of today – you know, part of the celebrations.'

'Why?' Tomasso handed her a plate of bread and butter. 'Table Four. Your grandfather hates the Royal Family. He's an old fascist.'

'He just pretends to be,' Marionetta said, handing the plate to Mario, who was passing. 'Table Four ... You know he wouldn't have missed today for anything ...'

The door of the café crashed shut as the family who had been by the window left. The queue at the counter had diminished, and for a moment the café seemed almost quiet.

'There!' Marionetta poured another cup of tea for her grandfather. 'The rush is over now.' She poured a cup for herself and went over to join the old man, who was lighting another cigarette.

'Nonno!' She was despairing. 'You shouldn't, not with your chest –'

'Don't nag, girl, you sound just like your mother.' He was secretly pleased that she had brought her tea over to sit with him. He had a definite soft spot for Marionetta, even though she was a girl.

She was leaning back in her chair, exhausted after a long day, her eyes closed, and he was able to study her face surreptitiously. Yes, she had exactly the same fine bones as Giulietta had had, the same arched brows and full mouth, the same habit of biting her lower lip when she was angry ...

4

'Have I got a smudge on my nose?' Marionetta was looking at him wide-eyed.

He leaned across and touched her cheek. 'Just a bit of jam,' he said gruffly.

'What a day!' Marionetta sipped at her tea. 'It's been wonderful, hasn't it? I just wish I could have got away and seen the coach . . .'

Princess Elizabeth had married Lieutenant Philip Mountbatten that day, and the streets of London were packed with people who had come to see the procession to Westminster Abbey. Even the sharp November chill had not dampened the spirits of Londoners who desperately needed cheering up after a long and dreary war. The cafés of Soho were doing splendid business, and the Imperial Café, situated in the middle of Old Compton Street, had benefited from those weary procession-goers who had wandered away from the crowds on Charing Cross Road and Tottenham Court Road in search of a sandwich and a cup of tea.

The Peretti family had not worked so hard since before the war. Even on VE day, the café had not been so crowded. Marionetta surveyed the floor of the café glumly: the paper flowers, the discarded flags, the squashed crumbs and the stained lino. It would be her job tonight to mop the floor and render it spotless before she was allowed to turn off the lights and take her weary body home to the family's cramped flat in St James's Residences. Princess Elizabeth and the glamour of the day seemed very far removed from the back-breaking hours she had spent that day in the café. She sighed.

Her grandfather caught the sigh and misunderstood its origin. 'I know,' he said conspiratorially, following her eyes. 'That lino – *orribile* – dreadful. The old wooden boards – they were fine. Just a quick sweep and a good scrub once a week, that was all the floor needed then . . .'

Marionetta smiled at him ruefully. She patted his wrinkled old hand. 'You're not very happy about Papa's changes, are you, Nonno?' She stirred her tea wearily, looking round at the place she knew better than the living-room at home. Papa had painted the walls blue, the paintwork white, and Mamma had made bright red curtains for the windows. It was all very patriotic, to go with the café's new name. But a change in the colour scheme could not change for Marionetta the dreadful, grinding boredom of day after day spent serving snacks to the people of Soho. She knew every stain in the sink, every crack in the lino, every cup on the groaning shelves behind Mamma's sink. And to increase her frustration, she also knew that *out there* on the streets of Soho, there was a teeming, exciting bohemian world, full of eccentrics, women of the night, artists, poets, painters, madmen! They passed by the windows of the café early in the morning as they emerged from their mysterious late-night activities, they reappeared on the streets late in the afternoon, bleary-eyed from sleep, and she glimpsed them as exotic shadows late at night, flitting past in the gloom, intent on lives that seemed so much more exciting than her own.

Occasionally they would actually come into the Imperial for a late-night cup of coffee or an early-morning bacon sandwich, and Marionetta would stare at them, transfixed, until her mother nudged her crossly and told her to stop daydreaming. Sometimes Papa would hurriedly cross to the door as they entered and murmur something apologetic and ask them to leave.

'Why?' Marionetta would ask, angry. 'They can pay like everyone else!'

'Your mother doesn't want their kind in here,' Papa would say, nervous, refusing to give further explanations. But Marionetta knew who these people were, she had not

6

lived in Soho all her life for nothing. These were the pimps
and the prostitutes, the people whose names appeared in
the newspapers, who lived off 'immoral earnings' and
made their money from sex. Marionetta, good Catholic
girl that she was, knew that these were sinners, wicked
souls beyond redemption. So why then did they inspire in
her such envy, these women with their fox furs and glossy
red lips, these men in their beautifully cut suits and their
two-tone shoes? And why was theirs the only café that
refused to serve these people and got away with it?

She stirred her tea thoughtfully. Perhaps it was because
her family were Sicilians, she mused. After all, they seemed
to be the only Sicilians for miles around. All their neighbours in St James's Residences came from Southern Italy,
to be sure, but none from Sicily. The other Italian families
in the tenement block where they lived were all *compaisani*,
all shared friends and relatives from the same area. Only the
Perettis were different, having no family along the passage
or down the hall or even in Clerkenwell, London's 'Little
Italy'. Marionetta knew that everyone feared Sicilians; they
believed everyone from Sicily was in the Mafia. It was ridiculous – as if anyone could seriously imagine that Tomasso
and his hard-working family, slaving away in this little café,
could be anything other than hard-working immigrants
trying to survive . . . Marionetta smiled grimly to herself.
If anyone in her family was in the Mafia, she thought, they
must be superhuman, because they all worked so hard and
for such long hours that there was no time even for
pleasure, let alone to join the Cosa Nostra . . .

Her thoughts were interrupted by the arrival of her
brother at the table, his coat slung over his shoulders.

'Bye, sis,' he said, grinning. 'If I see the Princess I'll send
her your regards, shall I?'

Their grandfather stirred and frowned. 'When my

Marionetta gets married,' he said, 'her wedding will be ten times more beautiful.'

'Nonno!' Marionetta laughed. 'I'm only seventeen!'

'Princess Elizabeth's only twenty-one.' Antonio's face was solemn, but he was nudging his sister, unseen by the old man. 'Only four years, Marionetta! Time's running out . . .'

She threw a napkin at him, cross. 'And I'll be a spinster for ever, stuck in this café all hours of the day and night!' she said, trying to sound good-humoured. 'Go and play with your silly friends and leave the women to do the work, as usual.'

Antonio headed towards the door, whistling, waving a careless goodbye in the general direction of the counter. 'Ciao, Mamma!' he called to Francesca, and then he was gone, the door slamming shut behind him, making the bell dance and jangle as he went.

The old man frowned. 'Where's he going?' he asked.

Marionetta stood up stiffly, her tea finished. 'Who knows? Out with his policemen friends again, I expect.'

Her grandfather snorted derisively. Marionetta patted him on the shoulder as she retrieved his teacup. Antonio was going to join the police force, and this meant one less person to help in the café. For the old man Franco Peretti, it meant the death of a cherished dream that he had brought with him from Sicily – to start a business and hand it on to his son, and then to his first grandson. For Marionetta it merely meant the prospect of fewer helping hands and more hard work.

She glanced up as the doorbell jangled again. It was a huge party of procession-goers, elated and noisy, in search of a sandwich before moving on to a pub. Marionetta forced a welcoming smile. 'Good afternoon!' she said. 'There's a large table over by the window, and another one there by the counter . . .'

*

It was getting late. Marionetta felt as though her knees would buckle if one more customer came through the door. Her dark curls stuck damply to her forehead, and the rough material of her dress scratched at her skin in the heat from the stove. If only it was time to close! But it was still early, even though darkness had fallen outside and the flashing lights of Soho were illuminated; and still the customers came and went relentlessly. As the clock struck eight, Francesca Peretti wearily put on her coat and called for her younger son. It was time for her to go home and do the washing, and it was time for Mario to go to his singing lesson.

'Mamma, your collar's in a muddle.' Marionetta crossed the café and rearranged her mother's coat collar, trying to hide her concern at the worn face so close to hers. Impulsively, she kissed the faded cheek, and was shocked to feel her mother's flesh burn against her mouth. Francesca was feverish. She had probably been like this all day.

'What was that for?' her mother asked, surprised at the kiss.

Marionetta shrugged. 'No reason. Will you promise me something?'

Her mother raised an eyebrow, waiting. 'Will you promise me you'll sit and have a cup of tea and a rest before you start the washing, Mamma? You're exhausted . . .'

'*Come mai?*' Francesca was irritable, 'Whatever for? I'll just get to bed even later.' She shook Marionetta away. 'Are you coming too, Papa?' She asked as she headed for the door, pushing Mario ahead of her.

Marionetta's grandfather was still at his place in the corner, nodding sleepily over a small brandy. The old man shook his head, stubborn. 'I'll stay. It's early yet . . .'

Marionetta's mother made an irritated noise. 'And who's going to get you home if you feel tired before closing time?'

9

'I won't get tired! In fact I may even help Tomasso behind the counter for a bit.'

Marionetta grinned at her long-suffering father, busy frying potatoes at the stove. 'Papa would be very pleased to have extra help, wouldn't you, Papa?' she said, teasing, as Francesca and Mario left.

Tomasso pulled a face at her through the heat haze of the chip fat. 'Of course you can stay, Papa,' he said wearily, ladling the fried potatoes onto a plate. 'Why not?' He could not resist adding sarcastically, 'It's not as if I need the table.'

'Papa!' Before Marionetta could admonish her father, the door swung open again and Antonio appeared, flushed and excited.

'I just met Mamma and Mario.' He was breathless. 'I told them they'd better scarper.' He paused. 'There's going to be a raid,' he said loudly, 'over the road!'

His words had the desired sensational effect. Customers craned their necks to see and climbed on their chairs to peer over the net curtains at the windows, as the familiar sound of a police-car bell approached. Marionetta joined her brother at the window.

'Who's being raided?' she asked, excited.

'The Triple X Club – chap in CID said they're pulling in some tarts,' Antonio said importantly, revelling in what he thought was police jargon. Sure enough, two police cars had screeched to a halt outside the darkened windows of the building opposite the Imperial, and several uniformed men leaped out and rushed inside. A ripple of excitement ran through the crowd in the café, and a large man jostled Marionetta out of the way to get a better look.

Marionetta turned to her brother, frustrated. 'Take me out there, Tony, I want to see –'

'No, Marionetta, stay here.' Her father had heard and was calling from behind the counter.

But it was too late. Antonio, pleased that he had infected Marionetta with some of the excitement he felt himself, had ushered his sister out onto the pavement.

The night air was intoxicatingly cold, and for a moment the harshness of it took Marionetta's breath away. She moved to the edge of the pavement, her hand clutching Antonio's sleeve.

'Here they come,' he was saying grimly. 'God, what a collection!' The police were ushering out a handful of women, pushing them across the road towards Marionetta and her brother and into a Black Maria which had materialized outside the Imperial. As the women were shoved past and into the van, Marionetta caught a whiff of exotic perfume, and the softness of chiffon brushed her face as someone's trailing scarf blew in a wintry gust. The women were stiff and dignified, only their faces reflecting their anger. One of them stopped for a moment in front of Marionetta to retrieve a corsage of violets that had fallen from her jacket into the gutter. As she straightened up, she seemed to see for the first time the wide-eyed girl in her waitress's uniform standing shivering and excited on the pavement in front of her. She hesitated for a moment, then held out the flowers.

'Here,' she said, 'You might as well have these.'

For a moment it seemed that no one moved or spoke, then all at once Antonio was shouting, 'She doesn't want your flowers, you tart!', a policeman was shoving at the woman from behind, saying, 'Get in there, you!', and Marionetta, in a swift movement, had shaken off her brother's restraining arm and had taken the flowers from the woman, looking her straight in the eye.

'Thank you,' she said, her voice a little fearful but her face brave. 'Thank you very much.'

The moment was over. The doors of the van slammed shut, the police cars revved their engines and the convoy moved off. The small crowd that had gathered on the pavement began to move away. Her nose buried in the sweet-smelling flowers, Marionetta turned and saw that the Lee Fungs, the Chinese family occupying the rooms above the café, were moving away from their windows, from which they had been observing the arrests. Even Bella, the café cat, had re-emerged onto her place on the window-sill, satisfied that the fuss was over and she could resume her feline study of Soho night-life.

'Honestly, Marionetta!' Antonio's voice was pained. 'Fancy accepting flowers from a prostitute! What do you think Father Joseph would say?'

Marionetta looked at her brother thoughtfully. 'I hope,' she said, 'that he would remember the story of Jesus and Mary Magdalene.'

Antonio snorted. 'How typical of you to turn it all into some romantic fairytale!' He snatched the flowers from her. 'Those women are filthy, diseased whores, and if Mamma knew you'd accepted flowers from one of them —'

Determinedly, Marionetta prised the crushed violets from her brother's hand. 'Ah,' she said, 'but who's going to tell her? Surely not Tony Peretti, the boy who went off drinking with his friends the other night when his dear mamma thought he was at the Church boys' club?'

Their disagreement was halted by the arrival of a large, gleaming Bentley which drew up silently opposite them, outside the Triple X Club's doors.

Antonio nudged Marionetta, excited, all thought of the violets forgotten. 'It's the Moruzzis!' he breathed. 'I might have known they'd turn up when it's all over.' He gulped a little as a tall, well-dressed man with an eye-patch over one eye emerged from the car and glanced casually in their

12

direction. Antonio pulled his sister towards the safety of the café. 'We'd better go in . . .'

But the man had turned away, indifferent, and was following his two companions into the club. Marionetta watched them go, intrigued, as always. The Moruzzis were the kings of Soho. They ran everything – the gambling, the vice, the prostitution. Their reputation was fearsome.

'Marionetta!' It was her father, at the door of the café, anxious. 'Get inside, you'll catch your death in that wind!' Slowly she went inside, still holding the violets, distracted by the sudden moment of excitement in an otherwise dreary day.

Immediately there were orders to take and tables to clear, and it wasn't until an hour later, as the last paying customer left and Tomasso wearily locked the door, that she was able to think about what had happened. Papa was sitting with Nonno and Antonio, drinking liqueur, when Marionetta, still clearing up at the sink, found the violets where she had discarded them on the draining-board. They were a little dry now, and a few were already fading. She pressed the soft petals to her cheek. How wonderful they felt, how soft and exotic . . . She filled a tumbler with water and sat the flowers in it, placing the glass on a small shelf in the back room near where her coat was hanging, so that she wouldn't forget to take them home.

Wearily she went back into the café. 'Silvia's coming to collect me at eleven, Papa,' she said, 'so can I leave the floor until the morning. . .?'

'Yes, yes!' Her father waved her away, impatient, engrossed in his conversation. 'So you're saying the Moruzzis are looking to expand their business?' He was addressing Antonio. Both he and Franco were leaning forward, intent.

13

Antonio was enjoying his role as temporary centre of attention. He shrugged. That's what my friends at West End Central tell me. They're saying that Barty Moruzzi has scared off some of the other pimps and so he's got more girls on his books than anyone else in the area. And that new club in Greek Street, the one that just opened – they're saying it's Carmelo Moruzzi's, even though it's in someone else's name . . .

'Carmelo's the one we just saw, isn't he?' Marionetta was interested. 'The one they call the Pirate, because of his eye-patch?'

'They're in a bit of trouble though,' Tony carried on talking to Tomasso as if his sister had not spoken. 'They had a handy contact in West End Central, and he's just gone down for three years on a corruption charge.'

Tomasso raised an eyebrow. 'A bent policeman?'

'Apparently. He used to meet Carmelo Moruzzi every Friday night in Soho Square and tell him what was going on. Then Moruzzi would hand him a brown envelope and they'd go their separate ways. Nice little arrangement.'

'Carmelo?' Marionetta persisted, 'Carmelo Moruzzi, the Pirate? The one we just saw? He paid a policeman to tell him things?'

'None of your business!' Her father was agitated. This was no conversation for a young girl. 'I thought you said Silvia was coming at eleven. I just heard the clock strike.'

'So if he's the Pirate,' Marionetta persisted, 'which one is Barty? Is he the one in the black hat?'

Tomasso exploded. 'The Moruzzis are nothing for you to concern yourself with!' he snapped. 'All you need to know is that they're evil men and they'd slit your throat without thinking twice about it.'

'Well, in that case,' Marionetta continued, rendered more than usually brave by her earlier encounter with the prostitute, 'don't you think I ought to know who they are? So that I can avoid them?'

Her grandfather, who had been silent, chuckled a little to himself, although his face remained grim. 'She's right, Tomasso,' he said. 'Just like her grandmother, she's always right . . . You might as well tell her about the Moruzzis.'

'Why?' Tomasso was annoyed. 'It's just to feed her silly excited ideas about criminals. She'll only go home and have nightmares.'

Antonio, annoyed at having lost the dominant position in the discussion, slammed his glass down on the table. 'Oh, for heaven's sake, Marionetta,' he said, pouring himself another measure of liqueur, under the disapproving eye of his father, 'it's quite simple to tell them apart. There are three of them.'

'And their father,' put in Tomasso, not to be outdone. 'Don't forget the father. Alfonso, he's called.'

'Alfonso . . .' The old man stared into space, remembering. 'Alfonso Moruzzi . . .'

'But no one ever sees him these days,' Antonio explained to his sister, a little condescending. 'He's retired. It's the sons who run things. A, B and C.'

Marionetta looked puzzled. 'What do you mean?'

'Just what I say. That's their names. A, B and C. There's A, Attilio. He's the big boss, keeps himself to himself. Barty – he's the middle one, B – a nasty piece of work by all accounts. Got a broken nose. And then Carmelo – C – he's the one they call the Pirate, with the eye-patch.'

'And what do they do?'

'That's enough, Antonio!' Tomasso's voice was stern. 'She's only a girl.' The doorbell jingled, and Marionetta's friend Silvia came in, still wearing her cinema usherette's uniform.

'*Ciao*, everyone!' she said. 'Ready, Netta?'

Marionetta ran to fetch her coat and, after a second's hesitation, pulled the violets from their makeshift vase, shook them a little, and then pinned them to her coat. Defiant, she went back into the café. For a moment her brother looked at the drooping purple flowers, then at his sister. Then he grinned, admiring her stubbornness. He wouldn't say anything.

'Goodnight, Papa! Goodnight, Tony! Goodnight, Nonno!' And she was gone, happy to leave the stifling little café at last, and too eager to escape to notice that her grandfather had not answered. He was staring into space, his mind full of memories. The beautiful Giulietta, Alfonso Moruzzi . . .

And what Marionetta did not see either, in her haste to leave the café, was a tall figure crossing Old Compton Street from the Triple X Club. The man strolled across the road and entered the Imperial Café. The only witness in the street was Bella the cat, crouched on her perch outside, her yellow eyes staring. Only she heard the gasp of fear from the men inside the café, and only she saw the gloved hand turning the 'Open' sign on the door to 'Closed', as the man with the eye-patch came to visit the Perettis.

Marionetta and Silvia, arm-in-arm, took their time heading towards their respective homes in St James's Residences in nearby Brewer Street. Neither was in a great hurry to enter that grimy tenement with its stale odours of too many people trying to inhabit a small space. There was never any room for entertaining friends or sitting up late and chatting. There was always a brother or a sister waiting to get to bed, or a weary parent in the sitting-room. The only privacy the two friends ever had was this kind – late-night walks home through the dark streets of Soho, clutching each other and gazing, transfixed, at the evidence of other more sordid lives unfolding around them.

Yet, like most Soho residents, in spite of the night-time vice and its accompanying sense of continual danger, the two young women would not have dreamed of living anywhere else in London. This magical network of tiny streets was to them the best place on earth, hidden away between the department stores of Regent Street and the bookshops of Charing Cross Road, bounded north and south by the bustle of Oxford Street and the theatres of Shaftesbury Avenue. They loved the sights and smells of Soho, from the early-morning blocks of ice melting on the pavement outside its restaurants, to the last eccentric drinker being ejected from the pubs at closing time. They loved the smell of *petits pains au chocolat* wafting from Madame Valerie's, the traces of perfume hanging in the air outside nightclubs. Happy in this melting-pot of races and cultures, where you could buy your coffee beans from an Algerian on Old Compton Street, fresh pasta from Italians on Brewer Street, and suspiciously cheap nylons from spivs in the Berwick Street market, they were completely at home even when the daylight faded and the cafés closed for the night. That was when the second layer of Soho society came into its own – the gamblers, the prostitutes, the late-night revellers. Girls like Silvia and Marionetta were told time and time again by over-zealous parents about the dangers of this nether world. They were exhorted to 'hurry home after dark, don't stop for anyone, don't speak to anyone'; sensible advice, but for two young girls the lights and sounds of late-night Soho were as seductive as the more familiar daytime Soho they knew so well. Consequently these night-time walks home were laced with a heady combination of fear and fascination, and they did not hurry quite as eagerly as perhaps they ought to have done.

They were passing Isola Bella, the smart Italian restaurant, and as usual, they paused for a moment to wave at Lino, a young Italian waiter who always managed to be hovering near the door at the time they passed each evening.

Marionetta nudged her friend. 'See? He was blushing!'

Silvia giggled, pleased. 'Of course he wasn't!'

'He was, I tell you! He's got a soft spot for you, that one.'

Silvia looked wistfully at her friend. 'Don't be silly. You know all the boys are after you. I can't compete with your looks, Netta.'

Marionetta squeezed Silvia's arm, ignoring her flattery. She dreamed of having a strong face full of character, like Joan Crawford or Bette Davis. She hated it when she saw men become transfixed by her startling, doll-like prettiness, when she was trying to say something interesting. In any case, she rather envied Silvia her pert, rounded features and her peroxide blonde waves – she was so much more fashionable than Marionetta, who still had long girlish hair and an old-fashioned, soulful look.

'I'm telling you,' she insisted, tugging Silvia away from Isola Bella's imposing entrance, 'I've seen the way he looks at you – it's you he's after, not me . . .'

Her voice faded as they negotiated their way past a group of prostitutes chatting on the corner outside Delmonico's Wine Store.

'Did you see that fabulous fox fur?' Silvia wistfully turned back for another look. 'Silver-grey fox! It must have cost a fortune . . .'

'Don't even think about it.' Marionetta was firm. 'You know how she earned that fox fur?'

'Of course I do!' Silvia was rueful. 'But surely there must be easier ways . . .'

As if in reply, a couple suddenly emerged from a dark

doorway in front of them and headed towards the kerb, the man calling loudly for a taxi. The two girls stopped, breathless at the sight of so much glamour. The woman, a glossy red-head swathed in a satin stole, picked her way through the late-night debris of revellers with some disdain, revealing a delicate satin-tipped toe beneath her ballgown.

'They've been to the Pavilion Club,' Marionetta guessed under her breath. 'Upstairs there's a casino . . .'

'See?' whispered Silvia triumphantly. 'I bet *she* isn't a tart!'

Marionetta smiled wryly as the smart couple disappeared into a taxi. 'No? I don't expect she'd call herself that, but maybe she's no different to those women back there –'

'Wise words from one so young.'

The voice startled them both and they turned, shocked. An old man had been standing in the dark shadows of the entrance to the Pavilion Club, and he had heard what they said. As the two girls turned and their faces caught the light of the street-lamp, he drew in his breath sharply, as if he had seen a ghost.

Marionetta was indignant. Usually the late-night prowlers of Soho left them alone. 'Come on, Silvia,' she said, turning, 'I think we should leave.'

The old man stared at Marionetta, his face white with shock. Silvia's kind heart took over. She stepped forward, concerned. 'Are you all right?' she asked, ignoring Marionetta's hissed 'Silvia!'

'I don't know.' The man's voice was trembling, and he held on to a nearby window-ledge for support. Silvia grasped his elbow. 'I think we should take him home, Netta.'

Marionetta was appalled. 'Well, I don't! Papa would be furious! And your father would beat you! You know we're not supposed to talk to anyone –'

Silvia frowned at her, embarrassed by her words. 'Netta, can't you see?' she said. 'This man's a *compaisano* – he's an Italian, one of us!'

The old man seemed to recover. He pulled himself upright, suddenly indomitable, powerful. Marionetta noticed for the first time his expensive overcoat, the soft leather gloves, the aura of money about him. He looked at Marionetta closely. 'And who', he said, 'is your papa, exactly?'

'None of your business!' Marionetta's head was up, defiant. This man was not a *compaisano*, he was rich and arrogant and belonged to the other world of Soho, not theirs, with its downtrodden workers scraping along trying to make a living.

Silvia, however, evidently felt differently. Her father had brought her up to believe that other Italians were automatically accorded respect. And the older they were, the more polite a young girl like Silvia should be. 'Her papa is Tomasso Peretti,' she said, glowering at Marionetta.

The old man stepped forward a little, studying Marionetta's face, a gleam in his eye. 'What a coincidence,' he said quietly. 'Peretti. And your name?'

Marionetta looked back at him, fearful. There was an air of menace about this old man that filled her with foreboding, in spite of his mild expression.

'Her name', said Silvia determinedly, 'is Liliana, *signore*. But everyone calls her Marionetta. And mine –'

But the old man held up his hand imperiously. 'I do not want to know your name,' he said. He looked at Marionetta again. 'I want to be taken to your father.'

'The café will be closed. He works in a café. It will be closed . . .'

The old man waved a hand, and a black car nosed its

way down the street towards them. 'The café will not be closed,' he said, as the car pulled up alongside them. 'Your father will be expecting me. Get in. You can show me the way.'

Marionetta's heart pounded in her ribs. She was about to be abducted. Terrible tales of white slave traders sprang into her mind. This man was going to drug her, take her away, sell her to a sheikh. A swarthy-looking man had emerged from the car and was holding the rear door open, standing stiffly to attention, for all the world as though he were a chauffeur at Ascot rather than a thug in a dimly lit Soho street witnessing the abduction of a young girl.

'Call the police!' Marionetta called to Silvia as she was bundled into the car.

Silvia's white face peered in. 'What do I tell them?'

The old man laughed incongruously and smiled at Silvia as he settled himself into the soft leather upholstery. 'Exactly. What indeed? I tell you what,' he had closed the door of the car and was speaking to Silvia through the rolled-down window, 'why don't you give your friend here half an hour, and if she's not back in St James's Residences by then, *then* you can call the police.'

The car moved away, leaving Silvia open-mouthed on the pavement. Too angry and curious now to be frightened, Marionetta turned to her captor. 'How did you know where I lived?' she asked, amazed.

She could see his eyes watching her, lit by the neon of a passing striptease club. 'You're Italian, aren't you?' he asked, his voice casual. 'So if you're Italian it's ten to one you live in St James's, isn't it?'

'I don't gamble,' she said frostily.

He laughed again, a low, gentle laugh. 'You have a strong character,' he said mildly. 'I like that.'

'It's not yours to like or dislike,' Marionetta was saying,

angry. But the car had already arrived outside the Imperial and had come to a smooth halt. Marionetta stared out. The lights were still on inside, and she could just make out four figures sitting round the table where she had left her father, brother and grandfather such a short time before. Someone else was with them . . .

Angrily she pushed past the old man and climbed out of the car. 'Papa!' she called, rushing inside the café, setting the bell off into a loud clanging and sending the terrified cat under a table. 'Papa –' she stopped. The fourth man at the table was the Pirate, none other than the dreaded Carmelo Moruzzi. He looked at her, interested, and then at the old man who had followed her inside.

'Papa,' he said, 'We've been expecting you. Tomasso here has put the coffee on.'

Marionetta was aware of the faces of the men in her family – Antonio, Papa, Nonno – all staring at the old man, their expressions reflecting different emotions: Antonio's numb amazement, Tomasso's anger, and grandfather . . . Marionetta gazed at him. He had risen to his feet, trembling, anguished, a look on his face that she had never seen before. It was a look of absolute terror.

'Alfonso Moruzzi,' he said, his voice suddenly sounding tremulous and small in the silence of the empty café.

The other old man looked at him and smiled a cruel smile. 'Franco Peretti,' he said. 'It's been a long time.'

Time seemed to hang suspended as the two old men faced each other, one in his shabby jumper and worn trousers, the other in his immaculate camel-hair coat, turning a smart trilby in his gloved hands.

Finally Alfonso Moruzzi spoke. 'It's time, old friend,' he said.

Franco seemed to shrink. 'No . . .' His voice quavered. 'No, Alfonso, not yet . . .'

'I'm afraid the hour of reckoning has come.' Alfonso Moruzzi began to peel off his gloves, loosening each finger carefully. 'I have come to claim my debt.'

Franco sat down suddenly in his chair, his face a strange, waxy grey. Marionetta moved forward anxiously. 'Nonno!' she said. 'Nonno, let me help you –'

But her grandfather put up a quivering hand. 'No, Marionetta,' he said. He looked up suddenly at his adversary, his face full of venom. 'Do me one favour, Moruzzi,' he said, his voice determined.

The other man raised an eyebrow inquiringly.

'Let her go.'

'Marionetta?' Alfonso Moruzzi turned to look at her. The look of desire in his eyes made Marionetta shudder. It was obscene – he was an old man. 'She's very beautiful, your Marionetta.'

'Let her go!'

The old man shrugged. 'Very well. My driver will take her home.'

'I don't want to go in your filthy car!' Marionetta burst out, 'I want to stay here, I want to hear what this is all –'

'Do as you're told, Marionetta!' It was her father, speaking to her savagely, in a way that she had never heard before.

'But I don't want to –'

'Just go!'

She stood there for a moment, at a loss. Seated round the table were three of the people she loved most in the world, something terrible was about to happen to them, and she was going to be sent away! Alfonso Moruzzi nodded imperceptibly at his son, and Carmelo the Pirate got up and went silently to the door, holding it open for Marionetta. He inclined his head politely, his one eye fixed on her implacably. She had no choice. She turned stiffly and walked out on to the darkened street and into the waiting car. The driver closed the door and went round to the driving-seat. Quietly, he started up the car and edged his way out of Old Compton Street, taking her home.

CHAPTER TWO

1948

Marionetta's shoes clipped the cool tiled floor of the corridor. A nurse passed her and smiled. Marionetta smiled back with a cheerfulness she did not feel. For Mamma was here, in Ward Four of the Italian Hospital, and it was increasingly evident that she would not be leaving.

Marionetta hesitated at the entrance to the ward. It was such a strange world, the murmuring voices of women as they spoke quietly to each other from their beds, the rustle of starch as the ward sister went about her inspection of the sinks, the unearthly combination of deathly calm and organized bustle that characterizes long-stay institutions. Marionetta had always harboured dreams of being a nurse. She watched a young woman taking the pulse of a patient sleeping in a bed close to the entrance. The nurse's fingers lay gently on the thin wrist, her other hand holding her fob-watch as she counted quietly to herself. She seemed so capable, so at one with her work, her life. To be doing some work that *mattered*! Marionetta sighed. Whenever she had tried to say such things to her mother, Francesca had only frowned at her and said, 'But the café matters, you silly girl! Feeding people – that matters, doesn't it?' It had been impossible to explain.

Slowly, she walked down the ward towards her mother's bed. She hated coming here, yet even the thought that she hated it filled her with such guilt that she always went straight from the hospital to St Patrick's to confess to Father Joseph. How could she be so selfish, so cruel, at a time like this? Poor Mamma was dying, and all she could think about was the awful suffocating atmosphere of death, her mother's feeble body propped up against the pillows, her chest heaving as she fought for air, and her own desperate desire to be free of the hospital, out of that sad place and into the sunshine of a world full of young people, pain-free, having fun, glad to be alive. It was a sin to think such things, so why did these evil thoughts keep sliding back into her head, unbidden?

'Flowers!' Her mother was managing a tired smile. 'How pretty!' Marionetta kissed her mother dutifully on the forehead.

'I'll put them in water, shall I?'

Francesca waved a skeletal hand. 'No, leave them . . . Nurse will do them later.'

Marionetta was shocked at the change in her mother even since the previous day. She seemed to have shrunk in the bed, her head enormous on the tiny shoulders, her eyes black-ringed and staring. Why, Marionetta thought in anguish for the hundredth time, why was death so cruel?

Her mother had reached a hand towards her, beckoning, conspiratorial. Marionetta leaned towards her, concerned. 'Pull the chair over,' her mother gasped, coughing a little 'I want to tell you something . . .'

The ward sister was passing. She smiled at Marionetta. 'Not too long, dear,' she said, 'we don't want the *signora* exhausted.' She sailed regally down the ward.

Marionetta pulled a chair close to her mother's pillow. 'Yes, Mamma?'

'When is your father coming?'

Marionetta looked at her in surprise. 'As soon as I get

back, like he always does. You know we can't leave Nonno running the café on his own with Mario.'

Her mother frowned a little, irritated, not wanting the explanation. 'Fine, fine ... So long as we have a little privacy. Look in my locker, would you, *bambina*? There's something I want to give you ...' Marionetta peered inside the locker. 'Bottom shelf ... there's a shoe box ... that's it! Here, give it to me ... Now sit yourself down ...'

Marionetta obeyed, curious, staring at the battered-looking box, dusty against the starched white sheets. Her mother fingered it pensively.

'Marionetta ...' she said, savouring the word. 'You know what your name means?'

'Of course!' Marionetta was surprised. 'It means little puppet.'

'And you know why you have always been called Marionetta?'

Marionetta pulled a face. 'Papa always says it's because I looked like a little doll when I was born. And Nonno always says it's because everyone in Sicily loves puppets. He says more people go to puppet shows in Palermo than to the cinema.'

Her mother sighed, and the sigh turned into a rasping cough. Marionetta tried not to notice the strange bubbling noise in her throat which descended to her chest. 'Both of them are right,' Francesca managed to say finally, her voice little more than a whisper, 'But it's not the whole truth. Look. Look inside the box.'

Marionetta carefully removed the cardboard lid and peered inside. Something wrapped in a piece of cloth was lying in the bottom of the box. She looked at her mother uncertainly. 'Take it out,' Francesca encouraged her, smiling weakly. 'Unwrap it ...'

Marionetta did so, and let out a little gasp. She held up a delicate little wooden puppet wearing the costume of the *Siciliana*. Its cheeks were rosy-red and its mouth was painted in a perfect wooden smile. Glossy black tresses mingled with the lace on the colourful costume. 'It's beautiful!' Marionetta whispered, holding it aloft, untangling the strings.

'It belonged to your grandmother in Sicily,' Francesca told her. 'She brought it all the way to England with her when she and Nonno made the great journey to London. You know she used to be called Marionetta too?'

Marionetta was entranced. 'No, I didn't! So I was named after my grandmother!'

Her mother patted her hand gently. 'It's only right you should have the doll now. You're so much like her, you know – in looks and in the way you are . . .'

Marionetta fingered the puppet's faded red felt skirt with its embroidered apron. 'How did my grandmother afford such a lovely thing?' she asked, puzzled. 'I thought they were penniless.'

'Ah. That's the story I want to tell you.' Francesca tried to pull herself up a little on her pillows. 'Pass me that glass of water, would you?'

Marionetta did so, concerned. 'Mamma, you're not well enough. You can tell me the story another day.'

But her mother shook her head, determined. 'There may not be another day.' She looked across at the ward sister, who was tending a patient by the window. 'And I must tell it now,' she pulled herself up a little, '*Now*, Marionetta.'

Marionetta covered her mother's hot hand with her own. '*Calmati*, Mamma,' she said softly. 'I'm listening . . .'

Francesca's head rested back against the pillows. She

closed her eyes for a long moment, then opened them again and looked at her daughter. 'Imagine,' she said, 'Sicily. Eighteen ninety-four. Fifty years ago. Your grandfather was twenty-two then . . .'

Marionetta smiled. 'Hard to imagine Nonno ever being a young man!'

Francesca patted her hand. 'Well, he was, and a very handsome one too, so he would have us believe. He was a peasant, working on the land – and he was in the *fasci* – she saw Marionetta's expression change, and added hastily, 'No, *cara*, not the *fascio*, it wasn't like the Fascist party then – it was a league of peasants, it was socialist. It was like a union.' She looked down for a moment, her bony fingers playing with the sheet, folding it into a row of sharp little creases and then unfolding it again. It was evident that she was not finding it easy to tell this story.

'Go on, Mamma,' Marionetta urged.

Her mother sighed. 'You have to know, I suppose . . . The village where Nonno lived – it was called Moruzzi.' Marionetta stared at her mother, silent. Francesca nodded, unsmiling. 'Yes. Moruzzi. The Moruzzi family, they owned everything – the land, the people. They ran the police force, they decided who was to be mayor, they decided how much tax the *paesani* should pay.'

Marionetta's heart was pounding. Was she about to told the secret that had been eating at her family for the past year, ever since that night when the Moruzzis had appeared and struck the fear of God into the men of the Peretti family? Marionetta had never been able to find out what had happened after she had been driven home in that smart, silent car smelling of expensive aftershave and new leather. Her father would only snap at her if she asked questions, and tell her it was none of her business. And Nonno had retreated into a kind of silent madness, staring at her like a frightened rabbit if she so much as mentioned the Moruzzis.

She leaned forward eagerly. 'So that old man I met – Alfonso Moruzzi – he knew Nonno in the village in Sicily?'

Francesca nodded. 'They were rivals. They were the best-looking boys in the village, the strongest, the bravest – only of course your Nonno had no money at all, and Alfonso Moruzzi had everything money could buy.'

'Were they friends?'

Her mother nodded. 'In a strange sort of way, yes, they were friends. Alfonso had a kind of respect for your grandfather, perhaps because he managed to be popular and well-loved, in spite of being poor.'

Francesca gave a dry little cough, and Marionetta, eager to hear the rest of the story, hurriedly poured her mother some more water.

'Thank you, *bambina* . . .' Francesca sipped at the water and then lay back against the pillows, exhausted. But she was determined to continue. 'They both fell in love with the same girl,' she said, her voice almost inaudible.

Marionetta leaned forward, her face very close to her mother's, her eyes intense. 'My grandmother?'

'Yes, your grandmother. Your father's mother. Giulietta.' She closed her eyes again, as if picturing her all those years ago in Sicily. 'She was very beautiful.'

'I know. I've seen her picture.' On the sideboard in the cramped living-room at St James's Residences, there was a small and indistinct photograph of her grandfather as a young man, standing stiff and unblinking in a photographer's studio in Whitechapel; and next to him, wearing a large feathered hat, the dimpled face of his beautiful young wife, frozen forever in sepia.

'They both fell in love with her,' Francesca repeated.

'And because they respected each other, they agreed that they would both try to win her. And that one would accept defeat honourably if she chose the other.'

Marionetta thought about the photograph on the sideboard. She tried to imagine Giulietta as she must have been in Sicily – young, brown, barefoot – not as she had become when she came to England, in her stiff Sunday collar and best hat. To have two suitors! She sighed. 'And she chose Nonno,' she said.

Her mother put out a hand and touched the little puppet that Marionetta had laid gently on the bed. 'As part of his quest to win Giulietta, Alfonso Moruzzi gave her this,' she said. 'He had it made specially – the costume is the one your grandmother danced in at *feste*.'

'How romantic!' Marionetta breathed.

'And he told her that if she married him, he would treat her just like a doll, as a precious, fragile thing.' She laughed a little, but the laugh became another racking cough. She tried to sit up, and uttered a little strangled cry as something in her chest gave way. The ward sister had looked up from her desk in the centre of the ward, and was getting up.

Marionetta, terrified, whispered, 'Stop, Mamma! Stop, you're too tired!'

But her mother pushed the restraining arm away and carried on in a choked voice. 'Alfonso Moruzzi could not have been more wrong. This was exactly the opposite of what Giulietta wanted to hear – she was a strong-minded girl, very independent, very like you, Marionetta . . .' She picked up the puppet and its box and pushed them into her daughter's hands. 'So she married your grandfather,' she gasped. 'She could have been rich, she could have had everything, but she chose your Nonno, who had nothing . . .' She coughed again, a desperate, dry little sound.

The sister had arrived at the bedside and was frowning at Marionetta. 'You must go,' she said sternly. Francesca was coughing in earnest now. Marionetta was about to object, when to her horror she saw a trickle of blood ooze from the corner of her mother's mouth. The coughing was getting louder, more uncontrolled. Marionetta stepped back, aghast, as another nurse appeared and began to draw curtains around the bed.

'You must wait outside,' the nurse told her. 'We'll call you.'

As the last of the curtains was twitched closed, leaving Marionetta stranded outside, she could still hear her mother's voice calling urgently in between the terrible sounds of her slow suffocation. 'Be like your grandmother,' she was calling, 'follow your heart, not your head!'

'Yes, Mamma!' Marionetta had a terrible feeling that she was saying goodbye to her mother, that this brutal parting was the final one.

'Don't be weak, like your brothers! Don't be weak, just because men find you beautiful . . .' Her mother's voice was fading. 'And look after my little Mario!'

'Mamma!' Marionetta called, fighting back a sob.

The nurse appeared, frantic, from behind the curtains. She propelled Marionetta down the ward, a firm hand on her shoulder, until they reached the entrance. 'You must stay here,' she said gently. 'You can't help her now.'

And so Marionetta was left standing dazed in the silent vestibule, too shocked to cry, still clutching the puppet that had been made to woo her grandmother in a distant land, and somewhere closer, her mother's words still echoing, 'Follow your heart, not your head . . .!'

Francesca Peretti's funeral was a quiet affair. It seemed to Marionetta that she drifted through it all like a sleepwalker, numb with despair, feeling more alone than she had ever felt in her life. Mamma gone! Mamma, who, in spite of her briskness and her relentless, endless work in the café, had always found time to be an affectionate mother to her daughter, finding in Marionetta something special, perhaps like all mothers. Now she was gone, and Marionetta knew, with a terrible heavy feeling in her heart, that this meant her own youth was now well and truly behind her; all dreams of nursing would have to be forgotten. She would be expected to take up where her mother had left off in the café, working twice as hard as she had done before, and now taking on the burden of all the domestic work her mother had undertaken at home, uncomplaining, for so long: the cooking, the washing, the ironing, the mending, the cleaning . . .

No wonder, then, that on this August evening Marionetta savoured her first outing since her mother's death. True, she was only going to meet Silvia for tea, but it would be a blessed hour without someone yelling, 'Two teas over here, miss!' or complaining about the lack of currants in the teacakes. Now that the hectic two weeks of the Olympic Games were over, and the crowds of visitors had thinned a little, Papa had looked at his daughter's pallor, patted her cheek and said, 'Get outside and breathe in some air, girl! You'll be putting the customers off with that face!' He hadn't noticed her speaking quietly into the telephone in the corner a few moments later, arranging to meet Silvia, or perhaps he would not have been so generous . . .

It was that strange twilight time in Soho, about six o'clock, when the late-night clubs had not yet opened, and the afternoon drinking clubs were emptied of their motley alcoholic clients, who hung about on the street corners or lounged in the cafés, trying to sober up a little before proceeding to their favourite pub. Many of them were familiar figures to Marionetta: the one-legged card sharp who regularly operated from a packing-case outside Madame Valerie's Pâtisserie, until he was moved on by a weary policeman; the shrill-voiced, drunken Suzanne Menlove, who could usually be found at this hour in an unseemly heap outside the York Minster pub, waiting for a kindly passer-by to load her into a taxi. People said she was a brilliant artist, but Marionetta couldn't help wondering when she was ever sober enough to paint. There were seedy-looking men with parcels under their arms, who avoided Marionetta's eyes if she stared at them. These were the purveyors of what the sisters at St Patrick's called filth – although Marionetta was never entirely sure exactly what form this 'filth' took. Antonio would shake his head wisely when she asked, pat her condescendingly and say, 'You don't want to know, believe me . . .'

Marionetta did not, of course, speak to any of these people although she waved at an onion-seller crossing Wardour Street, and called a greeting to several of the vendors standing behind their stalls in the Rupert Street market. These were the workers of Soho, like herself – the invisible army up at the crack of dawn and working ceaselessly in this odd, vibrant corner of London, just to make ends meet and feed their families. The drinkers and revellers, the fun-seekers, bohemians and artists – they were exotic and separate, like people from another tribe who had invaded a foreign land and decided to stay. But each group had a healthy respect for the other; after all, they needed each other to survive . . .

Silvia, looking fresh and pretty in a new lavender frock, was waiting for her friend in the doorway of St James's Residences.

'Hello!' said Marionetta, surprised. 'What are you doing down here? I said I'd come to your flat –'

Silvia took her elbow and propelled her back along Brewer Street. 'We're going to have tea out,' she said. 'My treat!'

'I've only got an hour,' Marionetta warned. 'Papa will kill me if I'm late back.'

'It's not far.'

Silvia seemed nervous, Marionetta thought, as they threaded their way past a group of West Indians arguing on the pavement outside Richards' fish shop. 'Are you all right?' she asked her, concerned.

'Fine!' Silvia's wobbly smile belied her words. Life had not been kind to Silvia. Her father had died, leaving her completely alone, and in order to supplement her meagre wage at the cinema, Silvia had begun working as a hostess in a club. At least, that's what Marionetta told her family. Only she knew that in reality what Silvia was doing was far more dangerous than mere hostessing: she was 'clipping'. She had explained it all to Marionetta in her innocent, bubbly way, excited by the prospect of easy money for so little effort. 'All I have to do is promise the customers a few favours after hours. They cough up the money in advance, I arrange to meet them outside, only I don't turn up, do I? I'm busy leaving by the back entrance, while the strong-arm boys hang about at the front and deter the punters from making any complaints.'

Marionetta had been appalled. 'But surely you're going to get caught!' she had expostulated. 'One of those men will get angry and follow you home and maybe kill you – or at least hurt you –'

But Silvia had laughed. 'Don't be silly, Netta! This is a proper business! All the girls do it. You should think about it, seriously. You'd be quite safe. It's all organized by the club – the boss protects us. Barty would never let anyone get near us –'

Marionetta had felt her blood run cold. 'Barty?' she had whispered. 'Barty Moruzzi?'

'Of course Barty Moruzzi! It's his club – or at least his brother's. Barty's the boss, though. We never see the other Moruzzis.'

No amount of pleading on Marionetta's part had succeeded in dissuading Silvia from this new line of work. For once in her young life she had some money, and, more importantly, it meant she could hang on to the flat she had shared with her father, and continue to live in Soho, which was the only home she knew.

Silvia was pulling her friend down Dean Street. 'This way,' she said brightly. 'We don't want to go past your dad's café, he might drag you in and make you go back to work!'

Marionetta was propelled, reluctant, past the Isola Bella Restaurant, where she could see Lino polishing tables. He looked up and blew Silvia a kiss as she passed, and laughingly, she returned it. Marionetta wondered how he felt about Silvia's work – or if he even knew about it. He worked such long hours that he only saw Silvia on his one evening off, and sometimes on a spare afternoon. He probably thought she worked as a cinema usherette and that was that. She had tried to interrogate Silvia about how much Lino knew, but her friend had been evasive, fingering the delicate silver cross he had given her for her eighteenth birthday which she always wore around her neck.

'Lino will look after me,' was all she said. 'He cares about me. He's the only person in the world apart from you, Netta, who cares whether I live or die.'

Marionetta had fallen silent, accustomed to Silvia's somewhat melodramatic pronouncements. But she could not help feeling anxious at the intensity of her friend's words.

What if Lino found out what she was doing? His declarations of love would very quickly cease, Marionetta was sure: decent Italian boys would never have anything to do with a girl from a clip-joint — not publicly, at any rate, and certainly not with a view to marriage.

They had turned the corner into Bateman Street, and Silvia slowed down now, hovering near the entrance to the Dog and Duck public house.

'We can't go in there!' Marionetta laughed. 'The landlord knows my dad.'

But Silvia had turned to a doorway next to the pub, and was knocking on a wooden door. Marionetta peered at the discreet brass plate on the wall and read it aloud: 'The Satin Club'. She was aghast. 'Silvia! This is where you work, isn't it? Why have we come here?'

Silvia gave a nervous little laugh. 'Don't worry, Netta, you're not going to be sold into slavery . . . I just thought we could have a quiet cuppa here, before the club opens. I have to start work at seven, so I haven't got a lot of time.' She was tapping discreetly on the door, but Marionetta pulled at her arm, appalled.

'Silvia, I can't go in there! Are you mad? Papa would have a fit.'

Silvia shrugged defiantly. 'So don't tell him.' The door was opened by someone unseen inside and Silvia stepped over the threshold, saying, 'Thanks, Wally,' to the invisible doorman. She turned, to see Marionetta, who had taken a step back onto the pavement, nearly collide with a passer-by.

Silvia giggled. 'Come on, Netta,' she called, 'before you get done for soliciting!'

Nervously, Marionetta stepped into the shadowy doorway. 'Only for ten minutes,' she said, annoyed with her friend for forcing her into such a situation. 'And if you ever tell my dad . . .'

The door closed behind her. The man standing there looked familiar to Marionetta. He did not smile at her, in fact he did not seem to have looked at her, his eyes were discreetly fixed somewhere in the middle distance. Marionetta had a fleeting impression of a pock-marked face and sandy hair slicked back with hair oil.

'Come on!' Silvia was leading Marionetta up a carpeted flight of stairs. 'There's a kind of dressing-room place up here for the girls. I'll put the kettle on.'

As they turned the corner at the top of the stairs, Marionetta glanced down into the darkened foyer and caught a glimpse of cold eyes watching her. That face . . . she knew it from somewhere – but where? He was hardly likely to be a customer at the Imperial. He was clearly from the twilight world of the clubs and the gambling joints, with his smart Italian suit and his gold tie-pin. It was only a fleeting moment, but it made Marionetta shudder. For she had realized, in that split second, that he had recognized her too . . .

She followed Silvia into a tiny, windowless room, no more than a cupboard, smelling of stale scent and face-powder. There were a couple of upright chairs standing against a small cupboard, a table with a mirror propped up on it, and a peeling picture of Frank Sinatra pinned to the wall.

Silvia was bustling about, searching in the cupboard for cups. 'You don't take sugar, do you?' she was saying brightly. 'There's some milk in the fridge behind the bar – oh, hello, Barty. 'She straightened up, nervous, her hand flying to her hair. Marionetta turned. 'I was just giving Marionetta some tea –'

The man smiled at Marionetta, the smile somehow not reaching his eyes. 'Marionetta Peretti, isn't it?' He stepped forward. He was rather a short man, very ugly, with a pointed nose. He held out his hand. 'How do you do. I've heard a lot about you.' Marionetta, with a courage she did not feel, looked him in the eye and ignored his hand. She could sense Silvia, anxious, at her shoulder. Barty Moruzzi laughed a little, amused by this small act of rudeness. He withdrew his hand and put it back in his coat pocket. 'Tea, eh?' he said to Silvia, 'Sure you wouldn't like something stronger?'

Marionetta turned to Silvia, mute appeal on her face. 'No, honestly, Barty, tea's fine.' Silvia avoided her friend's eye, ashamed.

The man was suddenly brisk. 'Good idea,' he said, 'I'll have one too. We'll have it in the club.'

'No, thank you,' Marionetta began, 'I'd better be getting back . . .'

Barty Moruzzi ignored her. 'Bring it in when it's made, would you, Silvia? There's a good girl. Follow me, Miss Peretti.'

'I'd really rather –'

'Nonsense . . . Don't be a silly girl, I won't eat you.' He had a firm hold of her arm now. Short of screaming and struggling, there was little Marionetta could do but follow him reluctantly down the dark plush corridor and into the Satin Club.

Barty Moruzzi installed her at a table in the corner of the darkened club. As her eyes grew accustomed to the gloom, Marionetta could make out a curved bar at the other end, gleaming with glasses and bottles. To her relief, there were a couple of men in bow-ties busy working there, washing glasses and laying out ashtrays. Whatever was going to happen to her, at least there would be witnesses. The Satin Club was smarter than she had imagined. There were deep maroon satin drapes at the two high windows to one side, overlooking Bateman Street, she guessed. The tables surrounded a small, highly polished dance-floor, and near where she was sitting there was a small raised stage with some discarded music sheets in a pile next to a drum kit. The place smelt of lavender furniture polish, and the atmosphere was one of calm.

She realized that Barty Moruzzi was watching her as she looked around. 'Nice, isn't it?' he said with some pride. 'Not quite what you expected, eh?'

Marionetta did not reply. Barty leaned back in his chair for a moment, contemplating her. 'So,' he said finally, 'I hear you're looking for work.'

This had the desired effect. Marionetta turned to him, angry. 'Who told you that? I'm not looking for work – and even if I was, I'd die rather than work here!'

He was busy lighting a cigarette, his face amused. 'Has Silvia told you what kind of money she's earning?'

'I told you. I'm not interested.'

'And that's only the beginning. She could earn a small fortune, given the right training.' He looked up. Silvia was approaching. 'Where's the tea?' he asked.

'Wally just came up.' Silvia was panting a little, anxious, avoiding Marionetta's accusing stare. 'He said to tell you your brother's car is outside. He must be coming in!'

Barty's expression changed. 'Attilio? But he never comes here –'

'Honestly, Wally says it's definitely him.'

Barty pushed his chair back and stubbed out his cigarette. 'Right.' His voice was decisive. 'Get lost, you two. I've got a visitor.'

Marionetta stood up, relieved at the prospect of escape. This unexpected release would also give her time to tell Silvia what she thought of her, tricking her into entering such a place. Silently she followed Silvia to the exit. Barty Moruzzi had evidently lost interest in her as a potential

40

employee. He was calling to one of the barmen to come and empty his ashtray, and smoothing back his hair, tense.

'How could you, Silvia!' Marionetta was whispering, furious, as they emerged on to the gloomy landing. 'I'll never forgive you for this –'

'I'm sorry.' Silvia's voice was almost a whimper. 'Barty said I had to ask you, I had no choice, he said I had to invite you here.'

Their way was barred by a tall figure standing against the light. Silvia instinctively stepped back, frightened, but Marionetta, too angry now to be afraid, pushed her aside and stood, defiant, glaring.

'Excuse me, please,' she said, her voice firm, 'we're in a hurry.'

The man stepped forward into the glow of a cheap chandelier hanging from the ceiling above. He was in his forties and handsome, with a smoothly tanned skin, black hair and an air of money about him. He had an expensive-looking dark overcoat slung over his shoulders, and a large gold signet ring on the third finger of his left hand, which he turned thoughtfully as he looked at Marionetta, absorbing her bright, doll-like features, the flush of her cheek.

'Who's this?' he asked no one in particular.

The man who had let them in stepped forward from the shadows. 'It's Marionetta Peretti,' he said. He had a broad cockney accent with an odd, nasal twang. 'Her dad owns the Imperial.'

The other man studied Marionetta's face, a slight smile on his lips. 'Ah,' he said. 'I remember. Something to do with our papa, wasn't it?'

'Last year,' said the doorman. 'I took him and Carmelo there. To renew the lease on the place.'

In the midst of her anger, fear and confusion, a thought crystallized in Marionetta's mind. Of course! The mystery

41

was solved. The man with the red hair and the face pitted with scars was the Moruzzis' driver. It had been he who had driven the big black car back to St James's Residences on the night of the mysterious visit to the café. It had been he who had silently opened the door to release her, and who had then driven off into the night, never saying a word.

She stared defiantly up into amused dark brown eyes. So this was the famous Attilio Moruzzi. 'If you've quite finished discussing my family business,' she said coolly, 'I have to get to work.'

The man smiled at her and made a mock bow. 'Of course,' he said, 'forgive me, *signorina*.' He was letting her pass! Dignified, she hastened down the stairs, Silvia hot on her heels, and flung open the street door. Silvia was pulling at her arm.

'Netta!' she called. 'Wait! Please! I want to explain —'

Marionetta shook her off, furious. 'How dare you, Silvia! I thought you were my friend, and you take me there! How dare you!'

She pulled away and ran off, ignoring the desperate call from Silvia behind her. She turned the corner into Frith Street, her face still scarlet, and then slowed down a little. She would be passing Bianchi's in a moment, and the proprietor was a friend of Papa's, so she must try to look calm, as if nothing had happened. She took a deep breath. Nothing *had* happened, had it? Of course not. Silly, unthinking Silvia had persuaded her into that awful club, under the mistaken impression that she was doing her friend a favour, persuading her to consider a job that for Marionetta was completely out of the question. Silvia ought to have known better; but Silvia wasn't to know that Attilio Moruzzi, the most feared and hated man in Soho, was going to show up. Marionetta took a deep breath and began to walk again at a more normal pace. Papa would be expecting her. She must get back to the café. She turned into Old Compton Street and hurried along to the Imperial, glancing at the big clock in Wheeler's opposite. Seven-fifteen. Good, Papa would be pleased, she was actually early . . .

One of Marionetta's greatest assets, her mother had always told her, was her sense of humour. She had a real knack for saying something witty at just the right moment, and many of the Imperial's most faithful customers came to the café simply to be cheered up by their favourite waitress. On the morning following her reluctant visit to the Satin Club, Marionetta was on top form. She was desperate to forget that dimly lit place and those sinister men. She felt tainted by the whole experience, and so angry with Silvia that she doubted she would speak to her again. But then, how could she explain that to Papa? Desperately she tried to put the entire distasteful experience out of her mind. Today was, after all, just another ordinary day. Mario was at school, and would go straight to his singing lesson afterwards and then to the Imperial for tea. Antonio was walking the beat somewhere in the Charing Cross Road and would pop in for a cup of tea this afternoon. Papa and Nonno were here, as always. Life was safe and sweet. She joked with the customers, pretended to juggle three tea-cups for the benefit of a complaining toddler, and even did a Betty Grable impersonation for a group of sailors, all to the distress of her grandfather, ensconced in his place in the corner, but to the delight of everyone else.

'Disgusting!' he snorted. 'You should be more modest, girl.'

'Great legs!' enthused a fresh-faced young man buying a Danish pastry at the counter. Marionetta's grandfather quelled him with a look.

'Don't be so grumpy, Nonno,' Marionetta admonished, more cheerfully than she felt. 'It's a lovely summer day, the café's doing well, you've got a grandson in the constabulary, another one set to sing at La Scala, and a granddaughter with great legs. What more could you ask for?'

'What indeed?'

The café had gone very silent. A terrible chill fell over Marionetta. She knew, even before she turned round, who would be standing behind her with that wolfish smile, turning the big gold ring on his finger.

'*Buongiorno*,' said Attilio Moruzzi.

Marionetta stood frozen next to her grandfather, a million thoughts buzzing in her head, a million unanswered questions. What was he doing here? And should she acknowledge him? Would he reveal to Papa that they had already met? Would he mention the Satin Club? Would he mention Silvia and what she did for a living?

Then the moment – an eternity – was over. Attilio Moruzzi turned to the counter where Marionetta's father stood, scared, his hand gripping the big knife he used to cut the sandwiches. For a ridiculous second, Marionetta wondered if Papa would lean across the counter and plunge the knife into the intruder's heart; but of course the reality was much more mundane.

'Good morning, sir.' Tomasso Peretti's voice was a little unsteady. 'Cup of tea?'

Attilio Moruzzi smiled and shook his head. 'No, thanks. Signor Peretti, isn't it? I believe you know my father.'

'We have met.' A couple of people were sidling out of the café, their faces tense. Others looked away, murmuring among themselves, trying to pretend everything was all right, too scared to leave.

Irrationally, Marionetta thought to herself, he *is* handsome. Evil but handsome. As if he could read her mind, he turned again and smiled at her. She looked away, blushing. 'I wondered if I might take your daughter out to tea for an hour or so? I promise you I will return her safely.'

There was a stunned silence. Finally Tomasso said, 'Marionetta? You want to take my Marionetta out *to tea*?' His voice was little more than a squeak.

'That's right.' Attilio looked at Marionetta again. 'She's very beautiful, your daughter. I hope you don't mind, *signore*. I will take great care of her, I assure you. And today is the fifteenth of August. *Ferragosto*. If we were in Italy today would be a holiday.'

There was a stunned silence. Tomasso put the bread knife down with a nervous clatter. All eyes were on Marionetta, who stood, ridiculously clutching a tray laden with dirty teacups, listening to these two men discuss her. She could feel her grandfather's frail hand tugging at her apron. She looked down at him. He was shaking his head imperceptibly, too afraid to speak. But she understood the gesture. *Don't go*, he was saying, *whatever you do, don't go* . . .

Then, amazingly, she heard her father say, 'Very well, Signor Moruzzi. If you are sure you mean her no harm.'

'On the contrary. I mean her nothing but good, I assure you.' The voice, with its flat London accent, was smoothly polite.

'Papa!' Marionetta could not believe her ears. 'Papa! I don't want to go with this —'

'*Basta!*' Her father snapped at her, unable to meet her eyes. 'It's a national holiday in Italy. This gentleman is right. Take your apron off and go!'

Almost in slow motion, Marionetta relinquished the tea-tray which someone took from her. She untied the strings of her apron, folded it carefully and handed it to her grandfather. He gazed up at her, desperation in his eyes. She patted his arm. Finally she said. 'Very well, Papa. If that's what you want.'

Attilio Moruzzi was holding the door open for her. He raised an eyebrow. 'Ready?'

And together, they left the café.

They walked silently in the sunshine. Marionetta was aware of the nudges and murmurs of passers-by. Of course. She was with a celebrity. Everyone in Soho knew Attilio Moruzzi, it seemed, and now it was going to be her turn.

They did not have far to walk. They had arrived at a familiar wooden door with a brass name-plate outside. 'The Satin Club,' Marionetta said bleakly. 'You told my father you were taking me for tea.'

'And so I am, Marionetta. But I'd like a little privacy, and Madame Valerie's is a little crowded at this time of day.'

The pock-faced, red-haired man had silently opened the door. 'Have you met Wally Wallace?' said Attilio. 'He's a colleague of mine. Go on up the stairs, there's a good girl. Wally, put the kettle on, would you?' His voice hardened as he caught Wally's look of surprise. 'Yes, Wally, the kettle. You know what a kettle is, don't you?'

He ushered Marionetta along the now familiar passage-way and into the club. This time, Marionetta saw with a sinking heart, it was completely empty.

'Shall we sit down?' Attilio was holding a chair for her, waiting. Instead, she walked across to the window.

'I'd prefer to stand,' she said. She pulled the satin drapes to one side and peered through the net curtain. On the street below she could see shoppers hurrying to Berwick Street market, their faces intent on their task, thinking about nothing more important, perhaps, than what to put in tonight's stew, or whether the nylon stockings were

46

cheaper in Rupert Street. How lucky they were, she thought, to have such quiet, ordinary little lives. Suddenly she longed with a desperate vehemence for such a life. She was sure now that this was not to be.

Attilio Moruzzi was standing next to her. 'Wonderful, isn't it?' She looked at him, not understanding. 'Soho,' he said simply.

'What do you care?' she asked bitterly. 'It's you and your sort who have ruined it, turned it into a sewer. I know what you do, Signor Moruzzi. I have a brother who is a policeman.'

Surprisingly, he laughed. 'Antonio? Oh, I know all about him.' She turned to look at him. 'I'm afraid he won't be coming to rescue you.'

'Do I need rescuing?'

'Of course not. I was joking. But you're wrong about me and Soho.' His face was serious. For a moment she thought she glimpsed a human being beneath the suave exterior. 'I love this place. I grew up here. I know every inch of it – like you do, Marionetta. We're not so different. We're both of Sicilian descent, we both love Soho. We have a lot in common.'

She moved away from him slightly, disgusted. 'I don't agree. We have nothing in common, *signore*. And if you want me to work for you, forget it. Your brother has already asked me, and I've told him what I think of your – your – enterprise!' She spat out the word, surprised at her own courage. But what did she have to lose? Her own father had betrayed her, forcing her to come here and be humiliated by this gangster.

He moved in closer and touched her face gently with his hand. She was shocked somehow to feel the softness of his flesh. 'That's the last thing I want,' he said, his voice very quiet. He pulled her face round towards his, forcing her to look at him. His eyes were far from kind. She was trapped, unable to move, the window behind her and Attilio Moruzzi blocking her escape. Her heart was beating so hard she was sure he must be able to hear it. 'Don't look so frightened,' he said, 'like some little trapped bird . . . I'm not going to hurt you, Marionetta. I think you're a very beautiful young woman.' His face was very close to hers. She was frozen. Surely he wasn't going to kiss her? But he suddenly moved away and walked briskly towards the bar at the other end of the room. 'I like your spirit, I like your courage.' His voice echoed across the silent space. He had reached the bar and was helping himself to a Scotch from one of the optics on the wall. 'And I won't deny that I like the way you look. What that boy said in the café – about your legs. He was right. You could be a real stunner, with the right clothes.' He looked at her from across the room and took a gulp of whisky. 'I'd like to supply you with those clothes. In fact, I'd like to supply you with anything you want.' Marionetta was silent, shaking, stunned. 'Are you listening, Marionetta? I'm saying I want you to be my woman. My *fidanzata*.'

He leaned across the bar, admiring her slender body as she stood framed in the window. She remained mute, too shocked to speak.

'Well?'

Marionetta shifted a little and looked first at Attilio Moruzzi and then at the door.

'Never,' she said.

He raised an eyebrow. The smile had disappeared from his face. 'I suggest you give my offer some serious thought,' he was saying, his eyes never leaving her. 'I don't want to put any pressure on you, Marionetta, but your little friend – Silvia, is it? – well, she's one of my employees. This club has been very good to her. I understand she needs the income rather badly. Do you get my drift?'

48

She still could not believe this was happening. His words were somehow ridiculous, the kind of thing James Cagney said in one of the many gangster films she had sat through, courtesy of Silvia, at the Odeon. Yet this was here, now. This was no hoodlum from Chicago. This was London, England; and the man saying these things was no celluloid fantasy – he was flesh and blood. But the realist in Marionetta finally took hold. Attilio Moruzzi may be a crook and an evil man, she thought, but he can't *really* hurt me, he can't really hurt my family, or Silvia. He would be deported if he did anything stupid . . .

Marionetta looked at that cold face and made a decision. 'I understand everything you have said, Signor Moruzzi,' she said. 'And now I wish to forget every word. So if you'll excuse me, I'm going home. Unless, that is, you want to hold me here by force?' And she walked across the room towards the exit with a steadiness she did not feel, her heart thudding. Attilio did nothing to stop her. He merely watched her go, cradling his glass of Scotch, thoughtful.

Marionetta stepped out into the sunshine, blinking. She wandered towards home in a daze. She ought really to go back to the café, she supposed, but she could not. How could she face her father, who had forced her to go out with that horrible man? What could she say? Now that she was safely out in the street, she began to tremble. She remembered Attilio Moruzzi's breath on her face, the pressure of his hand. If only Mamma were still alive! She would not have allowed this dreadful thing to happen . . .

'Hey, miss! Are you all right?' A young man had stopped her on the pavement as she turned into Brewer Street. She was vaguely aware, through her tears, of sympathetic brown eyes in an anxious face. He was wearing battered cord trousers and a polo-neck sweater, the uniform of the young Soho habitué.

'Of course I'm all right!' she said sharply, shaking him off. The kindness in his voice almost made her snap. She fought a desire to collapse, sobbing, into this stranger's arms, and instead shouted, 'Leave me alone!' and ran off down the street towards the shelter of St James's.

The young man watched her go, interested. His companions nudged each other and laughed.

'Well done, Micky!' A bespectacled youth carrying a huge double-bass case clapped a sympathetic arm round his companion's shoulders. 'You really charmed that one!'

But the young man was watching Marionetta as she turned hurriedly into the entrance to St James's Buildings, scrubbing her face with a handkerchief as she went inside. He thought she was the most beautiful girl he had ever seen.

Marionetta held her face up to the sun, closing her eyes against the glare, and let the warmth seep into her skin. Bella, the café cat, was stretched out next to her on the fire escape, basking in the heat. The only sound Marionetta could hear out here in the back yard of the Imperial was the clatter of Mario washing dishes, and the occasional shout of one of the waiters in Bianchi's calling to a worker in the Italia Coffee Bar next door in Frith Street. Perhaps, Marionetta thought sleepily, this was what it was like in Sicily. Perhaps somewhere in Palermo another girl was dreaming in the sunlight, wishing she could escape. Marionetta sighed. At least that other girl would not have to contend with her own father handing her over to a crook. Most Sicilian men would die rather than do such a thing – at least, that was what Marionetta believed.

The atmosphere between her father and herself had been decidedly frosty since her enforced outing with Attilio Moruzzi the day before. When she had berated her father

50

about his actions, he had merely tried to hug her, saying, 'You don't understand, *bambina*, you mustn't cross the Moruzzis. They're serious people, they could hurt you —'

She had pulled away angrily. '*Codardo!* Coward!' She was inconsolable. Even sweet Mario, with his innocent brotherly concern, had not been able to placate his sister; and Antonio, returning home from a day's beat, had merely shrugged wearily. 'Papa's right, Netta. Just play along with Moruzzi – he'll get tired of you in a few days and move on to someone else. You know they say he's been seen about town with that blonde woman who starred in the film about the docks? You know, that thriller –'

'Oh, shut up, Tony!' she had shouted. 'You don't understand!'

He had raised an eyebrow, ignoring his grandfather's warning nudge. 'I'm only trying to point out that there are some beautiful women around only too happy to please him, and you're only a girl. Not his type at all.'

Marionetta had turned to her grandfather, eyes full of mute appeal. But Nonno, somehow rendered almost dumb by this recent event, merely shook his head and mumbled something incomprehensible, retreating out of the room.

So now, she decided, she was completely alone. She hated her papa, hated the café, was angry with her best friend – it felt as if the whole world were conspiring against her.

'Hey, miss! Miss!' She opened her eyes, surprised. From the floor above, Mrs Lee Fung was calling her. Curious, Marionetta scrambled to her feet. The family who occupied the rooms above the café rarely spoke to her and never really communicated with the Perettis, other than with a series of polite nods as they passed the café on mysterious errands to the Chinese shops on the other side of

Shaftesbury Avenue. Now here was the mother of the family most definitely trying to attract her attention, looking around furtively, as if afraid someone would stop her.

Shielding her eyes against the glare of the sun, Marionetta looked up. Mrs Lee Fung was beckoning to her. She headed up the fire escape until she was level with the window out of which the tiny black-haired woman was leaning.

'Miss. Some women come for you. Urgent.'

'Me? What women? Where are they?' Marionetta fleetingly wondered if Mrs Lee Fung's English could cope with questions.

The woman beckoned her closer, her pale face nervous. 'Some women. They went to the café. Your dad, he throw them out. They knock on my door.'

Marionetta still did not understand. 'Where are they, these women? Who are they?'

The Chinese woman leaned further over the sill and clutched her sleeve. 'Bad women. You know. They ask for you.'

Marionetta shook her head firmly. 'They can't have. I don't know any women like that.'

'They said to see you outside Lina Stores. Only quick, quick. They in a hurry. Say it's very important. About your friend.'

Marionetta's heart skipped a beat. 'A friend? Did they say a name? Mrs Lee Fung, this is very important – did they say a name?'

Mrs Lee Fung's brow furrowed. 'Friend. Name.'

'Silvia? Was it Silvia?'

The woman brightened. 'Silvia! Yes. Your friend. Hurry.'

Marionetta was already clattering down the fire escape, her mind racing. But Mrs Lee Fung called her back. 'Miss!' Marionetta paused. 'Yes?'

The woman above looked down at her, evidently in some distress. 'You not tell your dad about me and those women, eh?'

'No, of course not.'

'And you not tell my old man, neither?'

'No, of course not, Mrs Lee Fung. And thanks!'

She ran inside, flustered. Mario was singing 'Ain't Misbehavin'' as he washed a pile of dishes. Tomasso was filling the tea urn. He glanced round as Marionetta came in. 'Table in the corner wants toasted teacakes –'

'Sorry, Papa, got to go out –' She searched in her mind for a plausible excuse and had a moment of inspiration. She leaned towards him, conspiratorial. 'Women's trouble – know what I mean?'

Her father reddened, embarrassed. 'Sure, sure – you go ahead.'

With a sigh of relief Marionetta hurried through the café and out into the street, heading towards Brewer Street. Her mind was racing. Surely Attilio Moruzzi hadn't sacked Silvia already? Or worse . . . ? She slowed down as she crossed the corner of Rupert Street. Sure enough, there were two rather brassy-looking young women hovering outside Lina Stores, causing some consternation among the Soho housewives entering to buy their fresh pasta. Ignoring the stares of the women, most of whom knew her, Marionetta approached the pair.

'I'm Marionetta,' she said, 'I came as soon as I –'

The older of the two women pulled her gently to one side. 'Can't stop, dear,' she said. 'Just thought you ought to know – Silvia's in a bit of a bad way. She asked for you, so we come to get you, only your old man chucked us out.'

'Where is she?'

'At home.' The younger woman pursed her very red lips, looking around nervously. 'Come on, Violet, we'd better go.'

And they went, hurrying away round the corner and disappearing into Great Windmill Street. After a second, during which time Marionetta managed to nod a polite greeting to two curious old Italian ladies, she had absorbed what the women had said. Silvia was in trouble. Never mind what Silvia had done previously, never mind that she had sworn to herself to drop Silvia as a friend. None of that mattered now.

She hurried into St James's Residences, the tenement home the Italians called 'the Buildings', just a few doors away from the shop. Silvia's flat was on the first floor. Marionetta ran up the concrete stairs that smelled of bleach and old vegetables, and hurried along the corridor to number fifty-three. The door was not locked and there was no sound from the interior. Quietly, Marionetta went inside.

Silvia was curled up asleep in what had been her father's bedroom, and which was now hers. Her body was turned against the wall and her breathing was loud and even. Marionetta looked around her for some clues as to Silvia's condition, but found none. Silvia had tried to give the small room a more feminine touch with a couple of chiffon scarves draped over the bedside lamp, and some new net curtains at the window, but it did not disguise the bare poverty of the place. Only some marcasite earrings and a rope of imitation pearls on the bedside table revealed a change in Silvia's previously austere lifestyle.

Tentatively, Marionetta approached the bed. 'Silvia,' she whispered, 'Silvia – are you all right? Oh!' She gasped. She had peered over and seen Silvia's face, bruised and blackened, incongruous against the white cotton pillowcase. One of Silvia's eyes opened slightly. The other was glued shut, blood congealed round the lashes.

'Silvia! Silvia! What have they done . . .?' Impulsively, as the battered face tried to move and then contorted in agony, Marionetta leaned forward to hug her friend, only to hear a scream of pain. She pulled away, horrified. Evidently Silvia's injuries extended beyond her face. 'I'll get a doctor –'

This suggestion only brought another agonized yelp, more desperate than the last. 'No, no, I won't – I promise –' Marionetta was fighting angry tears. Silvia's face was beaten almost beyond recognition. Whoever had done this would not have cared if he had killed her, she realized. She stared at her friend. 'Was it Attilio Moruzzi?' she asked finally, abruptly. Silvia tried to shake her head. A hand emerged shakily from beneath the covers, its knuckles bruised and discoloured, and reached out to Marionetta.

'B – Ba –' Silvia was trying to say something.

Marionetta understood. 'Barty? It was Barty Moruzzi who did this?' Silvia attempted a nod. 'But – why?'

'Wanted me to –' Sylvia burbled through thickened lips, 'wanted me –'

'No, don't speak,' Marionetta said grimly. 'Let me guess. He wanted you to sleep with him?'

Silvia shook her head. Marionetta was puzzled. 'No? Then why . . .?' Then she understood. 'He wanted you to start saying yes to the customers, is that it? Silvia? Is that it?'

Silvia nodded dumbly, a painful tear oozing out of her closed eye, her features distorted with fear.

'He wanted you to become a prostitute, and you said no? Is that it, Silvia?'

Again, Silvia tried to nod. A thousand reproaches sprang to Marionetta's lips, a hundred I-told-you-so's; but she said nothing. She stood up slowly and looked down at her friend for a long moment. Then she said, 'Go back to sleep, Silvia. I'm going to the chemist, get you some ointment for those bruises, and something to help the pain. All right? Go on – go back to sleep. There's nothing to worry about.'

Silvia seemed to believe her, and relaxed back into the pillows, drifting away into sleep.

Marionetta closed the flat door quietly behind her. Mrs Rocca, Silvia's nosy neighbour, was hovering in the passage.

'Everything all right?' she asked Marionetta.

'Everything's fine, Mrs Rocca,' Marionetta replied absently, brushing past her. 'Or it will be,' she murmured to herself, 'once I put a certain person behind bars . . .'

She found her brother strolling along Meard Street, gazing in shop windows, secretly admiring himself in his new constable's uniform. He was surprised to see his sister at this early evening hour, and even more surprised as her account of Silvia's beating came tumbling out. He tensed, and pulled his sister into a doorway.

'Don't go shouting that all over town,' he said, his voice nervous. 'You'll get us into trouble.'

'I *want* trouble!' she exclaimed angrily. 'I want the police to do something! I want Barty Moruzzi prosecuted, he could have killed Silvia! You haven't seen her, Tony, she's in a terrible state – you must do something –'

He backed away from her uneasily. 'Don't be daft, sis,' he said. 'You know the score. The police can't touch a Moruzzi, not unless someone's prepared to give evidence against them.'

Marionetta stared at him, absorbing his words. 'Your friend Silvia,' he went on, his voice sarcastic, 'she'd be prepared to do that, would she? Stand up in a court of law and speak out against the Moruzzi brothers?' He gave a little ironic laugh. 'I'd like to be there the day that happens. No, on second thoughts, I wouldn't. I don't want

56

to end up dead in a gutter somewhere with a knife in my back.'

Marionetta looked at her brother, surprise mingling with disgust. Suddenly he seemed like a stranger, not someone she had loved and cared for all these years. 'So you're not prepared to help?'

He shrugged. 'I can't. I feel bad for Silvia, but what can I – Marionetta! Come back!'

But she was running off, intent on some new mission. He watched her go, annoyed. Honestly, girls! They should stick to face paint and love songs, he reckoned, not go messing about in men's business. He turned and continued on his beat, whistling a little to hide his anxiety.

The shadows were lengthening as Marionetta turned into Bateman Street, her face determined. She went straight to the door of the Satin Club and hammered on it loudly. Wally Wallace's pock-marked face appeared instantly.

'For God's sake,' he said, 'cut it out! You want to wake the dead?'

She pushed past him and ran upstairs.

'Wait!' he called after her. 'Is Mr Moruzzi expecting you?'

She ignored him and continued along the passage to the club. She pushed open the doors and stood for a moment, blinking in the gloom. The club was fairly crowded, and a listless combo was playing dance tunes on the stage, while couples moved slowly, like somnambulists, on the polished dance-floor. No one noticed her entrance. She peered around for a moment, her eyes becoming accustomed to the half-light. Sure enough, there was Barty Moruzzi presiding over his empire, ensconced like some evil dwarf at the same table where he had brought her for the cup of tea she had never had.

He was sitting with a bored-looking young woman in a

silk blouse, who smoked languidly and stared away across the dancers. Between them was an ice-bucket with a bottle of champagne in it, two full glasses on the table.

Without a moment's hesitation, Marionetta walked across to his table. He looked up, surprised. 'Hello,' he said. 'And what can I do for you?'

Wordlessly, Marionetta picked up the glass nearest to him. His mouth made a surprised 'O' as he realized what she was about to do. The young woman gave a little scream.

'This is for Silvia,' Marionetta said calmly. With a quick movement she threw the entire contents of the glass into Barty Moruzzi's face. There was a split second of total shock and then his hand came up and delivered an agonizing blow to Marionetta's face. She staggered back, almost knocked to the floor by the force of his hand. 'You little bitch,' he said quietly, mopping his face with a handkerchief. 'You little bitch.'

Wally Wallace had appeared behind Marionetta and grasped her arm in a clamp-like grip, making her wince with the pain of it.

'Chuck her out, Wally,' said Barty Moruzzi, his face ugly with anger.

She was being propelled towards the door. She was faintly aware that the music played on, that the young woman was staring at her with something oddly like admiration on her face. She struggled in Wally's grip and turned to face Barty Moruzzi again. 'It's not over!' she shouted, beyond caring what happened now. 'I'm going to go to your brother and I'm going to tell him what you did! Are you listening to me?'

Barty's face had changed slightly. She could see that she had made an impact at last. 'I'm going to see Attilio,' she repeated, breathless, as Wally Wallace hauled her to the door, 'I'm going to tell him his brother's a psychopath! You think he'll be pleased? You think this is how he wants you to carry on, half-killing young girls?'

'Get her out, Wally!' Barty Moruzzi yelled. He gestured to the band, who nervously played a little faster, a little louder.

'He likes me, your brother, didn't you know?' Marionetta was still shouting. 'He wants me to be his *fidanzata*! And I'm going to tell him, I'm going to tell him –'

But it was too late. She felt the whoosh as the double doors opened against the weight of Wally Wallace's shoulders, and then he was hustling her down the stairs and into the street.

The doors of the Satin Club slammed shut decisively, leaving Marionetta alone in the shadows on the pavement. A couple of young men, slightly the worse for drink after an afternoon at the Artists' and Models' Club, eyed her appreciatively. She glowered at them and turned on her heel. At least she had said her piece for Silvia. She had shown Barty Moruzzi that not everyone was afraid of him.

Slowly, her heart still beating, she made her way along Bateman Street. She had been gone a long time. It was dark now. Papa would be starting to worry. Or maybe he would just think she had gone home to lie down . . . And she must go to Fortuna's the chemist and get Silvia some pain-killers, as she had promised . . . Her head was buzzing with anxious thoughts, and she was so preoccupied that she did not notice the figure following her quietly, side-stepping into darkened doorways whenever she paused, hanging back if she looked as if she might turn around.

It was not until Marionetta was crossing the dark alley-way by the pub that she became aware of the presence of someone close at hand, and by then it was too late. Suddenly she was pulled swiftly and efficiently into the darkness. I'm going to die, she thought, surprised, how stupid. Before she had time to scream or cry out, she felt the arm round her throat tighten, and she heard the swish of something close to her face. Then suddenly there was a hot gush of pain on her cheek, a terrible blinding scream, the murmur of a man's voice in her ear, and she was alone, crumpled on the ground, clutching her face, gasping.

She heard the sound of feet running, disappearing into the lights of Frith Street and beyond. The scream had been her own. Her hand was wet. She knelt there, too shocked to move. She had heard what the voice said, in that odd nasal whisper. It had told her that Attilio would never look at her now, that no man would look at her now. Terrified, still holding her face, she stared after her assailant, now long gone. She had recognized that voice. She pulled her hand away from her cheek, and trembled at what she saw. For her hand was dripping with blood.

Someone was running towards her. It was the girl who worked behind the bar at the Dog and Duck.

'Are you all right?'; she called. 'I heard a scream –' She slowed down, recognizing Marionetta. 'Oh, hello, Netta, what are you –' And then she stopped, staring at Marionetta's face. Marionetta looked up at her and held out her bloody hand.

'Anna?' she said. 'Anna, help me.'

But Anna's face was contorting into a scream, and she backed away. 'Your face, Netta!' she said. 'Your face!' And her scream began to echo down the dark alleyways, unrelenting, full of fear, as darkness mercifully descended on Marionetta and she crashed to the ground.

CHAPTER THREE

1950

'Well, I didn't like it much,' Mario declared, unfurling his umbrella as they stepped out of the foyer of the Odeon into the damp evening of Leicester Square. 'Apart from Jean Simmons, of course.'

'Oh, you!' Marionetta playfully dug her brother in the ribs. 'Just because it didn't have a hundred songs by Mario Lanza!'

He snorted. 'And just because you're a sucker for Dirk Bogarde, you say it's the best film you've seen all year.'

She tucked her arm in his as they huddled under the umbrella, heading back towards Soho. 'I may change my mind,' she grinned at him, 'after all, it is only March! Oh, hello, Mrs Rocca, how are you?' She paused for a moment, forcing a smile. Silvia's old neighbour was the last person she felt like chatting to, rain or no rain.

'Good evening Marionetta.' The old lady turned to Mario, simpering a little. 'I heard your solo at St Patrick's last week, Mario. Simply wonderful.'

Mario nudged his sister, his face serious and soulful. 'Thank you, Mrs Rocca. I try.'

'Try, he says!' Mrs Rocca turned, mock-ironic, to her companion, another old lady in a damp headscarf. 'This is Signor Peretti's boy – you know, the one who sings in the choir.'

Mario politely began to steer his sister away. 'So sorry, Mrs Rocca, we're in a bit of a hurry . . .'

'Any news of Silvia?' she was calling after Marionetta, determined not to let the young Perettis escape so easily. Marionetta sighed and paused. 'Not a thing, Mrs Rocca. I haven't seen her for months.'

'Ah. Such a pity. Such a good family . . .'

'We must be going, Mrs Rocca. Nice to meet you!' Mario was pulling his sister away. 'And I'm a liar,' he muttered, rather too audibly.

'Mario!' Marionetta whispered, shocked, as they dashed through the rain up a side alley and away from their persistent neighbour. 'That was rude!'

'I don't care!' Mario's clean-cut features were contorted with anger. He kicked at a dustbin, and the lid clattered to the ground. 'Stupid, nosy old woman!'

'She used to be Silvia's next-door neighbour, remember.'

But Mario was not to be placated. 'She knows damn well what's happened to Silvia! She was one of the bitches who got her evicted!'

Marionetta sighed. 'What else could they do? Silvia was on the game, Mario. She had started bringing men back to her flat. They had to do something.'

'She's one of us!' He looked very Italian in the lamplight, as he turned suddenly towards her, indignant. 'She shouldn't have just been thrown out on to the street!'

Marionetta patted his arm. Sometimes Mario seemed even younger than his nineteen years. 'Silvia's all right,' she said quietly. 'I've seen her, on Shaftesbury Avenue. And someone told me she's rented some rooms in Lisle Street and got herself a maid. She's doing all right, by all accounts.'

Mario laughed grimly. 'All right for a prostitute, you mean.'

Marionetta tried to forget the image of the Silvia she had glimpsed one night out on the streets – a small, pale, tired face framed by the kind of furs Silvia had always dreamed of. She had looked defeated, in spite of the smart new coat and the expensive perm; and she had also looked very alone. To her eternal shame, Marionetta had stepped into a doorway to avoid being seen by her old friend, and had watched the small, defiant figure make its way down towards the lights of Charing Cross Road; a desolate sight.

'I wonder if she still sees Lino,' she murmured aloud.

'Lino who?' Mario was interested.

'I'm not sure. Rivaldi, I think. Or was it Rinaldi? He was in the year above us at school. Works at Isola Bella.'

'He was Silvia's boyfriend?'

Marionetta shrugged. 'He was always very keen on her. He lived in Newport Dwellings, but he spent so much time hanging about outside St James's Residences waiting for a glimpse of Silvia that Mrs Rocca once chased him away with a broom.' She smiled at the memory.'He was crazy about Silvia. But I don't suppose he sees her now.'

Mario was still fuming. 'Anyway, it's none of that old biddy's business any more. She sent Silvia out on to the streets, and now she wants to know how she is!'

Marionetta hugged his arm a little harder and said nothing. She knew that it was not Mrs Rocca's curiosity about Silvia that had made Mario so angry. She had heard the whispered comment the old lady had made to her companion as they left: 'Poor girl, such a dreadful scar, quite ruined her looks . . .'

Marionetta was used to overhearing such remarks, and unlike her younger brother, had learnt not to resent them. People did not mean to be unkind, she reasoned. It was the shock of seeing her face, it always made people behave oddly, as though somehow the fact of having a gash from eye to mouth made her not quite human, not quite capable of seeing their looks of horror when she turned her scarred cheek towards them. She had learnt to pretend that everything was normal, that they were not staring at her, their mouths open, or worse, trying *not* to look at her, looking anywhere but at that ugly red gash that defiled her face. She had learnt that when a person is scarred or disabled, or in some way not the same as everyone else, it is that person who must make life comfortable for everyone else, pretending they don't mind, assuring others that they have learnt to live with it, offering soothing words to alleviate their discomfort.

Never again would she look away when she saw a war veteran with a limb missing, or met one of those jolly, desperate ex-RAF pilots, many with horrific burn scars, who sometimes had tea in the Imperial. She felt now as though they had something in common. All right, she had not fought the Germans, but she had borne the burden of other people's pity, which was surely worse than all the horrors of warfare. Something in Marionetta had changed, hardened. She felt as if she had lost her innocence, and it was all because of the Moruzzis.

She had not been able to tell the police anything about her assailant. A mysterious, unprovoked attack, she told them – someone must have mistaken her for someone else. Only her brother Antonio looked at her in disbelief when she told the same story to her distraught family through lips stiff with pain. What was the point, she had decided, of publicly accusing Wally Wallace? She knew enough of life in Soho to be sure that a convenient alibi would be found for her assailant if she named him. Why prolong the misery, why embroil her family in more trouble? No, she had decided, it was best to put the whole sorry mess behind her. The one good thing to emerge from the horror of that night was that her badly scarred face had had the desired effect on Attilio Moruzzi. He had been seen in Soho with a new mistress, indifferent, it seemed, to the cause of Marionetta's scar. He had merely crossed her off his list of potential victims, Marionetta reflected wryly, and found another woman, one not flawed by a razor, and more willing to play along.

Meanwhile, Marionetta had returned to her humdrum life at the café, working hard to be mother, sister and support to the men in her family, and trying to ignore the looks of pity at her face. It had been very hard at first, when the stitches were still congealing on her left cheek, and the pain of the cut so close to her lips forced her into an unaccustomed silence. Moving her mouth had felt as though someone were digging a knife into her jaw. Then, when the stitches were at last removed, she had begun to adjust a little, almost able to look in the mirror without flinching. She realized that if she smiled, the corner of her mouth did not move, which gave her a strange, lopsided look. So be it, she thought, I must just remember not to smile. And so much of the laughter that used to echo around the Imperial was now gone, along with the pretty girl who brought a smile with her when she served the tea. Sometimes she felt as if her life had finished almost before it had begun – between them, the Moruzzis had seen to it that she would never be able to enjoy what small pleasures being young and beautiful might have offered her.

But all of this, she reasoned, should not be placed on Mario's shoulders. Of all the Perettis, Mario was their great hope for the future, the one who would rise above their humble existence and make something of himself; and Marionetta did not want his young life to be overshadowed by bitterness on her behalf. Consequently she decided it was time to change the subject.

'How are you getting on with your Sinatra song-book?' she asked as they turned the corner into Shaftesbury Avenue.

Mario was slowly learning all the words to the songs of Frank Sinatra – a huge task. He looked at her and smiled wryly to himself, understanding perfectly well why his sister was introducing a new topic of conversation. His heart went out to her. She was still beautiful to him, the sister who had replaced his mother and who, he knew, would die rather than let anything happen to him. He patted her hand, overcome with an emotion he could not express. In reply to her question, and typically of Mario, who found it easier to explain himself in song, he began to sing, oblivious of the stares from passers-by. 'Embrace me, my sweet embraceable you,' he sang, his voice perfectly in tune as always. Mario could mimic any singer, and the smooth tones of Sinatra echoing along the rainy street made people turn and look. Marionetta laughed mischievously. 'You may sound like Frank, pity you don't look like him!'

Mario was indignant. 'At least I'm Italian like he is, that's more than most of these English crooners can say.' He carried on singing, his voice lilting above the roar of the traffic.

As the pair of them ducked under the awning of the bookshop in Greek Street, neither of them saw the young man leafing through a book on the other side of the window. At the sound of the song he had looked out to see who on earth in Soho was able to produce such pure, clear sound, and at the sight of Marionetta he had forgotten the song in an instant, and had gasped a little. He had seen this girl before somewhere, he knew, but he could not remember the occasion. What he did remember was the line of that cheek, so perfect, the pale skin translucent under the lights of Soho as she turned towards her companion, smiling. It was then that the young man had seen her face, with the livid red scar. He stood staring, still holding the book.

'Dreadful business,' someone was saying at his elbow. He looked up. It was the shop owner, smoking a cigarette and staring out of the window. 'The Peretti girl. Comes from that café round the corner. Got involved with the Moruzzis, so they say, and got her face done. You want that book, Micky, or do you intend to read the whole thing by closing time?'

The young man handed him back the copy of *The History of Jazz* he had been leafing through.

'No . . .' he said, distracted, 'Thanks, Peter . . . some other time.'

The shop owner laughed, and replaced the book on a nearby shelf. 'When you get paid by the Black Cat Club, eh? I won't hold my breath . . .'

But the young man was not listening. He was still staring out of the window as the couple stepped off the kerb and crossed the road, out of sight.

Mario and his sister headed towards the Imperial rather than home. It was seven o'clock, and the café should be closed by now, but there was just a chance that Papa and Nonno would still be closing up, and they could all walk home together. As they rounded the corner by Kettner's wine shop, Marionetta paused, staring at a uniformed figure standing in the doorway of the Imperial.

'What are the police doing outside the café?' She clutched her brother's sleeve.

'Isn't it Tony?' Mario asked. Their brother was on duty this evening, and it wasn't unusual to find him having a quick cup of tea in the Imperial if he was passing.

'No, it's not Tony.' Marionetta's voice was tense.

Something was definitely wrong. This was a policeman on duty, not some friend of Tony's hanging about waiting for a free cup of tea. 'Come on!'

The two of them broke into a run, dashing out in front of a taxi cab in their haste to reach the café, and causing the driver to curse and reach for his horn as they reached the opposite pavement.

'Idiots!' he yelled as the cab swerved off again in the rain, but neither of them heard him. They hurried inside the café, past the policeman yawning in the doorway, and stopped short at the devastation they saw. Tomasso Peretti was sitting with his father-in-law at the window table, his head in his hands. A man in a brown overcoat was writing notes in a small book, occasionally licking his pencil wearily. He looked up at the new arrivals.

'These your kids?' he asked Tomasso.

Tomasso nodded, still numb with shock.

'Papa!' Marionetta stared around her. 'Who did this?'

The man in the coat answered. 'We don't know,' he said. 'You got any ideas?'

The floor was littered with broken china. One end of the counter was leaning drunkenly outwards, its wooden supports shattered. Several tables had been overturned and a chair by the door had been smashed. The huge tea urn was balanced at an odd angle against the wall, and Marionetta saw that it had in fact landed there after smashing its way through the glass display stand where the pastries were kept. Bella the cat was profiting from the chaos, contentedly eating her way through a slice of squashed cake on the floor by the counter.

Dazed, Mario stepped towards his grandfather. 'Nonno, are you all right?'

Franco merely nodded, but the hand that lit his cigarette was trembling.

'Nonno, you shouldn't be smoking,' Marionetta said absently, righting a cup on its saucer on a nearby table. She turned back to her father. 'Who did this, Papa?'

She saw with a shock that Tomasso was struggling to hold back tears. 'All my years of work,' he was murmuring, his hands covering his face, his voice broken. 'All ruined, all ruined . . .'

Marionetta went over and knelt by his chair, overcome. 'It's all right, Papa,' she said quietly, 'it's all right . . .' She looked at the policeman. It was obvious that he was the only one who was in a fit state to offer her any kind of account of what had happened.

'We don't know who it was,' he said, closing his note-book. 'A couple of men came in here, according to your dad. They seemed harmless enough. Sat over there, drinking tea. Then some kind of fight broke out between them, one of them started letting loose a load of punches, and before you know it – they've wrecked the place.'

Mario let out a long, low whistle. 'They made a right mess, that's for sure.'

Marionetta looked around her, and then back at the policeman. 'They certainly did,' she said. Then, after a moment, 'Don't you think, officer, that they made rather a *lot* of mess, considering there were only two of them having a private argument?'

The man stood up. He was tired, and his shift was nearly over. 'Look, miss,' he said, 'if you've got any theories about who did this, I'd be happy to hear them.' He looked at her for a moment, his eyes drawn to the ugly scar across her cheek. Of course. This was young Tony Peretti's sister. There was some talk down at the station that she had got herself tangled up with the Moruzzis and had paid a high price for it. He looked at her with new interest. 'Well? You got an idea who did this?'

Marionetta shook her head. The man was staring at her scar, in spite of himself. Her hand automatically flew to her face. She met his eyes defiantly. 'Of course I don't know who did it. You think I'd be standing here if I knew?'

He turned towards the door with a shrug. 'Right, then. I'll be in touch if we get any leads.' And he was shouldering his way out of the door and into the street. The blue-uniformed figure disappeared with him past the window in the rain.

Mario righted the overturned chair. 'We won't hold our breath,' he said ironically.

'Why?' Tomasso was asking brokenly. 'Why us? Why now, when we were doing so well? I haven't got the money to do the repairs . . .'

'Hush, Papa,' Marionetta said soothingly. 'I'll put the kettle on, shall I?'

'You'll have a job,' Nonno said quietly. 'They managed to tear the electric wires out of the wall.'

'What?' Marionetta stormed over to the place behind the counter where the electrical junction box was fixed to the wall. Sure enough, there were wires protruding from it, and an ominous hissing noise.

'How on earth . . . ?' She stared at her father, angry. 'They must have meant to do this.'

Her father shrugged, defeated. 'Maybe they did. It doesn't matter, does it? The result is the same – no café. We might as well close it down.'

Marionetta could not believe what she was hearing. 'Papa! It's a setback, all right, but we'll recover, I know we will.'

Tomasso's tone was bleak. 'So – we recover,' he said dully. 'And for what? So they can come and do it again?'

Marionetta could hardly contain herself. How could her

father be so defeatist, so – so *cowardly*? Mario saw the expression on her face and withdrew hurriedly to the back kitchen.

'I'd better turn the electricity off,' he said hastily.

Mario's action seemed to rouse his grandfather from his stunned immobility. He scraped back his chair and got to his feet unsteadily. 'I'll find some candles,' he said, and shuffled out after Mario.

Marionetta was left alone with her father. After a moment's silence she spoke. 'We're not giving up,' she said. 'I don't care what you say, Papa. We're not giving up.'

He looked at her standing, angry, by the counter. She looked so much like her mother sometimes: the same energy, the same passion. Only the terrible weal across her cheek reminded him that this was not Francesca come back to life to berate him for his weakness.

'I can't afford another glass display case,' he said. 'And the counter will cost a lot to repair . . .'

'So we'll just have to have the cakes on plates for a while,' Marionetta said determinedly. 'And Tony will be able to patch up the counter. It may not look very good, but it'll hold up.'

'What's the point?' he asked. 'What's the point, Netta?'

She made an angry sound, thumping her fist on the counter, causing some shards of broken glass to tinkle to the floor. 'The point', she said, 'is that the café is *us*, it's everything. It's the Peretti family, Papa. If we don't have the café, we don't have anything.'

He gazed at her, his heart softening. Of course Marionetta would fight like a tigress for the café. What else was there for her in this world? Not a husband, not children, not all the things other women had. At twenty, her life had changed irrevocably, thanks to some thug with a razor. Small wonder that she stood there white with anger at the thought of losing her one source of comfort, the one place where she could forget herself in hours of backbreaking work.

'All right,' he relented, unable to prevent a sigh from escaping his lips. 'We'll patch it up, and we'll see what happens.'

Nonno came back into the room, holding a couple of lighted candles stuffed into bottles. 'Here.' He handed one to Marionetta and took the other over to the table where Tomasso sat. Then he called loudly, 'Right, Mario!' There was an answering muffled shout, a loud click, and the café was plunged into darkness.

It took a moment for their eyes to adjust to the gloom. Marionetta's pale face loomed out of the darkness, lit only by the candle she was holding. She walked carefully towards her father and grandfather at the table by the door.

'Where is Mario?' she asked her grandfather. 'He sounds as if he's been locked in a cupboard.'

'In the basement. That's where the big junction box is for the electrics.'

As if in answer, there was a loud thud under Marionetta's feet. Mario was banging on the ceiling below.

'He's found the trapdoor,' her father said absently.

Marionetta was surprised. 'I didn't know there was a trapdoor. I thought the only entrance was round at the back, in the yard.'

'There's a trapdoor under your feet as well,' Nonno told her. 'It got covered by the lino when Tomasso did the redecorations. There's a proper staircase, too.'

Marionetta stared at her grandfather, an idea beginning to form in her mind. 'A staircase?'

'The people who had this place before used to rent the basement out to a barber,' Nonno explained. 'So his customers would come in up here and then go down the stairs by the door.'

The Perettis had only ever used the basement as a store-room. Marionetta thought about the grimy walls, the boxes of tea, the empty crates. There was, she remembered, a pile of rubble in one corner, the remnant of some long-forgotten air-raid, heaps of old newspapers, and a lot of cobwebs.

Mario appeared, holding a lighted candle balanced on a tin lid, his face streaked with dust.

'We should get Mr Colpi in tomorrow to fix things,' he said, 'He's good with electrics –' He stopped when he saw Marionetta's face, illuminated by the candlelight. 'What's the matter?'

She turned to her brother, her eyes shining. 'That's the answer! The basement!'

Her father was beginning to follow her train of thought, and he made an irritated movement with his hands. 'Don't be silly, *figlia*, we can't open the basement to customers. As it is, I can't afford to put the café to rights, let alone think about opening up downstairs.'

'I didn't mean as part of the café, Papa! We could open it up as a club – for young people. We could have music, dancing . . .'

Mario looked at his sister, catching her excitement. 'A club in the basement? *Brava*, Marionetta! Why not? We don't use it for anything, Papa –'

Tomasso was dismissive. 'Don't waste my time with your wild talk, you two. If we're to re-open the café in the next few days we must start planning what repair work we can do ourselves –'

'But, Papa,' Marionetta interrupted him, her voice pleading, 'this is a good idea. If the club makes just a little money, we can pay to repair the café properly, make it

73

look just like it did before – maybe even put in the new counter you're always talking about –'

Her father stood up, annoyed. 'That's enough, Marionetta! Enough of your silly schemes. Come on, we should go home – we can't talk here in the dark. Up you get, Papa . . .'

As far as Tomasso Peretti was concerned, the subject was closed. He concentrated on helping his father to his feet in the half-dark; and as he blew out his candle, he failed to see the look of excitement that passed between Mario and his sister. A Soho club! A chance to reach out to that other, nocturnal world and embrace it, the whole exotic ragbag of danger and excitement that was Soho after dark . . . Marionetta felt a hand reach out and squeeze hers. She smiled to herself in the gloom. For she knew that a streak of stubbornness and determination ran in the Peretti blood. The same determination that had brought Nonno all the way from Sicily with his new bride, the same grit that had helped Mamma and Papa make a success of the café – this same family trait was equally present in the Peretti children. The club *would* happen – she and Mario would make sure of it!

Tomasso did not argue for long. Perhaps the shock of the damage to his precious Imperial café had weakened his resistance; or possibly he did not really believe that his children were capable of such an ambitious enterprise, for in his opinion the idea of opening a club in the basement, however small and humble, was preposterous. People like the Moruzzis controlled clubs. Club owners were a different breed – sophisticated, world-weary, knowledgeable about Soho night-life. They certainly were not green young working-class Italians who only knew about waiting at tables.

The only member of the family who supported his dislike of the scheme was Antonio, who saw nothing but trouble ahead. 'I know about these places,' he warned his sister. 'You'll get all the wrong types in – drunks, drug addicts . . .'

But Marionetta was adamant. 'Just one night a week,' she argued. 'It won't be open every night, Tony, you and your policeman friends will hardly know we're here . . .'

'You'll get no decent customers,' he scoffed. 'Who would want to come and sit in the basement of the Imperial on a Saturday night? You'd have to be drunk to want to spend an evening down there . . .'

Nonno was excited by the idea. It had breathed new life into the defeated old man. He had even insisted on paying for the paint out of his savings, and it had been all Mario could do to prevent his grandfather from climbing up the ladder and applying whitewash to the bricks himself.

The Imperial had re-opened after a few days' concerted hard work. It now had a patched-up counter and no display cabinet, but the customers, although a little ruffled by the unexpectedly violent incident in this usually peaceful corner of Soho, soon returned. Their duty done, Mario and Marionetta were able to work late at night, after the café was closed, turning the filthy basement into a place where people might like to come and enjoy themselves on Saturday nights. This was a formidable task. First, they had to remove the years of decomposing rubbish that had accumulated in the forgotten corners of the basement. Every bit of junk and rubble had to be hauled up the back stairs into the back yard, past the interested gaze of the Lee Fung family, to be dumped on the front pavement to await the council rubbish cart. A rag and bone man had been happy to take away the old cooker they had un-earthed, but the piles of damp, ancient newspapers and rags

75

had been harder to deal with. Marionetta's worst moment had been when she had pulled back a pile of rotting *Daily Workers* and found a writhing nest of blind baby rats, squealing for their mother. She had almost given up then, but Mario, determined, had called in the local rat catcher, who had dealt with their problem in exchange for a week's-worth of free breakfasts in the Imperial, grudgingly cooked by Tomasso.

Gradually the basement began to look less like a dumping ground for the café's accumulated rubbish, and more like a club. The walls were painted white, and Marionetta had persuaded a local travel agent to give her some out-of-date travel posters of Italian scenes to decorate the walls. They had found a stack of folding chairs under some sacking in one corner, a relic, no doubt, of the long-disappeared barber's shop, and they had bought some card tables at a junk shop.

'We can bring coffee from upstairs,' Marionetta had told her brother, 'and if people want to bring their own wine, they can. After all, they only have to cross the road to Kettner's to get it!'

'So how will we make a profit?' Mario asked.

'We'll charge an entrance fee,' she decided. 'The same for everyone, no exceptions – not even your friends, Mario!'

'And what about music?'

Marionetta remembered the men she often saw congregating in Archer Street, chatting on street corners, looking like a ludicrously large collection of gangsters, with their violin cases.

'There are a hundred unemployed musicians in Soho – you've seen them all hanging about near the Windmill Theatre, haven't you? I'm sure we could find a few who would play some tunes in exchange for a few cups of coffee . . .' She looked round the tiny 'club', pleased.

'We'll move the tables and chairs down a bit, so there's space at the far end for musicians to play.'

And so they had transformed the dank basement with their enthusiasm and hard work, until they were both so exhausted that Marionetta sleep-walked through her days at the café and Mario's singing lessons began to suffer as the dust and the damp affected his throat.

One evening, they had finished hanging an old fishing net on to the ceiling and were sitting together at a rickety card-table wearily drinking a cup of tea.

Mario looked around the room and then at his sister, who was busy writing out a notice advertising the club to stick in the café window. As her tea went cold beside her, she was wondering out loud whether or not they should be supplying food for their future customers.

'Perhaps,' she was saying, her head bent over the card she was writing, 'perhaps just some snacks – maybe spaghetti or ravioli. Or should it not be Italian at all? What about beans on toast? Or just omelettes?'

'Hey,' he said. 'Guess what!'

She looked up. 'What?'

He grinned at her. 'Never mind about omelettes. We've done it, sis! I think we're ready to open!'

Together they surveyed their handiwork, Marionetta's excitement mounting to match her brother's. 'You're right, Mario,' she said finally. They looked at each other. 'What are we waiting for?'

'I know,' Mario announced. 'The grand opening ceremony of the trapdoor!'

Amidst much grumbling from Tomasso, the Imperial's lino was ceremoniously rolled back to reveal the trapdoor beneath. With a little judicious rearranging of the tables near the door, it would be possible for the basement customers to walk straight in and down the steps without

77

disturbing anyone in the café. Tomasso watched these manoeuvrings grumpily.

'And what will you call this great palace of entertainment?' he asked sarcastically.

Nonno proudly put his arms round the shoulders of his two younger grandchildren. 'They're going to call it the Mint,' he told his son. 'Get it? The café's the Imperial, so the club is the Mint. Mint Imperial. Good, eh?'

Marionetta produced her small poster advertising the opening of the Mint the following Saturday. 'Can I put this in the window, Papa?' she asked. 'Please?'

He hesitated. Surely there could be no real harm? Probably nobody would turn up anyway. Surely one little club would not be a problem? And it had been worth it, he had to admit to himself, just to see Marionetta smile again. He sighed. 'Very well,' he said, 'Put your notice up. And *le faccio i miei migliori auguri*! Good luck!'

Antonio, who had turned up for the stair-opening ceremony still in his policeman's uniform and tired after a long day on the beat, took his sister to one side and spoke to her quietly. 'I have to warn you, sis,' he said, 'you're likely to get some trouble. The Moruzzis won't let just anyone open up a club in Soho, you know that.'

Marionetta shrugged. 'I don't think the Moruzzis are interested in me any more, Tony. I don't believe they'll bother with the Mint. It's hardly going to be a casino, is it? I should think it's far too humble to interest them.'

Her brother frowned. 'I wouldn't be so sure. You know Barty Moruzzi collects protection money from a lot of the clubs round here. And if people don't co-operate – well, I leave it to your imagination.'

Marionetta's hand crept up to her face. 'I know,' she said absently, 'I know what the Moruzzis get up to, Tony. But I'm telling you, I don't think they'll bother with me.'

Tony sighed. 'Maybe not. But what about Papa? Has it occurred to you that the fight in here that caused all the damage wasn't an accident?'

'Of course it's occurred to me!' Marionetta was impatient. 'I'm not stupid, Tony. But nothing's happened since, has it? No one's been back to threaten us, the Moruzzis haven't been in touch.'

He drew her a little further away from the family group by the window, who were arguing over the best place to stick the notice advertising the club's opening.

'I haven't mentioned this to Papa,' he said quietly, 'but there's a club in Meard Street had a bit of trouble recently. Two men, minding their own business, having a quiet drink together, and suddenly there's an almighty fight, and they wreck the place.'

Marionetta stared at him. 'And then what happened?'

Antonio shrugged. 'You think the club owner's going to tell the police what happened after that? They never tell us anything, Netta, they're all too frightened. All I can tell you is that the two men trashed the place, disappeared, and no one knows who they were.' His mouth tightened. 'But we all know who they work for, don't we?'

'What club was it?'

'The Black Cat Club. A jazz club – near the Gargoyle.'

Marionetta knew the Gargoyle by reputation – it was, by all accounts, a fabulous place with mirrored walls and a rooftop dance-floor. But the Black Cat Club she did not know. This was not unusual. Even though she was a permanent resident of Soho, it was difficult to keep up with the endless opening and closing of the hundreds of tiny clubs in the area, some exclusively for drinking, others for dancing, or gambling, or illicit sex. As soon as one closed down, another would open in the next street to replace it, and somehow the party-goers who invaded Soho as darkness fell always knew where to go.

Over by the door, Tomasso and Mario had finally agreed on the placing of the notice, and they called Marionetta over for her approval. 'Don't worry, Tony,' she whispered, as they joined the others, 'the Mint is *not* going to go the way of the Black Cat Club. I intend to stay open for a long time!'

'We've run out of onions,' Marionetta told her father the following morning, untying her white waitress's apron. 'I'd better nip along to Berwick Street and get some.'

Tomasso, busy at the sink, barely looked up. 'All right, Netta. Get me some more parsley as well, would you?'

She stepped out into the sunshine, relieved to be out of the smoky atmosphere of the Imperial, even if just for a brief moment. Hurrying away from the café, she turned into Dean Street, narrowly avoiding two Greeks having an argument on the corner by the shoe shop, their voices raised in an incomprehensible babble. Away from the Imperial, she slowed down a little, savouring the late morning atmosphere of Soho. The smell of fresh coffee and newly baked croissants wafted along the pavement from Madame Valerie's. A stray dog in a doorway wolfing a morsel stolen from a nearby dustbin, growled at Marionetta as she passed. A group of West Indian men were leaning on the railings of a shabby office building, enjoying the sunshine in a relaxed, aimless sort of way, and they grinned at Marionetta, seemingly oblivious to her scarred face, as she paused to cross the street. Like many of the Soho regulars, they knew her by sight, and her disfigured cheek was of no more significance to them than the huge handlebar moustache of Gaston Berlemont, the publican of the York Minster, or the swirling cloak and strange metal contraption on the foot of Ironfoot Jack, another Soho habitué regularly to be seen in this narrow network of streets.

Marionetta was not heading for the market, as she had told her father. She was going instead to the Black Cat Club, to find out for herself what had happened, and to reassure herself that the same thing would not occur at her humble little club. She turned into Meard Street and paused by the entrance to the Gargoyle, searching for a sign of the Black Cat Club.

'What you looking for, love?' A disembodied voice floated down from somewhere above.

Marionetta looked up. A window-cleaner was up a ladder nearby, puffing on a Woodbine. He had been swatting at a window in a desultory way with a dismal-looking cloth but had paused, grateful for an excuse to stop working.

'The Black Cat Club,' she told him.

'You a singer?' he asked, interested.

Marionetta shook her head, trying to disguise her impatience. 'Do you know it?'

The window-cleaner nodded his head in the direction of a doorway to Marionetta's right. 'In there, love. First floor. Good luck!'

She hurried up the narrow, sparsely carpeted stairs to the first floor, following the tatty signs to the club. She paused, hesitant, as she reached the landing. A man was sitting on a chair reading the *Racing Times*, ticking off horses with a stub of pencil. He barely glanced up, but indicated a door behind him with a jerk of the head.

'Black Cat Club?' he said. 'In there. Ask for Micky.'

She went inside. The club was nothing more than a small square room, painted a lurid red, with a piano at one end and a bar at the other. Someone was playing a desultory little jazz tune on the keyboard, and a very overweight, depressed-looking man was hammering at something near the bar. Marionetta approached him, looking around her, puzzled. She could see no sign of the damage to the club Tony had talked about, until she saw what the large man was doing. He was hammering a board across the bottom of the bar, where, she could see now, a large hole had been kicked.

'Micky?' she asked nervously.

He shook his head, his mouth full of nails, and waved in the direction of the piano. Marionetta looked across the room. The pianist, young and dark-haired, had not looked up from the keyboard, where he was picking out an odd, discordant little tune.

'Another one, Micky,' the fat man called. As Marionetta crossed to the piano, the young man sighed, straightened up some sheet music in front of him, and spoke. 'Right then, kid. What's your range?'

'I don't understand.'

Her voice made him look up at last, and Marionetta was surprised to see a look of recognition cross the pianist's face.

'Hello,' he said. 'You haven't come for the auditions, have you?'

She was aware of intense dark eyes staring at her. Had they met before? She had no memory of this good-looking, rather scruffy young man with the black hair seated at the piano, but he seemed to know her.

'Auditions?'

He grinned disarmingly. 'No, of course you haven't. It's your brother who's the singer, isn't it?'

She was surprised. 'You know Mario?'

His eyes moved back to the piano. He seemed suddenly shy. 'No, I don't know him. But I've heard him sing at St Patrick's.'

Marionetta stood, there, astonished by this revelation. 'You go to St Patrick's?'

He played a chord on the piano, still not meeting her eyes. 'Not very often.' She noticed a hole in his navy blue sweater at the shoulder seam, and the way his hair, rather longer than was conventional, curled on to the polo neck collar. 'So,' he said eventually, 'you're one of the Peretti family.' He seemed to be having difficulty finding things to say.

She held out her hand, trying to be businesslike. 'Marionetta Peretti. Pleased to meet you. Are you the owner of the club?'

He held her hand and looked up at her, a flicker of something she could not identify crossing his face. 'No,' he said, 'I wish I was. Bill over there – he's the owner. Bill the Bear. I'm just the piano player.' He was still holding her hand. 'I'm Micky. Micky Angel.'

She withdrew her hand politely. 'Pleased to meet you. I've come to talk to the owner, so I'll –'

She was about to walk away, but he called her back, his voice amused. 'I wouldn't, if I were you. Bill's like a Martian till he's had his lunch-time drink. He'll only tell you to get lost. I'd come back later, if you want to get any sense out of him. Or,' he held her with his eyes, his hands resting on the piano keys, 'or maybe I could help.'

She hesitated. She might not be able to get away again today. And it had taken her quite a lot of courage to get here this time. Micky Angel seemed harmless enough. In fact, she thought fleetingly, he was very good-looking. Then she pushed the thought away, angry with herself, and consequently when she spoke the words were brisker than she had intended.

'I've come to find out what happened the other night,' she said, turning back to the piano and resting a tentative hand on its polished top. 'The night of the fight.'

Micky Angel looked at her in surprise. He pulled a pack

83

of cigarettes from his pocket and offered her one. She shook her head. 'Why?' he asked, lighting one for himself, his eyes never leaving her face.

'I'm opening a club in the basement of my father's café,' she told him, 'and I heard there had been some trouble here. I want to know if it had anything to do with the Moruzzis.'

Micky inhaled on his cigarette and looked at the girl standing before him.

'You're opening a club?' He could not keep the incredulity out of his voice. 'You?'

'Yes, me!' She was indignant, her anger bringing a flush to her cheeks. 'And please don't tell me you think I'm crazy to do it, I've already heard all that from my father.'

He did not smile, as she had expected, and say something disparaging about women doing men's work. Instead he said, 'I wish you luck. What is it called, this club?'

'The Mint. It's only going to be open on Saturday nights, to start with.'

'I'll tell my friends.'

'Thank you.'

She was turning to leave. He leaned forward a little, his voice low. 'This fight you want to know about – I was there.'

She stopped. She was aware that he was studying her closely. For a fleeting second she wished foolishly that she was not wearing the plain white cotton blouse and black skirt that she wore every day at the Imperial. Then she swatted the thought aside. She felt mesmerized by the stream of sunlight pouring through the window behind Micky Angel, by the dark red gloom of the club, the incessant hammering from the far end of the room. She could almost feel the pulse in her wrist beating in time to the knocking of the hammer. She and Micky Angel seemed to be locked together in a mist of cigarette smoke and dazzling spring light, having a conversation about a night club but in reality having another conversation, one in which their souls suddenly recognized each other and reached out, tentative, to touch.

'What happened?' she asked, a little breathless.

Micky Angel crashed his brown hands down on to the piano keys, making a discordant sound. It was as if he wanted to shake off a spell. 'What do you think happened?' His voice was harsh. 'They smashed up the club. Bill is bankrupting himself trying to replace the furniture, and the police have done nothing. Any more questions?'

The moment had vanished, as if it had never happened, leaving Marionetta shaken and disconcerted. But she was determined not to give up. 'Yes,' she said. 'One more question. Did you have a visit from the Moruzzis after the fight?' There was silence. Micky Angel quietly closed the lid of the piano. 'Did you?' she persisted.

He looked at her, his face changed. His mouth was set in an angry line. 'Of course we did,' he said. 'Barty Moruzzi came round.'

Marionetta's heart sank. 'And he asked for protection money?'

Micky ran a hand through his mop of dark hair, sighing. 'No, I don't think you understand.' He was suddenly impatient. 'Surely it must have happened exactly the same for you?'

She did not understand. 'For me?'

He leaned forward and crushed his cigarette into an ashtray on top of the piano. His voice was cool, a little weary, as if he was sure she knew what he was going to say. 'The order of events – it must have been the same for you. One – Barty Moruzzi comes round and says pay me some money to look after your place, or I can't guarantee there won't be accidents. Two – you tell him to sling his hook. Three – a couple of blokes have a fight in your café or club or whatever it is you own, and they wreck the joint. Four – Barty Moruzzi comes visiting again and suggests you pay him protection again, only this time it's a little bit more expensive. Am I right?'

Marionetta stared at him. 'Barty Moruzzi came here and pressured the owner for protection money?'

'That's right. Only Bill is still saying no. That's why we're auditioning this morning.'

'Auditioning?' Marionetta did not understand. She felt herself being drawn into something she could not control or understand.

Micky Angel looked at her a little pityingly. 'For a new singer. The other one walked out. Said she didn't want to get her face slashed by the Moruzzis –' He stopped, aghast, realizing what he had said. 'I'm sorry. I didn't mean . . .'

Marionetta's hand had crept up to her burning face. Just for a moment she had forgotten about the scar, about the fact that she was not like other young women, that she could not even entertain the thought of a boy like Micky Angel looking at her and wanting her . . . 'It's all right,' she said. 'Really.'

But he would not let the matter drop. 'No, it isn't,' he said, aghast. 'Of course it isn't.'

She was angry now. He had looked at her so clearly, so honestly, but all the time he had only seen what everyone saw – a face razored by the Moruzzis. 'Anyway,' she said coldly, 'the Mint is opening on Saturday. And I intend to pack it with all the customers I can get. So you can tell your friend Bill and any other club owners you might know that it's not the Moruzzis they should be worrying about – it's me!'

She was turning to leave, triumphant at having the last

word, but the pianist had jumped to his feet and taken hold of her arm, his face full of anger. 'I'd like to wish you every success,' he said, his voice shaking a little. 'But I know that's not necessary. The Moruzzis will make sure everything goes swimmingly for you.'

She tried to shake him off. 'How dare you!' she panted. 'I have nothing to do with the Moruzzis, how can you say that, after —'

He let go of her arm suddenly, his face disgusted. 'I don't know,' he said. He sat down again, deflated. 'You're not what I imagined,' he said suddenly, inexplicably. 'Not at all.'

Marionetta did not understand what he was saying. She only knew he had insulted her. 'My family have nothing to do with the Moruzzis!' she said. 'Just because we're Italians doesn't mean we're all crooks and pimps and shysters! My family is decent, honest, hardworking —'

There were tears in her eyes, but Micky Angel was implacable. 'Go home and ask your father,' he said bitterly. 'Ask your father about the Moruzzis. It's all over Soho. The Perettis have finally paid protection to the Moruzzi family and now the Imperial will be left in peace! I hope it's worth it.'

Marionetta stared at him, her face drained of colour. 'I don't believe you,' she said flatly.

He shrugged, turning back to a pile of sheet music and pretending to look through it, unconcerned. 'Suit yourself,' he said angrily, 'but I'd have a word with your father before you go to anyone else with your holier-than-thou attitude.'

'You don't know my father,' she said. 'He would never have dealings with those people. There is such a thing as honour.'

Micky shrugged. 'Not in Sicily,' he said quietly.

She stood there, undecided what to do next. Part of her wanted to slap Micky Angel's face, but his words had left her confused, shocked. She was rooted to the spot, one hand unconsciously covering her cheek as she stared at his averted face.

'Micky!' Bill the proprietor was calling from the door, 'Another victim for you – shall I send her in?'

'Sure.' Micky looked up, his eyes still avoiding Marionetta's. A blonde girl in jeans and a checked shirt was standing in the doorway. 'Hi, Vicky,' he called, 'come on over. I thought you'd show up.'

The girl crossed the floor, her tiny feet in their black ballet shoes making no sound. She smiled at Marionetta as she approached, then leaned over and kissed Micky Angel on the cheek. 'Watcha, Micky,' she said in a cheerful cockney voice, 'I heard there was a job going. You want me to do my Peggy Lee number?'

Micky had begun looking through his sheet music. 'Sure, whatever you like,' he said.

The girl looked at Marionetta, an apologetic smile on her lips. She had a fresh, scrubbed face, not at all conforming to the image Marionetta had of a night club singer. This other world of Soho was full of contradictions, too confusing to understand. 'Oh, sorry,' the girl said, 'have you finished?'

'Yes, I've finished,' Marionetta said, her voice cold. Micky Angel would not look at her. 'I wish you luck with your audition with this idiot, this – *zotico*!' She stalked out with as much dignity as she could muster, tears of anger in her eyes. As she descended the seedy stairs, she could hear a soft, smoochy voice above her, and the gentle tinkling of the piano keys. 'Gonna take a sentimental journey, gonna put my heart at ease . . .'

She ran out into the street, distraught, scrubbing the

tears angrily from her face. How dare he speak to her like that! She was accustomed to the casual, everyday prejudice of the English against the Italians, the jokes about Mussolini, the assumption that they were all lazy, or cowardly, or dirty, or worse – but this! He had not only insulted Sicilians, he had insulted her own family, the Perettis! She found herself running back the way she had come, past the West Indians, still lounging on the railings where she had left them, past the stray dog gnawing at a bone thrown to him from Gennaro's kitchen, past the Greeks on the corner of Dean Street, no longer arguing but tearfully conciliatory, their arms about each others' shoulders.

Oblivious of the tourists strolling in their shirtsleeves, she pushed through the crowds on Old Compton Street and burst into the café.

'Papa, Papa!' she called, a sob still in her throat. 'Papa, I have something to tell you!'

But there was only Nonno behind the counter, pouring tea from the urn with a shaking hand, spilling some on to the counter top. 'Marionetta, *grazie a Dio*! It's starting to get busy, and I can't manage the sandwiches with my rheumatism –'

Pulling herself together, Marionetta joined her grandfather, tying on her apron. As usual, the demands of the café superseded everything else. 'What do you need?' she asked, sympathetic. Poor Nonno. He was far too old to be still here, still serving the public for hours on end.

'Cheese and tomato, cheese and pickle, two Danish pastries and a bowl of tomato soup for table three.'

She busied herself. 'Where's Mario? And Papa?'

'Mario's rehearsing for the *Messiah* at St Patrick's . . .' Nonno became intent on filling a sugar bowl, avoiding his grand-daughter's eyes.

'And Papa? It's not like him to leave you alone like this when he knew I'd had to go out –'

89

'What happened to the onions?' Nonno seemed nervous, distracted.

Marionetta stared at him. 'Onions?'

'The market,' he said gently. 'Weren't you going to get some onions?'

Marionetta's hand went to her mouth. 'I completely forgot!' she gasped. 'I'd better go out again.' Then she changed her mind. 'No, I can't leave you, Nonno. Where's Papa?' she repeated.

He hesitated for a moment before replying. 'Downstairs,' he said finally. Some grains of sugar spilled over the rim of the bowl on to the counter top. He began wiping them up.

'In the club?' Marionetta was puzzled. 'Why? Is there a problem?'

'No, no . . .' Nonno was scrubbing at the counter, intent on wiping away grains of sugar that Marionetta could not see. 'He's with a customer – a – customer, yes. A *cliente*.'

'Fine. I'll just go down and get him to take over for a minute.'

She did not see the futile gesture her grandfather made in an attempt to stop her, nor the look of fear and sadness that passed over his face as she turned away. She crossed to the door and descended the steps to the basement. In the gloom, she could make out Tomasso seated at a table by the makeshift performing area, and another man hunched over the table, smoking. A jug of coffee stood between them, half-empty.

Un tipo di furfante, she thought to herself fleetingly – an ugly customer! And then he looked up and smiled at her, his queer, crooked smile. It was Barty Moruzzi.

Tomasso made a sharp sound, something between a gasp and a sigh, at the sight of his daughter. 'Marionetta,' he said, his smile guilty, 'this is Mr Moruzzi. He's been very kind' – he hurried the words, as if the faster he said them, the less impact they would have – 'he's agreed to keep an eye on the café for us, to prevent any more incidents . . .' Marionetta stood silent. 'You know,' her father continued brightly, 'keep the trouble-makers at bay.'

Barty Moruzzi's eyes were fixed on Marionetta's scarred cheek. 'That's a nasty gash you've got,' he said.

Marionetta still said nothing.

Her father smiled, tremulous. 'And he'll watch the club as well, Netta,' he said. 'He'll look after the Mint, too!'

Marionetta turned silently and went back upstairs. She reached the door of the café and turned for a moment to look at her grandfather, alone and somehow vulnerable at the counter.

'Are you going to the market?' he called nervously. He had known all along who was in the basement with Papa, Marionetta realized. They were all involved, the whole family. She turned and walked out, her grandfather's voice echoing in her ears as she went. 'Don't forget the parsley, Netta!' he was calling, his words somehow incongruous in the light of the betrayal he and his son were perpetrating. 'Netta, the parsley . . .'

From that day on there was a space at the corner table of the Imperial reserved for 'Mr Moruzzi's friend', a silent, swarthy man in a cheap suit who appeared at irregular intervals and was given tea, free cakes and a discreet envelope full of cash.

The Mint opened quietly the following Saturday night, with enough customers to convince Tomasso that perhaps his daughter had hit on a good idea after all. But something had changed in Marionetta. She could barely disguise her contempt for her father, and would storm down to the basement when the Moruzzi henchman appeared for his payment.

The final straw had been when she heard that the Black Cat Club had closed down, forced out of business by the Moruzzis. Tony had told her, having collected the gossip at West End Central Police Station.

'And what happened to the owner – Bill the Bear?' she asked him.

Tony looked at her quizzically. 'How did you know about Bill?' he asked.

'Never mind. What happened to him?'

The intensity of her voice surprised him. He shrugged. 'Went off on a drinking binge, apparently. Hasn't been seen since.'

'And – and his musicians?' she had asked.

Her brother looked at her, puzzled. 'Don't ask me. How on earth should I know?'

Marionetta's question had been answered a few days later, when she had wandered, not entirely by accident, along Archer Street, where the itinerant musicians gathered to look for work, to compare notes and to commiserate with each other. She had found Micky Angel leaning against a 'No Waiting' sign, chatting to an earnest young man in horn-rimmed glasses carrying a giant double bass.

Feeling far from bold, she approached the pair. 'So I said if you think Satchmo is the best, you should hear this geezer –' The man in the spectacles broke off in mid-sentence as she stopped in front of them. She was looking directly at Micky.

'Hello,' she said. She could feel a strange lurching feeling in the pit of her stomach.

'Hello,' was all he said.

'Hello!' said the other young man enthusiastically. 'Do we know you?'

Marionetta's gaze had not left Micky, and it was him she addressed. 'You have every right to tell me to get lost,' she said.

Micky's friend was interested. 'Have I missed something?' he asked Micky.

He was ignored. 'How are you?' Micky asked. 'How's the club?'

'You were right. About my father. I'm sorry.'

He looked away, staring into the middle distance, his voice cool. 'So am I.'

'Look, are you going to introduce me, or am I supposed to just stand here like a wally while you two have this enigmatic conversation?' The boy in the spectacles was becoming indignant. Micky Angel seemed to pull himself together for a moment. 'Sorry,' he said. 'Marionetta Peretti, this is Peter Travis. He's a friend.'

Peter Travis shook her hand warmly. 'Nice to meet you. Have we met before?'

'I don't think so,' said Marionetta shyly, withdrawing her hand from his emphatic grip. She looked again at Micky Angel. 'I wondered', she said, 'if you would be interested in some work.' Micky looked down at her, unfathomable. 'In the Mint,' she carried on miserably. She might as well say her piece, she decided, in spite of the frosty atmosphere. 'We could do with a regular band – nothing big, just a piano and a bass and some drums, maybe –'

'Excellent idea!' Peter Travis could hardly contain himself. 'I don't think our engagement diary is quite full yet, is it, old chap? I'm sure there must be a few Saturday night slots we could make available to this good lady . . .'

'Forget it.' Micky was already walking away decisively.

His friend was appalled. 'Micky! Where are you going? Are you mad? We haven't worked since the Black Cat closed down and now you're turning your nose up at the chance of a regular spot! What's got into you . . .?'

Micky turned back, angry. 'The Bear drying out in that

93

seedy little clinic for alcoholics, that's what's got into me,' he said. 'And I don't work for villains.'

And then Micky Angel was striding off through the crowded street, shouldering his way past the groups of musicians arguing and talking on the pavement.

Peter Travis turned to Marionetta with an anguished expression. 'Don't go away, miss!' he shouted. 'Don't book anyone else! We'll be back – I promise!' And he too disappeared into the crowd, in frantic pursuit of Micky.

Marionetta turned away. It was no use. She knew that Micky Angel would never agree to take charity from her. After all, why should he? All he knew was that the Peretti family were no better than the Moruzzis, they were all Italians, they were all villains . . .

CHAPTER FOUR

1951

Marionetta was dreaming. She was standing in a field, somewhere very hot. She could feel the sun on her bare arms. She supposed it was Sicily. Someone was saying something to her in an urgent tone, someone standing a long way away, on a hill in the distance. 'Be strong, Marionetta!' It was her mother, Francesca, suddenly and miraculously well again, and she was waving something. Marionetta squinted into the sunshine. What *was* it? Just as she realized what the object was, the dream began to fade.

'The puppet, Mamma,' she murmured. 'Why have you got the puppet?'

'Marionetta!' She looked up, confused. The Sicilian landscape had disappeared. There was only the back yard of the café, the stifling heat of a July night, and her brother's face staring down at her in the darkness. 'Marionetta,' he was saying, 'I don't believe this! The club's full to bursting and you're out here asleep!'

She rubbed her eyes, confused. 'Sorry,' she murmured, 'I didn't mean to . . .'

But Mario was already hurrying inside. 'Second set starts in five minutes,' he was saying self-importantly, 'so you'd better get back in here!'

Marionetta sighed, and stretched. Mario was too caught up in his own minor success as Saturday night singer in the

Mint to notice how close his sister was to complete exhaustion. Now that Nonno was so ill, she hardly had a moment to herself, running backwards and forwards between the club and café and their rooms in St James's Residences, where Nonno was struggling to live out the last of his days in the lonely back bedroom. Papa tried to help, but the café took up all of his time, and when he noticed Marionetta yawning in the Imperial, he would simply frown and say, 'You should close that damn club, you haven't got the time to be there and here *and* look after your grandfather.' The injustice of this seemed to have escaped him, Marionetta thought wryly, getting to her feet. After all, the Mint was now the most successful part of the family enterprise; and she was determined not to relinquish the one small success she had found in her life. So it was that she filled every second of her days and nights with work – dealing with the customers in the café, coping with the crowds in the Mint at night, and dashing back to tend to Nonno in between. Small wonder, then, that she had developed the capacity to fall asleep in a moment, no matter what the hour.

She yawned and rubbed her eyes. This had been a particularly busy weekend. It was the Soho Fair, an annual event attracting people from all over London to take part in games, buy produce at stalls, picnic in Soho Square and, on Sunday, watch the famous Soho Waiters' Race. Both the club and the café had done a roaring trade, which was good for the family but hard on Marionetta, who would not have the reward next day of getting out into the sunshine to celebrate her corner of London, as others did. She had volunteered to stay with her grandfather, so that Papa and Tony could go to the race. After all, Mario was going to be a contestant, and many of the other competitors, all of whom were waiters in Soho cafés and restaurants, were their friends. It would have been unfair to expect one of them to stay behind . . .

She descended the steps of the fire escape slowly, straightening the seams of her stockings as she did so. Then she peered at her dim reflection in the dusty glass of the back door. Large, sleepy brown eyes looked back at her. Her mind was still in a field in Sicily, hand outstretched, trying to grasp the puppet that Mamma held out. Sadly, Marionetta reached up and touched her face. In her dream, there had been no scar.

'Beautiful!' someone called. She looked up. Mrs Lee Fung was shelling peas at the open kitchen window above. She was referring, no doubt, to Marionetta's new dress, bought specially for her nights at the Mint, and more glamorous than anything she had ever possessed. It was white georgette with tiny black polka dots all over it, a narrow bodice with fine shoulder straps giving way to a full, soft skirt, and had been the cause of many arguments with Tomasso, who thought it highly unsuitable for a respectable young woman to show so much of herself. Marionetta smiled up at her neighbour, grateful.

'Thank you, Mrs Lee Fung,' she called back. 'It *is* pretty, isn't it?' And she twirled round, laughing.

Mrs Lee Fung leaned out of the window and shook her head, suddenly solemn. 'Not the dress,' she said. 'You. Beautiful.' Marionetta's hand flew, as usual, to her face, but Mrs Lee Fung shook an admonishing finger at her. 'You must be in love,' she said. 'You keep smiling when you think nobody see.'

Marionetta felt herself blushing. 'When would I get time to fall in love?' she asked, edging towards the back door, anxious to end this probing conversation. 'I have far too much work!' And she disappeared inside, leaving Mrs Lee Fung gazing after her, thoughtful, as the pea shells flew through her tiny, competent fingers.

It was extremely hot inside the Mint. The walls seemed to be sweating. Marionetta sighed, as she breathed in the usual suffocating odour of cigarette smoke and too many people crammed into a small space. She was far from complaining, however; she loved the little club. This was her small kingdom, where she made the decisions. It was the only part of Marionetta's life where she felt she had some control – the rest of her existence was dominated by the Moruzzis and her own family, or so it seemed to her; and even here, in the world she had created, the Moruzzis' evil influence had penetrated. As she went over to the tiny bar to one side of the musicians' corner, she could see the Moruzzi henchman drinking whisky at the back of the room, near the stairs. He nodded at her, his face expression-less, but Marionetta ignored him. She loathed his presence, but was powerless to tell him to leave, thanks to her father's agreement with Barty Moruzzi. She supposed she should be thankful for small mercies: at least the Moruzzis had not sent Wally Wallace to sit in the corner and stare at her night after night.

She busied herself with the magnificent Gaggia machine she had recently purchased, making coffee for a queue of young people eager to settle down in time for Mario's second performance of the evening, which was about to begin. The drummer was already climbing into his seat behind his drum-kit, and the guitarist was tuning up. Mario was chatting to a couple of eager-looking girls, his hand running self-consciously through his black curls as he spoke. Marionetta grinned to herself. He really *was* taking this Frank Sinatra thing a bit too seriously – they'd be swooning on the pavement outside next!

'You look happy.'

Marionetta looked up with a start. It was Micky Angel, who had somehow materialized at the front of the queue.

This was the third time he had appeared at the Mint in as many weeks. His anger over the Perettis' co-operation with the Moruzzi brothers seemed to have abated. Or at least, Marionetta had decided, he no longer seemed to hold Marionetta responsible for her father's misguided actions. This was guesswork, since her conversations with Micky Angel had so far been limited to nervous exchanges about the weather. She was surprised to see that he seemed to be as tense about talking to her as she was about talking to him.

'Two espressos?' She could see Peter Travis sitting at a table near the stage. He waved at Marionetta and she smiled across at him.

'Yes, please.' As she turned to get the cups, aware of Micky Angel's eyes watching her, he spoke again. 'I said, you look happy.'

She turned back, her face serious. She hated it when people noticed her smile. It meant they had seen the odd way her lips remained immobile on one side, where the knife wound had cut into her mouth. 'Do I?' she said coolly. The machine spluttered noisily as she pulled a lever and hot coffee spurted into the tiny cups. 'The club's busy, I suppose that's why I look happy. Anything else?'

Unsmiling, Micky pulled the two cups towards him. 'No. How much?'

Marionetta bit her lip. She had been too brusque. He was here, trying to be friendly, and now her coldness was driving him away. 'On the house,' she said softly.

He looked up at her, suddenly braver. 'Will you come and sit with us when Mario starts his set?' he asked. She hesitated, and as if reading her thoughts, he said hurriedly, 'You know no one ever comes to the counter when he's singing . . .'

'Come on!' An irritable young man in a cravat was becoming impatient in the queue. 'They're going to start!'

'I'll be there in a minute,' Marionetta called to Micky as a drum roll indicated that the music was about to begin.

Mario was singing his fourth song, a ballad, before she was able to slip out, clutching a cup of coffee, and edge along the wall in the half-darkness towards Micky Angel's table. She had been clearing up thoroughly, doing the tasks she usually undertook after the customers had left. She only half acknowledged to herself why it was that tonight she had varied her routine; because perhaps someone would offer to walk her home through the dark streets of Soho, since Mario would be delayed packing up equipment with the other musicians, and he could lock up for once . . .

She sat down quietly at the table, as Mario sang, and allowed herself a small glow of pleasure when her eyes met Micky Angel's in the dark. Perhaps here in the gleam of the candle flickering in the chianti bottle on the table, away from the harsh light of the day, Micky Angel would not look at her face and see only a scar.

The song had finished, and the crowd applauded enthusiastically. Mario's popularity increased every week, and his growing reputation had guaranteed the Mint a lively and changing clientele. As Marionetta looked around her, she noticed a crowd of students from St Martin's School of Art arguing rowdily by the stairs, oblivious to Moruzzi's man, who eyed them with distaste from behind his whisky glass. Some chorus girls from the London Casino were having a final cup of coffee before wending their way home to their various bedsits in Kensington and Bayswater. The artist Suzanne Menlove was slumped at a table nearby, watching the proceedings with a jaundiced eye, a cigarette dangling from her lips. A group of American tourists opposite her clapped loudly, and a couple of sailors catcalled from the opposite corner, possibly more in appreciation of the chorus girls at the adjacent table than of Mario's singing, but it didn't matter. What mattered was that the Mint was full. The Festival of Britain may have acted like a magnet, drawing people across the river to the South Bank, Marionetta thought, but they all eventually drifted back to Soho, drawn by its exotic and eccentric nightlife, and the weekend of the Soho Fair still proved to be an attraction.

Micky Angel was leaning across the table towards her, his face tense, as Mario prepared to launch into his next number. 'Your name,' he whispered, 'what does it mean – Marionetta? Is it the female version of Mario?'

Marionetta, wanting to smile, put her hand up to her mouth. 'No,' she said, 'it most certainly isn't!' She pointed to the counter. 'You see the puppet hanging by the shelf?' He nodded. 'That's *la marionetta*,' she told him. 'It means puppet.'

'But why . . .?'

She shook her head at him, unwilling to explain. The song had started. Mario's baritone filled the room, silencing the gossip and laughter. 'They asked me how I knew my true love was true . . .'

Mario was transformed when he sang. It was hard to believe that the yearning, soulful voice echoing round the tiny basement club belonged to the irritating, chattering youth who plagued Marionetta's days. Like her customers, Marionetta listened transfixed as the song rang out.

'I of course replied something here inside cannot be denied . . .'

Micky Angel was nudging her. She looked up. He was pushing a paper serviette into her hand, his eyes never leaving the musicians on stage. Puzzled, she took the serviette and unfolded it. He had written something on it. She peered closer, leaning towards the candle, aware that Micky was watching her anxiously out of the corner of his eye. She began to make out the words, reading them slowly: '*Othello*, St James's Theatre. I've got two tickets for Thursday night. Can you come? It's Orson Welles.' She read the words again, disbelieving. Micky Angel was asking her to go out with him. She looked across the table at him, but he was pretending to concentrate on Mario.

She wanted to weep. She hardly dared admit to herself that this was what she had been dreaming about, that the sight of Micky Angel nervously descending the stairs of the Mint three weeks ago had started her spinning in a spiral of crazy dreams and imaginings she thought she had buried for ever the night that Wally Wallace had sliced through her face with his razor. She had longed for an indication that Micky was interested in her, that he really did feel something for her, that his sudden appearance at the Mint had not been a coincidence, or simply a musician showing his interest in the hottest new sound in Soho. He had done it, he had asked her to go to the theatre with him, such an ordinary thing, the thing that happened to other young women all the time – but not to her! She looked down at the scribble on the serviette again, fighting back tears. How could she tell him she would not be able to go? And yet she knew, with a sinking heart, that this was so. Nonno was dying. She could not go to the theatre. It was unthinkable; and in any case, Papa would not allow it, not his daughter, not a night out at the theatre with an unknown young man.

The song had ended. Peter Travis leaned forward in his seat, calling enthusiastically to Mario for an encore. Micky Angel looked across at Marionetta.

'I'm sorry,' she said, 'I can't.'

He took the serviette back. 'Forget it,' he said, his voice cool. He threw the serviette into the ashtray on the table, pulled out a cigarette and lit it, seemingly indifferent.

'But I want to explain . . .'

He had thrown his match into the ashtray, still alight, and it had caught the serviette, sending up a small bright flame as the paper curled and dazzled for a moment, then died. He looked at her, his eyes hurt. 'Go on then. Explain.'

But before she could speak, a voice interrupted. 'Hiya, Micky! They told me you were here. Get me a cappuccino before he sings his next number, would you?' It was Vicky, the blonde girl Marionetta had seen at the Black Cat Club, kissing Micky Angel on the cheek with a proprietory air and flinging herself down into the chair next to Peter Travis. 'Hello, Peter – who's this?' She looked across at Marionetta with a friendly smile. 'You got a new girlfriend?' She was wearing cyclamen coloured lipstick and a matching shirt tucked into tight black trousers. Marionetta suddenly felt very unsophisticated by comparison, in spite of her new dress.

She got up. 'No,' she said politely, 'I just work here. Cappuccino, was it?' And she left the table, heading back for the safe haven of her counter, fighting angry tears. And she had been dreaming of being walked home in the moonlight!

Somehow she got through the rest of the evening, trying very hard not to look at the table where Micky and Peter sat with Vicky, the three of them laughing and talking with the relaxed air of long-standing friends. She tried not to notice Vicky's hand on Micky's arm, or the way he laughed when she whispered something to him. Finally, as the hands of the clock crept round to two o'clock, and the band began to pack up and the customers started to leave, she hastened outside. Leaning against the cool metal of the fire escape, she breathed the musty summer air and allowed a tear to trickle down her cheek.

He could take Vicky to the theatre instead. After all, it was obvious that she was some kind of girlfriend; or if she wasn't, she would like to be. He had probably only asked Marionetta to the theatre out of pity, because he realized that she never went out, never had a social life.

She heard a sound behind her, and a small dark shape slithered past her to the ground. It was Bella, the café cat. Marionetta bent to retrieve her, burying her face in the warm fur.

'*Buona sera, donnina,*' she murmured. It was time to go home. Papa would be waiting up for her, worried as usual. She carried the purring cat inside and deposited it on the floor. The club was empty, apart from Mario, busy dispensing coffee to the musicians. 'You seem to have cleared everything up,' he said to his sister. 'Do you want to get on home? I'll lock up when we've had our coffee. Marionetta . . .?'

She was fingering the little puppet, which dangled from a hook on the wall. She touched its perfectly smooth wooden cheek. Be strong, Mamma had said. But that had been in her dream. That wasn't what Mamma had said at all.

'Marionetta!'

She shook herself a little, as if she were waking up again. 'Fine,' she said. 'I'll see you at home. Don't be too late, Mario. Papa will only shout.'

The drummer looked across at her, concerned. 'Will you be all right, walking about at this time?' He was a middle-aged man with a teenage daughter. Marionetta seemed to him to be far too young to be out alone in Soho.

She smiled at him, grateful. 'I'll be fine. It's less than five minutes to the flat, and I know almost everyone out there.'

Quietly she closed the door of the Imperial, careful not

to set the bell clanging. The Lee Fungs got up very early to open their Chinese supermarket, and sleep in the middle of Soho was hard enough to come by.

The Triple X Club was closing too. A group of very drunk men emerged from its dingy portals, incoherently trying to hail a taxi without much success. Marionetta waited in the darkened doorway of the café until they finally succeeded in persuading a cab driver to accommodate them all in his cab, then she stepped out and hurried off in the direction of Brewer Street. Her head was already buzzing with worries about Nonno. Would Papa have remembered to give him his medicine? Had he suffered from any more of the terrible chest pains that had so afflicted him last night?

She was so engrossed in her own worries that it was a moment or two before she noticed that something odd was happening in the darkened streets. The few late-night stragglers heading in the same direction along Old Compton Street had started to run. A couple hurried in the opposite direction, the woman sobbing into a handkerchief, the man accompanying her holding her up solicitously, murmuring, 'Sorry, darling, you shouldn't have seen that . . .' A bell clanged somewhere on the Charing Cross Road, and then an ambulance came racing round the corner, past Marionetta, disappearing down Wardour Street.

Curious, she followed it, and came to a surprised halt. A crowd had gathered, and the ambulance was struggling to nose its way through the throng. It couldn't be just the usual Friday night fight, she reasoned, otherwise why was everyone so quiet?

'Marionetta? I should go home if I were you . . .' It was Carlo, a waiter at the Trattoria in Romilly Street and a friend of Mario's. He, like Marionetta, had evidently been on his way home and had been diverted by the crowd.

She was relieved to see a familiar face. 'What happened?'

Carlo shrugged. 'Only a prostitute. She's been stabbed.'

'How awful! Is she dead?'

'As a doornail.'

Marionetta, in spite of herself, peered over the heads of the crowd to have a look. What she saw made her gasp and edge closer. Carlo tried to pull her back. 'Don't, Netta – it's a horrible sight –' But she shook him off and pushed her way through the people. One young policeman was trying to keep the crowd back, with little effect.

'Cover her up, for Gawd's sake!' an onlooker shouted in a horrified voice.

The young officer pushed at a particularly determined sector of the crowd. 'I would,' he panted, 'if you lot would just back off a bit!' Marionetta took advantage of his momentary loss of attention to slip in front of him and stare down at the body.

It was Silvia. She was lying on her side on the pavement, one hand outstretched, almost pointing. Marionetta gave a little sob. Silvia! The blonde hair was matted with blood, and a spreading stain discoloured the collar of her dress. Her eyes were open, their expression sad.

'Throat cut,' someone in the crowd said ghoulishly.

Marionetta could not look away, for she had seen something glittering in Silvia's outstretched hand. She edged forward a little, pushing at someone in front of her, to get a better look. Yes, it was the silver crucifix that Lino had given Silvia for her eighteenth birthday. Marionetta stared at that stiff, small hand, at the silver cross. 'Lino will look after me,' she had said. 'He's the only person in the world apart from you who cares whether I live or die.'

There was a sudden commotion at the back of the crowd. Everyone turned and surged forward, and as the young officer shoved her back into the throng, Marionetta was forced to go with them. On the other side of the road was Antonio, officious in his uniform, struggling to restrain an hysterical girl.

'He's round the corner now!' the girl was sobbing. 'Why don't you go and get him? He's sitting in the Granada Club cool as a cucumber!'

Antonio was trying to hold the girl at arm's length, his face reflecting his distaste. She was obviously a prostitute, judging from the cheap satin dress and the ostentatious jewellery. 'Just shut up, will you?' he was saying, roughly. Then he shouted desperately to the onlookers, 'Look – just move along, will you? This is police business . . .'

'Antonio!' Marionetta called to her brother, but he did not hear. The girl still struggled, terrified but somehow determined to say what she had to say in front of the silent crowd. She turned to them, her face appealing. 'I'm telling him who did it! I'm telling him and he's telling me to shut up!'

'Let her say her piece!' someone in the crowd shouted indignantly. Others murmured their agreement. Antonio looked nervously around him for support, and his face sagged with relief when a black police van appeared from Shaftesbury Avenue, its bell pealing.

'Get back everybody,' he shouted. 'Get back!'

The crowd was pushed back on to the pavement as the Black Maria arrived with a squeal of brakes. The girl was still struggling in Antonio's grip. 'It was Wally!' Marionetta heard her say, her voice now little more than a frightened squeak. 'It was Wally!'

'Save your statement for the station,' Antonio said, shoving her roughly into the back of the van and slamming the doors shut.

'Antonio! Tony!' Marionetta could not make him hear her. He hurried to the front of the van, climbed in, and it drove off. The crowd gave a collective sigh and turned back to where Silvia's body had lain, only to see a blood-stain on the pavement and the ambulance driving away. There was a murmur of disappointment and people began to drift away. The only evidence that a murder had taken place there was the white tape the police had strung round the spot, now sagging and fluttering in the night breeze.

Marionetta stood on the pavement, unable to think. All she could see was that small hand, and the silver chain glinting, and those sad eyes, staring into eternity. Silvia, her best friend, dead!

Someone put a hand under her elbow. 'Come on,' Carlo said gently, 'let's go home . . .'

'But it was Silvia,' Marionetta gulped. 'Silvia Conti.'

Carlo stopped, surprised. 'Silvia who was in your class at school? Silvia from the cinema?'

Marionetta nodded, unable to speak. Carlo bit his lip. 'I heard she'd gone on the game. Honestly, talk about giving the Italians a bad name! Now it'll be all over the papers.' He pulled at Marionetta's arm again. 'Come on, there's nothing you can do for her now . . .'

The day of the Waiters' Race was fine. Marionetta leaned out of the window and looked down at the passers-by, heading towards central Soho. She recognized many of the faces below, even those of the non-Italians. There were the Maltese brothers from the gambling club in Greek Street, the old lady who sold newspapers outside Leicester Square tube station, the tired-looking woman with too many children who lived above Bifulco, the butcher on Frith Street. Everyone except Marionetta seemed to be out on the streets today.

The Peretti flat in St James's Residences was at the front of the building, and every now and then someone would emerge from the entrance below her, step out into Brewer Street, look up and wave. The community in the building was tight-knit, and even though the Perettis were considered something of an oddity, being Sicilian, they were still part of that enclosed little world of immigrant Italian workers in Soho; and everyone knew that old Franco Peretti was dying. At Mass early that morning, several people had approached Marionetta and her brothers to tell them that they had lit a candle for the sick old man. Marionetta, lighting one herself in the gloom at the plaster feet of Our Lady, had felt warmed by their concern; but when she should have been praying for the safe journey of Nonno's soul to Heaven, she found herself thinking of Silvia, and those sad, dead eyes, instead. *'Aspetto la risurrezione dei morti e la vita del mondo que verra ...'* When she murmured the words of the Profession of Faith during the service, she found herself thinking not about Nonno's certain journey to the heavenly kingdom, but instead wondering where Silvia's soul would now be wandering in eternity ... 'We look for the resurrection of the dead and the life of the world to come ...' Mass had not offered her the comfort she had hoped for, not even when Father Joseph had said kind words to her on leaving.

'I'll come to see Franco this afternoon,' he had said, holding her hand, his face concerned. But Marionetta had hardly heard him, so distracted had she been by her thoughts of Silvia. For surely Silvia would go to hell? There could be no place in paradise for prostitutes, could there?

Nonno was calling her from the bedroom. Sighing, she turned away from the window and the seductive activity of the street below, back to the dark, stuffy rooms of their flat.

Nonno was lying propped up in bed, his face contorted

with pain. Marionetta stood crossly in the doorway, her hands on her hips. 'Nonno!' She was despairing. 'How many more times? You shouldn't be smoking at a time like this . . .'

He waved her away, coughing noisily, waving his cigarette, defiant. 'Too late now,' he panted. 'Only pleasure left . . .'

Annoyed, she crossed the room and tried to plump the pillows behind his head. She noted with a pang that there was a damp stain of sweat where his head had been resting. In spite of his attempted jocularity, Nonno was very ill. He struggled to push her away. '*Basta!*' he grumbled, his chest still heaving. 'Stop fussing. Why don't you go out?'

'Don't be silly,' she said firmly. 'I don't want to go out. It's too hot. Now be quiet and I'll read you some more from *La Voce*.' She picked up the Italian community newspaper from the chair where she had left it earlier, and sat down, turning the pages. 'There's an article about Italians coming to work in mines in Yorkshire,' she said, her voice bright, but her grandfather waved a disparaging hand.

'More immigrants,' he said, coughing. 'As if there aren't enough already! And so soon after the war! The British still hate us, what's the point of more coming over?'

'It says here the British Government asked for them.' Marionetta's eyes skimmed the article. 'And there's going to be more.'

Franco harrumphed intolerantly, waving his cigarette about and depositing ash on the eiderdown. 'More! There's too many already.'

Marionetta eyed him mischievously from behind the paper. 'It says here they're all Sicilians,' she said, her voice innocent, 'mostly from Trapani . . .'

He brightened. 'Sicilians, *finalmente*! In Yorkshire!'

There was a knock on the front door. Marionetta handed her grandfather the paper. 'Here,' she said. 'Read for yourself!' He grinned at her as she headed for the door, turning the paper over in his frail hands. That was more like Marionetta. The fact that Franco could not read, and would not learn, had always been a cause of friction between them.

'It's Father Joseph, Nonno!' She had returned followed by the old priest from St Patrick's. The two men were friends of many years, both sharing memories of arriving in London at the turn of the century as young men, eager to settle in this strange, damp country.

'How are you, old friend?' the priest was saying, settling into the chair by the bed. 'I've come to tell you all of the gossip.'

'He knows it all already, Father,' Marionetta smiled. 'He nags me for it every morning!'

'I heard about Silvia Conti.' Nonno was sitting up a little, coughing as he did so. '*La puttana*. Antonio told me this morning . . .'

The priest looked round, his eyes resting on Marionetta. 'Perhaps we'll talk of this later,' he said firmly. He did not believe the fate of a prostitute should be discussed in front of a young woman, particularly one who had known the girl in question. 'In any case,' he added, 'I thought we could let Marionetta go and look at the race for a while.' He held up his hand as Marionetta politely protested. 'Don't pretend you aren't longing to be out there, Marionetta.'

She kissed his hand, grateful. 'Thank you, Father –'

'Just be sure to be at Mass again tonight!' He patted her cheek. 'I can stay for an hour.'

Her face had brightened considerably at the prospect of a little unexpected freedom. '*Grazie, padre*! I'll be back before then, I promise!'

Through the open door, Franco could see from his bed that Marionetta had gone to the big dresser in the living-room and was searching for something.

'Hurry up, girl!' he grumbled. 'Why are you rooting about in the sewing-box?'

She emerged, triumphant, clutching a piece of black satin ribbon. 'I knew I had some!' she said. She returned to the bedroom and handed the ribbon to the priest. 'Tie this on for me, Father,' she said, her voice a little defiant, holding out her arm.

The priest placed the ribbon around her upper arm, as one did to indicate mourning and show respect for the dead. 'Who is this for?' he asked, automatically tying the ribbon.

She looked over his head at her grandfather. He knew what she was going to say. 'It's for Silvia,' she said. 'Silvia Conti. *La puttana*. The whore. She was my best friend.'

The start of the race this year was to be in Dean Street. Marionetta hurried through the crowded streets, calling greetings to people as she went. She might just be in time for the start of the race, and she wanted Mario to see her cheering him on. There would be stiff opposition this year – the Café Royal was rumoured to have put up a strong team, and the boys from Gennaro's had even been practising! Mario's team, made up from the small cafés that dotted Soho, did not stand much of a chance, Marionetta thought, but that was all the more reason to be at the starting-line, cheering them on.

She turned the corner into Dean Street and was relieved to see through the crowd the waiters in their black ties still hovering about, calling last-minute instructions to each other as the trays, bottles and glasses that the competitors had to carry were distributed. She pushed her way towards the starting-line, still slightly out of breath, when a voice startled her.

'Marionetta Peretti, isn't it?'

She turned. The face looking down at hers was unfamiliar for a moment, and then everything clicked into place. Of course. The wide-set brown eyes, the open smile – this was Lino, Lino Rinaldi. Or was it Rivaldi? He was wearing the smart, well-cut black jacket of a *commis* waiter, and a bow-tie. Evidently he was about to enter the race.

'Lino . . .!' She did not know what to say. Did he know about Silvia? From his smiling face, she guessed he did not. But perhaps he did not care, perhaps he felt, like all the others, that she had forfeited the right to be grieved over . . .

'You remember me, then!' Lino grinned at Marionetta, pleased. 'I remember when you and Silvia used to go past Isola Bella giggling away – thought I couldn't see you half the time! I'm working at La Dolce Vita now – do you know it? Corner of Frith Street and Bateman Street. Money's quite good but the hours are pretty long. Last night there was a private party until four o'clock. I've only just got up.' He chatted on about work, Marionetta staring at him white-faced.

'Lino,' she said eventually, 'do you know about Silvia?'

Her words stopped his flow. He looked at her, the smile gone. 'Of course I know about Silvia,' he said in a low voice. 'You think I don't spend every spare minute telling her to give it all up? I've told her – I'll marry her as soon as I can find us a place to live. I can't marry her and take her home, can I? My mum and dad know all about her, they'd never let her in the house. Only she won't stop what she's doing, not until we're married. Says if I loved her I'd move in with her to that place she's got in Lisle Street. She doesn't understand – my dad would never speak to me again. I've tried, Netta, I've tried to stop her, I've told her I love her.' His voice was desperate. He doesn't know,

113

Marionetta thought. No one has told him Silvia's dead. But then, why should they? She was just another prostitute, caught up in the dirty dealings of Soho. The fact that she was Italian would have been conveniently expunged from the minds of everyone to whom these things mattered.

Lino was looking around him. 'I'd better go – race will be starting in a minute – good to see you, Netta! I'll tell Silvia I saw you, she's always talking about you and the good old days.' As he turned, he saw the black armband on the sleeve of Marionetta's blouse. 'Did your grandad die?' He looked sympathetic. 'I'm sorry to hear that, they say he was a nice old geezer.'

Before Marionetta could even decide whether or not to reply, there was a sudden commotion nearby, and someone shouted, 'It's starting!'

With a wave Lino disappeared into the crowd. Marionetta struggled to follow, but could not force herself past the bulk of a large Greek family who had settled on the pavement to watch the race. She turned and went back down Dean Street as the shout of the crowd went up. The race had started! Never mind, she would go down to Old Compton Street and watch as the waiters came round from Greek Street.

She had decided; when the race was over, she would find Lino and tell him about Silvia. Better that he should hear it from Silvia's erstwhile friend than from some uncaring acquaintance – or, worse, from a bald paragraph in the *News of the World*.

This corner of Soho was quiet now, as the crowds surged forward to follow the race, or hurried round to Wardour Street where they could stand at the finishing-line. Someone crashed into Marionetta as she wandered along, lost in thought.

'Sorry, darling,' a slurred voice murmured, breathing

alcohol fumes into her face. The woman, wearing a stained jacket that had seen better days and a pair of sailor's trousers, clung on to the door-frame of the York Minster pub for support. 'Race over, is it?'

Marionetta drew back in distaste. This was the drunken artist, Suzanne Menlove, whose pictures hung in the Tate, according to Tony!

'They're coming now,' she said, backing away. The woman looked at her blearily. 'What happened to your face?' she asked sharply. Marionetta's hand flew to her cheek. The woman staggered towards her, peering. 'What a bloody awful mess! Was it a man? I bet it was a man . . .'

Marionetta turned. She could hear the shouts of the crowd. The waiters were coming closer. More people emerged from the pub, curious to see the runners pass. Suzanne Menlove gesticulated angrily at something invisible in front of her. 'Men!' She was shouting, her voice booming, 'BLOODY men!'

The noise of the crowd grew louder. The first waiter appeared, red-faced, sweating, still clutching his bottle of champagne and his wine glass somehow on the tray that he had to transport, intact, to the finishing-line. Hot on his heels came two more, running flat out, their faces contorted with effort, and then another. The crowd cheered.

Suzanne Menlove saw the waiters and her face went a strange purple colour. She pointed an accusing finger, as more men ran past in a blur of black and white. 'BLOODY men!' she roared. 'It's all your fault – all of you!' She staggered into the road. One of the waiters, disconcerted, dropped his wine glass, amid groans from the crowd.

Marionetta turned and hurried away. The winner would be at the finishing-line by now. She would have to forget about cheering Mario on, it was more important that she speak to Lino, that she tell him the terrible news. Perhaps she could take him somewhere quiet and tell him calmly – not here, not in this chaos; St Patrick's perhaps, or the garden in front of St Anne's . . .

The cheering as she turned into Wardour Street told her that the winner had arrived. She craned her neck over the crowds, searching for Lino. As more contestants completed the race, ragged cheers echoed around the street. Relatives in the crowd struggled to find their offspring to congratulate them on their effort. Jubilant waiters, their starched collars limp with sweat, slapped each other on the back and compared notes about their progress round the course.

'Giovanni dropped his tray on the first bend!'

'Did you see Enrico's face when I went past him . . .?'

Across the heads of the crowd, she suddenly saw him, laughing, in a group of waiters. At the same time, she saw something else, on the other side of the road. It was a small procession of blue helmets making its way through the crowd. She pushed past the spectators, struggling to reach Lino, and as she did so she glimpsed a familiar face.

'Tony!' she called. 'Tony!' She reached Lino at the same moment as her brother, in time to catch the words of the man in the brown suit accompanying him. It was the detective who had visited the café after the fight. 'Lino Rinaldi,' he was saying in that same world-weary, seen-everything voice, 'I'm arresting you on suspicion of murder of one –' he looked at his notebook '– one Silvia Conti. You are not obliged to say anything, but anything you do say may be taken down and given in evidence . . .'

Marionetta stared. Tony was there, her brother, in his uniform. He had produced a pair of handcuffs and was pulling Lino's hands roughly behind his back.

'Are you crazy?' Lino was saying, his eyes wide. 'Silvia's not murdered – I saw her last night!' The crowd around him had fallen silent. The waiters who had been standing with Lino stared at him, shocked. There was a click as Tony clamped the handcuffs into place. Lino turned to the detective, his face blank with shock. 'I saw her last night!' he repeated. The colour was draining from his face. He staggered a little, turning to Marionetta's brother, who was now holding his arm. 'She isn't really dead, is she?' he asked. Tony looked away and said nothing.

One of Lino's companions made an attempt to intervene.

'Listen, you can't just come here and –'

Tony shook him off. 'I'm afraid we can, sir,' he said politely.

The young man stared at him. 'Tony Peretti! How can you do this to one of us? We were in the same class at school . . .' Marionetta saw her brother's eyes slide away, his face an impersonal mask.

'Come along, sir,' said the detective to his charge. 'This way.' He began to push his way through the crowds, with Tony pulling a struggling Lino along and two more constables following. Marionetta stood rooted to the spot as they passed.

'Terrible . . .' someone in the crowd murmured.

'Doesn't look like a murderer,' someone else remarked.

'Spoilt the day,' said a third, a woman with a sour expression and several children in tow.

Lino turned and spotted Marionetta. 'Help me!' he called, desperate. 'I don't know what's happening! I didn't do anything, I didn't do anything, Marionetta!'

Tony turned sharply at the sound of his sister's name, but he was too late. He missed the look that passed between Lino Rinaldi and Marionetta, the look of an innocent man appealing for help to the one person he could see in the indifferent crowd who might care. Nor did Constable Peretti see Marionetta duck back into the crowd and slip away, her face taut and drained of colour, as the mass of people closed around the police van, eager to observe the event.

'I wonder which restaurant he works in?' Someone in the crowd asked of no one in particular.

'I dunno, but I won't be ordering stew for a while,' said a wag nearby. 'You never know what might be in it!'

'Typical bloody Italians,' someone murmured as the doors of the police van slammed shut, 'bunch of cut-throats!' And as the van revved up and prepared to leave, the crowd had already turned away, intent on returning to the business of a pleasant summer's afternoon in the exotic streets of Soho.

In St James's Residences, as the inhabitants prepared their supper that evening, they heard a terrible row erupt in the Peretti flat. Men paused over their perusal of the evening paper to listen; women hovered over boiling pans of pasta, ears straining to hear what was said. Even the children, who usually played noisy games of hide-and-seek on the landings and the stairwells, now stood in silent groups, somehow sensing the depth of anger emanating from number 104. They could hear the raised voice of Tony Peretti, and his father's deeper tones, but what had halted everyone in their tracks was the third voice in the argument, for it was Marionetta's – quiet little Marionetta with the scarred face, who hardly looked anyone in the eye nowadays, and kept herself to herself – and here she was, yelling like a fishwife for everyone to hear! Mrs Rocca, who had been sweeping the landing on the first floor outside her own flat, extended her activities to include all the stairs up to the third floor, in order to hear exactly what was said.

118

Inside the flat, Marionetta was pacing up and down, incongruously still clutching the large spoon she had used to stir the sauce for supper. Tony was sitting at the table, his hands over his ears.

'For God's sake!' he was saying. 'I don't make the law, I only enforce it!'

'Lino didn't do anything, Tony. He didn't do anything!'

'Netta, calm down!' It was her father, trying to impose some order. 'I won't have you speak to your brother like this –'

Marionetta rounded on him, furious. 'I will not calm down! I will not keep quiet, Papa! God knows I've kept quiet over so many things . . .' Her hand had gone to her cheek. Mario, who had been about to leave for St Patrick's to sing in the choir, hovered uncertainly by the door. Marionetta suddenly noticed him. 'Go on!' she said crossly. 'You'll be late!'

'I'm not leaving you like this,' Mario said. 'I don't see why I should be sent away like some naughty schoolboy so you lot can have your fight in peace.'

'Do as your sister tells you, Mario, *per piacere*!' The usually mild Tomasso was shouting now. 'This does not concern you!'

Mario slammed out of the flat, almost falling over Mrs Rocca on the landing. In a fury, he picked up her dustpan and hurled it down the stairwell. She stared after him, open-mouthed and indignant, as he stomped down the stairs. Well! she thought, so much for the saintly choir-boy . . .!

'Tell me,' Marionetta was demanding of her brother, 'tell me what evidence you've got against Lino.'

Tony was still at the table, staring at the chenille table-cloth. 'I can't tell you,' he said. 'It's sub judice.'

'Don't be ridiculous, Tony,' snapped Tomasso. 'This is

family! Tell her, for God's sake, so we can put an end to this.'

Tony sighed. He still would not meet his sister's eye. 'All right,' he said finally, 'though what business it is of yours I don't know. You hardly know this Lino bloke –'

'Tell me.'

Tony plucked at the chenille. 'This brass came forward. Young tart. Said she saw Lino at the club where she and Silvia worked. Said Lino was in a right state, begging Silvia to give it all up and marry him.'

'Rubbish!' Marionetta exploded. 'I spoke to Lino just before the race – he told me he couldn't marry Silvia at the moment, he was saving up for a place for them. Marriage was out of the question.'

Tony looked up at her for a moment. 'He was covering himself,' he said, 'getting your sympathy.'

'He's not like that! He's –'

'*Basta*, Netta,' her father intervened. 'Let Tony tell us what happened.'

Tony sighed again. He had no desire to continue, but in the face of Marionetta's fuming silence he had no choice. 'This tart,' he said, 'she says Lino was following her and Silvia when they left the club later that night. She says he suddenly ran up and stabbed Silvia, then he ran away.'

'Fine,' said Tomasso. 'Now can we have our supper?'

Marionetta looked closely at her brother. 'And this stabbing – it was where Silvia's body was found – in the alleyway off Rupert Street?'

Her brother nodded. Marionetta's voice was calm. 'You made her change her story, didn't you? That girl. The one who was there when they took the body away – you made her change her story.'

Tony said nothing. Tomasso didn't understand. 'What girl? What story?'

Marionetta's eyes did not leave her brother. 'There was a girl there – when Silvia was killed,' she told her father. 'She kept saying the murderer was Wally. Wally Wallace.'

'Who is Wally Wallace?' Tomasso was tired. It had been a long day. 'I can't keep up with you two, I don't know who these people are. Is he someone in the club, Netta? Is that it?'

She shook her head, turning suddenly to face her father. 'No, Papa. He works for the Moruzzis. He works for Barty Moruzzi –' She snapped the last few words. 'Yes, Barty Moruzzi, your dear friend!'

Tony was still hunched over the table, his face bleak. 'Just leave it, Netta, will you? Keep out of all this. It's none of your business.'

Marionetta turned back to him. 'You coward,' she said. '*Codardo*! All the men in this family are cheats and cowards! You sign up for the police force because you say you want to make the world a better place, and in five minutes you're as corrupt as the rest of them! How much did it cost, Tony, eh? How much did it cost the Moruzzis to buy you and your police friends off?' She stood helpless with anger for a moment, devoid of words. Then she threw the large serving spoon on to the table, where it clattered against a glass fruit bowl. 'I hate you and despise you, Tony, I don't ever want to speak to you again!'

There was nowhere for Marionetta to go. She slept in the living-room, so she did not even have the luxury of storming into her own bedroom and slamming the door. She stood trembling, fighting a desire to leap on her brother and punch him. Then she turned and stalked off to the only room where she knew she would not be followed – her grandfather's darkened bedroom.

She entered, closed the door and stood inside, panting a

little in the half-light, trying to control herself. Nonno would be asleep, Papa would not come in here and try to persuade Marionetta to calm down and carry on with the supper. She would stay for a few moments to calm her racing heart, and then she would return, with dignity, to finish the cooking. She would serve them their meal, as a good Italian daughter should do, but she would not speak to them, no, no matter how hard they tried, she would not speak to them – either of them –

'Netta . . .' She looked up, startled. Nonno was not asleep. Of course not – who could have slept through all that shouting? He was beckoning her towards the bed. She went over.

'*La lampada* – the light . . .' Obediently she clicked on the bedside lamp. Her grandfather's grey, sweating face was suddenly illumined, stark against the white pillows. She realized with a pang that his condition had deteriorated.

'Nonno,' she whispered, sitting down in the chair by his bed and reaching for his hand. It was cold, and the chill of his flesh as he squeezed her hand was a wintry reminder of his impending death. 'I'm sorry,' she said, tears of anger starting in her eyes, 'I'm sorry, Nonno, forgive me for being so selfish . . . I didn't mean to wake you.'

He shook his head, a movement which seemed to cause him some considerable pain. 'I was not asleep, Netta. I heard what you said in there.'

'Nonno, I'm sorry –'

'No,' he whispered. 'Listen. I must tell you something. I must –' She was trying to calm him, to persuade him to lie back quietly, but he shook his head, distressed. 'You must let me tell you this thing, Marionetta. It is important. It may help you to understand things, to understand your father, and your brother, and perhaps not despise them so much . . .'

Her lips tightened. 'They're cowards, Nonno. Both of them. You can't change that.'

The old man sighed, and the sigh turned into a cough, which rose from his chest and rattled in his throat. 'I want to tell you,' he gasped, 'about Sicily. About your grandmother, Giulietta, and me.'

Marionetta tried to soothe him, stroking his arm gently. 'I know all about it, Nonno,' she said. 'Mamma told me.' She told me on her deathbed too, just like you, she almost said, and then she bit her lip. It might be true, but you did not say it, you did not confront a sick old man with his own imminent death. 'You don't have to tell me anything. Try to sleep.'

He shook his head again, his brow furrowed. 'Listen,' he said, his voice almost a whisper, 'listen, will you?'

She nodded obediently. Best to humour him.

'I was a militant in my youth,' he said. 'In Sicily. I organized strikes against the landowners . . .'

'Mamma told me . . .' She remembered her mother's words about the *fasci*, how it had been a socialist league of peasants.

He smiled, proud of the memory. 'I was the leader in our village.'

She leaned forward and stroked his hair lightly. He looked so frail, lying there. It was difficult to equate this sad, sick old man in the bed with any militant activity, and harder still to imagine that the silver hair sticking damply to the clammy forehead had once been black, framing a strong peasant's face, as it was in the photograph on the sideboard.

'I know all about your rivalry with old Moruzzi, Nonno. Mamma told me. That's why I have the puppet now.'

He waved a hand impatiently, suddenly his old irascible self. 'Don't treat me like an idiot, girl! I haven't gone senile

123

yet. Of course you know the story about the puppet, I wasn't going to repeat the same old yarn to you –'

'Sorry, Nonno,' she said hastily, anxious to calm him. He had half-risen in the bed, leaning on one elbow, wheezing a little and glowering at her.

He subsided again, appeased. '*Bene*. I'll start again.' She sat quietly. 'Eighteen ninety-four . . .' he murmured, remembering. 'I ran the local *fasci*, the peasants' group. I organized a strike against the landowners. We demanded that the *latifundia* should be redistributed amongst the peasants . . .' Suddenly he looked at her sharply. 'You understand the *latifundia*?'

'I think so. They were huge pieces of land, weren't they? Like – like a ranch in America, I suppose.'

He looked grim. 'More like a prairie. Great swathes of farmland, all taken over by those rich bastards, Moruzzi among them.'

'And did the strikes work?'

He gave a wry little laugh. 'Of course not. But at least we were allowed to demonstrate and say what we felt. Then there was an election. Crispi became Prime Minister. Everything changed. The government dissolved the *fasci*, ordered the arrest of the ringleaders and declared a state of emergency in Sicily.' His face darkened at the memory, his eyes staring ahead into the increasing gloom of the room. The sun was setting outside and the shadows were lengthening across the threadbare rug.

Marionetta was intrigued, her quarrel with her brother temporarily forgotten. 'Were you arrested, Nonno?'

He closed his eyes. 'I went into hiding. I'd heard that a thousand peasants had been deported without trial to islands nearby. Others had the dubious honour of appearing before a military tribunal and being given a lengthy sentence. Either way I knew I had no chance. If they caught me, I would be locked up and they'd throw away the key . . .'

'Where did you hide?' She was sitting upright in her chair now, attentive.

The old man shrugged. 'Anywhere I could. In the hills, mostly. Caves.'

'How did you live?'

'Giulietta would bring me food. And the children from the village. People were very brave.' His face softened at the memory, and then became grim again. 'Moruzzi ran our local tribunal. He handed out terrible sentences to everyone involved. He decimated the village, broke up families, destroyed marriages –' He broke off, upset, biting his lip. He looked at his grand-daughter sitting in the glow of the lamp, looking so much like his beloved wife. 'Giulietta went to see Moruzzi,' he finally said. 'He still had a terrible soft spot for her, even though she had married me.'

'She went to plead for you?'

He nodded. 'I don't know what she said, but it worked. He agreed that he would turn a blind eye while we left the village at night and headed for Naples. He even gave her money to help us with the journey.'

Marionetta stared at her grandfather, surprised. She remembered the impassive face of the old man in the camel-hair coat she had met in Soho a few years previously. Alfonso Moruzzi. So he *did* have a heart after all!

'I know,' her grandfather was saying, 'it seems crazy, doesn't it? After all the rivalry, after him losing Giulietta. But it's true. He probably saved my life.'

Marionetta was confused. 'But I met him, Nonno! He seemed cruel, vindictive –'

Nonno shook his head. 'You want it to be simple, *ragazza*. Only it isn't simple. People are more complicated than you know.' He squeezed her hand again. He was coming to the end of his story. 'In Sicily, favours are not handed out lightly. "You are in my debt", Moruzzi told me, "and one day I'll call on you to repay that debt."' The old man sighed, remembering. He sank back into the pillows, tired. 'It was by the fountain, outside the church. It was midnight. Giulietta was waiting for me. Alfonso Moruzzi and me – we shook hands in the moonlight.' He looked at Marionetta. 'I told him I would repay the debt I owed him somehow before I died.'

There was silence for a moment. Then Marionetta said, 'And so you did, Nonno. You and Papa let the Moruzzis take over the café and the club.'

He shook his head, irritated by her lack of comprehension. 'No, no, you don't understand. I'm talking about a debt of honour, not some arrangement over the café. A debt of honour, Marionetta. The man gave me my life.' He moved restlessly in the bed, tired now that his tale was almost told. 'Giulietta and I left the village that night. Someone took us in a fishing-boat to the mainland, and then we walked to Naples. Only the relatives we had gone to find had disappeared.' He saw the look of horror on his grand-daughter's face, and waved a feeble hand. 'Oh, nothing sinister – they had just left the country, like so many Italians then. They were starving, they had no work – they had left to seek their fortune. So Giulietta and I – we had no choice. We had to do the same. We could not return to the village. So the next day we started walking again.' He looked at Marionetta, her ugly scar invisible in the gloom. How like his beloved Giulietta she looked at this moment! 'We walked and walked and we came to England,' he murmured, his head spinning off into a dream. He could feel his life ebbing away, and he was not sorry. Giulietta was waiting. But he had not finished . . .

'So you see,' he said, pulling himself back into the world with an effort, 'I still have a debt of honour to settle with old Moruzzi.'

She still did not understand. 'But Nonno, how could you pay him back? What can you give him?'

He looked at her, his eyes dim. 'Call your brother,' he said. 'Call Tony. And your father.'

His look brooked no refusal. She got up obediently, crossed to the door and opened it. To her surprise, her brother was sitting exactly where she had left him. Tomasso was standing by the window, staring out, his face bleak. It was as if time had not moved while she had sat in her grandfather's sick-room, listening to his story from the past.

'Nonno wants to see you both,' she said. They followed her into the bedroom, silent. Both stood at the foot of the bed, uncomfortable in the presence of the dying man.

'Should I get Father Joseph . . .?' Tony asked.

Franco Peretti waved his hand impatiently. 'There's plenty of time,' he said, a cough erupting from his lungs as he spoke. 'You can fetch him in a minute. Tomasso, come here,' the bony fingers beckoned, 'come here, where I can see you.'

Tomasso drew nearer, his eyes full of tears. His beloved papa was drifting away.

'Closer . . .'

Tomasso leaned over the bed, one hand on Marionetta's shoulder. She stiffened, still angry with her father, still angry with Tony – with both of them. Cowards!

The old man drew himself up a little. 'You must carry on, Tomasso,' he murmured, 'with the debt. You must carry on. It's my last wish . . .'

Tomasso sighed. 'I know, Papa,' he said, his voice breaking. 'I know.'

'And you'll obey me?'

'Of course, Papa. I may not have been born in Sicily, but I have the blood. I know what a debt of honour means.'

'So you will carry on with payment of the debt until Alfonso Moruzzi frees you from it.' This was more a command than a request.

'I will.' Tomasso's face was solemn in spite of his tears. He clasped his father's hand. He meant to keep his promise.

Marionetta, suddenly overcome with a terrible lassitude, leaned towards her grandfather. None of this made sense — or was she just too weary to understand? It had been a terrible day, a cruel weekend: Silvia dead, Lino falsely accused, her brother exposed as corrupt, her father a weakling, her grandfather slowly dying in the dark room . . .

'What is it?' she asked finally. 'What is this payment?'

There was a silence. She realized that both the old man and his son were looking at Tony, who stood immobile at the foot of the bed. Marionetta, too, turned her face towards him. She could see only his outline, rigid in his uniform, his head held high, and the gleam of his eyes in the dark.

'I am the payment of the debt, Netta,' he said. 'I belong to the Moruzzis.'

CHAPTER FIVE

February 1952

'Marionetta, there's another reporter wants to talk to you!' Mario was calling from the top of the stairs that descended to the Mint. His sister sat at one of the tables in the club, her head bent over a newspaper article.

'Tell him to go away,' she said, without looking up. She heard Mario speaking quietly, and then the clang of the café doorbell as someone left. The day's newspapers were spread out in front of her. She stared at the headlines. 'Rinaldi to hang tomorrow!' one trumpeted, 'No reprieve for prostitute killer', stated another.

Footsteps descended the stairs. Mario paused on the bottom step, his face creased with worry as he watched his sister. This was all too much. Marionetta was half-mad with exhaustion. Her campaign to prove Lino Rinaldi's innocence had escalated to the point of insanity. Her picture had been in all the papers, she had been interviewed on the radio, she had argued with Members of Parliament at Westminster, written countless letters to the Prime Minister, to the new Queen, to anyone who might listen and be able to change Lino's fate; and it had all proved fruitless. It was hard to imagine how she must be feeling. She had exposed herself to the public, she had forced herself to speak out, she had been braver than any of them – and yet it had all been in vain. Lino Rinaldi was due to be hanged the following morning at nine o'clock for a murder he did not commit.

Mario crossed the floor and sat down silently by his sister, reaching for her hand. She squeezed it absently, her eyes still on the newspaper. He peered over her shoulder. It was an editorial in a liberal newspaper, questioning capital punishment. He supposed that it gave Marionetta some kind of comfort to read the words of people who sympathized with her activities; but the hard truth was that for most of the country the death of Lino Rinaldi would be seen as just another young hoodlum getting his just deserts. Mario had spent countless months protecting his sister from the attentions of the virulent pro-hanging lobby, the wild-eyed ravings of the supporters of whipping and flogging, the mealy-mouthed pillars of society who pronounced against what they saw as the rise of the 'cosh-boy' and the thug, and who saw in Marionetta another shocking example of the uncontrollable arrogance of the young. Her scarred face, seen in every national newspaper, had only confirmed the suspicions of these denizens of law and order: this was an immoral young girl who had hung about Soho and had tangled in vice and criminality – that vicious weal across her face only served to show what penalties such activities exacted. Small wonder that she was the person who elected to fight the campaign to free that young Italian gangster.

Mario looked wearily round the walls of the Mint. The posters of Italian scenes had been replaced by endless cuttings from the press, all about Lino Rinaldi – the arrest, the trial, the verdict, the appeal. You could tell the date of the events, he thought wryly, by the degrees of ageing in the yellowing newspapers – dark ochre and curling for the early news of Silvia's murder and Lino's arrest last year, pale yellow and fading for the verdict, with a couple of cuttings completely disfigured by a dark stain. That was the remnants of the fight, he recalled, when a drunk had come into the club and made a disparaging remark about the 'Spics' getting what they deserved, and Marionetta had hurled a jug of scalding hot coffee over the offender, burning his hands and splashing the walls. He smiled grimly at the memory. Those musician friends of Netta's had grabbed the man and hauled him up the stairs, dumping him unceremoniously on the pavement outside and telling him never to come back if he valued his life. He had never returned . . . Odd, he realized: the musicians hadn't been seen in the club much after that either.

The latest cuttings, Mario saw, were about to be added to the collection; Marionetta's scissors were sitting on the chair next to her. Funny how even her obsession with the trial had not dimmed the popularity of the Mint, he mused – if anything, the club had become even more popular, a magnet for the curious and the sensation-seeking. After all, Marionetta was famous now; or was it notorious? In any case, the prospect of seeing someone in the flesh who had actually appeared on Pathe News and on the BBC was too enticing for the revellers of Soho to resist – they came in their hundreds to look at Marionetta for themselves, and of course they paid their entrance fee, they bought their drinks, and the Perettis, ironically, found themselves better off than they had ever been. The public came to stare surreptitiously at the club owner's dramatic scar, to feign sympathy and interest in the case, offering vague promises of help and support, but really they were just vultures, come to feed off bleeding flesh . . . And in the meantime, Mario thought to himself, depressed, their real friends had all disappeared, alarmed by the sudden notoriety of the Perettis, or perhaps jealous – it was hard to tell.

Marionetta began to snip round the article she had been reading.

'Whatever happened to that musician chap who seemed keen on you?' Mario asked her. 'You know – the one who looked like Dirk Bogarde.'

Marionetta smiled in spite of herself. 'Don't be silly, Mario. He didn't look a bit like Dirk Bogarde. You mean Micky Angel.'

'That's the one. And his friend – Peter, was it?'

'Peter Travis. With the double bass.' Her white fingers kept snipping neatly at the paper. 'Peter went off to play in a band on a cruise ship, I think.' There was a small silence. 'I heard Micky's been seen at the Artists' and Models' Club recently.'

Mario looked at her, surprised. 'But that's a prostitutes' dive, isn't it?'

She gave him a wry look. 'And how would you know, little brother?'

He grinned. 'Not so little, if you don't mind! What on earth is Micky Angel doing hanging about in there?'

Marionetta shrugged. She was tired. She must pin these up, and then catch the bus to the prison. Mr and Mrs Rinaldi had asked her to go with them to say goodbye to their son. She was dreading it. She had been rehearsing over and over in her mind what she could possibly say to Lino to ease his last few hours on earth. What words could make it easier knowing he was going to his death for a crime he did not commit? In the past at these meetings she had always been able to say something bright and hopeful about the appeal, but now that was all over. She could no longer smile and say, 'Don't worry, Lino, I've written another letter to the Home Secretary,' or 'I've just had a petition from a group in Yorkshire – thousands of people believe you didn't do it!' There was nothing left to say. Time had run out. Her head was spinning with exhaustion. She must think of something positive to say to Lino. The last thing she wanted to think about was Micky Angel and why he had deserted her. 'Maybe he's fallen in love with a prostitute,' she said drily.

Mario took the cutting from her, picked up a couple of drawing-pins and headed to the next empty space on the wall. 'Tony said he thought Micky Angel had fallen in love with *you*,' he said, lining the cutting up next to one which read 'Diary of a killer – we trace Rinaldi's last movements'. Marionetta was glad that her brother could not see her face.

'Nonsense!' she said briskly, folding the newspaper carefully. 'Anyway, I don't care what Tony thinks – about anything.'

Mario turned and watched her as she sorted the papers into a neat pile. She looked so tired, and she certainly would not sleep tonight; none of them would. 'You and Tony can't keep this up for ever,' he said. 'You're brother and sister! I don't understand you, Marionetta, how can you not talk to your own brother for months on end?'

Marionetta was silent. Mario had no idea about the moral debt that dogged the Perettis. When Nonno had died, drifting peacefully away in his sleep, satisfied that he had made his last wishes clear to his family, Tomasso had begged the two older children not to embroil Mario in the family's dealings with the Moruzzis. Consequently the explosive atmosphere at home, the wall of silence that had sprung up between Tony and Marionetta, the utter despair of his father – to Mario, this was all the result of the family's inexplicable involvement in the murder of Silvia Conti, and Marionetta's grim-faced determination to see Lino Rinaldi freed at all costs. He did not understand why the death of a prostitute – even if she had once been Marionetta's friend – seemed set to ruin all their lives. The family was fractured, unhappy, quarrelsome, and he did not understand why.

Mario sighed. Whatever the reasons, he could see that his sister was almost too tired to speak. 'Get your coat on,' he said, his voice kind. 'I'll clear up here . . .'

Grateful, Marionetta fetched her coat. She went to the back door and peered out into the yard. It was raining, and a grey, disconsolate sky hung sullenly over Soho. She would need her umbrella for the journey to Wandsworth Prison.

Under the dripping steps of the fire escape, she could see Bella, curled up asleep in a dry patch, oblivious to the dreary February evening. It was dark already, and as usual, Marionetta could hear the clatter of pans in the kitchens of the Dean Street restaurants and cafés, as cooks and waiters prepared for the evening's business. Strange to think that this time tomorrow it would all still be going on – the shouts of the chef in Gennaro's, the peals of laughter from the girls in Bianchi's, the sound of the radio blaring in the Bar Italia – it would all be the same, only Lino would be dead.

Mario joined her at the door, shrugging into his overcoat, and peered out at the rain. 'Filthy night,' he said.

'This time tomorrow . . .' Marionetta murmured. He squeezed her arm, not knowing what to say. 'You'll miss the bus,' he managed finally.

She turned back inside as he locked the door. 'Funny to think how quiet Soho will be,' he said, fixing the big padlock into place.

'Quiet?' Marionetta was already mounting the stairs to the café, only half-listening.

'Everything's closing – didn't you know?'

She stopped and turned to stare at him. 'Because of Lino?'

'I thought I told you.' He followed her up the stairs. 'Isola Bella obviously decided to close as a mark of respect because of Lino working there, and then it turned out he had worked at a couple of other restaurants too, so they decided they'd close as well.' They emerged into the gloom of the deserted café, which had shut a couple of hours previously. 'Word just sort of spread,' he went on, 'and gradually they all seemed to be closing. And not just the Italian places, either – Jimmy's, the Greek place, they're closing, and the Welsh Dairy as well.'

Marionetta stood by the door of the café, tears springing to her eyes. She must not cry; but people never ceased to surprise her with their small acts of kindness. She felt a pang of guilt that her friends in Soho had been planning this gesture for Lino, and she had been so busy rushing off to the solicitor's, acting as translator for Lino's stunned parents who spoke hardly any English, visiting Lino in prison, that she had ceased to be aware of what was happening on her own doorstep. She felt a descending wave of exhaustion, and sat down suddenly at the nearest table. Mario knelt down by the chair, concerned. 'Let me call you a cab to the prison, Netta. You can't go on the bus, not tonight, the weather's too dreadful.'

She was about to shake her head, stubborn, when she saw his face, helpless and anxious in the half-light. He wanted to help, she realized, and he could not find a way to reach her. 'I'll pay,' he was saying, reaching into his pocket impulsively, 'I made a lot of money singing yester-day . . .'

She looked at him reproachfully. 'Were you busking again? Oh, Mario!'

He grinned. 'It's fun. As long as Dad doesn't ever find out, it's worth it. Here,' he was pushing a ten-pound note into her hand, 'please, Netta. Please.'

She took the money and gave him a quick, gentle kiss on his cheek. 'Thanks,' she said simply.

'Stay here out of the wet,' he covered his embarrassment with briskness, 'while I get you a cab.' And he had unlocked the door of the café and was gone.

Marionetta rubbed her eyes and sat quietly looking round her. The café looked a little shabby, its cheerful red white and blue decor faded. It seemed incongruous now, this display of patriotism. The King's funeral had taken place only a few days previously, and the whole of London seemed to be suffused with gloom. It seemed to Marionetta that this was a time she would remember for ever, recalled in years to come in odd little vignettes: Silvia's funeral, with hardly any mourners; the King's coffin rumbling towards the chapel at Windsor, glimpsed on the new television set Tony had installed in the flat in St James's Residences; Lino's desperate face as he was marched from the Old Bailey, calling, 'I didn't do it, I didn't do it!'; the guilty and defiant face of the young prostitute in the dock as she committed perjory, swearing that she had seen Lino stab Silvia: 'I seen him! He crept up behind us!' It was like a crazy kaleidoscope, a speeded-up film, the Keystone Cops gone mad.

Wearily she stood up and went to the door, pressing her forehead against the glass. Small wonder that Mario was having trouble finding a taxi: the sound of the rain drumming against the windows was louder now, and small tides of water mounted the pavement whenever a car passed. She could see someone standing in the doorway of the Triple X Club opposite. She wondered fleetingly if he, too, was seeking a taxi. Then suddenly the figure crossed the road at a run, making straight for the doorway of the café, head lowered against the rain. Before she had a chance to put her hand on the lock, he had opened the door and was shouldering his way in, rain glistening on the shoulders of his mackintosh. It was Carmelo Moruzzi, his eye-patch just visible under the shadow of his hat brim.

'Hello,' he said. 'Is your dad in?'

'Get out,' Marionetta said, her voice shaking. 'Get out!'

He leaned against the door and smiled at her, his face polite. 'That's a very unfriendly greeting,' he said, 'considering the long relationship between your family and mine.'

'I want you to go,' she said, almost afraid of herself, shaken by the onrush of emotions she was experiencing at the sight of this enemy, tonight of all nights. She had thought her feelings were all buried for ever.

He took off his hat and smoothed his hair. He looked very like his father, Marionetta thought absurdly: the same strong features, the cold mouth. She wondered fleetingly how he had lost his eye. 'Please,' she said finally. 'Please – just go. Before I do something I might regret.'

He raised an eyebrow. 'That should be interesting. Perhaps I should stick around and see what you have in mind.'

She briefly contemplated crossing to the counter and grabbing the bread knife. The thought made her slightly hysterical, and a small giggle welled up in her throat. That would be too ridiculous. She would follow Lino to the gallows, and for what? For the murder of a Moruzzi!

'If you've come here to gloat,' she said finally, 'then gloat. I can't stop you. But if you really did want to speak to my dad you'll find him at home. Although I don't advise you to go to St James's – the people there are ready to lynch you and your family.'

He grinned at her, amused by the thought of a lynching party lurking in the tenements of Brewer Street. 'Don't worry,' he said, 'I have no intention of visiting your papa at home. No, you'll do.' He picked up an ashtray from the table nearby and turned it in his gloved hands. 'Just a message, that's all. Attilio says to tell you that he expects your café to be open tomorrow. We've heard a rumour that people intend to close.'

Marionetta stared at him. 'That's right,' she said. 'As a mark of respect for Lino Rinaldi.'

He replaced the ashtray gently. 'We're not interested in marks of respect for the killer of a common tart,' he said. 'We expect the Imperial to be open.'

An icy wave of anger washed over Marionetta. This was too much to bear. 'You can't make us open the café,' she said.

He stepped closer, examining her face in the dim light from the neon sign opposite. 'You forget,' he said mildly, 'I'm your father's landlord.' He put his hand up to her cheek. She flinched and moved away. 'We're rather alike, aren't we?' he said in a conversational tone. 'Both scarred, both not quite the good-looking specimens we once were.' He gave a mock sigh. 'Soho! What a place, eh! You can never tell who's going to be sliced up next, can you . . .?'

The little bell jangled as he left, closing the door behind him. Outside, a taxi drew up and Mario emerged triumphant, not seeing the tall figure of the Pirate pass by, stooping under the rain and smiling to himself.

The prison officer yawned and stretched. It was going to be a long night. No one in the prison liked this kind of occasion, it made the other prisoners restless and demoralized the officers. The young woman in the green coat stirred and opened her eyes. She had been fast asleep, her head on her arms resting on the table in front of her.

'Not long now, miss, I shouldn't think,' he said, and then regretted his words. Best not to talk about the passing of time, when every minute brought them all closer to nine o'clock the following morning, when Pierrepoint would do his duty. The discreet little man who had one of the most grotesque jobs in the country was already inside the prison, making his notes and taking his measurements

138

to ensure that the sentence was carried out as quickly and painlessly as possible.

The young woman at the table ran a hand through her hair, the curls still damp from the rain outside. The officer recognized her from the papers. Nasty scar, he thought; she had obviously been a very pretty girl before someone took a razor to her face. He wondered fleetingly, as countless others had before him, whether this Peretti girl was really Rinaldi's girlfriend. She had denied it in interviews, of course, but otherwise why on earth make such a spectacle of herself? She claimed it was because the dead prostitute had been a friend, but he was sure there must be more to it than that. 'Funny lot, the Italians,' his wife had said darkly over the ironing, only the other night, 'They don't do things like the British. No morals . . .'

There was a slight commotion in the corridor outside. The officer opened the door and then stepped forward to assist the weeping figure of an elderly woman crossing the threshold. It was Rinaldi's mother, in a state of total collapse. He helped her to the chair that the Peretti girl had vacated, and then stood politely by while the two women wept together. Lino Rinaldi's father stood helplessly, turning his hat in his hand, his face blank, his body sagging.

'Here, sir, sit yourself down a minute,' another officer said, proffering a chair. 'You don't have to leave yet awhile if you don't want to . . .'

The man turned to the girl and asked her something in Italian. She answered quietly in a soothing tone, wiping the tears from her face, appearing to recover from the excess of emotion the sight of the old couple had inspired. Then she spoke to the weeping woman, gently stroking her cheek. The woman stopped crying, gazing into her eyes with complete trust. They spoke again in Italian, then the Peretti girl stood up.

'Mr and Mrs Rinaldi are ready to leave now,' she said. 'Could you please make sure they are put into a taxi? I don't want them bothered by reporters at the gate.' She was holding out a five-pound note, but the governor, who had come into the room and heard this, shook his head politely.

'It's all right, Miss Peretti,' he said. 'I'll take care of it. Now – if you're ready?'

The young woman turned for a last look at the distraught couple. She kissed them both, then turned and walked from the room, still holding the damp headscarf she had removed on entering the prison.

She followed the governor along a primrose-yellow corridor. The prison seemed very silent. She could hear their footsteps echoing along the floor and wondered if the prisoners were all listening, sitting in their cells, thinking about Lino Rinaldi.

'In here, Miss Peretti.' The governor was indicating a door. 'I'll be here when you come out, if you wish to see me.'

Marionetta tried to smile at him. He had been decent and fair throughout this long and painful business. 'Thank you,' she said, 'I don't think there will be any need . . .'

She went into the room. An officer was standing by the door, his hands behind his back. He nodded at Marionetta, his face strained. The tension of these last farewells was beginning to tell on him. Behind the glass, Lino was waiting. Marionetta forced a wobbly smile. Lino looked back, bleak, serious. He slowly held a hand, palm facing her, up to the glass. Marionetta crossed the room and sat down in the chair provided. She raised her hand and placed it against the glass, against his. It looked very small compared to Lino's large, square-fingered hand.

'Hello,' she said.

140

'Hello.' There was a silence. The two prison officers, one either side of the glass, exchanged a look. This visit was not going to be as agonizing as the last; it was evident that both Lino and Marionetta were going to make a determined effort not to break down.

'It's not over, Lino,' she said finally. 'I've got a lead on one of the people who arrived at the scene of the murder just after it happened. It's in Kensington. I'm going there the moment I leave here.'

Lino's face brightened. 'You think they'll talk?'

She looked away, unable to meet his eyes. 'You never know . . .'

Of course they *did* know. Not one of the witnesses at the scene of the crime had come forward since Lino's arrest – fear of the Moruzzis was a powerful thing, and the fact that Silvia Conti had worked for the brothers had been made public by the press. Both Marionetta and Lino knew that there was little hope of a change of heart; but both played a determined charade, to keep up each other's spirits.

'And the governor says there can be a reprieve right up to the last minute,' Lino was saying.

Marionetta nodded, her eyes brimming with tears. She must not cry, not now, not when Lino was being so courageous. They talked for a while about mundane things – memories of their childhood years in the little school in Soho, of communion classes at St Patrick's, Lino's friends at the restaurant. Gradually the conversation petered out and there was silence. Then Lino leaned forward and pressed his forehead against the glass. 'You know I'm innocent, Marionetta,' he said.

She nodded, tremulous. 'Not just me,' she said, 'thousands of people. You'd be amazed, Lino –'

He shook his head. 'No – I meant – you really *know* it,'

he said, struggling to control his emotions. 'You know how I felt about Silvia.'

She nodded, not trusting herself to speak.

'And you know how good she was, how sweet –' He broke off, bit his lip and then continued, frowning with the effort not to break down. 'She never kissed them, you know,' he said.

'What?' Marionetta wondered for a moment if Lino had finally gone mad.

'Silvia. The punters. She never let them kiss her on the mouth. Only me. I was the only one who ever kissed her on the mouth.'

She was silent, absorbing this, not knowing what to say. 'I'm going with a clear conscience, Netta,' he said. 'And I'm going to go with my head held high, for Silvia's sake.'

She nodded again, biting her lip. It was impossible to know what to say in reply. Some occasions are not made easier by words. She pressed her own forehead against the glass, so that she and Lino mirrored each other, in a strange kind of Alice-Through-the-Looking-Glass embrace, brows together, palms together, but separated by the reinforced glass. They remained without moving, for a long time. Then Lino stood up.

'Thank you for everything, Netta,' he said.

'*Prego*. It was nothing, Lino.'

'And you're going to Kensington now? To talk to this witness?'

She nodded, pulling on her gloves. 'I'm sure something will happen,' she whispered, her head bent, pretending to concentrate on easing her fingers into the gloves. They both knew that they were saying goodbye.

'I've got to go now,' Lino said. This was patently untrue, but the officer on his side of the glass obediently straightened up, prepared to take his prisoner back to the condemned cell. Lino stood for a moment, looking at the slight figure in front of him. 'Look after my mum and dad,' he said. She nodded, the tears spilling down her face. 'I've got to go,' he repeated, attempting a wavering smile, 'there's a priest waiting to see me!' He nodded curtly at the prison officer, and before Marionetta could look up or speak, there was a flurry of activity, and Lino Rinaldi had left the room.

She stood there, dumb, still pressing the fingers of her gloves automatically, staring at the empty chair where Lino had been.

'All right, miss,' said the prison officer by the door. She stepped outside. The governor was standing where she had left him.

'I'm afraid I've had a call from Mr Haskell,' he said. Marionetta looked up, her heart sinking. John Haskell was the solicitor who had defended Lino at the trial, and who had worked tirelessly alongside Marionetta to find some cause for an appeal. The governor spoke quietly, knowing his words would have a devastating effect. 'The man in Kensington – he's changed his mind. He doesn't want to see anyone. He says he has nothing more to say.'

Blindly, she turned and left.

Outside the prison, a crowd had gathered. The taxi nosed its way through the throng, the driver cursing as people thumped on the bonnet and shouted incoherently. Marionetta stared out blankly, blinded by the flash-bulbs of the press photographers, deaf to the yelled questions: 'Did you see him?' 'Any last words?' 'Did he confess?' Suddenly they were through the crowd and heading away down the rain-soaked road. Marionetta turned back for a last look. It was a strange, ghostly scene, lit by the unnatural glare of the film crews' lighting equipment. Banners denouncing capital punishment jostled with others declaring

Lino's innocence. Hundreds of people had come to stand in the rain, she thought in wonderment, all strangers. Faintly she could hear the strains of 'Abide With Me' floating down the street in the darkness. The taxi turned down a side road and speeded up. 'Brewer Street, was it, miss?' The driver eyed his passenger discreetly in his rear-view mirror. They'd never believe him at the depot – he'd got that scar-faced tart in the cab! She stared out of the window and did not reply. Shrugging, he turned the vehicle in the direction of Soho.

'Here we are, then!' Marionetta came to with a start. She had lost all sense of time. The taxi had stopped in Brewer Street by the main entrance to St James's Residences. The pavement glittered in the lamplight, still wet although it was no longer raining.

Marionetta stepped out of the cab. She was so tired she thought she would weep. 'How much?'

The driver shook his head. 'On the house, love.' Worth every penny, he had decided, considering the mileage he would get out of it back at HQ. 'Hard-faced bitch,' he would say, 'never batted an eyelid, never shed a tear. Just sat there, cool as a cucumber, staring out of the window. Good legs, though . . .'

'You're very kind,' Marionetta said, touched.

He drove off. Marionetta stood for a moment. She could hear the sound of music floating across the rooftops from the Windmill Theatre. On the other side of the road, the one-legged man who did the three-card trick outside Madame Valerie's was hobbling past on his way to the pub. He nodded at Marionetta, the first time he had ever acknowledged her existence. Surprised, she raised a hand in response as he disappeared into Green's Court opposite. She looked up. The lights were on in the Peretti flat. She had known they would be, but she had hoped for a miracle. She was not sure if she could get through the night if Tony was home. It would be impossible to keep silent as the minutes ticked towards Lino's end . . .

Someone spoke her name and stepped forward from the shadows at the entrance to St James's. She gave a little start, certain it was Carmelo Moruzzi come to threaten her again, but there was no eye-patch, no wide-brimmed gangster's fedora. With a shock she recognized the face under the lamplight: it was Micky Angel.

'Marionetta – I must talk to you –'

In spite of everything her heart lifted at the sight of him – she couldn't help herself. The recognition of the effect he had on her made her angry with herself. 'Go away!' she said, more tersely than necessary. 'Not now, Micky, not now –' She pushed past him and made for the gate, vaguely aware that he was still behind her. She had the fleeting impression of rain-drenched hair and a dripping overcoat; he must have been standing there for hours.

'It's important, Marionetta – listen to me – I've got some news –'

'I don't want to hear it!' She slammed the gate shut just in time. Now Micky Angel was on one side of it, staring at her through the bars, in a heart-stopping parody of the scene she had just witnessed in Wandsworth Prison. She straightened up. Lino was about to die, and here she was, fighting back a stupid surge of happiness because this itinerant musician had shown up on her doorstep, after ignoring her for weeks!

'Go away, Micky,' she said.

'Marionetta, if you'd just listen –'

She walked away and hurried inside the building. How dare he show up here, tonight of all nights! She mounted the stairs. The way he said her name always made her heart turn over . . .

145

Mrs Rocca was hovering on the first-floor landing. Marionetta pushed past her, not caring if her behaviour was rude. She just wanted to get inside, away from everyone. She wished her family would disappear, so that she could spend the night in silence, not having to put on a brave face for anyone.

On the third-floor landing, Mario was waiting for her. 'Kettle's on, sis,' he said.

In the living-room of number 104, Tomasso was watching television. Gilbert Harding was being sarcastic on *What's My Line?* Tony was hunched in Nonno's old armchair with his constable's jacket draped over the back, pretending to watch but staring into space, tense, smoking a cigarette. As his sister entered, he got up and went into the bedroom, taking his cigarettes with him and slamming the door.

Mario exchanged a wry look with his father. 'So that's just three for tea, then, is it?' he said.

They sat in silence watching television, grateful for the distraction. Tony stayed in the bedroom, invisible. When it was time for the news, Marionetta made more tea in the kitchen, so that she did not have to see that same picture of Lino they always showed in the bulletins, and that same unflattering picture of Silvia, laughing in a restaurant, caught in a harsh light that made her look blank and soulless. As she poured the tea, she could hear the newsreader's voice solemnly confirming that the hanging would take place as scheduled. She paused for a moment, staring into space. To die so meaninglessly, punished for something he did not do, could never do . . . The face of Attilio Moruzzi sprang into her mind unbidden, smiling that cold smile that seemed to be the trademark of the Moruzzi brothers. For some reason she could not fathom, the face changed a little and became Micky Angel's, and for a frightening second he too smiled at her with that same unfeeling smile. The newsreader had moved on to an item about the abolition of identity cards; she picked up the tray, shaking off her visions, and returned to the living-room. There was nothing she could do now except pray for Lino's soul; and pray for God's forgiveness for her brother, who knew that Lino was innocent . . .

At eleven o'clock, as the National Anthem blared out signalling the end of the day's programmes, Tomasso got up, stretched exaggeratedly, yawned, and said, 'Bene, I think I'll turn in . . .'

Marionetta's eyes were still fixed on the white dot at the centre of the television screen, watching it recede to nothingness. Her father approached her nervously. 'Are you going to bed, Netta?' he asked. She slept on a bed in the corner of the living-room which they pulled out from behind the settee every night.

She shook her head from the sofa. 'I'll sit up, I think. I know I won't sleep, so I might as well stay here.'

Her father hovered, unsure what to say, reluctant to leave her. 'Would you like me to sit with you? If you want me to –'

'No.' Her voice was emphatic. 'I'd rather be on my own, Papa.'

He shrugged, unhappy. 'If you're sure . . . I'll say goodnight then.'

'Goodnight.' She still had not met his eyes, her tone subdued but polite.

'I'll be praying for Lino,' he said. She did not reply.

He reached the bedroom door and then turned back. 'Listen, Netta, I know how you feel about me, and about your Nonno and about Tony –'

She shook her head, grim, looking at him at last. Mario shifted uneasily from his place in the armchair. 'You'll never know how I feel, she said. 'Never.'

147

Tomasso tried to speak again, but she held up a hand. 'Please, Papa. Not tonight. I couldn't bear it. Please.'

Defeated, he opened the bedroom door and went inside. Marionetta sighed. The gulf between her father and herself seemed to be growing, and she felt powerless to mend things. Thanks to some ridiculous promise made fifty years ago, a man was about to hang – and the Perettis were as responsible for Lino's imminent death as were the Moruzzis! She had begged Papa to forget his promise to Nonno; after all, she had argued, surely what happened in the future was what mattered, not some ridiculous vendetta from years ago, in another country, another time? But her father had been adamant. A promise had been made to the Moruzzis. It must be honoured; and Tony was being a good son, he was honouring that promise at great cost to himself . . . The arguments had raged on until both sides were exhausted. They had all retreated into a stubborn silence, unable to find any common ground, Marionetta struggling with a feeling of contempt for both father and son. How could she ever forgive her father? How could she ever laugh with Tony again, and treat him as a sister should a brother? Thank God for Mario, she thought, the only untainted one in their sad, besmirched family. As if he sensed she was thinking about him, Mario stood up nervously. 'You want another cup of tea, sis? Cocoa? Ovaltine?'

Marionetta reached out gratefully and caught his hand, squeezing it. 'Go to bed, Mario. You've been an angel. But I just want to be here on my own.'

He stood, uncertain. 'I'll – I'll get up early – be here with you before nine o'clock . . .' he began, his face contorted with the effort of pronouncing that unspeakable hour tomorrow morning that would signal the end of Lino's life.

She nodded, and waved him away. There was the long night to be got through first . . .

She had been dreaming again. There had been a puppet, dancing stiffly on its strings, a painted smile frozen on its wooden face, and then she had looked down and had seen with horror that the red felt skirt, the delicate frilled apron and the velvet bodice were hers, she was wearing them, and the puppet was herself. She had tried to shake herself free, but the more effort she expended, the more she became entangled in the strings, and the more she danced . . .

She shook herself awake. The light was seeping in through the living-room curtains, and outside she could hear a milk cart clattering along the street. It was five-thirty. She had only been asleep for a few moments. She got up stiffly, stretching, angry at herself. How could she drift away? She must concentrate, she must put her mind inside Lino's mind, she must send him strength, courage . . .

She went to the window and opened it, surprising a pigeon that had alighted on the sill to survey Soho from on high. She breathed in the sharp air, thankful to feel the chill on her cheeks.

Perhaps Lino was sleeping. Perhaps they would have given him something – a pill, some brandy – to make his last few hours easier to bear. Down in the street a pale-faced girl was leaving the flats opposite, calling goodbye to someone, her face streaked with make-up, her evening dress rumpled. She did not look up, did not see the girl watching her from the third floor of the tenement opposite. Smiling sleepily to herself, the young girl teetered away on her high heels in search of a taxi. Marionetta watched her go without envy. Was she a tart? An actress? Or just a good-time girl? They were about the same age, but they might have come from different planets, she mused. The girl disappeared round the corner, heading towards Shaftes-bury Avenue. Marionetta closed the window. Less than four hours to go . . .

She wandered over to the radio in the corner, turned it on, and fiddled with it for a moment, tuning it to the Home Service, careful to keep the volume low so as not to disturb the rest of the family sleeping in the other room. The familiar murmur of the long-range weather forecast gradually became clear. Marionetta went wearily into the kitchen. Winds gale force five, Fisher, German Bite . . . Time for yet more tea . . .

Suddenly her hand froze on the kettle. Hardly daring to move, she stood and listened, paralysed, her heart beating. 'There has been a stay of execution for Lino Rinaldi, the Soho waiter condemned to hang this morning for the murder of a prostitute in Soho,' the matter-of-fact voice of the BBC announcer was intoning. 'Due to fresh evidence brought to light during the night, the Home Office has issued the following statement . . .'

Marionetta only half-heard what was said next. She stood, incredulous, trying to absorb what she had heard. Could it be true? Could a miracle really have happened? Was Lino really going to live? She turned impulsively to the small statue of the madonna on the sideboard that had belonged to her mother. '*Grazie, madonna mia,*' she mur-mured, picking up the statue and kissing it. Then she ran to fetch her coat. Lino was not going to die! When the clock struck nine, Lino would not be hanging from the end of a rope, silenced forever from protesting his innocence!

Without really knowing what she was going to do, where she was going, Marionetta flew down the stairs, her shoes clattering noisily on the concrete, something between a laugh and a sob on her lips. She felt the jangle of some coins in her pocket. She would go to the phone box on the corner of Archer Street and telephone the prison. She needed to hear the governor say it, she needed to hear his voice tell her that it was really true, that Lino really had been reprieved!

In the gloom of the downstairs hallway she almost fell over something in the doorway. It was someone sleeping, huddled under a coat, and the dark shape stirred and groaned as she stumbled and reached out to the wall for support.

'Sorry – I didn't see you – oh!' she gasped. A face had appeared, sleepy and confused, from beneath the coat, and then Micky Angel's eyes opened wide as he recognized her, and he staggered to his feet.

'Micky! What are you doing?' She grabbed his sleeve, suddenly overcome with the realization of what she had just heard. 'Lino – he's had a reprieve, Micky! He's not going to hang – I just heard it on the radio . . .'

'I know,' he said surprisingly. She stopped and stared at him.

'You know?'

He nodded, rubbing his eyes. 'I tried to tell you last night – I thought there was a chance . . .' He was leaning against the wall, his face grey and exhausted, his shirt collar rumpled. 'There's this other girl – another prostitute. Her name's Teresa – I tried to tell you –' He was only half awake, stiff from his uncomfortable night on the steps of St James's Residences.

Marionetta could hardly contain herself. 'Come on, Micky – tell me! What girl? What happened? Tell me!'

He sat down on the steps again, running a hand through his hair. Marionetta sat next to him, shivering, clutching her coat round her. 'Teresa –' he said, '– this girl – she's prepared to come forward and speak. She saw what happened, Marionetta. She was there.'

Marionetta stared at him in amazement. 'There? You mean – she saw the murder?'

He shook his head. 'Not exactly. But she was in the club with Silvia just before it happened. And she says Wally Wallace was shouting at Silvia, crazy with jealousy over Lino, telling her she wasn't to see Lino again, she wasn't to meet him after work, or he couldn't answer for the consequences.'

Marionetta tried to absorb this, her brain racing. 'You mean – this wasn't just Wally carrying out a killing for Barty Moruzzi?'

Micky shook his head grimly. 'No. He was crazy about Silvia, according to all the prostitutes who used the Granada Club. He was supposed to be managing it for the Moruzzis, but he spent all his time watching Silvia, wanting to know who she was with. He hated Lino. That's why he killed her – jealousy.'

Marionetta sat hunched, her knees under her chin, puzzled. 'And this prostitute,' she said finally, 'why is she suddenly prepared to speak out? If all the prostitutes in the club knew about Wally and how jealous he was, why is there just this one who's prepared to stand up against the Moruzzis? And where has she been up till now? Why hasn't she come forward before?'

Micky was looking uncomfortable. He fumbled in the pocket of his overcoat for a cigarette, and lit it silently. Marionetta watched him, puzzled. Then gradually the realization of it dawned on her. 'This Teresa,' she said, 'do you know her, Micky?'

Micky inhaled on his cigarette. Then he nodded.

Marionetta absorbed this new revelation without speaking. Then, 'How on earth,' she said, her tone a little cold, 'did you persuade this – this girl – to come forward with the truth and defy the whole Moruzzi family?'

'It must be my personal charm,' he said, his voice dry. They sat for a moment, neither speaking. In a flat on the floor above a baby began to cry.

'I was about to phone the prison governor,' she said eventually. 'I couldn't believe it was true.'

'It's true,' he said, tired. 'You don't have to phone. I came to tell you last night, but you wouldn't listen to me.'

'Sorry.' Her voice was bleak.

There seemed to be nothing more to say. She stood up, digging her hands deep into the pockets of her coat. It was suddenly very cold. 'I'd better go back in,' she said. 'I'll have a couple of hours' sleep, then I'll go to the prison . . .'

'Right.' He stood there awkwardly. He seemed to have something to say but was unable to say it. All Marionetta could think of, ludicrously, was that Micky Angel was involved with a prostitute. Somehow that thought tainted the joy of knowing that Lino would live. She began to climb the stairs and then turned. Micky was still standing where she had left him, his face upturned in the half-light, watching her. 'Thanks,' she said finally, and then continued up the stairs. Micky watched her go, and then turned away and stepped out into the street.

Marionetta let herself back into the flat. The radio still burbled away in the corner. She sat for a moment, still in her coat, trying to regain her composure and piecing together what Micky Angel had told her.

The announcer repeated his bulletin, confirming that Lino had been reprieved. Marionetta stood up and quietly went into the bedroom, crossing over to the bed which Tony shared with his brother. Mario slept peacefully, only a slight frown flickering across his forehead to hint at disturbed dreams. Tony's eyes opened the instant that Marionetta leaned over him.

'What is it?' he whispered, immediately awake. In the

153

bed by the window that had once belonged to Nonno, Tomasso turned, grunted and huddled under the covers.

'Is something wrong?' Tony asked.

Marionetta shook her head and beckoned for him to follow her back to the living-room. He obeyed, pulling on trousers over his pyjamas. Marionetta went through to the kitchen and put the kettle on. Funny, she mused, how very British she became at moments of high drama . . .

'What is it?' Tony asked, still in a whisper. These were the first words he had spoken to his sister for weeks, but he guessed that something momentous must have occurred for Marionetta to have woken him up.

'Sit down,' Marionetta said, her voice calm. 'I think you might need some tea.' She told him then, as she busied herself with the tea caddy and the cups and the milk jug, about Lino's last-minute stay of execution, about the prostitute who had suddenly come forward with the truth. Tony listened, his jaw slack with amazement.

'I don't believe it,' he said.

Marionetta poured the tea calmly. 'It's true,' she said. 'It was on the radio. Do you want some toast?'

He stared at her, the full implications of her words dawning on him at last. A look of terrible fear crossed his face. For a moment Marionetta felt almost sorry for him.

'Once this girl's statement is made public,' he whispered, 'I'll be finished! They'll know down at the station that I screwed a false statement out of that girl at the scene of the crime! I'll be done for!'

'Not necessarily.' Marionetta handed him a cup of tea, but he simply took it from her and put it on the table at his side, in a daze.

'They'll throw me out of the force.' His voice was choked. 'A bent copper! I'll never work again.'

'You could always come clean,' Marionetta said, sipping

her tea and looking at him. Sometimes it was hard to believe this was her own brother. They were so different. 'You could tell your superiors the truth – that you forced a witness to make a false statement. You could tell them you're prepared to take your punishment like a man. Surely that would make a difference.'

'No!' He interrupted her, anguished. 'You don't understand! It's not just the police.' She crashed her teacup into its saucer. She knew what he was going to say. 'It's the Moruzzis –'

His voice tailed away. He was already planning to run, she could see it in his face. He got up.

'I'll have to disappear,' he said. His face was white. He looked very vulnerable, standing there with his tousled hair and his rumpled pyjamas. Marionetta's eyes strayed to the photograph of Nonno on the sideboard. Tony looked so like his grandfather – but what a difference in character!

Tony hurried into the bedroom. She could hear him tiptoeing about, quietly opening a drawer, then the creak of the wardrobe door. He was packing. She picked up the photograph of her grandparents and gazed at it for a moment. Mamma had been right – the young girl gazing out from the picture could almost be Marionetta: the same direct gaze, the same unruly curls, the same look of determination; but of course Giulietta's face had been perfect. There was no scar blighting that flawless cheek, marring that soft mouth. Gently, Marionetta put a fingertip on to the glass, where Nonno's young face was. Giulietta had been fortunate. She had married the man she loved – but at what cost! Marionetta wondered if her grandmother would have agreed to the marriage if she had known what heartache it would cause to future generations. She sighed. But to have had the chance! To have really felt like you were living happily ever after . . . !

Tony emerged from the bedroom, dressed now and wearing an overcoat. He was carrying the small brown case he had taken with him to training college at Hendon — was it really only four years ago? He had been so full of hope then, so sure that he was going to be the people's hero, fighting crime wherever he found it.

'Goodbye,' he said awkwardly. 'Say goodbye to Dad for me, won't you? And Mario.' She was silent, staring out of the window. People were beginning to stir outside. A group of men on the corner were talking excitedly, one of them waving a newspaper. It seemed that the news of Lino's reprieve was filtering through Soho.

Tony tried to kiss her on the cheek, but she turned away, her hand automatically reaching up to where the scar cut into her mouth. She heard Tony reach the door. There was a short pause, then the sound of the door being opened, and closed again. His footsteps echoed on the steps outside and then faded away.

As the church clock on the tower of St Anne's struck nine that morning, the inhabitants of Soho were on the streets, laughing, talking, celebrating . . . even drinking. Gamblers emerging from the Maltese Club embraced the roadsweeper when he told them the news; two streetwalkers, buying their breakfast at King Bomba, wept when the *padrone* of the store told them about Lino. The musicians on Archer Street cheered when they saw the newspaper headlines, and the art students in Madame Valerie's stopped drinking their espressos and danced in the streets. It was not just the Italians, usually so private and self-contained, who gave thanks for the miracle that had saved Lino Rinaldi from the gallows. The tarts, the gamblers, the drinkers, the dancers — everyone celebrated in the kind of impromptu party that only Soho could provide. No one noticed that two people were missing. Marionetta was on the bus, heading towards Wandsworth to see Lino; and Micky Angel was sitting at his piano, in the cramped flat he shared with Peter Travis in Broadwick Street. He was playing 'Lullaby of Broadway', gently at first, his long fingers teasing out the notes, playing over the keys delicately, skilfully, then louder, more discordant until he finished with a crash and sat despairing, the final note still echoing around him like the murmur of a spectre.

CHAPTER SIX

November 1952

St Patrick's was quiet. It was Friday afternoon, and the workers of Soho had not yet appeared for early evening Mass. Marionetta had taken half an hour away from the café to come to confession, and had just spent her time in the ornate wooden confessional murmuring her sins to Father Joseph. Now she knelt before the altar dedicated to Jesus, Mary and Martha, whispering her penance.

This was her favourite corner of the church, with its delicately painted green and gold pillars framing the painting of Jesus standing between two young women, both wearing the clothes of peasant workers, and both with gilded haloes. Ever since her childhood, Marionetta had been transfixed by this painting. She knew the story by heart: this standing figure, her hand outstretched, was Martha, the sister of Lazarus and Mary. Mary had sat at Jesus's feet listening patiently as he preached, while Martha had complained about the amount of housework she was expected to do. Marionetta studied the faces on the painting, cracked and faded with age. These were the two faces of every woman, she had decided – the one submissive, at the feet of her Master, the other complaining about her lot, not prepared to accept her womanly role. Most women spent their lives teetering somewhere between the two positions, but Marionetta had always secretly identified with the upright figure of Martha, rather than the seated, silent Mary. Mamma had told her that Martha had become the patron saint of good housewives. This seemed to Marionetta to be most unjust, an ironic reproach, a punishment meted out to a woman who would not be silent. Guiltily, she realized she was not concentrating on her prayers, and she closed her eyes, trying to forget the look of appeal in Martha's face. She finished her Hail Marys, genuflected, and got up to leave. Then, hesitating for a moment, she turned back and took a candle from the box, dropping some coins into the collecting-box to one side of the altar. She lit the candle, placing it in a holder with the others, and stood surveying the rows of soft wavering lights below the painting. The haloes gleamed, bright against the dullness of the old oil paint. Silently, Marionetta mouthed a prayer for Martha, who had spoken out and railed against her existence, even in the face of Jesus.

Quietly, she headed for the door, turning back for a last look at her candle flickering away below the gilded words '*Dilegebat Jesus Martham et Mariam*'. Her heart rebelled at the thought of returning to the Imperial and the prospect of several hours' work, then rushing home to change and get ready for the Mint, which opened at eight. She was tired, and the church was a quiet, cool haven after the heat and bustle of the café. Sighing, she was about to turn away when she saw someone emerge from the confessional, and her body froze in surprise. It was Micky Angel, hunched into a duffle coat, his face preoccupied.

Hurriedly she made for the doorway and slipped out into the pale sunshine of Soho Square, anxious to get away. She had not spoken to Micky since the night Lino had been reprieved. She had glimpsed him hanging about in Archer Street with the other musicians, but he had never descended the stairs to the club, and his absence had hurt her. Peter Travis, Micky's bass-playing friend, returned from his work on the cruise ship, had often visited the Mint, and when Marionetta had plucked up the courage to ask after the missing piano player, he had merely looked sheepish and mumbled something about Micky being very busy.

She crossed the road into the gardens of the square. Bright red geraniums struggled to bloom in the fading warmth of a mild autumn. Apart from a couple of dogs fighting below the statue of Charles II and a few old people dozing on a bench, the gardens were almost deserted.

'Marionetta!' He had seen her. She turned, a little reluctant. Why start it all up again, the churning in her stomach, the *frisson* of excitement at seeing him? She was tempted to run, but it was too late, it would have looked absurd. She stood, her face stony, looking back at him. He was standing outside the church, clearly amazed at seeing her. He crossed the road, dodging a speeding taxi, and hurried to join her, his face registering his pleasure at seeing her. 'How are you? You're looking terrific!'

Angrily, she felt herself blush. How dare he use words like that? Terrific, indeed, with a gash across her face marking her out as someone who could never look terrific, no matter how hard she tried . . . !

'I didn't know you were a Catholic,' she managed to say.

He fell into step beside her as she headed, confused, towards an exit. 'There's an awful lot of things you don't know about me,' he said, teasing. Then, his face suddenly solemn, he put a hand on her arm to prevent her from continuing her way out of the square. 'Wait a minute, Marionetta,' he said. 'Can't you spare me five minutes? It's been such a long time, and it's a nice day . . .' He gestured towards an empty bench.

Marionetta hesitated for a moment and then acquiesced, smiling a little to herself. A few moments ago she had been standing in front of the painting of Martha, wishing she did not have to go back to the café, and Martha had sent Micky Angel; or at least it was nice to think so. Papa would not miss her for at least another ten minutes . . . She turned to face Micky, smiling self-consciously, her gloved hand reaching up to her mouth. 'And how have you been, Micky? I haven't seen you for months.'

He shrugged, not meeting her eyes. 'I've had a lot of work.'

'Lucky you.' She took this opportunity to study him as he sat next to her looking out across the square, seemingly engrossed in an old man nodding over a meths bottle opposite. Micky had a strong profile with a straight nose and a pronounced jaw. With his very black hair he could almost be Italian, she mused; or Greek, or Maltese, or any of the other Mediterranean nationalities that inhabited Soho.

'What about you?' he asked finally.

'What about me?'

He turned to her, his brown eyes surveying her face. 'Have you been busy? I hear the Mint's been a great success.'

'It has. I still can't believe it sometimes.' *Why don't you come and see for yourself*? she longed to ask, but instead she heard herself say, 'How's Vicky?'

'Vicky?' He seemed surprised. 'Fine, as far as I know. Singing in a club in Knightsbridge, last I heard, but that was a couple of months ago.' He was still watching her. 'And Lino? How's Lino?'

She was touched by his concern. 'Well, he's pretty shaken by what happened, of course, but he's putting a brave face on it. He's got his old job back at Isola Bella . . .'

161

'Micky nodded, frowning. 'I've seen him there.'

'Of course he won't really be able to relax until Wally Wallace's trial is over, but it looks as if the Moruzzis are staying away from the witnesses this time, so we're keeping our fingers crossed.'

Micky shook his head. 'That isn't what I meant. I meant – you and Lino.'

It was her turn to be surprised. 'Me – and Lino? What do you mean?'

He was still looking at her, his face intense. 'I thought you and Lino – the papers said –'

She felt laughter bubbling up inside her. 'You should never believe the papers, Micky Angel!' He had believed she was Lino Rinaldi's girlfriend – that was why he had stayed away! And Vicky – he hadn't seen Vicky for weeks, he had almost said as much! For once she smiled at him and forgot to disguise the smile with her hand. 'Lino was Silvia's boyfriend, Micky,' she said. 'He was never mine. I did everything I did for Silvia, because I was ashamed.'

'Ashamed?'

The smile faded. Marionetta looked down and plucked distractedly at her gloves. 'Silvia got into trouble, and I dropped her.'

Micky gave her a sympathetic look. 'Understandable, under the circumstances.'

But she shook her head vehemently. 'No, it wasn't! She was my best friend and I let her down and then she died.'

A hand reached over and took hers. She looked at that brown hand, the long fingers enclosing hers, and her heart turned over. 'It wasn't your fault, Marionetta,' he was saying. 'Silvia didn't die because of you. She died because of people like the Moruzzis.'

She hardly heard him. He was holding her hand. They were sitting in the dusty little park, close together on a bench, their hands entwined, just as so many lovers had sat before them, lovers that Marionetta had watched and envied. And now here she was, feeling so close to him that she could hardly speak. At that moment she felt as if she could trust Micky Angel with her life.

'I want to tell you something,' she said suddenly, impulsive. 'It's about the Moruzzis.'

He was staring at her again, an odd expression on his face. 'Whatever it is you've got to say about them, it won't shock me,' he said quietly. 'I've heard all the stories. I know what they're like.'

'No,' she said, 'you don't understand. This is about my family – the Perettis. The Perettis and the Moruzzis – they're connected.'

He was silent now. He still held on to her hand, and now he turned it in his, slowly, as if it were something precious. 'Go on,' he said.

So Marionetta told Micky Angel about the two young men all those years ago in Sicily, how they had both loved her grandmother, and the terrible consequences of that love. She told him about the debt of honour passed on from her grandfather to her father and how Antonio had paid the price of that debt by becoming a corrupt policeman. Micky listened in silence, his face revealing nothing. 'And now Tony has disappeared. So you see,' she concluded wryly, 'everything you thought about the Italians is true. We might as well all be in the Mafia. Plots and vendettas, deathbed promises – it's like a gangster film.'

He did not respond. Regretfully, she withdrew her hand from his. She wondered if she had made a mistake, telling him her family secrets. Standing up and pulling her coat around her, she looked down at him. 'I expect you think it's all stupid,' she said lamely.

He stood up too. 'Not stupid, no.' He seemed preoccupied,

163

distant.' 'I know what the Moruzzis are like – they're cruel, evil, ignorant people.' His voice was suddenly very hard. 'They're scum, Marionetta. I hate them.'

Taken aback by his vehement tone, Marionetta backed away a little. 'I'd better be going,' she said. 'Papa will be sending out a search party.'

He didn't try to stop her. As she reached the exit nearest to Greek Street, he called her name. She stopped and turned.

'Will you go out with me tonight?' he called.

Without thinking, she shook her head. 'I can't,' she began to say, 'the club –'

He walked up to her, a frown creasing his forehead. She noticed how brown his skin was. 'I can't –' she repeated, with less conviction. He was standing facing her.

His voice was very quiet. 'What do I have to do?' he asked quietly. 'What do I have to do, Marionetta?'

A moment passed, unspoken, between them. 'I have to open the club tonight,' she said. 'Mario's singing with his new combo. There's no one else besides me to work the bar.'

He hesitated for a moment. 'If I solved that problem,' he said, 'if I found someone – someone you trusted, who was competent to run the bar for one night – would you come out with me then?' He was standing very close. 'Would you?'

She backed away again. 'My father would be furious. Anyway, there isn't anyone,' she said.

'But if I found someone?' He was persistent.

Finally, she relented, not really believing him. 'All right, then.'

His face broke into a wide grin. 'Nine o'clock, then. And your father needn't know. Nine o'clock, Marionetta!' He was hurrying away across the square towards Oxford

Street, elated. 'And wear your glad rags!' she heard him yell. She turned and headed for Old Compton Street, confused by their meeting, happy and yet scared, not really believing she would see him again.

The old man on the park bench had been joined by the scrawny figure of Suzanne Menlove. Together they had watched the parting of Micky Angel and Marionetta Peretti, and now the old drunk raised his meths bottle in a toast. Suzanne Menlove fumbled in her coat pocket and produced a tarnished hip-flask, which she raised aloft and clashed against the man's bottle.

'To young love,' she said, her voice cynical. They both drank.

At ten to nine, Marionetta was behind the bar of the Mint, trying to concentrate on the coffee machine, while Mario and a couple of gloomy-looking young men set up their equipment.

'You're looking glamorous tonight, sis,' Mario remarked, studying her from his elevated place behind the microphone. The Mint had recently invested in the construction of a small stage in the musicians' corner.

'Don't be silly!' she said tartly, pulling one of the Gaggia's levers so that a spurt of steam hissed out. 'I look like I always look.'

Mario shrugged and returned to adjusting the sound level on stage. Tonight he would be singing with just a clarinet and a set of drums for company – an experiment. They were calling themselves the Peppermints, and tonight was their debut. 'Hadn't you better let 'em in?' Mario asked her. 'The punters are queuing down to the corner of Frith Street.'

'I'll do it if you like,' said the clarinet player, a thin, anxious, red-haired boy.

Marionetta threw him the keys. 'Thanks, Dave,' she said. 'Here – take the cash-box. You'll need it for change. And give us a shout if there are any trouble-makers at the door.' She repressed a sigh. Another frantic Friday night at the Mint, just like the last one, and the one before that. She knew she should be pleased that the family's financial troubles were over thanks to her, but sometimes she longed to be just an ordinary girl, not the proprietress of a nightclub . . .

Someone was hammering on the back door. She and Mario exchanged a surprised look; people rarely came to the back entrance of the basement. Marionetta went over and opened the door. Lino Rinaldi was standing there, wearing his bow-tie and smart black jacket.

'*Ciao*, Netta!' He kissed her on both cheeks and stepped inside, grinning. 'Am I on time?'

'On time for what?' She hurried back to the counter. She needed to sort out the coffee cups. There were still several dozen of the tiny espresso cups upstairs on the draining board in the Imperial, and already she could hear the crowds milling about in the doorway upstairs, paying their entrance fee to Dave. The first footsteps were descending the stairs to the club and she wasn't quite ready . . .

'Didn't I say it would be someone you trusted?' She looked up. Micky Angel was standing at the bar, grinning at her. He was wearing the standard musician's outfit of dark suit, dark shirt and narrow black neck-tie.

Lino was bustling about next to Marionetta, piling up cups. '*Presto*, Marionetta!' he was saying. 'Go on! I can do this with my eyes shut, so go away and enjoy yourself, will you?'

Marionetta was speechless. 'It was his night off,' Micky explained. 'He volunteered.'

Lino clicked his heels and bowed, the model of an efficient waiter. 'The least I can do,' he said.

'So,' said Micky Angel, his eyes not leaving her face, 'what excuse are you going to give me now for not coming out with me?' She looked back at Lino, and then at Mario, grinning from the stage. The crowds were already noisily descending the stairs, grabbing tables and heading for the bar.

'I'll get my coat,' she said. As she passed the stage, Mario leaned towards her, still grinning. ' "Don't be silly!" ' he mimicked, ' "I look like I always look!" '

Marionetta had the grace to blush as she grabbed her coat from its hook. She was glad she had bothered to wear her new black pedal-pushers and the patent shoes . . .

'There's more coffee upstairs in the cupboard behind the counter,' she called to Lino. 'They can get a pass out and go over to Kettner's if they want wine. Glasses are under the counter –' Micky was pulling at her arm.

Lino waved her away, unconcerned. 'I'll manage!' he called, turning to the crowd already gathering at the bar. 'Right, then, who was first . . . ?'

Friday night on the streets of Soho was always exciting, but never before had Marionetta been able to stroll along, arm in arm with someone, drinking in the sights and sounds and smells of it. Micky Angel seemed to know everyone; he was greeted with a cheer by a gang of students outside the Caves de France, hailed by the card-sharp packing up outside Madame Valerie's, and greeted cheerfully by the moustached proprietor of the York Minster, who was busy in the doorway of his pub trying to prevent a small terrier from biting the ankles of a passing drunk.

The unusually mild autumn weather had made Soho's visitors feel even more festive than usual, and the streets were alive with the shouts of partygoers, the throb of jazz emanating from dark cellars, and the hum of traffic as more and more taxis arrived and disgorged their occupants, dressed up and ready for a night on the town. The theatre-goers had all disappeared as the evening's performances began, and now the serious revellers, in Soho specifically to savour its delights, were taking over. The pubs were full to overflowing, the restaurants crowded and the night charged with excitement. Only Soho residents like Marionetta and Micky Angel were unmoved by the porn palaces, the seedy bookshops, the depressed-looking girls hanging about outside strip clubs; visitors from elsewhere were always easily identifiable by the look of frozen shock on their faces when they witnessed a girl soliciting for the first time, or staggered out of a clip-joint, having been fleeced of a week's wages.

'Where are we going?' Marionetta asked her companion as they wandered along Wardour Street. She asked the question out of politeness. She did not really care where they went; she was happy like this, strolling along under the neon lights, watching the other side of Soho come to life.

Micky looked at her. He seemed to understand what she was thinking. 'I thought I'd show you the Soho *I* know,' he said, 'The one you never have a chance to see.'

She grinned up at him, excited, her hand flying to her mouth. Gently he took hold of it and moved it away from her face. 'Is that all right with you?' he asked. The expression on her face was his answer.

'Good,' he said. 'We'll start with the Rockingham!'

And so he took Marionetta on a dizzy tour of the Soho known to the musicians who frequented it and supplied its music: the Rockingham in Archer Street, with its exotic membership of Peruvians, Mexicans, Russians and Arabs; Club Eleven in Windmill Street, packed with penniless musicians jamming together in a steamy, raucous cacophony; the Abalabi, where black youths and white girls danced sweatily together to the sounds of calypso. He took her to a café in Fitzrovia to eat moussaka and explained to her the complexities of New Orleans jazz, Chicago blues, bebop versus trad – all the topics that he and his friends debated endlessly over their espressos in clubs like the Mint. Then, their cheap but substantial supper finished, he took her to Humph's on Oxford Street, where Humphrey Lyttleton's band blasted out traditional jazz to a twitching audience.

'Not really my cup of tea,' he shouted to her above the noise as they left, ascending the stairs to Oxford Street, 'but I thought you should get a taste of it, see what it is your brother and his friends are always arguing about!'

They emerged into the relative quiet of Oxford Street, where only the blaring of car horns and the rumble of traffic competed with their conversation. They crossed the road and headed into Soho Street, where the darkened windows of the large post office contrasted with the sudden shaft of light opposite, as the door of a club opened and a group of people emerged, flushed with alcohol, squinting in the sudden change of light. Ahead of them, the trees around Soho Square rustled in the evening breeze. The group from the club raced ahead, whooping with laughter, and ran into the square, performing an impromptu tango around the brooding hulk of the statue. Marionetta, her arm in Micky's, thought she would probably never be this happy again. She had been entranced by this her first real taste of the bright side of Soho, so different from the daily grind of her own life. She was beginning to understand what made people return night after night, addicted to the pleasures of this eccentric nocturnal melting-pot.

Somewhere, a clock struck. 'One o'clock!' she gasped. 'I'd better get back to the Mint –'

Micky groaned. 'But it's still early! I thought at least we could go and have a last cup of tea at Mrs Bill's.' This was the coffee-stall in the bombed site by St Anne's Church.

Marionetta looked rueful. 'I'd love to, Micky, but I can't. I have to get back to the Mint before it closes, in case my dad decides to turn up and walk me home . . .'

They were crossing the square now, very slowly, both reluctant to let the evening end. 'Would he really be so angry if he knew you'd gone out with me?' Micky asked quietly.

Marionetta looked at him. She could see his serious expression, even in the shadows cast by the trees. 'He's Italian,' she said simply. 'You wouldn't understand. He thinks I have to go out with Italian boys. And even then they have to be boys from some family we already know.'

Micky was looking at her, unsmiling. 'Well, he'll just have to move with the times, won't he,' he said, 'because I intend to do this again – often. That is,' he stopped for a moment, causing her to stop too, 'that is, if you want me to – if you want –' For a moment he was no longer the seemingly sophisticated musician who knew everyone and everything in Soho; he was a nervous suitor, unsure of himself and stumbling over his words. Marionetta could hardly believe it.

'Of course,' she said, her voice soft. In this half-darkness she felt brave, for once not thwarted by her scar from looking directly at him. 'But let's not push it, Micky – not tonight, all right?'

'You're right.' He put her arm through his once again and they continued walking. She felt a little disappointed; she had thought for a moment that he was going to kiss her. 'There's plenty of time . . .'

'But you could come in for a last cup of coffee,' she suggested shyly, anxious for the evening to continue. 'If Papa isn't there . . .'

This was agreed. Together they walked silently out of the square and down Greek Street towards the Mint. The restaurants were closing now, and there was something a little forlorn about the empty tables visible inside the gleaming interiors, the lone waiters polishing glasses, the crash of cutlery as weary workers made ready for another influx tomorrow. Someone in L'Escargot waved and shouted at Marionetta. Further along, an exhausted-looking man wielding a saxophone case emerged from a darkened doorway and murmured a greeting to Micky Angel.

The couple grinned at each other. 'It seems that between us we know everyone!' said Marionetta, laughing.

'That', he said, 'is why we make such a perfect couple.'

She didn't know how to reply. Instead, to cover her confusion, she asked, 'How come you know so many people?'

He shrugged. They were turning the corner into Old Compton Street. 'I've been playing in Soho since I was sixteen,' he said.

'Did your parents mind you being a musician?'

His face closed up suddenly. 'My mother died when I was small,' he said. He moved away from her slightly, and she dropped her hand from his arm. She had evidently touched a nerve. 'I ran away from home,' he said finally. 'I live in Broadwick Street now. I share a place with Peter.'

They were nearing the Imperial. The new pink sign for the Mint was visible, shining above the door, with an arrow pointing down to the basement flashing on and off. Marionetta wished she had not asked Micky about his family. He was preoccupied now, his hands stuffed into the pockets of his jacket, no doubt thinking about his past.

'Coffee!' she said brightly, then halted. 'That's odd . . .'

The lights of the Imperial were shining on to the pavement.

'What's the matter?' Micky asked, pulling himself away from his memories.

Marionetta signalled for him to stay where he was. She 'crept forward, peering into the window nervously, keeping herself hidden. What she saw made her heart sink. It was happening again, then. The Moruzzis were back. Seated at a table, opposite the wretched figure of her father, was Attilio Moruzzi, the cruellest of them all, languidly stirring his cup of coffee with a teaspoon, apparently prepared to sit there for ever. She turned back, intent on telling Micky he would not be able to come in after all, when to her surprise she realized that he had been standing right next to her, peering in to the window too, his face frozen. She pushed him backwards, away from the window and into the shadows of the Lee Fungs' doorway. A soft miaow told her that Bella had taken up residence there for the night and was indignant at this intrusion.

'I should go,' he said, his face invisible in the darkness.

Marionetta, her heart thudding, shook her head. 'No,' she said. She had made a decision; she knew it was fool-hardy, defiant, designed to cause the maximum amount of trouble, but she didn't care – her evening with Micky Angel had made her strong. 'I want you to come in with me,' she told him, 'I want you to meet my papa.'

'No,' he said, 'no . . .'

She stared up at him, trying to make out the expression on his face. But it was too dark. Bella wound softly around her ankles, recognizing a friend, purring and butting her head against Marionetta's patent shoes.

'Please,' she said, hurt. 'You said Papa had to move with the times. Well, I've decided he might as well start now.'

Micky Angel gripped her arm suddenly, making her jump. 'That's Attilio Moruzzi in there,' he said unexpect-edly.

'I know,' Marionetta said, puzzled. 'I expect he's come to bully us about Tony. It's nothing to do with you, Micky, it's family business. He won't mind if I just bring you in to meet Papa –' A little bit of her thought defiantly that it would shock Attilio Moruzzi to see her with another man, someone who wanted her, even with her scarred face.

But Micky was pulling away. 'No,' he said, 'I can't –'

'Please!' She could not believe what he was saying. He had been so enthusiastic before, so eager to be involved with her, and now he was backing away down the street, his face white. 'Please!' she said, desperate, 'Micky, please! I'm scared of Attilio Moruzzi, I don't want to go in there alone . . .' He hesitated for a moment. 'Please!' she persisted. 'If I went in there with you, he wouldn't scare my papa by bullying me.' Her hand was up to her face, pressed against her scar.

Still he backed away. 'I can't,' he said, 'I'm sorry –' and then, to her astonishment, he turned and ran, racing away into the night, bumping into some people wandering along eating chips out of newspaper, and disappearing round the corner into Greek Street.

She stared after him. 'Want a chip, love?' the passer-by asked her, grinning, thrusting a greasy handful at her. Trembling, she turned away, back to the café. The laughing girl sharing the man's chips saw Marionetta's scar in the light from the windows and her smile faded. Marionetta, still numb with shock at Micky Angel's cowardice, opened the door of the Imperial and stepped inside. As she did so, a low black shape slithered in at her feet.

The ringing of the bell above the door made both Tomasso and Attilio Moruzzi look up. Attilio smiled at Marionetta, a smile that did not reach his eyes. From the floor below, the sound of the Peppermints wafted up.

'Miss Peretti,' he said, 'you have been a long time.'

'Mario said you'd gone over to Wheeler's,' her father said, 'but you've been gone fifteen minutes!'

She breathed a small sigh of relief. Thank God for Mario, who had invented a plausible lie to explain her absence. She dare not think of what would have happened if she had accepted Micky Angel's offer of a cup of tea at Mrs Bill's: both she and Mario would have been in terrible trouble, Mario for lying to protect his sister, Marionetta for daring to spend the evening with a stranger. Ever since Tony's disappearance, her father had become even more protective of his two remaining children.

'Sorry, papa,' she said quickly, taking off her coat, 'there was a queue a mile long in there –'

'So where's the brandy?' Tomasso asked, suspiciously eyeing her new outfit. Attilio Moruzzi's eyes were on her as well.

'Brandy?' She thought fast. 'Oh – they didn't have what the customer had asked for, so I left it.' She glanced at the clock on the wall and smiled nervously. 'I expect the customer's given up and gone home by now anyway . . .' She turned to descend the stairs to the club, but Attilio raised a hand and stopped her.

'No,' he said, 'don't go yet, *per favore*.' This was not a request, it was an instruction. Slowly, Marionetta returned to the table. The cat followed her and wound hopefully round Attilio's chair leg.

'Sit down.' Marionetta obeyed. 'Tomasso, fetch your daughter a cup of coffee from downstairs, will you? She looks like she needs livening up.'

Tomasso shot his daughter a look full of appeal. She nodded to him. 'It's all right, Papa. I'll be fine.' Tomasso left, descending the stairs with a heavy tread, leaving her alone with the man the papers described as 'Soho's vice king'. She found to her surprise that she was no longer afraid of Attilio Moruzzi. Her hand crept to her cheek. After all, he had not been directly responsible for Wally Wallace slashing her face – that honour went to his brother Barty. She shuddered. Barty Moruzzi was a psychopath; but Attilio Moruzzi would not stoop to slashing the faces of young girls – he had bigger fish to fry.

He was watching her. Bella had jumped on to his lap. 'Quite a little empire you're building for yourself here,' he said, his voice dry. He stroked the cat as it curled up, purring, on his knees. Marionetta waited for Attilio to knock the cat to the floor, but he didn't.

'My father is paying protection money already, if that's what you've come about –'

He held up his hand. 'My brother Carmelo deals with that side of things,' he said smoothly. 'That's not why I'm here.'

'No?'

'No.' He leaned back in his chair, surveying her. 'It's been quite a year for the Peretti family, hasn't it?' he said finally.

Marionetta shifted angrily. 'Look, if you've come here to make small talk –'

He continued as if she had not spoken. 'What with you making a name for yourself in the *News of the World*, your boyfriend getting a reprieve, Wally Wallace getting done for murder, your brother disappearing –'

His words hung in the air. Marionetta said nothing. What could she say? That she hoped Wally Wallace got the death sentence, that she hoped he went through twice the hell poor Lino had gone through, waiting to die?

'Lino wasn't my boyfriend,' was all she managed.

He shrugged, indifferent. 'No word from your brother, then?'

She could ask him now, the question that had been hanging over her family ever since that night when Tony had packed a suitcase and disappeared out of their lives. Now that Papa was not here, she could articulate the words that expressed the Perettis' greatest fear.

'Is he dead?'

He looked surprised. 'Sorry – who?'

'My brother. Antonio. Please, Mr Moruzzi. Tell me the truth. Is my brother dead?'

There was a long moment during which Attilio Moruzzi pulled out a packet of cigarettes and lit one with a gold lighter. He did not offer the packet to Marionetta. Finally he spoke, exhaling a plume of smoke upwards. 'Well, if he is,' he said, his bony fingers caressing the cat's ears, 'my family had nothing to do with it. Satisfied?'

Relief flooded through her. The Moruzzis had not found Antonio! Tomasso returned with a cup of coffee for his daughter. He was followed by a couple of students arm in arm, dressed in black, both yawning after a long night in the club. They headed for the exit, engrossed in each other, neither of them recognizing the figure at the table in the café. They called a goodnight to Marionetta and left, the doorbell jangling as they stepped out into the mild night. Marionetta watched them enviously. How uncomplicated their lives looked, how simple their affection for each other!

Tomasso sat down heavily at the table, and deposited the coffee in front of his daughter. '*Bene*,' he said. 'You wanted to wait until Marionetta was here, *signore*. Now she's here. So what is it you want to say to us?'

The troubles of the past few years had weighed heavily on the shoulders of Tomasso Peretti. He had aged suddenly, Marionetta thought. His hair was almost white, and his face had shrunk in on itself, leaving the proud nose and the fine bones prominent. She found herself comparing her father with the man seated opposite. They must be about the same age, but there the comparison stopped. Years of good living had taken their toll on Attilio, as was evidenced by the wrinkles around his eyes, the pallor of his skin; but he was still essentially a handsome man, his hair gleaming black, a powerful body encased in expensive clothes. He made poor Papa, hunched over the table in his worn shirt and cheap waistcoat, look like a pauper. She wondered fleetingly if Attilio Moruzzi had a wife hidden away somewhere, children . . .

'It's quite simple, really.' His voice interrupted her thoughts. 'I have a proposition to put to you.'

Marionetta frowned and turned to her father. 'We don't have to listen to this, Papa –'

'Ah, but I think you do,' Attilio said, smiling. 'Shall I continue?' There was silence. He spoke again. 'As you know, we are dealing with a debt of honour between our respective fathers, Mr Peretti – yours now dead, mine still very much alive.'

'Yes, and we have honoured that debt,' Tomasso was saying nervously. 'We have done everything you have asked of us –'

Attilio smiled again. 'But there is a problem. Antonio was the payment of the debt, as we agreed. He worked for us occasionally from within the police force, helping us when required. Unfortunately,' he surveyed them both, his face regretful, 'Unfortunately, Antonio has reneged on that debt by disappearing. So I am obliged to come here and renegotiate the terms.'

'No,' Marionetta said flatly. 'No. We have done everything that you asked. There is nothing to negotiate.'

Attilio's face hardened a little. He stared at Marionetta. 'Do you always allow your daughter to speak for you,

177

Mr Peretti?' he asked drily, his eyes not leaving Marionetta's. 'A sad state of affairs. I thought you were Italian.'

This hit home. 'Of course I'm Italian!' Tomasso blazed. '*Basta*, Marionetta! Speak when you're spoken to!'

Fuming, she subsided. It was pointless trying to argue. Attilio continued smoothly, 'So . . . the terms.' He examined a manicured fingernail for a moment. 'I've been having some trouble with my brother Bartolomeo –'

Marionetta could not repress a snort of derision. 'Trouble!' she exclaimed. 'Your brother's middle name is trouble.'

Her father quelled her with a look. Attilio raised an eyebrow but otherwise did not comment. 'My brother – Barty – you may know his business involves the running of certain clubs, and the hiring and firing of – what shall we call them –' he smiled slightly, '– hostesses.' He stared at Marionetta, silently challenging her to rise to the bait. What was the point in responding? she thought wearily. They all knew he was talking about call-girls, street-walkers, prostitutes – it did not matter what they were called for the purposes of polite conversation. 'Barty's getting a bit too involved with some of his girls,' Attilio went on, choosing his words carefully. Still his long fingers caressed the cat in an hypnotic rhythm. 'I've not been very happy with his treatment of certain young women recently . . . I want my brother to be married, respectable. I want him home in his own bed at night, I want a nice wife there, waiting for him with slippers and cocoa. You know the kind of thing.'

'And what has this got to do with us?' Tomasso asked, his voice full of dread. It was as if he already knew the answer.

'Your daughter,' Attilio said, looking across the table at Marionetta appreciatively, 'seems to have all the right qualities. She's Sicilian, so my papa will be happy. She's a Peretti, which will make him even happier. And –' his eyes lingered on her scar '– she's not likely to stray very far once she's married, is she?'

There was a shocked silence. Marionetta gripped the edge of the table, as though the world had suddenly moved on its axis and she feared solid objects might spin away. She looked at her father. He was staring at Attilio Moruzzi, his face grey with fear.

'Think about it,' Attilio said. 'There could be worse things than marrying into the Moruzzi family.' He stood up, scraping back his chair and gently pushing the cat to the floor. He stood looking down at them, his face grave. 'There are not a lot of options,' he said. 'If you don't agree to my proposition then I'll have to think again, of course . . .' He began to walk to the door, turning the collar of his coat up, his face full of regret, 'But it would be a terrible pity to have to interfere with the life of that nice boy down there, wouldn't it?'

Marionetta's mind was blank for a moment, and then it dawned on her: he was talking about Mario! He was saying that if she did not agree, he would turn his attentions to her younger brother!

'You wouldn't dare,' she said fiercely.

He opened the door. 'No?' The bell jangled above his head. 'Someone will be along in the morning,' he said. 'I'd like to hear your answer then. Sleep on it. I think you'll find that by the time you've had your breakfast, it will seem like the best solution.'

The door closed behind him and he was gone.

Tomasso stared at his daughter, mute, his face quivering with desperation.

'No,' she said, 'No, Papa. *Never!*'

★

It had rained during the night, and when Marionetta found the cat the next morning, its fur was matted and damp. Bella was curled up in the doorway and when the creature had not responded to Marionetta's voice as usual, she had knelt down to take a closer look. It was only then that she had realized Bella was dead.

'It was probably a car,' Mario said sadly as he dug a grave for the animal among the weeds, in the back yard. 'Bella wouldn't have felt a thing, Netta. She would have crawled back here to the doorway and just died quietly in her sleep.'

Marionetta exchanged a glance with her father. He looked away, unable to speak. They put the animal's stiff little body into the hole and Mario began to cover it with earth.

'*Ciao*, little *gatto*,' Marionetta whispered tearfully.

Upstairs, Mrs Lee Fung watched them from her window. Marionetta wondered fleetingly what on earth the Chinese woman made of such a sentimental little ceremony. Her father tried to touch her shoulder but she pulled away, walking briskly back into the café.

It was still early, and the Imperial was not yet open. Someone was knocking on the door, and Marionetta went to see who it was. Peering through the glass, she could see the distinct outline of an eye-patch. She unlocked the door. Carmelo Moruzzi politely took off his hat.

'My brother sent me,' he said.

'I know,' Marionetta said, her heart freezing over. 'Tell him I've agreed. Tell him he finally persuaded me. Tell him Marionetta Peretti says yes.'

The Pirate grinned down at her. 'He'll be pleased.' He turned to go. 'We'll be in touch.'

But she stopped him. 'Wait. I haven't finished. Tell him – tell him I'll marry Barty Moruzzi on condition that this is the end of the debt. From the day of my marriage, the Perettis will be free of your family completely.'

He considered her words and then nodded. 'Of course,' he said. 'Only you won't *really* be free, will you? – because you'll be one of us! You'll be a Moruzzi yourself!'

And so it was that on the fifth day of a drizzly December, Marionetta married Bartolomeo Moruzzi in a ceremony at St Patrick's Church. There were few guests. Mario refused to come, not understanding why his sister would choose to marry one of the most evil men in London. Marionetta's friends were too appalled and frightened to attend. Only a few wan-faced girls from the Moruzzi clubs had been coerced to come to the church and they stood in a be-draggled row, their furs dripping, their faces hard in the daylight. A motley collection of the Moruzzis' employees were in attendance, heavy-jowled men in expensive suits with coarse cockney accents, standing stiff and ill at ease, murmuring to each other. There seemed to be some terrible shadow casting itself over the whole proceedings from high above Soho, above the huddled streets and buildings, above the cross of St Patrick's piercing the grey sky. It was like the slow flapping of the wings of Lucifer hovering somewhere in the heavens, a malevolent, uninvited wed-ding guest, settling himself on the rooftop of the church among the shuffling pigeons peering down on the proceed-ings below with bright, indifferent eyes.

Marionetta went through the ceremony like a sleep-walker. She was wearing the kind of dress she had dreamed of, an expensive creation made for her by the best Knights-bridge dressmaker. She had stared at herself in the mirror and had seen not a beautiful, eager bride, but a sacrificial virgin going to be slaughtered. The sight of all that white satin, the gossamer veil, the delicate bouquet of lilies, had filled her with horror and she had almost vomited. But here she was, at the altar, and there was the familiar face of Father Joseph, and this was her voice, repeating the marriage vows. Only the man next to her was not the one she had dreamed of, except in her worst nightmares. Barty Moruzzi, ill-pleased at having this scarred café girl thrust on him by his family, simply scowled and avoided her eyes. This, she thought, was truly a marriage made in hell.

It was over. People were murmuring in the church, their voices reverberating in the emptiness. Slowly, Marionetta walked back down the aisle with her new husband. She saw her father staring at her, transfixed, as if he, too, could not believe this had really happened. Her eye fell on the painting of Martha and Mary and she smiled a little to herself; she had thought she was Martha – proud, independent – and all the time she had been destined to be Mary – the submissive wife, the listener, the silent, uncomplaining one.

They stepped out into the drizzle of a dank morning. A car was waiting. Some of the club girls, feigning enthusiasm after a prod from Carmelo Moruzzi, threw confetti and raised a feeble cheer. Marionetta felt strong arms clasp her, and she was pulled towards a grizzled cheek. It was Alfonso Moruzzi, her new father-in-law.

'I can't tell you what this means to me,' he murmured, pressing his trembling lips against her scarred cheek. She pulled away, silent, and got into the car, where her new husband was already lighting a cigar and loosening his tie.

'Get going,' he said tersely to the driver, 'I need a couple of stiff drinks before the bloody reception.' He turned to his new wife, a look of disdain crossing his pinched features. 'God,' he said. 'God!' He pulled the veil back and stared at her scarred face. 'What the hell have I got myself? You look like Boris Karloff on a bad day.'

The car drove away. Marionetta stared out of the

window, her face a blank. She was so busy trying not to cry that she did not see the sign outside Moroni's the newsagents as they sped past. It read: 'Wally Wallace hanged for prostitute's murder'.

CHAPTER SEVEN

August 1953

Marionetta woke up alone, as usual, in the big bed in the room at the front of the house. She looked at the clock on the bedside table. It was ten o'clock. Barty had left the house already, bent on some unnamed business in the West End. The day stretched ahead of her like all the others, endless hours to be filled – with what? She wondered what other wives did all day. She had never realized before what life was like for those women who never had to work, whose marriages brought them hours of liberty to spend as they pleased. For Marionetta, accustomed to a working life of getting up at six and never going to bed before two o'clock the following morning, these empty hours were desolate deserts to be crossed until night and sleep took mercy on her.

Her days in Soho as a waitress, her nights as a small club owner – it all seemed like a dream now. She sighed and sank back into the pillows. There was little point in getting up. Something landed on the bed with a little cry and nuzzled up to her. It was Nevata, the white Persian kitten her brother-in-law Attilio had given her as a birthday present. She was a beautiful little thing, with strange yellow eyes, soft, downy fur, and a magnificent plumed tail. Yet somehow Marionetta could never warm to Nevata as she had to Bella – little, ordinary Bella, the café cat, whose life as a working mouser had been so cruelly cut short. Every time Marionetta looked at Nevata she remembered Attilio sitting in the café, stroking Bella, his face thoughtful; small wonder she had such trouble loving the little pedigree cat when she was sure the man who had given it to her had killed her own pet. Nevata seemed oblivious to the lack of affection she received from Marionetta, and followed her about devotedly. Now she nestled into the crook of her arm, purring noisily, until Marionetta pushed her onto the floor.

'Go away, Nevata!' she snapped. 'You're not allowed on the bed –'

The door opened. 'Did you speak, madam?'

It was Mrs McQueen, duster in hand, poking her head round the door. Marionetta knew she had been hovering on the landing, nosily waiting to see what the lady of the house was up to.

'I was talking to the cat,' Marionetta said. 'And please don't call me madam.' She hated Mrs McQueen, who had a rather refined Scots accent and looked as though she had a bad smell under her nose. It was evident she regarded her employers as somewhat beneath her.

'Very well, Mrs Moruzzi, I'm sorry,' she said in a voice that indicated she was not. Marionetta was about to dive under the covers again, when she noticed something and sat up.

'Mrs McQueen,' she said, 'what *are* you wearing?'

Mrs McQueen entered the room. She was a small, spare woman with wiry grey hair and a sharp-featured face. She stood as if for inspection, smoothing her apron self-consciously with one hand. 'It's a uniform, madam – Mrs Moruzzi.'

'I can see that.'

'Your husband ordered it for me. He said I should wear it, madam.'

Marionetta sighed. 'It's ridiculous. You're only here three hours a day, doing the cleaning. Why on earth does he want you dolled up like a maid?'

Mrs McQueen bristled slightly. Evidently she was rather taken with her new outfit, with its frilly apron, severe black dress and white collar and cuffs. 'I'm quite happy to wear it,' she said stiffly.

Marionetta threw back the gold satin quilt and flung her legs over the side of the bed. She felt Mrs McQueen's eyes assessing her silk nightgown and silently calculating its cost. 'In that case,' said Marionetta, defeated, 'I suppose you'd better carry on.'

'Thank you, madam.'

Marionetta considered correcting the woman but then thought better of it. She was not sure she liked the sound of 'Mrs Moruzzi' any more than she liked being called 'madam', as though she were some member of the aristocracy instead of the wife of a Soho gangster. 'Please,' she said, as Mrs McQueen headed for the door, 'take the cat, will you?'

'Shall I open the curtains for you?'

Marionetta shook her head. 'I think I can manage to do that myself, Mrs McQueen.'

Silently, Mrs McQueen swept up the protesting Nevata and proceeded from the room, her eyebrows managing to express a wealth of disapproval.

Once the door had closed, Marionetta got up and went to the window, her feet making no noise on the soft carpet. She opened the curtains slightly and peered out. The branches of a chestnut tree cast dappled shadows over the window-pane, and below there were neatly cut grass verges lining the wide suburban street. She opened the window, leaned over the sill and held her face up to the sun, enjoying its warmth on her skin. Marionetta supposed that Muswell Hill was the very height of respectability. Certainly her neighbours, living their alien lives composed of nannies, commuter husbands, coffee mornings and small, well-scrubbed children, seemed to be the epitome of middle-class English life. Small wonder, then, Marionetta thought wryly, that they studiously avoided the couple at number 24 Endicott Gardens, despite the fact that theirs was one of the biggest houses in the street, and that Barty's car was larger and more expensive than any of the others parked by the kerb outside at the end of each day. She wondered for the hundredth time at the folly of the Moruzzis, who thought that money could buy acceptance in suburbia. It had been Alfonso Moruzzi, the old patriarch of the family, who had bought them the house as a wedding present, despite Marionetta's protestations. He had taken a liking to Marionetta. Not only did she remind him of his lost love (in spite of the facial scar, which he preferred to ignore), she also had spirit, which was something he admired, and which was sadly lacking, he often thought regretfully, in his sons. He had been delighted at this match between the Perettis and the Moruzzis; somehow it had seemed to him to even up old scores, to settle the balance. He expressed his pleasure by showering his new daughter-in-law with unwanted presents, each more lavish than the last, in the unrealized hope that she might one day smile and seem happy with her lot. Instead Marionetta remained an unsmiling, wraith-like figure who rattled about in the large house, surrounded by expensive furnishings and uncomfortable in her fashionable clothes.

Below her in the street, two women were passing, one of them pushing a magnificent pram containing a lace-bonneted infant. One of the women nudged the other and they looked up at Marionetta hanging out of the window daydreaming, her long black hair mingling with the leaves of the chestnut tree.

'Anyone would think this was Naples!' one said loudly, and the other tossed her head disapprovingly as they passed.

Hastily, Marionetta withdrew. She shouldn't mind. Those women were never going to be her friends; and they would never understand the world from which she had come, the sweaty proximity of the Buildings, where the sight of a young Italian girl leaning out of the window to bask in the sunshine was as common as a pan of spaghetti.

She washed and dressed in a kind of trance, wandering about among the gold fittings, the crystal lamps, the opulent marble tiles, the flocked wallpaper, like a lost spirit in the Underworld. Finally she descended the stairs to face Mrs McQueen and the rest of the interminable day.

Mrs McQueen was dusting the umbrella stand in the front vestibule with vigour. She looked up as Marionetta appeared, heading towards the kitchen.

'If you'd like to go into the breakfast room, Mrs Moruzzi,' she said, attempting to sound bright but succeeding only in emphasizing the disdain she felt, 'I'll be happy to bring you some tea.'

'I'd rather eat in the kitchen.' Marionetta tossed the words over her shoulder without stopping. 'And I'm quite capable of making tea, thank you.'

She was aware of Mrs McQueen, her face rendered an odd blue by the reflected light of the leaded windows in the hall, gazing after her, frowning. Marionetta sighed. She should not take out her loneliness and frustration on the only human being she saw all day apart from her hated husband. 'Perhaps you'd like a cup as well,' she called, relenting, not realizing that this gesture would be considered totally inappropriate.

'No, thank you, Mrs Moruzzi,' came the frosty reply.

More polish was applied to the over-ornate legs of the umbrella stand, and the sound of vigorous application of the duster followed Marionetta into the kitchen. She lit the gas and sat the kettle on the flames. Nevata wound round her ankles, yowling. She repressed the desire to kick the fluffy little bundle across the linoleum, and busied herself with the tea instead, reaching into the cupboard for a hefty china mug like the ones they used in the café and ignoring the over-ornate china stacked on the shelves, a wedding present from Carmelo Moruzzi.

In the hall, the telephone rang. She heard Mrs McQueen lift the receiver, and her strangled Scots vowels announce, 'The Moruzzi residence . . .' She waited, holding the teapot, hopeful. She had this foolish dream that one day Micky Angel would telephone her, would tell her it had all been a dreadful mistake, would take her away with him, they would elope together to some distant place, and there they would continue what they had once so tentatively started . . .

'It's your father, Mrs Moruzzi.'

Marionetta shook herself a little. 'Thank you, Mrs Mc-Queen,' she said, heading out to the hall and trying to suppress the small feeling of disappointment lurking in her heart. At least it wasn't Barty, or one of his brothers, or her father-in-law . . .

'Papa? *Buongiorno* . . .'

'Marionetta?' His voice sounded unnaturally loud. He had always hated using the telephone, holding it as if it were an unexploded bomb, shouting into the receiver. Marionetta smiled to herself, imagining him leaning against the wall in the Imperial in his shirtsleeves, cradling the dreaded machine and yelling above the noise of his customers and the hissing of the coffee machine.

'Is everything all right, Papa?'

'Very busy,' he boomed. '*Frenetico*! I just thought I should telephone, see if you're all right. Barty just passed in his car, and I wondered . . .'

She understood. Tomasso had seen his hated son-in-law in Soho, which meant he could talk to his daughter openly on the telephone, without fear of being overheard by a Moruzzi.

'I'm fine, Papa,' she said softly. 'Any news of Tony?'

'No. Nothing.' The question and the answer were both automatic; there was never any news of Marionetta's brother who had disappeared over a year ago. Marionetta wondered if Tony knew she had married Barty Moruzzi. Of course, he could have left the country, gone to Italy, perhaps, in which case he would have no idea of the change in her fortunes. Or perhaps he was dead, disposed of by the Moruzzis; perhaps Attilio had lied to her. These thoughts flashed through her mind as they did every day, but as usual, she presented a brave face to her father. 'I know he'll come back one day, Papa,' she said, her voice comforting.

Her father's voice quavered. 'But what's the use, Netta? We're a divided family, you were so angry with him when he left –'

'That's all over now, Papa,' she said calmly. After all, what was the point of anger now? She had married one of the Moruzzis; she was no better than Tony. 'If Tony comes back home, I promise I'll be as glad to see him as you are.'

'Hold on.' She heard the receiver clatter down, and then her father's distant voice asking, 'Two teas, mister? Dough-nuts are over there, or we have some nice Danish pastries . . .'

She waited patiently, listening, while at the other end of the line she could hear the sounds of the café in its usual mid-morning chaos. It was like music to her ears. She could hear the tinny clanging of the doorbell as someone came in, her father greeting a regular customer, the crashing of cups in the washing-up bowl. In the front vestibule, Mrs McQueen had returned to her polishing, clearly listening in.

Her father returned to the telephone, breathless. 'Sorry, *cara*,' he said, 'it's like a lunatic asylum in here. Coronation crowds already and still two weeks to go! A great big gang of Yanks just left, and now there's some Germans in –' He sounded excited but fraught. At that moment Marionetta envied him more than anyone in the world. 'I'll have to get some help,' he was saying. 'What with Mario always off singing somewhere, I can't do this on my own. I was thinking about the Falconis' little girl, she's just left school, seems a bright enough child . . . Netta? Can you hear me?'

'I'm listening, Papa.' She had never imagined someone else taking her place at the Imperial.

'What do you think, Netta?' he persisted. 'You think she can cope with the work? I could nip round to the Buildings and fetch her in five minutes, if you agree she's suitable.'

She made a decision then. 'You don't have to talk to the Falconis yet, Papa,' she said. 'I'm coming to help you.'

'You?' He snorted in surprise. 'But you're in Muswell Hill!'

'It's not Siberia, Papa,' she said reasonably.

'But it takes hours on the underground!'

'I'll get a cab,' she said decisively. 'God knows, I can afford it!' She felt rather than saw Mrs McQueen's little flinch of disapproval at the vulgarity of talking about money on the telephone. The small stiff figure stalked past her to the kitchen, intent on some new cleaning mission, no doubt.

'What about Barty?' her father was asking anxiously. 'He won't like it . . .'

'He won't mind,' Marionetta lied, 'not if I tell him it was an emergency.'

'If you're certain . . .' His voice still sounded unsure.

'I'll be there in half an hour,' she said, '*Ciao*, Papa!' And she replaced the receiver hastily, before he could change his mind.

Humming, she went into the kitchen. Mrs McQueen was pouring tea into a delicate bone china tea-cup. Evidently she had not approved of Marionetta's choice of crockery, and had returned the mug to the cupboard.

'It's all right, Mrs McQueen,' Marionetta said, smiling a rare smile. 'You have the tea – I'm going out.'

'Out?' Mrs McQueen raised her head, interested, but Marionetta was not about to give her any information. She headed for the hall again, about to grab her coat, when she looked down at herself and gave a little gasp.

'I can't go like *this*!' she said aloud. Mrs McQueen peered round the door at her as she raced upstairs, then shrugged and went back into the kitchen. It was none of her business, after all . . .

Marionetta tore off the tasteful wool dress she had been wearing and rummaged in the wardrobe, emerging triumphant with her old black waitressing skirt. She struggled into it, haste making her clumsy, and then groaned when she remembered that she no longer had the blouse that went with it; Mrs McQueen had torn it up and used it for dusters. Frantic, she rooted in the drawers of the mahogany chest of drawers, and settled on an expensive-looking crepe blouse patterned with tiny sprigs of daisies. It was far too fancy for the café, but it would have to do. Snatching up her handbag, she ran downstairs again, pausing in the hall only to collect her coat.

The door slammed behind her. Mrs McQueen stood in the polished vestibule sipping her tea and wondering why on earth her young employer had taken off a perfectly good dress in order to go out in a shabby skirt that looked too shoddy even for the rag-and-bone man. But of course it was none of her business . . .

The regulars in the Imperial were delighted to have their favourite waitress back, even if it was only a temporary pleasure. They were surprised, however, by this new Marionetta with her glamorous hairstyle, stylish blouse and expensive shoes. What was most noticeable was the change in her demeanour. Gone were the irrepressible sense of humour and the ready laugh; this new Marionetta was altogether more grave, more thoughtful. Hardly surprising, they thought privately, considering her choice of husband. Most of them were rather surprised that she was still alive, let alone surviving this odd marriage. Even though the customers of the café were now a little scared of Marionetta thanks to her new surname, most of them saw that she was still her father's daughter, still a Peretti at heart and not a Moruzzi at all.

No one asked about her husband, no one inquired about how she was finding married life: the name of Moruzzi seemed to be unpronounceable within the walls of the Imperial these days, and for this Marionetta was thankful. She wanted to forget about her awful daily existence, her virtual imprisonment in the house in Muswell Hill, cut off from everything she knew and cared about. Here at least she could recapture for a few hours the comfort of working in a world she understood.

The café was busy all afternoon, with a relentless flow of tourists, most of them visiting London for the Coronation. Marionetta and her father were soon working to their old rhythm, efficiently dispensing tea and cakes, sandwiches and coffee to a sea of ever-changing faces at the crowded tables of the Imperial. Tomasso had been busy with red,

193

white and blue streamers, and the picture of the Queen had been draped in Christmas tinsel. Marionetta had paused for a moment in front of it, smiling wryly to herself at this icon of Britishness, when someone grabbed her from behind and swung her round in a bear-hug. It was Mario, beaming from ear to ear with delight at seeing his sister.

'Netta, it's so good to see you!'

She hugged him back warmly, then laughingly disentangled herself in order to collect up some plates from a nearby table. 'I haven't seen you for ages, little brother. Why don't you come and visit me at the house?'

He pulled a face, helping her by piling up some teacups and following her to the counter. 'You know why.'

She smiled regretfully. 'I'm alone all day, Mario. If you came to see me before the evening, you wouldn't have to see Barty at all.'

He grinned. 'So the only problem left is my inability to get up before lunch-time.'

Tomasso heard this from his place at the sink, and grunted. 'Now he's got a regular spot at the Ambassador Club it's like living with Perry Como.' Only the sly wink he gave his daughter belied the gruffness of his tone. He was ridiculously proud of Mario's growing success as a singer, and seemed now to accept that his youngest son's destiny did not lie in the catering trade as he had once hoped.

Mario took off his overcoat, rolled up his shirt-sleeves and prepared to take over at the counter. He looked keenly at his sister. 'How does it feel to be back?' he asked.

She smiled, wiping a tired hand across her forehead. 'I'm sure you can guess,' she said. It was a mixture of elation and exhaustion, compounded by the fear that at any moment one of the Moruzzis might stroll in and catch her there, disobeying instructions that she should stay out of sight in Muswell Hill and be a dutiful wife. That had been the agreement; but how could the Moruzzis ever know what simple pleasure she had derived from an afternoon's hard work? She shrugged to herself. They would never understand.

It was odd; now that she was part of the Moruzzi family, now that she had experienced them all at close quarters, she did not fear them quite so much. After all, they were just egotistical men, drunk on their own idea of *virilità* – a childish fallacy about what makes men powerful. She knew them better now. She had seen her husband almost weeping with frustration because he had lost a game of poker. She had witnessed her brother-in-law Carmelo slapping the face of a cheeky newspaper boy. She had watched, disgusted, as Attilio had reduced a waiter in a restaurant to a quivering, toadying shadow because the wine had not been sufficiently chilled. All these actions, intended to prove that the Moruzzis had control, only served to confirm to her what a collection of cowards they were. She had to live with them, but she did not have to be defeated by them. The fear she now felt at being discovered working in the café was not for herself, it was for her father, and for Mario. She had made the ultimate sacrifice for them, and it would be foolish now to provoke the Moruzzis into further action against the Perettis.

Mario was still watching her, as she thoughtfully dried a pile of plates, stacking them on the shelf above the sink. 'Listen,' he said, 'why don't you nip out for a bit – have a bit of a walk around? It's slacking off a bit in here, and anyway, I'm here now.'

She looked across at her father, who nodded. 'Good idea. Go on, Netta. Get some colour in your cheeks.'

She took her apron off, pleased. 'All right, then,' she said, 'but there's one thing I must do first . . .'

She crossed the café, pausing at the stairs descending to the Mint, closed off as usual during the day by a red cord hung across the entrance. She hesitated for a moment, looking at her brother. He had been left in charge of the Mint since her wedding. Would he object to her wanting to look at it once more, to remember when it had been her own little kingdom? Mario was grinning at her. 'Go on!' he said. 'Just don't expect me to have done much dusting recently!'

In the half-light, she stood at the foot of the stairs, looking around the Mint. At first it seemed as if nothing had changed. The rickety card-tables were still ranged round the walls, the Gaggia machine gleamed on the counter, the little stage in the corner was still there. Then she began to notice changes. The newspaper cuttings about Silvia Conti's murder and Lino Rinaldi's trial had gone. They had been replaced by brightly-painted murals of what seemed to be giant trees, covering the walls in various shades of green, but which on closer examination were perhaps abstracts. Marionetta studied them intently.

'Well? What do you think?' It was Mario, who had followed her downstairs, anxious to see her reaction to the changes he had instigated.

'I love them, Mario!' she said. 'Or at least,' she stared at them again, 'I think I do.'

He was pleased. 'They didn't cost a penny. A gang of students from the art school offered to do them.'

'What exactly are they?' She peered more closely, hoping for a clue.

Mario laughed. 'Good question! When I asked them they looked a bit annoyed, as if I was supposed to have known the moment I looked at them. Apparently they're supposed to be various kinds of mints.'

'They are?' Marionetta tried peering at them from a different angle. 'I thought they were trees of some kind.'

Mario tilted his head and tried looking at them upside-down. 'Really? I would have bet my life they were beehives.'

'Or possibly hedgehogs?'

They giggled together like a pair of schoolchildren. Mario hugged his sister again impulsively. 'It's good to have you back,' he said simply.

'I'm not back, Mario,' she said sadly, 'not really.' She turned back towards the stairs. 'This is just a flying visit.'

He watched her, frustrated. 'I wish –'

She held up her hand. 'I know,' she said. 'Whatever you wish, I wish it, too.' She turned to go, and then remembered something, and crossed to the bar where the wooden puppet her mother had given her still hung, its arms and legs akimbo, its strings tangled and dusty.

'I didn't know whether to take it down or not,' Mario began.

Marionetta carefully unhooked it from the wall, and blew gently on the dusty folds of the little dancer's costume. The perfect painted face looked blandly up at her. 'If you don't mind,' she said, 'I think I'd like to take her home with me . . .'

'Of course,' Mario said, relieved she was not angry with him for having left it there. He had always felt it was a reminder of his sister, but this was better, having the real thing here instead.

She carefully folded the wooden limbs, winding the strings around the body of the puppet, and then, wrapping it in a handkerchief, pushed it into her handbag. She crossed back to the exit and began to climb the stairs. Mario watched her, thinking how pretty she looked, how innocent, how unlike the wife of a gangster . . .

'Have you seen Micky Angel at all?' he asked.

She paused, but did not turn round. 'No,' she said. 'I

197

haven't seen him since – well, a long time.' She began to climb again, her face hidden. 'I'll see you later, Mario.'

Once outside, she knew at once where she wanted to go. She hurried round the corner to Greek Street, ignoring the nudges and stares of some of the Soho regulars who recognized her, and headed for St Patrick's. Confession, they said, was good for the soul, and her soul was sorely in need of sustenance . . .

She was standing in the doorway of the church removing her headscarf, feeling more at ease with herself now she had made her confession and lit a candle for Mary and Martha at the side altar. She was about to step out into the bustle of Soho Square when someone tapped her on the shoulder. Turning, she was surprised to see a well-loved face beaming at her from beneath the familiar nun's shawl.

'Sister Maddalena!' Marionetta was genuinely pleased to see the old nun from the Don Bosco convent in Greek Street, where she had attended nursery school so many years ago. 'Sister Maddalena! I had no idea you were still in Soho.'

'I went away when the convent closed during the war,' Sister Maddalena explained, still clasping Marionetta's hand in hers, delighted to see her old pupil. 'But now I've come back. We're opening a new convent – just a small place – round the corner.'

'Where? I'd love to see it.' Marionetta's face fell. 'But I expect you're busy . . .'

The nun looked at her, and understood how lonely she was. She knew what had happened to Marionetta Peretti, but now was not the time to talk of it, not here in the street.

'Why don't you come to the convent and have some tea?' she asked. 'The place is a bit of a mess, we haven't been there long, but we've certainly got a kettle.'

Marionetta smiled again eagerly. 'I'd love to!' she said.

She was led to a tall, narrow building just round the corner from the square, in Greek Street. She must have passed it a hundred times and not realized what went on behind its anonymous black door. As they toured the almost empty building, Sister Maddalena explained, her voice echoing in the bare rooms, that this was to be a charitable rooming-house for young women who had, as she tactfully put it, 'fallen from grace' and needed a refuge.

Marionetta was touched. 'I think that's a wonderful idea,' she said, moved. 'When I think of what happened to Silvia, and how she needed a place like this to come to. . .' She bit back the tears.

Sister Maddalena patted her hand. 'It was partly Silvia's death that inspired us,' she said. 'Our Lord did the rest.'

They were standing in the hall among the packing-cases. Several religious paintings were stacked against the wall, and a small plaster *Pietà* stood rather forlornly by the door, waiting for a niche to be found for it. A young girl appeared, timid. 'Did you want tea, Sister Maddalena?' she asked.

'That would be lovely, Teresa.' The nun smiled at her, and the girl slipped silently away down the hall and into a room somewhere at the back of the building. Marionetta stared after her, curious. 'Is that one of the . . .?'

The nun nodded. 'Yes, Teresa had the misfortune to be drawn into bad ways,' she said, discreetly drawing Marionetta into the front room where a couple of very old armchairs had been placed either side of an empty fireplace. There were dusty boxes of books everywhere, and a stepladder stood in one corner, where someone had been hanging curtains. They settled into the chairs. 'She was brought to us,' the nun continued carefully, watching Marionetta for her response, 'after the Wally Wallace case. We are protecting her.'

Marionetta stared in surprise at her old teacher and adviser. 'Protecting her? From what?'

Sister Maddalena hesitated for a moment. After all, this young woman seated opposite her was now the wife of Barty Moruzzi. She looked at the honest brown eyes gazing at her, the open, guileless face, and chided herself for doubting Marionetta. She had known her since she was three years old. It was impossible that eight months of marriage to a Moruzzi could have changed her very radically from the steady, bright soul who had laboured so hard over her spelling all those years ago ... 'A young musician brought Teresa here,' she said eventually. Marionetta was staring at her, suddenly brought to life, sitting forward tensely on the edge of her chair. 'A young musician,' Sister Maddalena repeated. 'His name was Angel.' She heard Marionetta's sharp intake of breath. 'Teresa was the key witness at the trial, the girl who came forward and gave evidence against Wally Wallace.'

'So she's the one who saved Lino!' Marionetta said in a low voice.

The nun nodded, her eyes never leaving Marionetta's face, watching her reactions and choosing her words accordingly. 'She's a good girl at heart. She had been brought up to know right from wrong. It was only fear of the Moruzzi brothers that kept her silent, like all those poor unfortunate girls.'

Marionetta stared into the empty grate, her mind racing. Micky Angel had brought that girl here, to a refuge. Why?

The door opened and Teresa came in carrying a tray. Silently she knelt and placed it on the floor between the two women, her eyes lowered. Marionetta watched her as she arranged the tea-cups. She was a small, slight girl with a pale face and freckles, her hair scraped back in a ponytail. It was hard to imagine this waif walking the streets, selling her body.

'Thank you, Teresa,' Sister Maddalena said gently, and silently the girl withdrew.

The old nun sipped her tea and studied Marionetta's face again. She was clearly shocked by what she had just been told, and seemed to be lost in thought. Sister Maddalena carefully talked of inconsequential things, her voice murmuring soothingly as Marionetta tried to collect her thoughts. Finally there was silence. Marionetta looked across at her old teacher and saw that she had fallen asleep, her head nodding gently, her breathing regular. Quietly Marionetta got up and gently removed the trembling tea-cup from the old woman's hands, placing it back on the tray. Then, on tiptoe, she left the room.

She was quietly closing the door, careful not to let the handle squeak, when Teresa suddenly appeared in the hall.

'She's asleep,' Marionetta whispered. 'I would get the tray later if I were you.'

Teresa nodded and was about to retreat again to the back of the house when Marionetta stopped her.

'Can I speak to you for a minute?' she asked. Teresa hesitated, fearful. 'I'm Marionetta Peretti.'

It was evident that Teresa remembered the name from all the publicity surrounding Silvia's murder and Lino Rinaldi's trial. Her face cleared. 'You were the one who was Silvia's friend,' she said in a soft foreign accent, which Marionetta guessed to be Spanish.

Marionetta nodded. 'And you were the one who stood up in court and told the truth,' she said, keeping her voice low so as not to disturb the sleeping Sister Maddalena on the other side of the door. 'I want to thank you. You saved my friend Lino's life.'

Teresa smiled, a wan little smile. 'Don't thank me,' she said. 'What I did was nothing.'

Marionetta hesitated for a moment, and then said, 'Micky Angel brought you here, is that right?'

Teresa nodded, her face lighting up. 'Micky is a real hero. He risked his life for your friend, you know. He spent many nights talking to the working girls on the streets, trying to get to the truth about how Silvia died.'

'And he found you?'

Teresa shrugged, suddenly very Mediterranean. 'Eventually. I was hiding. But he talked to me,' she smiled softly at the memory, 'he persuaded me to tell the truth. He promised me an end to my horrible life out there,' she nodded in the direction of Soho, beyond the stout front door, 'and he told me he would take me somewhere safe, where the nuns would look after me.' She smiled animatedly at Marionetta. 'And he told the truth! For once, a man who does not lie!' She looked around her at the cluttered hall with evident happiness. 'I have found a home here. I can't believe I have escaped.'

Then her expression changed. She had just realized something. She stared at Marionetta, suddenly afraid. 'I have remembered. You are now Mrs Moruzzi. You married Barty.'

Marionetta put a hand reassuringly on the girl's arm. 'You think Sister Maddalena would let me in here if she thought I would tell my husband where you were?' She felt the girl relax. 'In the same way Micky Angel made his promise, Teresa, I give you my word. The Moruzzis won't find out you are here from me.'

Teresa's face filled with relief. She was a pretty girl, Marionetta thought sadly to herself, such soft, clear skin, such a smooth flawless cheek . . . 'You're very lucky,' she managed to say eventually.

Teresa laughed a little. 'Yes, I am lucky to have the sisters to care for me. Lucky to have escaped . . .' She hesitated, and then continued defiantly, 'to have escaped your husband, Barty Moruzzi.'

Marionetta shook her head. 'No, that's not what I meant.' She began to turn towards the front door. 'I meant you were lucky to be loved by someone like Micky Angel.'

To her surprise, Teresa giggled. 'Micky doesn't love me, Miss Peretti.' She paused a moment. 'I'm sorry. I cannot call you Mrs Moruzzi. I cannot say that name.'

Marionetta had not registered these words. She was still trying to absorb what Teresa had said about Micky Angel.

'He's not your boyfriend?'

Teresa grinned. 'Certainly not! I'm much too common for someone like him. No, Micky was my guardian angel, Miss Peretti. He saved my life. I think God must have sent him.'

She had followed Marionetta to the door, but stood back in the shadows when Marionetta opened it. Shyly, she held out her hand, and Marionetta took it and held it for a moment. Briefly, she wondered if Teresa was one of the many prostitutes who had shared her husband's bed over the years. It didn't matter. What mattered was that Micky Angel was a man they had not shared.

Behind her, the door of the refuge closed, keeping its secret from the streets of Soho just outside. Marionetta began to walk, lost in thought. It was all falling into place. Micky Angel, who had seemed almost incidental in the story of the freeing of Lino Rinaldi, was in actual fact the key figure in the drama. It was he who had found Teresa, the terrified witness, he who had persuaded her to speak out and save Lino from the gallows, he who had managed somehow to get her to court to be a witness against Wally Wallace. Micky Angel. How on earth had he done it? And why?

She found herself in Archer Street. It was early evening, and already there were groups of musicians gathering, preparing to look for work in the clubs that night. She searched the faces, hoping to recognize someone, but not admitting to herself who it was she was seeking. Sighing, she turned into Rupert Street, wandering disconsolate among the market stalls, deaf to the shouts of the street vendors and oblivious of the jostling shoppers.

Then, out of the corner of her eye, she saw him. He was sitting at a crowded table in the window of a smoke-filled café. Among the people gathered there she recognized the horn-rimmed spectacles of Peter Travis, and the blonde hair of Vicky, the singer she had met at the Black Cat Club, the one she had thought was Micky's girlfriend. She stood paralysed, watching. They were joking and arguing noisily among themselves. Micky Angel, wearing his usual scruffy blue jumper, was smoking a cigarette and laughing at something Peter Travis had said. Suddenly he caught sight of her, standing alone outside the café, looking in, a young slim woman in an expensive coat. Instinctively her hand went up to her face to cover her scar. For a second their eyes met. Then, deliberately, he turned away, leaning across the table to light Vicky's cigarette, joining in the laughter at some witty remark. When he looked back, a few seconds later, the young woman had gone.

The taxi arrived outside number 24 Endicott Gardens at seven o'clock. It was already dark, with a chill descending over the chestnut trees. Marionetta peered out of the cab, and her heart sank. The lights were on; her husband was home.

She paid the taxi driver and went up the front path, her heart hammering. She was never sure what kind of mood Barty would be in. Some days he played at being a kind of ironic textbook model husband, almost considerate, almost thoughtful; at other times he would suddenly erupt into ferocious rages over nothing, finding fault with everything Marionetta said or did, lashing out at her with his hands, knocking the furniture over. She was not sure which of these moods she feared more. When Barty was being nice to her, she knew it meant he was feeling amorous, and the nightmare of his hands all over her flesh, his forced penetration of her body, was the greatest anguish of all. She would have preferred a hundred blows, a thousand curses, a million sudden, hot rages to one of the many acts of marital rape she had been forced to endure since her marriage to this hateful man.

Quietly, she let herself into the house. In the hall Barty was on the telephone as usual, pacing up and down the gleaming parquet floor so energetically polished by Mrs McQueen that morning, shouting into the receiver.

'Of course I meant tonight!' he was yelling at someone. 'You want the whole of CID on your head?' He barely glanced at Marionetta as she slid past him. 'If I tell you to do something, dumbo, you do it, got it?'

Relieved, she quietly hung up her coat and went into the living-room. The television was on, very loud. It was some kind of variety show, with a ventriloquist and his dummy grinning into the camera. It reminded Marionetta of the puppet in her handbag, and she was reaching to retrieve it when she heard the click of the receiver being replaced. Barty had finished his phone call. Hastily she snapped the bag shut, leaving the puppet where it was.

'Hello, Barty!' she said brightly. 'Would you like a drink?' Without waiting for an answer she hurried over to the cocktail cabinet and lifted the stopper from the whisky decanter. Barty never refused a drink.

He had sunk into one of the armchairs and sat watching her, smoking a cigarette, unsmiling but calm.

'Where have you been?' he asked.

She did not dare meet his eyes. She knew it was pointless to lie. She had probably been seen by one of the Moruzzis' spies anyway. 'I went to the café,' she said, concentrating on pouring the whisky, 'to help Papa out. You wouldn't believe the crowds, Barty, people are so excited about the Coronation . . .'

'I wish you'd phoned me,' he said, his voice pleasant. 'I wish you'd phoned me and asked me if you could go into Soho.'

Her heart sank. 'I'm sorry, Barty,' she began, but he interrupted her.

'I'd like you to remember in future,' he was saying smoothly, tapping the ash from his cigarette into an expensive onyx ashtray, 'you don't move from this house unless I say you can. Is that clear?'

She nodded, scared. She picked up the glass of whisky and crossed the deep-pile carpet to hand it to him. As she did so, he grabbed her wrist, looking up at her, his small eyes gleaming. He always reminded her, disconcertingly, of a squirrel, with his pointed nose and narrow mouth. 'It's done you good,' he said, his eyes admiring her, 'you look almost human.'

She understood the signs. She wanted to weep. 'Is there anything good on the television?' she asked him, trying to sound carefree. 'Did you look in the *Radio Times*?' She tried, without success, to free her wrist. 'I could be making your supper while you watch –'

He shook his head. 'We're not eating in tonight,' he said. 'I've got a few bits of business I need to do, and I need you there. Moral support.'

She tried to keep the look of despair under control. She loathed going out with Barty and his friends. They inevitably made too much noise, drank too much, bullied the

206

waiters and intimidated everyone else. Marionetta invariably returned home from these outings ashamed and even more desperate to escape.

She managed, finally, to free her hand. 'I'll go and change,' she said flatly.

Upstairs she stood in her slip at the open wardrobe door, staring blankly at the array of evening dresses hanging there. The pink chiffon, perhaps. Or the blue sequins. It didn't matter much. No one would look at her once the first bottle of wine had been drunk. Barty and his friends would tell each other coarse jokes, exchange racing tips or plan obscure revenge on some rival gangster while she sat in a corner, bored and alienated, waiting for the time when she could go home and seek the oblivion of sleep . . .

A hand was on her shoulder. Her husband stood there, looking at her in the ornate mirror on its stand by the wardrobe door, his eyes admiring the curves of her body through the thin silk petticoat. Her heart began to beat. No, please, she thought, not yet, not now, not today. I couldn't bear it.

'I thought the black lace top . . .' she said lamely.

'Good idea.' His voice sounded thick. She could feel his breath on her shoulder, smell the whisky fumes. Very gently, he slipped the strap from her shoulder, grinning stupidly, possessively. 'But there's no hurry, is there . . . ?' And he pressed her back on to the bed, burying his face in her neck, groaning, his hands pulling at her. She closed her eyes, trying not to weep, willing herself not to cry out. This had to be endured. For what choice was there? She was trapped in this hateful marriage with a man she wished dead, and there was no prospect of escape.

At the foot of the bed, unnoticed by Barty Moruzzi, the little puppet lay where Marionetta had hidden her in the shadow of the counterpane, her skirt in disarray, her wooden limbs twisted grotesquely by the pull on the tangled strings, her face staring into the middle distance, revealing nothing, a perfect wooden mask.

CHAPTER EIGHT

December 1953

Marionetta sat at the kitchen table wrapping a Christmas present for Mario, and humming along to the radio. She had bought her brother an expensive Dansette record-player, which she knew would be the envy of his friends. Why not? She mentally shrugged. The only pleasure she was likely to get this miserable Christmas was hearing Mario's shout of joy when he unwrapped his gift, and watching Papa's face when he opened his present and saw the new suit she had bought him.

Mrs McQueen came into the kitchen, buttoning her coat over the ridiculous uniform she persisted in wearing. 'I'm off now, Mrs Moruzzi,' she said, pressing a sensible felt hat over her permed curls.

'Thank you, Mrs McQueen,' Marionetta said absently, her mind on the gifts she was wrapping.

Mrs McQueen hesitated in the doorway. 'Are you sure you don't want me to stay a wee while?' she asked, indicating the closed living-room door with a jerk of her head. 'If Mr Moruzzi would like some more tea brought in . . .'

Marionetta shook her head firmly. Barty had expressly told her to 'get rid of the old bat as soon as possible'.

'It's very kind of you,' she said politely. 'But you should be getting home to your own family. It's Christmas, after all.'

The small Scotswoman gave her a sour little smile. 'I live alone, Mrs Moruzzi,' she said. 'But thank you for the thought.'

The front door slammed shut behind her. Marionetta sighed guiltily. She really must try to be kinder to Mrs Mc-Queen . . .

'Netta!' Barty was yelling at her from the living-room. 'Any more Johnny Walker out there?'

She got up and searched in the cupboard, breathing a sigh of relief when she found an unopened bottle of whisky on the upper shelf. At least she wouldn't be humiliated in front of everyone for having forgotten to supply her husband's needs.

She took the whisky into the front room. The Moruzzi brothers were gathered round the imitation log fire, hunched forward in the low armchairs, intent on conversation. Cigar smoke hung heavily on the air. Marionetta skirted the room, trying to stay out of sight. Barty was sitting on the opposite side to the door, deep in conversation with a large, red-faced man in an expensive suit. Marionetta did not recognize him. She heard the whispered names of some of Soho's most famous criminals as she passed nervously behind the backs of Carmelo and Attilio. 'I don't believe Billy Hill did the 'fifty-two mailbag job,' she heard Carmelo saying, and then Attilio's supercilious reply: 'You been drinking with Jack Spot or something? Who the hell else could have done it if it wasn't Hill?'

As usual, they were discussing past crimes. They reminded Marionetta of the old women gathered in the wash-houses, scrubbing their sheets and gossiping. Only these were vicious men, she had to remind herself, and the stories they exchanged involved murder and violence and misery.

She put the bottle of whisky on the table at Barty's

elbow, hoping to escape before he noticed her. Unfortunately the bottle crashed rather loudly on the glass table-top, causing her husband to look up. He scrutinized her, grinning a little drunkenly, squinting up at her through the smoke of his cigar.

'Ah,' he said. 'The little wife. Allow me to introduce you.' The large man in the suit got up clumsily, causing Barty to guffaw. 'Sit down, man!' he said. 'She's not worth getting up for.' Hastily, the man sat down again. Like most people, he feared the Moruzzis. 'Say how do you do, Marionetta. This is a friend of mine. Mr Smith. Mr John Smith.'

Automatically, she shook his hand. Everyone who called at the house was called John Smith. 'How do you do,' she said politely. The man smiled at her nervously, unsure how he was supposed to respond to the unexpected spectacle of Barty Moruzzi's wife. 'Beautiful, isn't she?' Barty said to his companion, holding his wife's arm tightly, smiling up at her, his lips drawn back in a mean grin.

'Certainly is,' the man stuttered.

Carmelo laughed loudly from his place on the other side of the electric fire. 'You like razor scars, do you?'

The man's eyes slid away from Marionetta's face. 'No . . . I mean . . . yes . . .'

Attilio suddenly spoke, irritated. 'For God's sake, Barty, let her go! We've got things to discuss here.'

To Marionetta's relief, Barty let go of her arm. 'Where were we?' Attilio asked. 'New Year's Eve. Right. So we make sure the nightwatchman gets a few extra drinks . . .' He paused, watching Marionetta, waiting for her to leave the room. More than happy to oblige, she hurried for the door, rubbing her arm where Barty had squeezed it. 'And make yourself scarce for a few hours, would you, Netta?' Attilio's words were more of a command than a request.

Marionetta closed the door behind her and stood in the hall, absorbing what he had said. He had told her to go away! That meant she could leave the house, go to Soho – he had practically given her permission! Nervous and excited, she unhooked her coat from the hall stand, snatched up her bag and let herself quietly out of the house, careful not to slam the front door.

Outside it was raining, that relentless grey drizzle that characterizes an English winter, and a sharp wind whistled through the bare branches of the chestnut trees. Marionetta, struggling with her umbrella against the wind, made for the High Street, where she would be able to hail a taxi to take her into the West End.

As she walked, she peered into her handbag. Yes, her cheque-book was there ... She had plans for her free afternoon in Soho, part of a larger plan that had been crystallizing for many weeks now. She could hardly believe her luck, that her brother-in-law had almost pushed her out of the house in his keenness to be rid of her. It meant she could carry on with the work she had started in secret, work her husband must never know about. Every time she was able to escape from the confines of the large house in Muswell Hill, she would go to Soho, to see how the secret plans she had been nurturing for so long were coming to fruition at long last ...

A taxi loomed through the rain, its yellow sign illuminated, and Marionetta waved at its driver. He pulled up and she climbed inside. 'Soho, please,' she said. 'Greek Street.'

The driver was a garrulous, cloth-capped cockney, full of opinions about the state of the world. Marionetta sank back into the upholstered seat of the cab, content to look out of the window and listen as he expounded on the Korean War, Winston Churchill and finally, as the cab neared Oxford Street, the death penalty.

'That Christie geezer,' he was saying, 'I mean, I know he did all those murders, and he had to pay for it, but it makes you think, doesn't it? I mean, they hanged the wrong man for some of those murders, and who's to say it hasn't happened before? There's always a chance of that, isn't there – hanging the wrong man?' The cab swung out in front of a bus. 'No miss, the way I see it, they've got to abolish the death penalty, it's only 'uman . . . ' Marionetta absorbed his words as she stared out of the window at the brightly-lit shops with their Christmas decorations. Everyone in England seemed to be arguing about the death penalty these days. 'Do you realize,' the cab driver was saying, intent on the traffic, 'it's a year since that young boy died? What was his name?'

'Bentley,' Marionetta said, 'Derek Bentley.' How could anyone forget? A year ago, a nineteen-year-old boy had gone to the gallows for a murder that had been committed by his under-age partner-in-crime. And this year John Christie had met the same fate for four murders, including some for which another man, Timothy Evans, had already been hanged. The British justice system seemed to be faltering under the weight of public opinion, and the death penalty no longer seemed to be the automatic fate of the accused; there were too many doubts, too many questions.

Marionetta smiled wryly to herself, remembering the night when Lino had almost gone to the gallows. It came flooding back, the same wet streets, the same grey skies, only then she had been the unwitting focus of attention, her face in all the newspapers, her opinions sought, her words quoted. Now she was just another housewife going to do an afternoon's shopping . . .

'Mind you,' the cab driver was turning into Soho Street, 'there's some as deserve worse than hanging, if you ask me. Take that Wally Wallace case – you remember him?'

213

Marionetta looked up in surprise. It was as if the man was reading her thoughts. But he was concentrating on manoeuvring his way round a stationary van, his eyes on the road ahead, oblivious of his passenger.

'I remember,' Marionetta said. 'I got married the day he was hanged.'

'You did?' They were heading slowly round Soho Square now, through the steady drizzle. 'Well, that lot – they should all be hanged, if you want my opinion. The gangsters. The pimps. The Italians. The Maltese. The world would be a better place without those Moruzzis, for a start.'

They had arrived at the corner of Greek Street. 'Here will do fine,' Marionetta said.

She got out and reached in her purse for the fare. 'You want to be careful, miss,' the cab driver said, as he took the money and sorted through his pockets for some change. 'You don't want to be hanging about round here for too long – this isn't a nice area . . .'

Marionetta smiled at him, suppressing the desire to burst out laughing. She handed him half a crown. 'Thank you,' she said, enjoying his amazement at her generosity, 'but I think I can look after myself . . .'

The cab drove off, and Marionetta turned towards the tall building behind her. She looked around her, nervously. No one on the street seemed to be taking any notice of her. Suzanne Menlove was shuffling out of the off-licence next door, clutching a packet of cigarettes and a bottle of whisky and talking to herself. A street cleaner pushed his broom along the gutter, whistling. Soho was having its quiet time, after the businessmen had left the restaurants and their expense account lunches, and before the night-time revellers made their appearance. No one was going to notice Marionetta. She knocked on the black front door. After a few moments the door opened, and Sister Maddalena stood there, her face registering surprise at this unexpected visitor.

'Marionetta!' she said. 'I wasn't expecting to see you – I thought we arranged it would all be done by post – '

'I know,' Marionetta said, smiling, 'But I couldn't resist the chance to come and see what you've been doing since my last visit.'

'Come in, come in!' The old nun looked out anxiously into the street for a moment, her face registering the same fear Marionetta's had done a few moments previously. Then she reached out and took her arm. Marionetta stepped inside, and the black door closed behind her.

It was five-thirty when, her business done, Marionetta stepped out into Greek Street again. It was already dark, and the rain had stopped, leaving the pavements glistening under a hundred multi-coloured lights, a neon-tinted fairyland. She allowed herself the luxury of a slow stroll round Soho Square under the dripping trees, and crossed into Dean Street. She would go and see Papa and Mario in the Imperial, but first she wanted a few quiet moments to herself, to think about Sister Maddalena, about the peaceful rooms in the refuge she had just left, about the bright smile on Teresa's face when they had said goodbye . . . She was passing the imposing portal of Leoni's Quo Vadis when someone hammered on the window. She looked up, startled. It was Lino Rinaldi, his waiter's uniform hidden behind a stiff white apron. He gestured to her to come inside the restaurant. She hesitated, but the door had suddenly opened, and Lino was there. He kissed her on both cheeks in Italian fashion.

'It's all right,' he said, 'Mr Leoni said I could have five minutes to talk to you. You want a coffee?'

He ushered her inside, taking her umbrella. Mr Leoni nodded at Marionetta from behind the bar, and several waiters, busy laying tables, called to her as she passed. The restaurant was opulent, with soft carpets, white linen and gleaming cutlery, but Marionetta did not feel at all intimidated. This was the world of catering, where she knew everyone and everyone knew her. Lino was ushering her into the cloakroom.

'Wait there,' he said eagerly. 'Take your coat off, make yourself at home! I'll get you a coffee.'

He disappeared. Marionetta took off her coat, hung it up, and sat down on the velvet-covered bench. Through the alcove she could see one of Leoni's chefs arguing in Italian with a barman. Somewhere, someone dropped some glasses, and there was a loud curse and then laughter. She grinned to herself. She felt at home here.

Lino reappeared carrying a tray and two gold-rimmed coffee cups. He settled himself on the bench next to her.

'So,' he said. '*Come vai?* How are you?'

Marionetta sipped her coffee. 'I'm fine, Lino.'

He snorted. 'Fine! She's married to the biggest pig on earth and she says she's fine!'

'Don't,' she said. This was a discussion they had had before. Lino had received a half-hearted, garbled explanation for Marionetta's bizarre marriage, a murmured apology about duty and family loyalty that he had not understood. Because he was Italian, and because he had already tangled with the Moruzzis to his cost, Lino wisely said nothing, apart from the occasional outburst about Marionetta's poor choice of husband. It was a subject that made them both uncomfortable, and they were both relieved when Lino changed the subject.

'Listen, Marionetta,' he said, 'I must show you something.' He put his coffee cup on the floor and searched in the pocket of his apron for his wallet. 'Here.'

He handed her a photograph. She studied it, interested. It showed a smiling girl, rather ordinary, holding a cat. 'Who is it?' she asked.

Lino was grinning. 'Her name's Peggy,' he said. 'Peggy Whitmore.'

'And who is this Peggy?' Marionetta asked. She looked up and saw his face, sheepish and rather pink. 'Oh!' she said, laughing, teasing him a little, 'I *see*.'

'She's someone I met,' he said, seemingly having difficulty explaining himself. 'She's a nice girl, Netta, really she is . . .'

Marionetta looked at the photograph with more interest. The girl had a sunny smile and a lot of curly hair which tumbled over her shoulders. 'She looks very nice,' she pronounced.

Lino's face was anxious. 'I wanted to tell you,' he said, 'because of Silvia. I didn't want you to think I'd forgotten Silvia. I'll never forget –'

'Oh, Lino!' She put her hand on his, touched. 'Of course I wouldn't think that! And Silvia would want you to be happy, she would want you to find another girl . . .'

She had said the right thing. Lino's face relaxed into a smile. He gazed at the photo fondly. 'She's a great girl,' he said, 'I'd like you to meet her.'

Marionetta stood up. 'I'm sure I will one day, Lino,' she said, handing him her empty cup.

'No,' he said, 'Marionetta, don't go yet, I want to ask you something . . .' He stood there, uncomfortable, holding the coffee cup, his face contorted as he searched for the right words.

Marionetta looked at him, surprised. 'What is it?' she asked. 'You know you can ask me anything, Lino. I'm your friend, remember?'

'I know.' He sat down again heavily. Marionetta

hesitated for a moment and then sat down again too. It was obvious that Lino was having trouble telling her whatever it was that was on his mind.

'Come on!' she said, her voice bright. 'Cough it up!'

Slowly, he put her cup on the floor next to his. He turned the photograph in his hands slowly. 'It's about what you're doing,' he said finally. 'Your work at the refuge for fallen women, or whatever it's called.'

'What about it?' she said, suddenly fearful. This was meant to be a secret. She had told Lino about it, but she had not expected him to mention it ever again. She had asked him not to.

He hesitated again. 'I just thought you might be willing to help a girl in another way,' he said. He looked at her suddenly, the large brown eyes anxious. 'It's Peggy, you see,' he said. 'She's in a bit of trouble.'

Marionetta stared at him. 'Pregnant, do you mean?' she asked.

He shook his head. 'No, nothing like that. She's, well . . .' He was still having trouble finding the right words.

'Start at the beginning,' Marionetta suggested gently. 'You might find it easier.'

He was staring at the photograph again, his face miserable. 'You'll think I'm stupid,' he said finally, 'getting myself tangled up with another Soho girl . . .'

Marionetta's heart sank. 'You mean she's a prostitute?' she asked. 'A hooker?'

He shook his head emphatically. 'No, nothing like that. Only she's been working in a club. A strip club. The Treasure Chest in Wardour Street. Do you know it?'

Marionetta shook her head. The clubs changed every night. It was difficult to keep up with the name changes and the different faces of the girls that appeared on the boards outside. 'Is it one of Barty's clubs?' she asked.

Lino nodded. 'I think so,' he said, his voice low, 'although Peggy says she never sees the Moruzzis in there.'

'That doesn't mean anything.' Marionetta failed to keep the bitterness out of her voice. 'They own half of Soho, but they prefer to keep out of the way. They usually put other people in charge.'

'I've been trying to get her to stop,' Lino said. 'I told her she could easily get a job in a department store – you know, something a bit glamorous, the cosmetics counter, or lingerie or something – but she says she won't.'

Marionetta sighed. It was like Silvia all over again. She could imagine just what kind of a girl Peggy was – the same kind Lino had fallen in love with all those years ago at school – pretty, vain, easily led, but essentially good-hearted. She hoped that Peggy's naivety about Soho would not lead her down the same path as Silvia; but it seemed almost inevitable.

'The thing is,' Lino said, 'she lives in a bedsitting-room on the other side of the Charing Cross Road – or at least she will do until the New Year. Then she's getting evicted.'

'Don't tell me,' Marionetta said, 'let me guess. Her landlord is my dear brother-in-law. The Pirate.'

'Carmelo Moruzzi. Exactly.'

Marionetta groaned. 'Lino, please don't ask me to –'

'The thing is,' he interrupted eagerly, 'she told them at the club she was thinking of giving up the stripping, and the next thing is Carmelo Moruzzi tells her he needs the room. Says he only rents flats to girls who work in Soho.'

Marionetta nodded grimly. 'I get the picture.' She looked at him. It was a familiar story. The Moruzzis had Soho sewn up between them. If a girl employed by one brother seemed to be losing interest in her job, it was easy for another brother to threaten her with eviction. With Barty's management of the clubs and Carmelo's activities as a landlord, Marionetta knew that this kind of thing was common practice; it was how the Moruzzis kept control of the girls who worked for them. 'I know what you're going to ask me,' she said. 'I can't, Lino. I'm sorry, but I just can't.'

'I haven't asked you yet,' he said indignantly.

'I know,' she said, 'but don't deny you're going to.'

A waiter appeared in the doorway. 'Lino,' he said, 'Chef wants you.'

'Just a minute!' Lino got up again, agitated, turning to Marionetta. 'I just thought if you could have a word with this Carmelo, explain that Peggy's a friend of a friend of yours –'

She stood up slowly, turning her face away from him. 'I must go,' she said.

He pulled her coat off the peg and helped her into it, ever the gentleman. 'Please,' he said.

She turned to him, her face sincere in its regret. 'I'm sorry,' she said. 'You don't understand. If I told any of the Moruzzis that a friend of mine was in trouble and needed their help they would go to the ends of the earth to make sure that help never arrived.'

Lino looked at her, taken aback. He knew Marionetta's marriage was an old-fashioned, arranged affair, but he had no idea she was this unhappy.

They walked slowly out of the cloakroom and crossed back through the restaurant. 'I'm so sorry, Lino,' Marionetta whispered, 'I wish I could help you. I wish I could help Peggy.'

He pressed his lips together regretfully. 'Don't worry,' he said, 'you've done enough for me to last a lifetime. I'm sorry I asked.'

They had reached the door. She had a thought and

turned to him. 'Why don't you persuade Peggy to go to Sister Maddalena and stay there? She wouldn't have to pay any rent, not until she's got a job, and the sisters would take good care of her.'

'You think I haven't tried?' His voice was bleak. 'You think I haven't told her all that? But she won't listen, Netta. She just won't listen. She just says she'll have to keep stripping to keep the flat.'

She could see in his eyes the haunted look of a man reliving a recurring nightmare. She reached up and kissed him on both cheeks. 'I'm sorry, Lino,' she said. 'I wish I could help . . .'

And she stepped outside, saddened by the encounter. The traffic had increased now, and cars circled the streets looking for parking places. The sound of jazz emanated from Richmond's Buildings opposite, and in the entrance to St Anne's Court, a couple of weary prostitutes hovered in a doorway. Soho was coming alive . . .

The festive season passed quietly enough. Marionetta was obliged to cook a Christmas turkey for the entire Moruzzi family and various henchmen, but cooking had never held any fears for her. She was glad of the distraction, and the opportunity to stay hidden in the kitchen while the Moruzzis drank themselves noisily into oblivion in the dining-room. Barty had bought her a new fur coat, which he had ungraciously thrown at her across the bedroom on Christmas morning. She was sure that he had bought it for one of his girlfriends and it had been rejected, otherwise she would never have received such an opulent present. She in turn had bought Barty a silk dressing-gown and a new hat, knowing that she must appeal to his vanity and his unerring lack of taste. The dressing-gown was in a bright red paisley and the hat was a lurid tan colour with a bright band. Barty was delighted with both gifts, and spent Christmas morning parading the rooms of number 24 Endicott Gardens wearing them and smoking a large cigar.

On Boxing Day, the brothers had decided to call yet another meeting at the house, and were happy to send Marionetta to St James's Residences in a cab, to spend the day with her family. As she was leaving, she had seen the red-faced 'John Smith' entering the house, and she wondered idly what horrors the family were planning with this particularly unsavoury character. But no matter: at least she had a day with her beloved Mario and Papa! – and there was always the chance, however slight, that she might glimpse Micky Angel wandering along the empty streets, on his way to play in a club . . .

Of course she did not see him. The day at the Buildings passed uneventfully. Peretti father and son loved their presents, but even more they loved having Marionetta back with them, and they both settled happily back into the routine of sitting slothfully in front of the television set and allowing Marionetta to wait on them hand and foot, just as she always had done at Christmas. She didn't mind; it was just so good to get away from the suffocating atmosphere of the house in Muswell Hill. The only shadow cast over the day was the absence of Antonio. No one spoke of it, but the empty chair where he always sat at dinner said more than words, and there were three un-opened gifts for him under the Christmas tree, one from each of them. Later that evening Marionetta noticed, as she was washing up in the tiny kitchen and Mario dozed in front of a festive televised Arthur Askey show, that her father had gone quietly to the tree and picked up the presents for Antonio. He took them to the sideboard, opened the top drawer and placed them inside, revealing a glimpse of more brightly coloured paper and ribbons.

Evidently there were other gifts there, awaiting Antonio's return, birthday presents no doubt, perhaps an Easter egg ... Sighing, Marionetta had turned back to the sink and continued scrubbing vigorously at the saucepan she was holding. It was unlikely that Antonio would ever come back now, she thought. It had been more than a year since he left.

All too quickly the day in Soho had come to an end, and Marionetta returned to Endicott Gardens, battling with herself not to succumb to a sense of total despair as the cab deposited her at the front gate. I must be strong, she told herself, I must do this for Mario's sake, and for Papa ...

In the week following Christmas, Marionetta sensed a tension in the brothers she had not seen before. Barty in particular was so preoccupied that he almost forgot to be rude to his wife. Carmelo and Attilio seemed to spend more time than usual in the Muswell Hill house, neglecting their usual collection of gum-chewing, bored-looking girls, closeted away having murmured meetings and furtive telephone conversations. Both would cease if Marionetta came into the room. She was glad of their preoccupation; it meant she was left in peace. The only communication she had for most of that week was with Mrs McQueen and the little white cat, Nevata.

On New Year's Eve she was busy in the kitchen as usual, warming a *panettone* for tea, and half-listening to a diatribe from Mrs McQueen about Princess Margaret and Group-Captain Townsend. The small, grey-haired figure, bustling about with tea-cups, was declaiming volubly on the unsuitability of a divorced commoner as a princess's husband when the telephone rang. Carmelo's deep voice echoed in the high-ceilinged hall as he spoke into the receiver. Marionetta was piling plates on to a tray when to her surprise her brother-in-law appeared at the kitchen door.

'It's Papa,' he said. 'He wants to speak to you.' He seemed to be as surprised as she was by this fact.

'What about?' She could not prevent the fear in her voice. It was unusual for old Alfonso Moruzzi to require a conversation with her; he was usually content to visit once a week on Sunday afternoons, when he would sip tea and stare fixedly at Marionetta, thinking, no doubt, about her long-dead grandmother.

Carmelo's single visible eye glinted, curious. 'He didn't say,' he said. Then, as Marionetta moved towards the door, 'No, not on the phone. He wants you to go to the flat.'

She stopped, now even more apprehensive, aware that Mrs McQueen, busy at the sink, was absorbing every word. 'What – now?'

'That's what he said. He said I was to drive you over there straight away.' Carmelo leaned against the door, surveying his sister-in-law with a supercilious smile. 'What have you done to upset Papa, eh?' He looked thoughtful. 'Must be serious, to get him on the phone demanding to see you.'

Marionetta reached for her bag, trying to hide her mounting terror. 'I haven't done anything, Carmelo,' she said, her voice even. 'How could I do anything? I'm practically a prisoner here.'

She moved towards him, intent on passing into the hall, but he did not move out of the way. 'I've told you,' he said quietly, smiling, 'if you're ever bored I'm always around . . . just give me the nod when Barty's out.'

She pushed past him, disgusted. 'I'll get my coat,' she said. Mrs McQueen crashed some cutlery expressively in the sink.

Barty was standing in the hall, replacing the telephone

224

receiver. He stared at his wife. 'What's all this about Papa wanting to see you?' he demanded. 'What have you been up to?'

She struggled into her coat, trying not to let him see how she was trembling. 'I haven't been up to anything,' she said. 'Perhaps your father's lonely, that's all. After all, you're all going out, and it's New Year's Eve.' Barty had been making lavish plans for the brothers to dine out in the West End in a smart new restaurant.

Carmelo was standing behind her, the car keys in his hand. 'We'd better go,' he said. 'Papa said we must come at once.'

'You'd better be back here by eight o'clock,' Barty told his wife. 'I've booked the table for nine. I want you in your best dress, and an inch of make-up on your face. Got it, Scarface?'

She turned to leave, biting back her anger. He was just a cruel, ignorant man. It was pointless to rise to the bait.

'Just a minute,' he said suddenly. She turned back to him, controlling her emotions, so that the face that met his was calm, expressionless. 'Yes?' she said.

'Why aren't you wearing my present?' he demanded. 'What's the point in me forking out for the best beaver-lamb in London if you aren't seen out there wearing it?'

'I thought – perhaps I'd keep it for best –' she murmured.

'Best!' Barty exploded. 'My old man *is* the best, you silly cow! Now run upstairs and get it, and stop trying to shame me by going out looking like the tatty little waitress we all know you are!'

Silently she ran upstairs. I must not cry, she told herself, I must not cry . . .

She pulled the luxurious fur out of the box in the wardrobe and wrapped herself in it, catching sight of her

225

reflection in the dressing-table mirror, a wide-eyed, tense young woman swathed in luxury, with a bright red furrow down her face. I look like what I am, she thought wearily – a gangster's moll. Mechanically, she picked up a hairbrush and brushed her hair. Then she patted some face powder over her scar, and applied some lipstick to her pale mouth, making it blood-red. She studied herself again. Now the reflection looked even more incongruous, even less like the Marionetta she was used to seeing. I look like a painted doll, she thought, depressed. Or a puppet. *Una marionetta*. She smiled wryly, thinking of the wooden puppet hidden in a shoe box under the bed, then turned and headed downstairs.

Alfonso Moruzzi lived alone in a small but expensive flat in Mayfair. Marionetta had only visited her father-in-law a few times at home, and then she had always been accompanied by Barty and had kept a low profile, politely offering to make tea or wandering out on to the small balcony and staring down into the pretty gardens below. This time, crossing the silent marble entrance hall in the apartment block, she felt intimidated, unsettled by this sudden summons. She and Carmelo took the lift to the fourth floor, neither of them speaking. They arrived at Alfonso's front door where, mysteriously, the name on the gleaming brass door-plate was not his. Marionetta thought it best not to ask why.

Carmelo pressed the doorbell and a loud pealing rang through the apartment. 'He's getting deaf,' Carmelo said by way of explanation. After what seemed like a lifetime, the door was opened slowly, and there stood Alfonso Moruzzi in his carpet-slippers, smoking a cigar. 'There you are,' he said, his voice benign. 'You'd better come in. Not you, Carmelo,' as Carmelo tried to cross the threshold after Marionetta. 'You go and smoke a cigarette in the car,' he told him. 'Come back in fifteen minutes. This won't take long.'

Obediently Carmelo turned on his heel. Marionetta was inside the apartment now. Alfonso closed the door and stood in the vestibule, studying her. 'Nice coat,' he said.

'Thank you.' Was he going to stand here all day, just staring at her? She shrugged the coat off, and he took it and laid it down on a nearby chair.

'This way,' he said finally. He led her into the living-room, which was furnished with dark leather armchairs, the walls lined with antiquarian books. A few table lamps cast a soft glow in the corners of the room, and a fire burned in the grate. By the window, a grand piano gleamed in the glow from the fire. It looked like something out of a Hollywood film set, staged and unnatural. Marionetta realized something for the first time: her father-in-law was play-acting, playing at being a high-class gentleman . . .

He gestured towards an armchair by the fire, and as she sat down, he handed her a glass of brandy he had ready on a small table. He settled himself into the chair opposite her, took a sip of brandy and sighed, staring into the fire.

'Did you have a good Christmas, Marionetta?'

Why was it that everything he said somehow sounded menacing, loaded, making her feel as though her life might depend on the answer? 'It was all right,' she said politely. 'You?'

She noticed his hand trembling as he replaced his glass on the table, the ropy veins standing out on his knuckles, the fingers curled with the beginnings of arthritis. He was getting old, she saw. This did nothing to evaporate her fear.

'Christmas was pleasant enough for a lonely old man,' he said, leaning forward to tap the ash from his cigar into the fire. His eyes had gone to a silver-framed photograph on the mantelpiece. Marionetta tried to make it out. It seemed to be of Alfonso Moruzzi and a small boy. The old man gazed at it for a moment, lost in thought, and then shook himself a little, sighing. 'But I was worried about you,' he said unexpectedly, leaning back in his armchair again and surveying her with his hooded eyes, so like his sons'. She waited, surprised, to hear what he would say next. 'I worry about all my family,' he said blandly, 'but I worry in particular when I hear that one of them is spending money in places where they shouldn't. Do you understand me?'

Marionetta's heart was pounding now. Alfonso Moruzzi had found out her secret. He would probably have her killed.

He sucked on his cigar for a moment, thoughtful. 'I know you don't approve of my business, Marionetta. That's up to you.' He looked at her steadily, and she willed herself not to look away, not to reveal her dread of what he would say next. 'But it seems that not only do you despise the way I make a living, you are prepared to spend my money on undermining my business interests.'

There was silence. He was waiting for an answer. Finally she was able to speak. 'There's no point in denying it, is there?' she said.

He shook his head, satisfied. 'None.' At least, he seemed to be pleased at her honesty.

'So what are you going to do?' she asked him, suddenly aware that her fear had dissipated. In an odd way, it was rather a relief to have been found out.

He shrugged. 'I understand what you did and why you did it,' he said, 'surprising as that may seem. You are very like your grandmother, Marionetta. You have the same open-hearted goodness. That is why I don't intend to punish you . . . for the moment.'

She felt her body go weak with relief. Whatever her head had told her, her body told her otherwise: she *had* been afraid, and it had been a mortal fear. Wisely, she chose to remain silent, sipping at her brandy with trembling lips as the old man continued. 'I will ask you this just once,' he said. 'I want you to stop what you're doing, these good works of yours. I want you to stop writing out cheques for the young women's refuge. I want you to stop sending my girls to the clap clinic and forking out for the doctors' bills when they need abortions. I want you to stop funding accidental pregnancies and organizing adoptions.' He looked at her, his eyes steady, his voice low and calm. 'You're interfering with my business,' he said. 'And you're making Barty look like a fool.'

'That's not difficult.' She couldn't resist a small spark of defiance.

Alfonso's expression darkened. 'I don't want to hear wisecracks about my son,' he said. She subsided, a flutter of fear returning. That was foolish, she thought. I nearly made him very angry. 'Barty hasn't found out what you're up to,' he said, 'but it's only a matter of time. Your good works are the talk of Soho.' She stared at him, horrified. How could they be? She had been so careful to keep quiet, she had not even told her own father what she was doing . . .

'I'm waiting,' he said.

'I'm sorry, father-in-law,' she said, trying to sound penitent. 'Forgive me . . .' He was probably lying, she had decided; he had probably heard a whisper about what she was doing, and hoped that by telling her that everyone knew about her 'good works', he would frighten her into stopping . . .

He shook his head impatiently. 'No,' he said. 'That isn't enough. You must promise me – promise me, Marionetta! –

that these activities of yours will stop. *Pronto*. As from now.'

She lowered her eyes. 'I promise.'

He stood up suddenly, furious. 'No!' he shouted. 'Do you think I'm stupid?' She saw suddenly why this old man had managed to hold every gangster in London in thrall. As he stood silhouetted against the fire, his eyes gleaming, she thought suddenly of the devil. If a forked tail had suddenly appeared and the stench of sulphur had filled the room, she would not have been surprised. He had been play-acting all along; the refined old gentleman had disappeared, to be replaced by a malevolent, crazed bully.

'Stand up!' he shouted. Her knees like jelly, she obeyed. Had he changed his mind after all? Was he going to strangle her, here among the leather-bound tomes and the tasteful furnishings? 'Stand and face me!' he thundered. 'Hold up your hand! Look me in the eye, girl!' She did. 'Now, repeat after me — I promise I will not interfere in my husband's business again! Say it!'

Stumbling over the words, terrified by her father-in-law's evil glare, Marionetta repeated the words. There was a moment of silence. Then as suddenly as Alfonso Moruzzi's anger had erupted, it subsided again. He sat down wearily, like someone who was physically exhausted and on the verge of collapse.

'Good,' he said, his voice indifferent. 'We understand each other. You stop what you've been doing, and I say nothing to Barty. That's the deal.' He looked up at her, trembling in front of the fire. 'If you break your word, I will no longer be responsible for what happens to you,' he said. 'And you know what Barty can be like when he's angry . . .'

He turned to pour himself another brandy. The moment of his terrible, blinding anger was over, as if it had never happened. 'You had better get your coat,' he said, his voice calm and indifferent. 'Carmelo will be waiting for you outside. Goodbye, Marionetta. Happy New Year.'

She remained silent during the drive home, ignoring Carmelo's attempts to find out what it was his father had wanted to say to her. Gradually her mind stopped racing and she began to feel calmer. It had mostly been a bluff, she was sure; hardly anyone knew what she had been doing in Soho. Probably her father-in-law had heard a whiff of rumour and had over-reacted. She settled back in her seat, staring blindly out of the car window as the grey wisps of mist settled over the last evening of 1953. She would just have to be more careful in future. There were ways round this. She would have to find a way to make it look as if she was spending money on the house, or buying clothes in the West End. She would have to move money into a secret account ... She had decided. She was not going to stop the work she had started; it was the only way she could keep her sanity in the spiral of misery that was her daily life. No, she would carry on, but she would be much, much more careful ...

The car drew up in Endicott Gardens by the front gate. Carmelo made no effort to move. 'Tell Barty I'll see him at the restaurant as planned,' he said as she got out, and then he drove away without a backward glance, annoyed that Marionetta had not let him in on her mysterious meeting with his Papa.

Wearily, Marionetta pulled her fur coat around her and headed up the path. Mrs McQueen was just leaving, pulling the front door shut behind her, knotting a headscarf under her chin.

'Have you finished, Mrs McQueen?' Marionetta asked absently, as they passed each other by the dripping hydrangeas.

'Marionetta!' The urgent hiss of the other woman's voice made Marionetta look up sharply. Mrs McQueen had never called her by her first name before. She was staring at Marionetta, her face taut with fear. 'I'm so sorry,' she was whispering, 'I didn't mean to get you into trouble – I would never have said anything if I'd known . . . It was the cat, playing under the bed –'

Before Marionetta could respond to this puzzling outburst, the front door crashed open, and Barty stood there in his shirt-sleeves. He was clearly very drunk.

'Get inside, you!' he commanded his wife, and then to Mrs McQueen, 'And you – bugger off! And don't come back – ever, all right? We won't be needing your services any more. I'm giving you your cards. Shove off!'

Marionetta stared after the little Scotswoman who was sobbing uncharactistically into a handkerchief as she hurried away. She turned to face Barty. 'What is it?' she asked.

In reply he stepped out on to the path and pulled her into the house with such force that she lost her balance and almost fell. 'In there,' he said, propelling her roughly into the living-room. There was no sign of Attilio. He shoved her towards the low table in front of the electric fire, slamming the door behind him. What she saw made her tremble. Laid out on the table was the little wooden puppet she had treasured for so long, its strings in a tangle, its legs awry. But there was worse. Next to it, Marionetta saw a folded letter. She had hidden it in the box with the puppet.

Barty pushed past her and snatched up the paper. 'Shall I read it?' he asked sneeringly.

'I know what it says.' The sound of her own voice surprised her. Her throat was so dry and constricted that she had not thought she was capable of speech.

'So tell me,' he said, standing with the letter in his hand, the veins in his neck pulsing.

'It's from Sister Maddalena – you know what it says, Barty.' She just wanted this to be over with. If he was going to kill her, she wanted it to be quick.

He leaned over and grabbed the front of her dress, dragging her towards him so that her face was only inches from his. 'You're fucking right I know what it says.' His breath was sickly-sweet, reeking of whisky, and she turned her head away. He grabbed her chin and wrenched her head back towards his. 'It says thank you for playing the lady bountiful with your husband's money. It says thank you for giving handouts to every brass in Soho who's too knackered to carry on working, it says thank you for playing Florence Nightingale to a bunch of clapped-out whores, and it says please make the cheques payable to the Mary and Martha Hospice!'

He slapped her once, very hard, and she fell to the floor. Thank God, she thought, lying there, her brain reeling, it's over. 'Mrs McQueen does her job properly,' he was saying, his voice somehow coming from behind a thick, damp curtain of continuous noise. 'She hoovers under the bed as well as round it. She found your little box of trinkets, wifey of mine.' The noise, she realized, was inside her head. Her ears were ringing. He was kneeling over her, pulling at her hair, forcing her to raise her head. 'You stupid little bitch,' he said, his voice cracking, 'You silly, stupid little bitch.' And he slapped her again, this time around the mouth, and she cried out. He had hold of her hair in a tight, agonizing knot and he pulled her head round sharply again, forcing her upper body against his. He was shouting at her, she couldn't understand the words, only the continual beating of his fist against her face, pummelling at her until she could feel almost nothing, until her mind was empty and the pain became almost pleasurable. Every punch was a relief from the terror of the moment before it arrived, every blow was better than the fear of anticipation. Sometimes a word penetrated her confused senses, a phrase. Barty was shouting about the restaurant, how they were meant to go out, how she had wrecked their plans, made them vulnerable.

Vulnerable! The irony of the word made her giggle stupidly amid the punches, and for Barty this seemed to be the turning point, where violence became power, and she felt his hands tearing at her dress, his breath on her neck. Somehow, his rage had excited him, and now he was going to exact the ultimate punishment from his wife. He shoved himself at her, grunting, forcing himself inside her, spread-eagled on the floor. He was hurting her, not caring what he did, excited by her resistance, inflamed by his own violence. It was useless to struggle. Instead, inside Marionetta a small flame of hope was gradually extinguished as he pushed himself greedily at her body, invading and defiling. She let herself go limp, and opened her eyes. She was lying with her head under the table, and as Barty raped her, she stared across the room to where Nevata, the little white traitorous Persian kitten, was watching her, unblinking, from the sofa. People were wrong to compare rapists with animals, she thought fleetingly. Animals did not hurt each other in this way, they did not want to destroy each other's souls. And then for a moment she drifted away, losing consciousness, somehow floating above the terrible things that were happening to her body, above the pain and the indignity and the perversion. None of it mattered, really, since she was going to die . . .

Mary and Martha, Mary and Martha . . . There was a dim, regular beating, cavernous and insistent, coming from somewhere close by. She tried to open her eyes but she could not. All was a murky, bloody darkness, with just the sound banging continuously like a sledgehammer. She heard Barty's voice somewhere very far away, still shouting, something about a restaurant, about the family, then she felt herself being hauled to her feet. She managed to open one eye, and was temporarily blinded by the light. She wondered vaguely why the other eye would not open. Barty had hold of her by the collar of the beaver lamb coat she was still wearing. The banging sound faded for a moment at his face loomed close to hers, then she felt herself being dragged along, her limbs weightless, aware only of the difference between the soft texture of the living-room carpet and the cold surface of the hall tiles. How shiny they are, she thought dreamily, Mrs McQueen must have been polishing them again . . .

There was a sudden rush of cold air, and then she felt herself being hurled into space. She landed with a thud on the soft mud of the front lawn. Slowly, she crawled on to her hands and knees, bewildered. There seemed to be an avalanche of softness around her and she wondered just for a moment if it was snowing. Something velvety-soft fluttered near her face and she put her hand up to catch it. It was a chiffon scarf. Barty was throwing her clothes out into the garden.

'Don't come back,' he was saying. 'Not if you want to live.' Lights were being turned on in the houses nearby. People were hovering behind their net curtains, curious, attracted by the noise. She sat bewildered on the wet grass, holding her torn dress together, trying to focus out of the one eye that would open, aware only that the banging in her head had not abated. Suddenly the front door slammed, and she was plunged into darkness. Barty had gone inside.

She could feel blood oozing from the scar on her cheek. Barty had opened the old wound with his fist. She sat there for a long while in the darkness, not moving, until the lights in the neighbouring houses had been extinguished again. Then she moved slowly and painfully across the grass on her hands and knees, groping in the bushes, searching for something. Finally she gave a little sigh – she had found it! Under her hand she felt the smooth wooden face of the puppet her mother had given her. She had banked on Barty throwing it out of the house with all her other possessions, unaware of its value to her. Then, comforted, she found enough strength to resume her crawl round the hydrangeas in search of her handbag, which she retrieved eventually from beside the front-door step where it had landed in a holly bush.

Slowly, she stood up. She wondered if Barty had broken her legs. One of them seemed to have been mashed to a pulp and when she tried to walk she almost fell over again. Somehow she made her way out of the front gate and began to walk unevenly and slowly down Endicott Gardens towards the High Street. Once she saw a cab and waved at it, but when the driver pulled over and saw her he accelerated away.

She knew where she was going. She knew nothing else. She had almost forgotten her name, but she knew where she was going, and why. She turned into Muswell Hill Road and began the long walk along the edge of Highgate Wood towards the tube station. Oddly, in spite of the dripping trees and the flickering shadows of a damp December evening, she was not afraid. She felt as though she would never be capable of fear again. On and on she walked, sometimes stumbling, ignoring the rush of traffic heading towards New Year's Eve parties, the lighted bus that passed, the stares of the occasional passer-by. Somehow the endless, painful walk through the dark became the brightness of city streets again, the gleam of shop-window decorations, the glimmer of tinsel and signs proclaiming the January sales. Somehow she managed to find the underground and bought herself a ticket, causing a concerned man at the ticket office to ask her if she needed any help. Dumbly she shook her head and proceeded at a snail's pace down the stairs towards the platform. The journey passed in a haze of doors opening and closing, people staring, the thunder of the train as it roared through the tunnels, the rush of escaping air when it rattled to a halt in a station. Kentish Town, Camden Town, Mornington Crescent, Euston . . . Suddenly she had arrived. Tottenham Court Road.

Stiff now, she stumbled off the train on to the platform, giddy from the effort. A kindly man touched her arm. 'You all right, love?' he asked. She was not able to reply, only waved a hand at him and made blindly for the stairs to the street. It was easy now. Right into Oxford Street, left down Soho Street, into the square, then right . . .

It was raining again, big heavy drops that fell out of the sky as if reluctant to land on the unwelcoming earth. Marionetta stood, trying not to lean against the doorpost, pulling up the matted collar of her fur coat, feeling a dampness on her neck and pulling her hand away to see blood, black in the lamplight. A man had approached her.

'How much?' he had asked, and then he had pulled back, aghast, on seeing her face, and hurried off into the rain, muttering to himself.

Another man was passing. She tried to smile at him. He made a sound of disgust and turned away.

A woman's voice spoke suddenly, close by. 'You shouldn't be here, you! Are you on drugs, or what?' A face was peering into hers, eyes heavy with black eyeliner, carmine lips, the sweet smell of face powder and cheap perfume.

'I know you,' Marionetta said, or thought she said. 'You gave me some violets once . . .'

There were three of them now, gathered round her, fussing, anxious.

'She can't stay here,' she heard one of them say. 'She'll have us all put away!'

'We should get her to a hospital . . .'

'You'll have to go home, dear,' one of them said loudly in her ear, above the insistent drumming noise. 'I'll call you a taxi.'

She became incoherent then, shouting and struggling, until they managed to convince her that they would not send her home. 'This is what I'm good for,' she told them, her voice pleading, 'I'm just like you, really. Please – leave me alone . . .'

Miraculously they left her, murmuring among themselves, unsure what to do but not wanting to attract attention. Theirs was a difficult enough profession at the best of times . . .

She did not know how long she stood there in the rain, shivering. Sometimes men would hover and stare; one even came up and touched her, but they went away again, eyes averted, recoiling.

I'm not doing this right, she thought. I have to go into the road. I have to stand on the kerb. They can't see me properly, that's the trouble.

She walked, still unsteady, out into the rain, and made her way to the junction. There was a small shoe shop there, its window illuminated, and she stood in front of it so that the light shone directly on to her. It seemed very quiet in Soho, she reflected, for New Year's Eve. Where were the drinkers, the theatre-goers, the revellers? There was only the insistent drumming sound in her ears. She heard a car approaching. Painfully she turned, unable to focus with one eye shut. The car pulled up. She stepped forward, trying to smile. She had no idea what she was supposed to say. Suddenly the door opened and a hand reached out and pulled her unceremoniously into the passenger seat, reaching across and slamming the door shut. She felt the pull of the car's acceleration as she turned to look at the driver. It was Micky Angel.

CHAPTER NINE

January 1954

She had no idea where she was at first. She knew that a doctor came and stitched up her face. She knew that Micky Angel was there. Most of the time she slept, a deep, dreamless sleep, her mind finding oblivion and a way to lessen the pain.

When Marionetta woke, she was in a small room with dark blue walls. The room seemed to glow with a strange, luminous azure light – like being underwater, she thought sleepily to herself before drifting into unconsciousness again. She never wanted to leave this room and the dark blue shadows moving slowly across the floor as the days passed; here she felt safe.

Then there came a time when she was aware of people bringing her tea, and soup, and bowls of cornflakes. Peter Travis appeared in the doorway, she was sure it was him, peering at her with concern over the rims of his spectacles. The blonde singer – was her name Vicky? – came in and helped Marionetta change into another nightdress, taking away the bloodstained one she found, to her surprise, she had been wearing.

'Mine,' Vicky explained. 'I brought it round when Micky phoned and said he'd found you.'

Marionetta blinked at the bloodstains through her swollen eyelids. 'Sorry,' she said. Her voice sounded strange – thick and muffled.

Vicky grinned at her. 'Don't be daft,' she said. 'Now go back to sleep . . .' And Marionetta did.

Most of the time she knew that Micky Angel was in the room. Sometimes she would open her eyes and see him at the window, staring thoughtfully down into the street. She knew it was Micky who gently helped her to sit up when it was time for her to sip, reluctantly, at some soup; and Micky who quietly closed the curtains if the sun shone too brightly on to the bed, making her wince.

Once, she was woken by the sound of music drifting in from the adjacent room. She realized that Micky was playing the piano, very softly. She did not recognize the song, but the sound, redolent of a hundred smoky little Soho clubs, made her feel comfortable, and smiling, she drifted off to sleep again.

She found Micky's presence comforting, even if at first he barely spoke to her, other than to ask if she was all right, if she wanted more soup, if her pillows were in the right place. As she gradually recovered and began to sleep less and think more, she regretted his silence, longing to talk to him, to explain what had happened, and why he had found her on a street corner in Soho.

One evening she awoke again to the sound of the piano. This time she recognized the tune, it was one Mario used to sing to their mother in the café: 'Embraceable You'. Tears stung her eyes. It seemed a very distant and innocent world now, when the Perettis had all worked together in the Imperial, and the highlight of Marionetta's week had been a trip to the pictures, where she could lose herself in celluloid fantasy, dreaming of marrying Dirk Bogarde . . .

She had not noticed that Micky had stopped playing the piano until she realized he was standing in the doorway, looking at her. He was wearing a rumpled shirt and jeans and no shoes.

'Do you want a cup of tea?' he asked her.

She shook her head, and as he turned to go, she reached out impulsively. 'Micky!' He turned as she pulled her arm back, grimacing.

'You shouldn't move too much,' he said. 'You're covered in bruises.'

'Please,' she said. 'Please come and talk to me.'

He came and sat carefully on the edge of the bed, avoiding her eyes. 'It's getting late,' he said. 'Maybe you should try and sleep.'

She attempted a laugh. 'I've done nothing but sleep for days. I don't even know what the date is.'

'It's January the fifteenth.'

She stared at him, amazed. 'You mean I've been here more than two weeks?'

'The doctor gave you some sleeping pills. You were out for the count for the whole of the first week, practically.'

She looked down and saw the yellow and brown smudges on her arms. 'I must look a sight,' she said ruefully.

Now he looked at her, his brown eyes serious. 'You'll be fine,' he said. 'You just need time.'

She leaned back against the pillows. 'Time ...' she murmured. 'That's one thing I don't have ...'

'You do.' He had got up and stood for a moment gazing down at her, his expression grave. 'You can stay here for as long as you want.'

She shook her head. 'I can't. If Barty found out –'

He shook his head, adamant. 'Never mind him. You're welcome to stay as long as you like. Do you understand?'

She nodded, too weak and too relieved to answer. He had reached the door again. 'I've got a gig,' he said apologetically. 'The Mambo Rooms. I'm really sorry. But Peter's here. He'll be in the other room if you want him.' He seemed eager to leave.

She realized with some surprise that Micky Angel was slightly afraid of her. She put her hand slowly up to her face. Did she look that grotesque? 'Have a good night,' she said automatically, and then the door closed behind him.

Later, she called to Peter Travis, who had been installed in the room next door listening to jazz on the radio. He was pleased to see Marionetta so wide awake. 'You've perked up a bit since the last time I popped in,' he said.

She patted the bed, determined. 'Sit down, Peter,' she commanded, feeling more certain of her ability to deal with him than she had been with Micky. He sat down willingly, glad of the company. 'Tell me,' she said, 'tell me everything that has happened.'

'What do you want to know?' he asked ingenuously.

'Well, I presume I'm in the flat you share with Micky,' she said. 'Am I right? Are we in Soho? How did Micky find me? Are the Moruzzis looking for me?'

Peter Travis told her everything, beginning with what she had already surmised: that she was indeed installed in the flat in Broadwick Street. 'This is Micky's room,' he told her. 'Funny colour scheme, eh? Typical Micky. He's fond of blue.' She absorbed this information silently. She knew so little about Micky Angel.

'And as to how he found you – maybe he should tell you all that himself.'

'Oh, he has,' Marionetta said, unashamedly lying, attempting to sound airy. 'Only I want the details.'

So Peter told her how they had been playing in a jazz cellar on New Year's Eve and how there had been a terrible commotion because Suzanne Menlove had staggered in demanding to talk to Micky. At first, they had all assumed it was another of the woman's hallucinatory fantasies, when she declared that she had something urgent to tell Micky Angel. It was only when she had started

243

smashing glasses and shouting incoherently at the dancers on the tiny jazz club dance-floor that Micky had been forced away from his piano to find out what was troubling her.

She had told Micky that she had been drinking in the Caves de France earlier when a prostitute she knew had come in and reported that 'the Peretti girl' was soliciting on the corner of Dean Street and St Anne's Court. 'She said you were all bashed up' Peter Travis said bluntly, 'and somehow that rang alarm bells with Suzanne Menlove. So she came staggering round to the club to tell Micky.'

Marionetta stared at Peter, amazed. 'Suzanne Menlove! But I don't know her.'

Peter shrugged. 'Neither does Micky. But apparently she knows you. Seems she sees a lot more than you'd think, in spite of the booze.'

They both pondered this for a moment. Marionetta decided she would never again pass by in distaste when she saw the strange, stringy figure of Suzanne Menlove staggering about in the gutter outside the York Minster at closing time. She had probably saved Marionetta's life.

'And the Moruzzis?' she asked him finally. 'Are they looking for me?'

Peter shrugged. 'No one seems to know. It doesn't seem to be public knowledge that you've left Barty. I don't think the Moruzzis are telling anybody anything. They're lying low at the moment. Keeping a low profile.'

'Why? What have they done now?'

Peter got up off the bed and disappeared into the other room for a moment, returning with a copy of the *Evening Standard*. He handed it to her. 'Page ten,' he said.

Marionetta leafed through the paper with swollen fingers until she came to the page. There was a photograph of a man handcuffed between two policemen, under the headline 'Bungling bank robber gets ten years'. She recognized

244

the man; it was the red-faced John Smith who had spent so many evenings at number 24 Endicott Gardens. 'I see . . .' she said quietly to herself.

Peter Travis studied the photograph over her shoulder. 'Everyone knows the bank job was organized by the Moruzzis,' he said. 'But as usual they've managed to steer clear of the blame. Apparently when the robbery took place on New Year's Eve, they were all very publicly having dinner in some posh restaurant in Knightsbridge. Someone even took photographs.'

Marionetta smiled grimly to herself, feeling the stitches in her face tighten. Of course. The Moruzzis always thought of everything . . .

At two o'clock in the morning, long after Peter Travis had left her to sleep, she woke with a start. Someone was standing over the bed, looking down at her.

'Sorry,' Micky Angel said, 'I didn't mean to wake you up. Just wanted to check that you were OK.'

'I'm fine,' she said sleepily. His face was lit by the street-lamp outside. He brushed back a lock of black hair, and looked away towards the window. 'Do you want me to close the curtains?' he asked.

She nodded, watching him as he went quietly to the window and pulled the curtains shut. He was wearing the dark suit he always wore when he played, only he had pulled the neck-tie loose and his shirt collar was open.

'Was it a good night?' she asked. She could hardly see him now, the room was almost completely without light.

'It was all right,' he said, his voice penetrating the darkness, calm and quiet. 'I'll let you sleep now, Marionetta. I'll see you in the morning.'

She did not want him to go, but she could think of nothing to say to keep him there. She heard him cross the room and open the door. Just before he left, he stood for a moment in the doorway, illuminated by the light from the living-room, looking at her. Then the door closed and he was gone.

She tried to drift back into sleep, but she could not. Suddenly the room felt hot and stifling. The nylon night-dress Vicky had kindly donated was clinging to her body, wrapping itself round her legs, aggravating her bruises. She wished she felt strong enough to go to the window and open it, to lean out and inhale the cold winter air, to breathe again the atmosphere of Soho . . . She could hear the clock next to the bed ticking away in the silence. She closed her eyes again, trying to sink into oblivion. From the next room she heard Peter Travis murmur something to Micky. They were sleeping uncomfortably on a mattress on the floor, since Marionetta had the only bed. She wondered what Micky Angel was thinking about. Did he ever think of her? Or was his head full of half-learned tunes, snatches of song, fragments of jazz? Was he tossing in his bed, sweat trickling down his back, fighting insomnia too? She opened her eyes again. There was a small ripple of light on the ceiling as a curtain moved in the draught from the ill-fitting bedroom window. Marionetta was wide awake now, her heart thumping in her chest. She sat up slightly, turning the thought round in her mind, examin-ing it, fearful, excited. She knew why she could not sleep. She hardly dared recognize the sensation, but she knew. What was keeping her awake was a feeling she had never experienced before, not as a woman, not as a wife, not ever; she had thought about Micky Angel before, but not like this. The strange knot she experienced in the pit of her stomach, the fluttering in her body, the sudden, physical awareness of herself meant that she wanted him.

The strip of light which shone from under the door was suddenly extinguished. Peter Travis and Micky Angel were going to sleep. But in the small blue bedroom, Marionetta lay awake still, her eyes open and staring unseeing into the darkness, as she struggled with an unfamiliar sensation and wondered if she should weep or be happy.

The days came and went. Gradually Marionetta's bruises changed from blue-black to an ugly yellow, and then began to fade. The doctor returned and removed the stitches from her face. 'You want to look?' he had asked, holding up a mirror. She shook her head, shuddering. She knew without looking how ugly that scar was.

When Peter Travis came in later and had looked at her face with an expression of surprise, saying, 'But he's made a good job of it – it's better than before!' she did not believe him. He was trying to be kind, as people had been when she had first been scarred by Wally Wallace's razor. Still she would not look in the mirror, and when Micky returned later with an armful of groceries and did not comment on her face, she was relieved. She found Peter Travis's well-meaning lies harder to bear than Micky's silence.

She found it difficult to stay in the same flat with Micky now; everything he said or did had taken on a new meaning. She struggled not to stare at him too much, not to touch him when he came close. She was confused by these new feelings, slightly shocked by them. Was this what kept those street girls with their pimps, this suffocating, hysterical feeling? Was she just like them, ruled by her sexual instincts and not by her common sense? Or was this what Mamma had meant when she had talked about being ruled by your heart, not your head? Surely not . . . This was being ruled by your body, by carnal lust. What did that have to do with your heart? For Marionetta, sex had been the unspeakable acts performed on her by a greedy, sensual man who had no feelings for her as a human being, let alone as a woman. The horrors she had experienced when she had felt Barty's hands on her were her only sexual experiences. Small wonder that the stirrings of physical attraction she felt for Micky Angel threw her into such turmoil.

The change in her feelings had brought a change in the atmosphere of the tiny flat in Broadwick Street. As Marionetta recovered, became mobile, was able to participate in things by doing a little cooking, making cups of tea, so she became more distant from Micky, hardly able to meet his eyes, confused by the new sensations she was experiencing. He, in turn, hurt by this new, frosty Marionetta, began to distance himself from her, staying out more, playing late in impromptu sessions long after the clubs closed, spending his days with other musicians on Archer Street, preferring to sit morosely in cafés drinking coffee and wine rather than go home.

Peter Travis and Vicky noticed the change, whispered between themselves about it, but did not interfere. Peter tried to take Micky out as much as possible, and Vicky attempted to distract Marionetta with bright items of clothing she lent her from her own wardrobe, and girl-chatter about make-up and hair-styles; but Micky became increasingly silent and irritable, and Vicky, in mid-flow about a new perm or the latest hemline, would suddenly realize that Marionetta had not been listening, but was staring into the middle distance, her brow furrowed, one hand as usual touching the scar on her face.

January turned to February. Marionetta felt as though she knew every inch of the little flat, every cobweb, every cockroach, every wretched creak in the floorboards. Still she did not go out, fearful for her life if the Moruzzis discovered where she was. She wondered about her father and Mario. What had the Moruzzis told them? Did Papa believe she had disappeared into thin air, just like Antonio before her? And what would happen to Mario now? Would the Moruzzis return and demand Mario, the final Peretti child, as payment of the cursed debt of honour? She would circle the cramped living-room, lost in thought, listening unhappily to the radio. This could not go on.

One rainy afternoon she was curled up on the sofa, reading *The Catcher in the Rye*, which she had found on the rickety bookshelf above the piano, when she heard the kitchen door slam.

'Is that you, Peter?' she called, not looking up from the book, which she was enjoying. 'Stick the kettle on, will you?'

The door opened. It was Micky, hair wet from the rain, taking off his raincoat. 'It's me,' he said.

There was a moment's embarrassed silence. It was not often they were alone together.

'I thought Peter was going to be here,' Micky said finally. 'He said we were going to try out for some session work . . .'

Marionetta did not raise her eyes from the page she was studying with exaggerated attention. 'Someone came round and took him off to a football match,' she said. 'Arsenal versus someone or other.'

'Oh.' He hesitated for a moment, then grabbed a towel from the kitchen and headed towards the bedroom, towelling his hair as he went.

'I'll get a dry shirt,' he said. He and Peter still kept their clothes in the blue bedroom, even though Marionetta occupied it at night. The door closed behind him. Marionetta closed the book with a sigh. Why did he have to come back now, disturbing the respite of a quiet afternoon alone? She got up, resentful, and went to the kitchen. She filled the kettle with water and sat it on the hob, lighting the gas, then returned to her book by the glow of the single bar of the electric fire. When she heard the whistle of the kettle she returned to the kitchen and made a pot of tea, hesitating for a moment before putting two mugs on the tray along with the milk jug and the sugar.

She would go and offer him a cup of tea, it was only polite. She hesitated again outside the bedroom door. He had not made a sound since he had come in – perhaps he had fallen asleep? Very quietly, she opened the door and peered in. Micky was sitting on the bed, having removed his shirt, with a clean one hanging ready over the bed-head; but he had become distracted by something. He was holding the wooden puppet Marionetta had brought with her, holding it gently in his lap, looking at it, his face full of tenderness. Marionetta watched his white fingers encircling the tiny waist and felt again the strange flutter inside her, the overwhelming desire she had been struggling against.

The look in his eyes made her brave. Slowly, silently, she crossed to the bed and touched his bare shoulders. He started and turned, his eyes wide with shock.

'Micky,' she said, simply. He turned away, his expression unfathomable, and looked at the puppet again. 'It's only a doll,' she managed to say. 'This is me. I'm real.'

'I know,' he said, his back still turned. She did not remove her hand, touching the cool flesh of his back. Gently she moved her fingers, feeling the muscles in his shoulder. 'Micky,' she said, terrified of what she had started, knowing there was no turning back, 'please kiss me.'

He shook his head, ashamed. 'I can't,' he whispered. Her fingers still caressed his shoulder, gentle and insistent.

'Why not?' She felt the air tremble between them, the tension quivering, tangible.

He did not answer, still holding the puppet, still staring at it, his face averted from her.

'Why not?' she persisted. Still he did not reply. She closed her eyes. He was rejecting her. He had never felt anything for her, only pity. There was a moment when she thought she would die, when she thought she should run from the room weeping, out into the street, out into the darkening February afternoon, weeping and wailing, and never return. Then she felt his fingers tentatively reach out to hers, where she still touched the flesh of his neck, and he spoke, his voice barely a whisper. 'If I kiss you I won't be able to stop.'

'I don't want you to stop,' she said, amazed at her own bravery. She had never imagined herself saying these words.

Micky was looking at her now, his expression unsure. 'I can't,' he said. 'I can't. Not after what Barty did to you – I can't do that.'

Marionetta leaned across and took the puppet from him. Carefully she laid it on the bed, wrapping it in Micky's discarded shirt, folding the fabric over its wide-eyed wooden face. Then she stood up and pulled her dress over her head, dropping it on the rug by the bed. Micky watched her, saying nothing, his face white. Then she knelt next to him on the bed. She took his hand, guiding it to her back, to the fastenings of her brassière. 'Barty never existed,' she said, suddenly strong, knowing what she was doing, certain, for once, that this was right. 'Only you exist,' she whispered, her voice faltering, as she felt his fingers loosening the hooks, felt the fabric fall away from her. She took his hand again and placed it on her breast. 'Only you . . .'

And they fell together on the bed, his lips on her neck, sinking down into the dark blue oblivion of the little room, eager to become lovers, to consummate a passion they had both harboured for so long . . .

They both had a lot to learn, mistakes to erase, memories to confront. But now it seemed they had gone from being two lonely souls wandering separately in the universe to become one being, with eternity ahead, all the time in this world and the next to be together. Because they were young and because the young are fearless, they discovered each other without shame and with a growing impetuosity and sense of excitement, as if they were the first lovers in the world: Adam and Eve, discovering the joys of the flesh in the Garden of Eden and wondering how on earth anyone could call this sin . . .

There was only one shadow hovering, and Marionetta pushed it away, lost in the feverish exploration of her own passion. There was no time for doubts now . . .

Later, much later, she remembered the tea and sat up irrationally, saying she would put the kettle on again, but Micky only laughed and pulled her to him, saying tea could wait, tea could wait for ever for all he cared, bloody stupid British institution . . .

She woke with the sun on her face, streaming in through a gap in the curtains. For a moment she was confused. What was different, why was the world no longer the same? Then she felt the warmth of Micky's body next to hers and smiled to herself. Of course. She had Micky now, that was what made the world suddenly brighter, more beautiful. She turned to look at him, expecting him to be asleep, but he was watching her.

'Hello,' he said. 'You want breakfast?'

'Is it morning?' she asked him sleepily.

He kissed her shoulder. 'I heard Peter go out about ten minutes ago. Let's hope he's gone to get some bread, or it'll be Weetabix again.' He studied her face, his own serious. 'Are you – do you – how do you feel?'

She leaned over and put her cheek next to his, gentle as a butterfly. 'I couldn't be happier,' she said, shyly, her face above his, her hair brushing his face. Then, sighing, she sank down into the pillows again next to him, silent.

He could see that she wanted to say something, but could not find the words, and he propped himself up on one elbow, pushing his dark hair out of his eyes and looking at her quizzically. 'What is it?'

She looked away, troubled. Micky leaned across the bed. 'Marionetta,' he said, 'we can't have secrets. What is it?'

'It's stupid,' she said.

'Try me.'

He was waiting, his face open and curious. She hesitated for a moment. He was right. Her life seemed to be a fragile structure of lies and half-truths and secrets. Now was the time for that to end, or there was no hope for either of them.

'You haven't kissed me on the mouth,' she said finally, the words no more than a whisper.

There was a moment when he looked astonished. Then, surprisingly, he grinned. 'You idiot,' he said at last, 'do you think I don't want to?' He leaned over and touched her scar with gentle fingers. 'I can't,' he said finally, still seemingly amazed by her anxiety, 'I can't, Marionetta. I'd hurt you. You've only just had the stitches taken out. That's the only reason.' She closed her eyes. Of course. She was being stupid. 'I'm scared the scar will open up again,' he said. 'I don't want to put you through all that a third time.'

'I'm sorry,' she said. 'I'm being ridiculous.'

He leaned over her again, his face full of concern. 'Yes, you are. I'm in love with you,' he said. 'Didn't I tell you that?'

She allowed herself a grin. 'Only about a hundred times.'

'Well, then,' he said, 'that's all you need to know, isn't it?' He looked at her, suddenly very serious. 'Isn't it?'

She smiled up at him. 'Of course,' she said. She could not tell him how she had been haunted by the spectre of Silvia the previous night, how when they had been locked together in their sexual fervour, clinging together in the heat of their bodies, she had heard Lino's voice floating across the darkness, that desolate, lonely voice from the past, saying, 'Not on the mouth, that's what Silvia told the customers. The mouth is for lovers, not punters . . .'

Micky sat up, relieved. He swung his legs over the side of the bed and began to pull on his clothes. 'We're mad,' he said from somewhere inside his sweater.

'I know.' Her smile disappeared. She had remembered the Moruzzis. Slowly, her hand went up to her face. Micky, his head emerging from the neck of the scruffy blue sweater, saw what she was thinking. He grabbed her hand and put it gently to his lips.

'Don't worry about them,' he said simply. 'You've got me.'

She did not say what she was thinking, which was: *how can you fight something so powerful, so corrupt, so determined to win at all costs?* Instead, she touched his face, overcome with such overwhelming feelings that she could hardly speak. Micky was the most courageous person she had ever met: he was prepared to love her in defiance of the Moruzzis, and that would surely mean trouble, terrible trouble.

The moment was interrupted by the slamming of the front door, and the sound of Peter Travis calling excitedly. Micky grimaced. 'The real world,' he said. 'I knew this couldn't last.' He got up and went to the door, pausing only to grin at her. 'We've got to face them sometime,' he said, his voice teasing. 'First Peter, then the rest of Soho!'

She got up slowly, pulling on the exotic red silk kimono Vicky had lent her from her extensive wardrobe. In the other room she could hear Peter and Micky talking. Distractedly, she went to the small dresser in the corner and picked up a hairbrush and the shaving mirror propped against a pile of sheet music. Almost without thinking, she peered into it. Her reflection showed her hair tousled, her skin white against the bright silk of the kimono – and her mouth! She touched her face, disbelieving. Peter Travis had been right, the scar was not so bad this time; true, it was still very red, the small marks where the stitches had been still visible, puckering the flesh on her cheek. But she knew this would fade to a pale pink – still visible, but not so garish. The main thing was that this was definitely a smaller, neater scar than previously. She experimented with a smile. Her mouth curved upwards in perfect symmetry, and she felt her heart give a joyous little lurch – she could smile again!

'Marionetta!' It was Micky, calling from the living-room, his voice excited. 'Quickly, come here!'

She hurried to join him, blushing a little at the sight of Peter Travis, who merely grinned at her and lit a cigarette. 'Look at this!' Micky was saying. He was holding open a newspaper. Marionetta went and peered over his shoulder.

'It's Barty,' she said, her heart sinking. Why did he have to intrude in her life, today of all days, when she wanted to bask in her happiness with Micky Angel? It was a picture, under the caption 'NEW MOLL FOR MORUZZI', of Barty leaving a nightclub, arm in arm with a smiling young girl, her face emerging like a flower from the large collar of a fur coat. Marionetta stared at the picture, silent.

'See?' Micky was saying. 'He's moved on to someone else!'

'Maybe he won't come looking for you after all,' Peter Travis said hopefully.

Micky was looking at Marionetta. 'Maybe he'll even let you have a divorce,' he said.

She shook her head, still gazing at the picture, transfixed. 'We're Italians, Micky, we don't get divorced.'

'I think this calls for a party,' Peter was saying. 'Time to introduce you to some of our friends, Marionetta, seeing as it looks like you might be more of a permanent lodger than I thought . . .'

'Good idea!' Micky's face lit up. 'A party! Brilliant!' He handed the newspaper to Marionetta, preoccupied by this new idea. 'I could get Vicky to tell the girls at the Windmill to come after the show, and Big Jack isn't playing tonight, so he can come . . .'

He and Peter went into a huddle of excited plans and preparations. Marionetta stared at the photograph. She knew that girl from somewhere. Where? She searched her memory but found no answer. She scanned the text below the picture, hoping for a clue. 'Barty Moruzzi, brother of vice king Attilio Moruzzi, seen emerging from the Treasure Chest in Soho's Wardour Street last night with a woman he described as his "fiancée"'. The Treasure Chest. That rang a bell . . . It was difficult to see the girl clearly, but she seemed ordinary enough. Ordinary . . . Of course. It was Peggy Whitmore, the girl in the photograph that Lino had shown her that day in Leoni's, the girl with the ordinary face and the nice smile, holding a cat. Peggy Whitmore, the girl who worked at the Treasure Chest, the girl that Lino had fallen in love with! Her heart went out to him. Lino, who had suffered so much already – and now he had lost someone else to the Moruzzis . . .

The party was a success. By midnight the narrow staircase leading up to the front door of the flat was crowded with people leaning against the rickety banisters or sitting in argumentative groups sharing bottles of wine. Inside the tiny living-room a crowd had gathered round the piano, where Micky was playing ridiculous boogie-woogie versions of songs from the Hit Parade to howls of laughter. Vicky was perched on the arm of the sofa telling jokes to an appreciative and admiring audience of art students from the Slade, and Peter Travis was engrossed in a political argument with several serious-looking Russians he had found in a coffee bar when he went out to buy more wine. The flat was full of the sound of laughter and the air was heavy with cigarette smoke. To Marionetta it was overwhelming. In the Buildings there had been parties, certainly – Italians love to celebrate – but those had been occasions dominated by people of her parents' age, with grandparents always present, and aunts and uncles, small babies, gauche adolescents, priests, neighbours. This was completely different: a party at which no one seemed to be over the age of thirty!

She liked Micky's friends. They accepted her presence in the flat without comment and did not ask awkward questions. If they saw the intensity of the looks she exchanged with Micky Angel, they did not say so, and as the night progressed into early morning and the atmosphere relaxed into a sleepy somnolence, no one commented when Micky Angel and Marionetta danced slowly together, circling the floor, lost to everything but each other.

It was only at two o'clock in the morning, when people were beginning to leave, and others nodded off over their drinks, and Marionetta was making herself a cheese sandwich in the kitchen, that she had her first inkling of the true feelings of Micky's friends. She was busy spreading pickle on her sandwich when an amused voice behind her interrupted her thoughts.

'Makes you hungry, doesn't it?'

It was Susie, a willowy dancer from the show currently playing at the Duke of York. Marionetta knew she was the girlfriend of one of Micky's friends, but she had met so many that she could not remember which.

The girl grinned at her and perched on the draining-board, pulling a packet of cigarettes from the pocket of her toreador pants and proffering it to Marionetta, who shook her head.

'Love,' Susie said, by way of explanation, lighting her cigarette with a flourish. 'Makes you hungry.'

'You want some?' Marionetta began unwrapping the cheese again. 'There's plenty more –'

Susie shook her head, looking at Marionetta thoughtfully through a cloud of smoke. 'You've got a good figure,' she said. 'Ever thought of being a dancer?'

Marionetta laughed. People like Susie had no idea of the kind of restricted life Italian girls led. She had a sudden, ridiculous vision of her Papa's face as she stood before him and announced her desire to be a dancer. He would have a fit. It had been bad enough when Mario had said he wanted to be a singer . . . A sudden longing to be with her family overwhelmed her. What on earth was she doing here, pretending she could live this bohemian life, when just around the corner Papa and Mario would be worrying themselves sick?

'Are you all right?' Susie was still studying her, concerned now.

Marionetta nodded and bit miserably into her sandwich. She was suddenly tired. She wished the people would all go home, and she could curl up in bed with Micky Angel and forget about the world.

'Micky's very keen on you, you know,' Susie said, as if reading her thoughts. Marionetta looked at her. Susie was sipping from a teacup without a handle, and she grimaced suddenly. 'Awful plonk!' she announced, holding the cup out to Marionetta. 'Want some?'

Marionetta shook her head. Susie set the cup carefully on the draining-board next to her. 'I know this is none of my business,' she began slowly, 'but do you really think that you and Micky . . . that it can work?'

Marionetta busied herself putting the cheese and bread away. 'Why not?' she said brightly, not meeting Susie's eyes. 'If two people care about each other –'

Susie was shaking her head, very serious now. She got off the draining-board, still managing to be elegant, and crossed over to the door. In the living-room, Marionetta could see Micky getting coats for some departing guests. He caught her eye and blew her a kiss. She smiled back at him helplessly. Susie sighed and closed the door, leaning against it to keep out intruders. 'I know you care about each other,' she said, 'that's bloody obvious. Can't keep his hands off you, we can all see that.'

Marionetta, surprised, wondered what was coming next; surely not some kind of moral lecture, not from a Soho showgirl! But Susie's face was compassionate, not stern.

'I know it can't last,' Marionetta said finally, her voice very quiet.

'You mean the Moruzzis,' Susie said.

So they all knew who she was! She supposed it was inevitable. 'The Moruzzis will find me,' she said bleakly. 'It's just a matter of time . . .'

Susie inhaled on her cigarette, saddened by too much wine. 'And when Attilio Moruzzi finds out you've been having an affair with his son, he'll probably kill you both,' she said.

It took a moment for her words to sink in. Marionetta stared at her. 'What did you say?' she whispered finally.

Susie's eyes widened. 'Oh, God, Marionetta,' she breathed,

her face stricken, 'don't tell me you didn't *know* . . .!'

Somehow Marionetta managed to get through the next hour, as the last of the guests drifted away and out into the sharp air of a grey February morning in search of taxis. Susie had left almost immediately after her conversation with Marionetta in the kitchen, genuinely aghast that she had revealed something she had not known was a secret. She had kissed Marionetta on the cheek, her face anxious. 'I'm so sorry,' she had murmured, 'please don't tell Micky I put my foot in it . . .' before hurrying away into the dawn.

Like an automaton, Marionetta helped Micky and Peter to clear up the ashtrays and the discarded mugs of wine, laughing at their jokes, joining in the party post-mortem, making some instant coffee to revive them after the long night. Finally, Peter Travis announced it was time for bed and began to pull out the mattress from the cupboard on the landing where it was stored during the day. Micky looked at Marionetta and smiled. Her heart turned over. He took her hand.

'Come on,' he said. 'Peter and I have got to get up in a few hours – we've got a gig at some posh lunch in the City . . .'

They went to the blue room and huddled together under the eiderdown in the narrow bed, still too intoxicated by their new relationship to want to sleep. Instead they made love until the sun pushed its way through the grey dawn and filtered through the curtains, and they were both exhausted and silenced. Marionetta turned to look at Micky's profile as he dozed next to her, his head close to hers on the pillow. The faint blue shadow of stubble was beginning to appear on his jaw. His eyelids quivered. 'What are you looking at?' he murmured, without opening his eyes.

She touched his face gently, feeling the rough texture of his cheek. Now was the time. 'I know who you are,' she said, her voice very quiet in the early-morning silence.

His eyes opened immediately and he turned to look at her. She was surprised to see the fear in his face. 'Of course you do. I'm Micky,' he said, 'Micky Angel.'

She shook her head slowly. 'Your name is Moruzzi,' she said.

He turned from her, sitting up in bed. He reached over and grabbed a cigarette from the bedside table. 'How did you find out?' he asked. The flare of the match illumined his features for a second, and she saw a nerve twitching in his cheek. She wanted to weep, but knew that she must not.

'It doesn't matter how I know,' she said, weary, 'only that it's true.'

He blew a plume of smoke towards the window, staring into space. 'You should be pleased.' His tone was bitter. 'That makes me an Italian, just like you. That's good, isn't it?'

'Micky . . .' She reached out to touch him, but he shook her off.

'All right,' he said finally. 'All right, I'll tell you. My name is Moruzzi. Michelangelo Moruzzi. Michelangelo – Micky Angel, get it?' He turned to her, his expression one of appeal. 'Marionetta,' he said, 'I'm still the same person I was before you knew my name . . .'

She stared at him. 'You even look like him,' she said, transfixed. 'Why did I never see it before?' Now she could see the strong jawline of Attilio Moruzzi echoed in this face, only softer, not so uncompromising; and the mouth had that same strong curve, the same sensuality, only in Micky not cruel, not narrowed, but gentle.

'Would it help if I told you I haven't spoken to my

father for five years?' he asked her, still angry. 'Or will you still just see a Moruzzi?'

She could not take her eyes off his face, comparing, remembering, too shocked to take in what he said. 'Attilio never even said he had been married,' she murmured. 'I never knew . . .'

'Hardly surprising,' Micky said. 'My mother died when I was fifteen. I was brought up by my grandfather.' She remembered then the photograph in Alfonso Moruzzi's flat, the small boy she had not recognized. And, of course, the grand piano. It would have been the dream of a doting grandfather to have a concert pianist for a grandson. She wondered fleetingly what Alfonso would have made of Micky's penchant for jazz and his badly paid work in the seedy clubs of Soho; but of course he would know what Micky was up to – the Moruzzis knew everything. She had so many questions she wanted to ask, but her brain was spinning, still trying to absorb the devastating fact that Micky Angel was a Moruzzi.

Micky was looking at her now, trying to read the expression on her face. 'I left my grandfather's when I was eighteen,' he said. 'I couldn't take it any more – not the private schools, not the piano lessons, not the hypocrisy of going to Mass every Sunday – not when I saw what my family were doing,' his voice was harsh, 'what my father was doing.' He leaned over her and stubbed out his cigarette in the ashtray on the bedside table, his arm brushing hers. Strange, the touch of his skin against hers still made her tremble . . . 'My father disowned me,' he was saying, sitting hunched up next to her now, his knees drawn up, his face stony at the memory. 'I have nothing to do with the Moruzzis any more, Marionetta – nothing.' He had turned to her, his eyes pleading. 'I've only ever used the name to get me something once in my life. Only once.'

'When was that?' she asked.

'Can't you guess?'

She shook her head. There was the face she loved, gazing at her, so close, only a kiss away, but now it was another face, the face of the family she loathed.

He had picked up her hand, which had lain limp on the sheets, and was holding it. 'Teresa,' he was saying. 'The girl at the convent with Sister Maddalena.'

She looked at her hand, enfolded in his. It seemed so right, somehow. How could she hate him? How could she be angry? If he had told her who he was, she would have gone to the ends of the earth to avoid him. Instead he had remained silent, and they had had the most wonderful moment of discovery, the kind of moment you only dream about, the kind of moment you see in films, where the lover meets the woman of his dreams and suddenly, miraculously, there is a happy ending. Only this was not a film, and there would be no final moment of blissful union, of happy-ever-after, because she knew who he was. 'Teresa . . .' she echoed, confused.

'How do you think I persuaded her to come forward and identify Wally Wallace?' he asked. 'I told her who I was.'

She looked at him, surprised. 'You told her you were a Moruzzi?'

He nodded grimly. 'It's a magic name in Soho, especially among prostitutes.' His face took on a distant look as he remembered. 'Oh, I was kind to her, promised her I'd find her a place to hide if she spoke out, told her about Sister Maddalena. She wanted to see Wally Wallace go to prison, she wanted to see justice done for Silvia's sake, but in the end she was just like all the other girls – terrified of the Moruzzis.' He sighed. 'So I played my trump card. I told her who I was. To a working girl in Soho, a Moruzzi is a

Moruzzi, no matter how kind they might appear to be on the surface.'

Marionetta reached up and tenderly smoothed back a lock of Micky's hair, 'Why?' she asked 'Why did you take such a terrible risk? If the Moruzzis had found out what you had done –'

'Can't you work it out?' He put her hand to his lips, his eyes never leaving her face. 'I did it for you, Marionetta. because I love you.' And he leaned across and kissed her gently on her unscarred cheek, his lips trembling, careful not to touch her mouth. She longed to pull his face round, to place her mouth on his, but she could not. A tear slid down her cheek unnoticed, and dissolved into the red gash, the salt biting into the wound.

I must go,' Micky Angel said. 'We've got a gig.'

She sighed and lay back against the pillows, watching him as he pulled on a pair of jeans. He blew her a kiss and headed for the bathroom on the landing. She heard him yelling to Peter to get up as he passed through the living-room, and then Peter's stirrings and groanings as he gradually woke up.

Half an hour later, Micky and Peter, both transformed into respectability with the aid of bow-ties and black jackets, were ready to leave. Peter discreetly packed his double bass while Micky and Marionetta exchanged a whispered, fevered farewell in the bedroom doorway.

'You'll be here when I get back?' he was asking her anxiously.

'Of course I will,' she said.

'I love you.'

'I know. I love you, too.'

Peter Travis coughed ostentatiously and looked at his watch. 'Come on, Romeo and Juliet,' he said, 'time's up.'

Micky kissed her, full of tenderness, on her forehead,

and then lifted her up in an exuberant bear-hug. 'It'll be all right!' he shouted to no one in particular. 'I know it will!'

He was following Peter to the door, reassured by Marionetta's laughter. 'To hell with the Moruzzis *and* the Perettis!' he said, and blew her a kiss as they left.

She heard them clattering down the stairs, struggling with the double bass, and Peter sarcastically intoning, 'From forth the fatal loins of these two foes a pair of star-cross'd lovers ...' Then their footsteps crossed the downstairs hall and were gone.

Slowly, Marionetta went back into the bedroom. Automatically she tidied up, made the bed, pulled back the curtains. Below her, Broadwick Street was quiet – a combination of Sunday morning and a sharp February frost. An occasional passer-by stepped into the newsagent's on the corner of Lexington Street opposite, but no one looked up and saw the pale face of Marionetta at the window, her eyes focussed into the distance. At the other end of Lexington Street was Brewer Street and St James's residences: the familiar comfort of home, the sights and smells of her childhood, Papa, Mario ... So near, and yet so far. She could have put on her coat and walked into the familiar courtyard of the Buildings in a few short minutes, yet the distance between this bohemian musicians' flat and the home where she had been brought up might just as well have been a million miles.

She sighed and turned away from the window. It was no use dreaming of home, and of how it used to be. That was all over now. So was this. She thought about *Romeo and Juliet*. She had seen a version of it at the cinema as a child many years ago with her mother; Leslie Howard had played a rather unconvincing Romeo, and Norma Shearer a misty-eyed Juliet. She went into the living-room, pulled down a heavy tome from the bookshelf above the piano,

and began leafing through it. *Romeo and Juliet*. She found
the piece she was looking for, the lines from the prologue
she had heard Peter Travis quoting on the stairs. It had
reminded her of something. Sure enough, there it was.

> A pair of star-cross'd lovers take their life:
> Whose misadventur'd piteous overthrows
> Do with their death bury their parents' strife . . .

Sighing, she closed the book with a snap and replaced it on
the shelf. It was time to leave.

She pulled on a pair of trousers and a red sweater
donated by Vicky. She would have to send them back to
her later. She had no coat; she had begged Micky to get rid
of the bedraggled fur one she had arrived in, because it had
hung on the wardrobe door like a malevolent animal,
reminding her of Barty and everything she hated. Now she
pulled out a donkey jacket of Micky's. The sleeves were
too long, but it would have to do. She found her handbag,
untouched since she arrived, under the bed. She opened it
and found a few pounds in her purse. Good. At least she
would not have to take Micky's money. She went to the
chest of drawers and pulled a bundle from the top drawer.
It was the wooden puppet, still wrapped in Micky's shirt.
For a moment she hugged it to her, burying her face in the
fabric, breathing in the aroma of smoky clubs and aftershave that still lingered. Then she slowly unwrapped the
puppet, leaving the shirt on the bed, and untangled its
strings. She held it up, letting it dance for a moment in the
blue light of the bedroom, like a strange little sea creature,
its face bright and blank. Then she folded the strings away,
bent the sturdy wooden legs over and around the puppet's
head, and put it in to her bag.

She wondered about leaving a note. What could she
possibly say? It seemed better just to disappear. Micky

266

would understand, or at least he would think he did. He would imagine that she could not live with a Moruzzi, that the name would always come between them, that she had done the dishonourable thing and disappeared because she could not face telling him it would not work. But this would not be the real reason why Marionetta was leaving Micky Angel.

She closed the door of the flat carefully behind her and made her way downstairs. It seemed odd to be outside the flat. It had been her haven, her happiness, for so long. She lifted her head. It was no good thinking about that, about the past, about what might have been. She pushed open the door and stepped into the street. Quickly, shocked by the icy air, she headed into Poland Street, away from Soho. And as she walked, the words of Shakespeare she had been reading echoed in her head, their meaning solidifying, taking on a new coherence. She was doing the right thing. She had to leave Micky Angel. She had to stop this crazy circle of deceit and fear, or they would both be killed. She had to sacrifice what they had found in order to keep them both alive.

A taxi was meandering down the street behind her, its yellow sign illuminated. She waved to the driver and he pulled over.

'Where to, love?' he asked.

CHAPTER TEN

February 1954

Alfonso Moruzzi must have been looking out of his window and seen the taxi pull up in the forecourt, because when Marionetta stepped out of the lift on the fourth floor he was waiting for her.

He raised an eyebrow at the red sweater and the slacks, the oversized donkey jacket. Marionetta was a far cry from the fur-coated, painted young woman who had visited him on New Year's Eve.

'So – you've come back,' he said finally.

'I must talk to you, father-in-law.' Then, when he remained motionless, expressionless, her voice rising a little, 'Please!'

Silently, he held open the door of his flat and she went inside. 'You know the way,' he said.

He made her sit by the fire, took her jacket politely and offered her a drink.

'Brandy? Whisky?' He studied her, his face still revealing nothing. 'You're shivering. You must have something.'

When she did not answer he poured her a large brandy and placed it on the table next to her before settling into the armchair opposite. He waited for her to speak, but instead she looked round the room, seeing it with new eyes. Here was where Micky Angel had grown up. There was the piano on which he had practised his scales day after day, there on the mantelpiece was the photograph of Micky and his grandfather, a little boy dwarfed by the powerful figure next to him. How had she not recognized that face last time she was here? Micky's dark eyes looked out at her solemnly from the photograph. How unhappy he must have been here, stifled by the expensive, soulless furniture, the carefully tasteful decor. No wonder he had exchanged it all for the scruffy blue room in Broadwick Street . . .

'Marionetta?' Her father-in-law's voice brought her back to the present with a start. She must not daydream about Micky – that was all over. 'Are you going to tell me what it is you want, or will I have to guess?' he was asking, watching her curiously.

'It's quite simple.' The clarity of her voice surprised her. She took a sip of the brandy, comforted by its warmth. 'I want to ask you to set my family free.' Alfonso was about to speak, but Marionetta held up her hand. 'Hear me out, please,' she said. 'You must know what Barty did to me, father-in-law. He almost killed me. He doesn't want me any more. He threw me out. Doesn't that make us quits? I was the debt, now I've been rejected. So I'm asking you to cancel the debt.'

She looked at him, her heart thudding. He was staring into the fire. It was as if he had not heard her. 'Father-in-law?' she said tentatively.

'I heard you,' he said. The silence between them grew. Still he stared thoughtfully into the fire. Marionetta waited, agonized. Finally he looked across at her, and her heart sank. She knew his answer even before he spoke.

'I warned you,' he said, 'I warned you what would happen if you carried on with your charitable work in Soho.' He shrugged, very Italian. 'So you disobeyed your husband and he smacked you about a bit. That's your

269

business – yours and Barty's. I don't interfere in my sons' private lives.'

She almost choked at the hypocrisy of the old man's words. He interfered all the time, whenever possible! He had even told his son who to marry, and the disastrous liaison between Barty and Marionetta had been the result.

He leaned over and took a cigar from an ornate-looking box. 'Your duty is to be with your husband,' he said in a tone of finality.

Angrily, Marionetta opened her bag and pulled out the newspaper cutting she had taken from the flat when she left. 'He doesn't want me!' she repeated, thrusting the cutting at Alfonso. He paused in the act of lighting his cigar and glanced at the cutting, his eyes registering no surprise as he absorbed the photograph of Barty with Peggy Whitmore. After a moment he handed it back to her and returned to lighting his cigar, making small gulping noises as the tip of the cigar glowed and faded, then glowed again.

'A man can have a mistress if he chooses,' he said. 'You were born in this country, you wouldn't understand. In Italy . . .' His voice faded as he leaned back in his chair, memories of his past seemingly invading the present.

Marionetta made a small impatient movement. He reminded her of Nonno sometimes – the same obsession with how things were done in Italy, even though they were in England. That wasn't so surprising, she realized; after all, Nonno and this man had grown up together in the same Sicilian village. It dawned on her then that trying to persuade this proud old man that she should be released from her marriage was exactly the same as if she had been trying to persuade Nonno, her dead grandfather, to do the same. Nonno, with his nineteenth-century views on the world, his old-fashioned, stern morality, his unbending sense of what was right in the Old Country which he had rigidly demanded of his family in London. Remembering the inflexibility of her dead grandfather, who had played in the fields with Alfonzo Moruzzi, who had fought with him, who had fallen in love with the same girl as him, she knew then that she would fail; but she had to keep trying, this was her only hope. 'I don't care if Barty has a hundred mistresses,' she said vehemently. 'I just want to be free of him. Is that so hard to understand?'

He was watching her now, his face in the shadows, only his eyes faintly visible in the glow of the fire, his expression unreadable. 'You're a good Catholic girl, Marionetta,' he said, his voice calm. 'Surely you're not suggesting I should condone any idea of divorce?' He coughed a little. 'What would the Church think, what would Father Joseph think, if he could hear you?' He leaned forward a little, his face intense, his eyes still fixed on her face. 'I believe in the sanctity of marriage,' he said. 'Why do you think I left your grandmother alone once she had married Franco Peretti, your Nonno? Because their union had been sanctified before God, Marionetta, just as yours was. What do they say in the marriage ceremony?' he asked pensively. '"Let no man put asunder" . . .' He watched Marionetta as she battled with her tears. 'Marriage is for life,' he said finally, in a dismal tone. 'For better, for worse. In my case, it was for worse. In yours, too, it would seem.' He sighed. 'Other people, like your grandfather, are more fortunate. That's the luck of the draw, *figlia*.'

She had to try once more. 'What about a legal separation?' she asked, trying to keep the desperation out of her voice. 'What about if I promised to stay out of trouble in exchange for leaving Barty?'

The old man shook his head slowly and decisively. 'Out of the question,' he said. 'You had your chance to stop your stupid charity work – you chose not to. There's nothing more to say.'

'I was going to stop,' she said, her voice shaking. 'But then Barty hit me . . .'

She was scrabbling in her handbag for a handkerchief, furious with herself for crying, when she had been so determined to be strong in the face of this challenge; but she had failed. 'Go back and try a bit harder to make it work,' Alfonso was saying dictatorially. 'Have a baby. Have two. I'm waiting for grandchildren, Marionetta.' His expression was bleak. 'I have none to speak of . . .' He was talking about Micky Angel. She forced herself to look indifferent, as if the question of his grandchildren was of no interest to her. He must never know about her and Micky.

There was no choice now. She would have to return to that hated suburban house, to Barty, and face the terrible consequences. She was sure she would be killed. She dabbed at her face.

'You're looking very beautiful,' Alfonso Moruzzi murmured, his eyes still fixed on her face. 'I can hardly see that scar from here . . . It could be Giulietta sitting there. Same eyes, same mouth, same neck . . .' She felt her flesh creep as the old man stared at her, devouring her with his eyes. 'I gave your grandmother a puppet once,' he said, his voice wavering a little at the memory, 'a little wooden *marionetta* . . . so beautiful . . .' There were, she realized with surprise, what looked like the beginnings of tears in his eyes. It seemed grotesque, this display of emotion in someone she knew only as a bullying autocrat. His voice wavered, dealing with emotions he had probably buried for many years. 'Women are precious, fragile things,' he said. 'They are there to be cherished by their men, to be caressed and loved.' He was leaning forward now, his breathing uneven, rasping. 'Little puppets . . .' He laid a gnarled hand on her knee, and she stiffened, appalled. 'I lost my *marionetta*,' he said, his eyes gleaming, 'but I'm happy my son has got his . . .'

She stood up suddenly, disgusted by his attentions. He was a loathsome old man, transferring his long-buried lust for a dead woman on to her, and in some warped excess of guilt, imagining that what he had felt for Giulietta Peretti could be displaced on to his psychopathic son.

'Where are you going?' he asked, looking up at her.

She crossed the room and collected her coat, her body like ice, her brain numb. 'I'm going where you are telling me to go, father-in-law,' she said. 'I'm going back to Muswell Hill. Back to my husband.'

And she walked out of the warm living-room into the draughty expanse of the hall, opened the front door and stepped out, slamming the door behind her.

She did not have enough money for a taxi. Instead she was obliged to take the underground to Highgate and walk along Muswell Hill Road towards Endicott Gardens, reliving in her mind the last time she had been here, under the gaunt trees and the faded undergrowth on the edge of Highgate Wood. It had been New Year's Eve and she had been running away. Now it was February and she had to go back. Her feet clipped eerily on the damp pavements. She walked rapidly, staring ahead, afraid that if she looked around or paused for a moment she would change her mind and turn back. She had no choice. She had to go back to Barty. No choice, no choice . . .

A fine drizzle cooled her face as she walked. A car passed, and for a moment she heard a snatch of a popular song blaring from the car radio, a tune she had heard Micky playing in the flat in Broadwick Street. She saw him then so clearly, sitting relaxed by the window in the untidy living-room, picking out the tune with one hand, humming a little to himself, then looking up at her with a grin and saying, 'Come on, then, join in!' She saw again the way he had smiled at her, and the light in his eyes whenever he had spoken to her. Micky Angel had really loved her. He had not cared about the scar on her face, he had not cared that she was married to someone else, nor that the someone else was one of the most evil men in London. He had not cared that loving her had put him in the most terrible danger: nothing had stopped him from simply loving her.

She had turned into the Broadway now, and was passing shops, people, the bustle of suburban life. She stared around her at passers-by: a tired-looking woman with two children in a pram, a grim-faced matron with an enormous amount of shopping, a girl in a mohair jumper emerging from a record shop. Were they in love, these women? Did they have their own Micky Angel waiting for them somewhere? Perhaps it didn't happen that often, she mused. Perhaps old Alfonso Moruzzi was right about something after all. What was it he had said? Something about for better or for worse, and it usually being for worse. She turned into Endicott Gardens. Perhaps she was luckier than she had thought. At least she had had the chance for a little happiness, a few short weeks discovering the potential for a story-book ending. Perhaps most people, like Alfonso Moruzzi, had never even had that chance. Perhaps the majority of people in the world simply plodded through life from birth to death and never really encountered much ecstasy in between. Perhaps, perhaps ... It didn't really matter, any of it. She had no choice. She must remember that. She was shivering. She had reached the gate of number 24.

For the first time since she had left Alfonso's Mayfair

flat, she paused. The house looked exactly the same as ever, with its neat net curtains at the windows, its tiny clipped front lawn, but to Marionetta it was the exterior of a prison, the respectable outer trappings of a torture chamber. She had no choice, she had to go back . . .

Slowly, she pushed open the gate and walked up the path to the front door. She knew that any minute now her husband would open the door, pull her inside, and the old nightmare of her life as Mrs Barty Moruzzi would begin again. Sure enough, she heard footsteps in the hall as she fumbled on the step for her front-door key, and before she could insert it in the lock, the door swung open. Filled with dread, she raised her eyes.

'Barty –' she began, and then stopped. Standing on the threshold was Antonio, her brother. She stood, blinking, the keys in her hand, dumbfounded. 'Tony?' she said disbelievingly. 'Tony?'

Without speaking, Tony simply held open the door and motioned for her to step inside. Speechless, she obeyed. Standing in the hall, wringing her hands, was Mrs McQueen. At the sight of Marionetta she let out a little cry and rushed forward. 'Mrs Moruzzi!' she exclaimed, her voice quavering. 'Madam!' She clasped Marionetta's hands, genuinely pleased to see her. 'I was so afraid of what that man was going to do to you – and it was all my fault! I'm so sorry, I'm so sorry . . .'

Dazed, Marionetta squeezed the woman's hand, too shocked by the sight of her brother in this house of all places to say anything. She stared at him over Mrs McQueen's heaving shoulders, her eyes questioning. 'Tony?' she said again. 'What are you –?'

He held up his hand, indicating Marionetta's former housekeeper with a small movement of his head. This was not the time for explanations.

Someone was emerging from Barty's study. Marionetta turned, bracing herself for her husband's first words. Of course. Tony had always been mixed up with the Moruzzis. They must have allowed him to emerge from hiding at last. The thought had hardly formed itself in her mind when her eyes registered that the figure standing in the doorway to Barty's private domain was not the man she was expecting: it was a uniformed police officer. 'Mrs Moruzzi?' he said politely. 'This way, please. The inspector would like a word . . .'

She was ushered into Barty's study. This was not a room she had been in often, since Barty forbade it; but she knew it had never looked like this. The entire contents of the filing cabinet in the corner had been emptied into piles on the floor, and a man in a dark suit was kneeling on the carpet, sifting through it, putting documents into various envelopes. Another man was perched on the corner of the large mahogany desk, gazing thoughtfully at a sheaf of papers in his hand. He looked up as Marionetta entered, and she knew she had met him before.

'Mrs Moruzzi,' he said, standing up politely. 'I'm Inspector Davis. We met a few years back – when your dad's café got smashed up. Of course I was only a sergeant in those days.'

She remembered then. He was in the Vice Squad and consequently would be involved in any investigation of the Moruzzi family. He was signalling to the uniformed officer to empty the room, and before Marionetta could say anything, she saw Tony being ushered away. Inspector Davis saw the look on her face and said, 'Don't worry, Tony's only going into the living-room for a minute or two. You'll have a chance to talk to him later.'

She stared down at the chaos on the floor. 'What are you looking for?' she asked.

He smiled again. 'It's more a question of what aren't we looking for,' he said. Then he became serious. 'Can I ask you where you have been, Mrs Moruzzi?'

She shook her head. 'No.' Her tone was emphatic.

The inspector raised an eyebrow. 'Very well,' he said after a pause. 'In that case, can I ask you when you last saw your husband?'

She moved carefully among the papers on the carpet, and sat on the edge of a small upright chair opposite the desk, unable to stand on her shaking legs for a moment longer. 'That's easy,' she said. 'I left here on New Year's Eve.'

He nodded, looking down again for a moment at the papers in his hand. 'That's what Mrs McQueen said.' His voice was thoughtful. He looked at her again. 'She said she was afraid for you. She thought your husband was going to hurt you.'

Marionetta shrugged. 'Well, as you can see, she was wrong.' She hated this. She was becoming like them, like the cursed Moruzzis. She was surprised at how smoothly the words rolled off her tongue, as she lied to protect her hated husband. But what choice did she have? Barty would be home at any moment, and he would be furious to find the police here, ransacking his desk. Still, she mused, at least it would mean his anger was redirected against something other than herself . . .

'I presume you have a warrant to search my husband's house?' she asked the inspector, daring to meet his eyes across the room, the tilt of her head defiant. He seemed to expect the question, and looked back at her, a disappointed expression on his face. 'Of course we have a warrant,' he said wearily. 'So are you going to tell me where your husband is?'

'I don't know where he is.'

He shrugged, indifferent. 'It doesn't matter. We'll pick him up sooner or later.'

She felt a small quiver of hope. 'Are you going to arrest him?' she asked, trying to keep her voice emotionless.

The inspector was looking at her again, this time more closely. 'Of course we're going to arrest him,' he said. 'We've got enough evidence against him to keep him locked up for at least twenty years, I'd say.'

Somewhat to his surprise, the young woman began to sob. She scrabbled in her bag for a handkerchief, and he pulled one from his breast-pocket and handed it to her. 'Very touching.' His voice was dry. 'It's nice to know Barty'll have a devoted wife to visit him in Strangeways ... Pity you'll both be collecting your pension by the time he gets out.'

She was shaking her head, her face hidden in the folds of the voluminous handkerchief he had handed her. 'You don't understand,' she said, her voice muffled. Then, suddenly, scrubbing at her tears in a gesture of irritation, she looked at him, and he saw that she was smiling. Funny, he couldn't remember the Peretti girl ever smiling before ... 'I'm glad you're going to arrest him,' she was saying, 'I'm glad ...'

The door opened and the uniformed officer appeared. 'The housekeeper wants to know if we want tea, sir,' he said, his face hopeful. The inspector was still looking at Marionetta, his face puzzled. He turned to the door. 'Fine,' he said. 'I was just going to suggest it –' he looked again at Marionetta '– if it's all right with you, Mrs Moruzzi?'

She was turning the handkerchief over and over in her hands. 'Of course,' she said, not really listening. Barty was going to go to prison! She would not be free, of course, there was still the debt to the Moruzzis to be lived through, but at least she would be free of him. She would not have

278

to live with a psychopath, would not have to fear his temper, his violent outbursts, nor bear his hands on her . . .

'Take Mrs Moruzzi into the other room,' Inspector Davis was telling the officer. 'She probably wants a quiet chat with her brother.'

Marionetta stood up gratefully. 'Thank you,' she said.

'Don't leave for a while yet, will you?' he said, returning to his scrutiny of the papers on the desk. 'I may have some more questions to ask you later.'

She followed the policeman out into the hall where Mrs McQueen was hovering, anxious to make amends for the past. 'Tea for everyone, is it, Mrs Moruzzi?' she asked.

Marionetta nodded absently. 'For everyone,' she said. Then she pushed open the door to the living-room and went inside. Tony was standing staring into the ornate electric fire. Marionetta went to stand beside him. 'It's cold in here,' she said. 'I'll put the fire on.'

Her brother turned to look at her. She gently put a hand up to his face. 'Tony,' she said, 'you look so tired . . .' And then she reached up to him and hugged him, too happy to see him again to say all the angry things she had been storing in her head for this day, if it ever came. She felt her brother's arms grip her tightly, and knew that he was as close to tears as someone with his strict ideas of manliness would ever be.

'I'm so glad you're alive,' she whispered. 'We thought we'd never see you again . . . We've all missed you so . . .'

'Have you?' his voice was husky. 'Even Papa? I thought he'd never forgive me −'

She pulled away a little and looked at him. 'Tony,' she said, mock-reproachful, falling easily into her old, teasing role, 'this is Papa we're talking about! You were always the apple of his eye − you think a little absence of a few years would change that?'

'I didn't know,' he said gruffly. 'I had no way of knowing . . .' He turned and sat down on one of the overstuffed settees, rubbing his face, overcome with a mixture of emotions. She went and sat next to him, drawing her legs up under her. 'Where have you been all this time?' she asked. 'We had no idea where to look for you . . .'

He shrugged. 'Various places. Bradford for a while. Then Glasgow.' He smiled bleakly at the memory. 'I even did a spell in the Hebrides for a few months.' He saw her blank expression. 'I was working,' he said, by way of explanation. 'Factories mostly. Engineering works. A cotton mill. Even a fish factory – that was the Hebrides.'

'You never even sent a postcard,' she said.

He shook his head, not meeting her eyes. 'How could I?' There was silence. Then he spoke again. 'I was afraid,' he said, a slight quaver in his voice. 'What am I saying?' He laughed bitterly. 'I was terrified, Marionetta. One whiff of where I was, and the Moruzzis would have had me killed.' He ran his fingers through his hair in a desperate gesture. 'But of course you know that, don't you?' His voice was filled with despair and self-loathing. 'Of course you do. You're married to one of those bastards. And it's all my fault.'

She took his hand, squeezing his fingers, not knowing what to say.

'My fault . . .' he was saying. He pulled his hand away, ashamed. 'You were right when you called me a coward all that time ago. I *am* a coward. I ran away and left you to face the music.'

'But you came back.'

'I heard you'd gone missing.' His voice was little more than a croak. 'I thought they'd killed you. I thought, it'll be Mario next, and that would finish Papa. I *had* to come back . . .'

'I know what that must have cost you,' she said quietly.

He shrugged. 'I went back to the Vice Squad offices,' he said. 'I told them everything. About how I'd got that tart to make a false statement about Silvia's murder.' He was staring at the floor. 'I told them I was a bent copper,' he said.

She touched his arm gently. 'And what did they say?'

'That it didn't matter now, that the Silvia Conti case had been concluded successfully, the right man had gone to the gallows, so the case was closed.' He laughed, a harsh sound. 'No thanks to me, of course.'

'But it's true,' she said. 'Lino Rinaldi didn't hang, Tony, that's the important thing to remember. You did a stupid thing – a – a dangerous thing – but it's over now. Justice was done in the end.'

He nodded slowly. 'I read about it in the papers. I was living in Glasgow then. I remember everyone talking about it in the pub, all the blokes from the factory.' He stared at her, his face full of pain. 'And I kept thinking, what if they knew I was the person that nearly got Lino Rinaldi hanged for a murder he didn't commit?' He buried his face in his hands again. 'I just kept on working, Marionetta. They made me foreman in the end, I worked so hard. I just wanted to forget – who I was, what I'd done – everything.'

'Your family?'

He nodded. 'Especially my family. I'd let you all down. I was supposed to be honouring the debt for papa, and I ran away. I was supposed to be your big brother who looked after you, and instead I left you to . . .' he could not finish the sentence, staring into space. 'Was it awful?' he asked finally. 'Being here? Being married to him?'

She did not want to talk to him about that. She had buried it for ever. Her heart was still singing because she

281

had realized she would never have to be alone in the same room with Barty Moruzzi again. He was going to jail! 'Tell me what they said when you went back to the police,' she said, changing the subject, 'tell me what they said about you disappearing.'

He looked at her again. 'They told me I'd be dismissed from the force,' he said. 'They told me they wouldn't be bringing any charges against me, since the case was closed. Then they started asking me questions about the Moruzzis' businesses in Soho, about what I knew. I told them everything. All about the key money Carmelo gets from the prostitutes when they want a flat; about which gambling clubs he owns under other people's names. I told them about Barty's protection rackets, and about the girls who got beaten up when they tried to leave Soho. I told them about the girl who died having a back-street abortion because Attilio Moruzzi wouldn't pay for her to see a decent doctor . . .' His face was contorted with the mounting anger and disgust he felt at his own involvement in these activities. 'I told them everything, Netta. Everything.'

She wanted to tell him how proud she was of him, even though she had hated him only a short while ago. She was proud that at last Tony had found the courage to face up to his mistakes, and to take the consequences; but she knew she could not tell him that, he would have broken down.

'Aren't you afraid of what the Moruzzis might do if they find out that you're telling the police all their secrets?' she asked instead, her voice mild.

He shook his head. 'I don't care, Netta. I've spent years on my own, in strange cities, sleeping in strange beds, and all that time,' his voice quavered dangerously, 'all that time, all I've wanted is to be with my family, back at the Imperial, in Soho, with you and Papa and Mario. That's what counts. To hell with the rest.' He brushed away a tear. 'Got a cigarette?' he asked abruptly. She shook her head. 'I don't care about the police force any more,' he said, his voice low. 'I just want a quiet life with you and Papa and Mario. I want to run the café. I want to help you with this club they talked about in the papers – what was it called?'

'The Mint.'

'That's it – the Mint. I read all about it – you know, when you and Lino were all over the *News of the World*. There was a picture. I was so proud of you, Netta.'

He was dangerously close to tears. Fortunately Mrs McQueen chose that moment to bustle in with a tea-tray, which she set triumphantly on the glass coffee table. 'Only powdered milk,' she said, 'I don't think anyone's been near the refrigerator since you left, Mrs Moruzzi . . . Shall I pour?'

Marionetta shook her head. 'No, it's all right, Mrs McQueen. I can manage.'

The woman backed away, eager to please. 'Well, if you're sure, madam . . . I'll go and see to those policemen.'

And she was gone. Tony grinned at Marionetta, his old self restored for a moment. 'Madam!' he exclaimed. 'I can't believe she called you madam!' Then he stared at his sister, as if seeing her for the first time. He registered the red sweater and the trousers, and the way she sat with her legs curled under her on the sofa, leaning forward to pour the tea, unaware of his scrutiny.

'You've changed, little sister,' he said.

She raised an eyebrow. 'I have?'

He studied her more thoughtfully. 'You've grown up,' he said finally.

She laughed, and handed him a cup of tea. 'I should hope I have!' she said. 'It's been a long time, Tony.' Then he saw the way Marionetta's mouth was turning up at the corners – both corners – in a smile, and he knew that this was the biggest change of all. He wondered what had happened. Had the Moruzzis paid for plastic surgery? Had they been kind to her, after all? Surely she hadn't been happy with Barty Moruzzi? The thought was so dreadful that he did not have the courage to frame it into words and to ask her. Instead he sipped at his tea, his eyes never leaving her face.

'You're looking good,' he said finally, in that grudging way brothers have of paying their sisters a compliment.

She laughed. 'I turn up here in a pair of tatty trousers and someone's old jumper and you tell me I look good!' She pulled a face at him. 'You should have seen me in my Moruzzi evening gowns and my posh fur coat,' she said, but somehow the joke fell flat, the very pronouncement of the name Moruzzi casting a shadow over their mutual pleasure at being together again at last, at being friends once more.

They both stared at the electric fire, as if willing some warmth to suddenly flicker into life there. Outside, a car pulled up with a screech of brakes.

'It's all there,' Tony said finally, 'the evidence. In Barty's desk. The police have never been able to get a warrant before, but now I've made my statement they'll be able to take him to court.'

'I know,' Marionetta said. 'Inspector Davis told me. All I can say is thank God.'

Tony looked at her, relieved. She was still the same sister he had left behind, then; she had not become part of the Moruzzi family, as he had feared. It was evident from the look of relief on her face that the thought of Barty going to prison brought her solace, not pain. He reached out and squeezed her hand.

284

'Drink your tea before it gets cold,' she said, smiling. Nothing more needed to be said. She got up and went to the window, peering out through the net curtains. 'It's another police car,' she said. 'Someone's coming up the path . . .'

They heard the front door open, and a muttered, urgent exchange in the hall, then silence. The door to the living – room opened and Inspector Davis stood there, his face solemn.

'What is it?' Marionetta asked, turning from the window to face him. He seemed uncomfortable standing there.

'You'd better sit down, Mrs Moruzzi,' he said. 'I have some news.'

She obeyed, returning to her place beside her brother, her mind racing. Surely it wasn't Papa. Or Mario. Dear God, had they found Micky Angel and hurt him? She looked up at the police officer. 'Just tell me,' she said.

He sat down in the armchair near the fire, looking at her, trying to gauge how she would respond to what he was about to tell her. 'Your husband's dead, Mrs Moruzzi. He was found shot through the head in a back room at the Treasure Chest club.' The young woman opposite was staring at him, her eyes large and dark in a white face.

'Dead?' she whispered. 'Are you sure?'

He nodded, his face grim. 'Certain.' He watched her as she absorbed this. It was difficult to say what she might be feeling. She looked as if she might faint. He leaned forward in the armchair, solicitous. 'Are you all right?' he asked. 'Can I get you a cup of tea?'

Tony Peretti stood up. 'I'll get some brandy,' he said decisively. 'Is this the drinks cabinet over here?' He headed in the right direction and busied himself finding glasses, sensible enough to see that his sister needed a minute to herself.

Finally she spoke, her voice little more than a whisper. 'Who did it?' she asked Inspector Davis. 'Do they know who did it?'

He sighed. This was the difficult bit. 'I'm afraid it's looking increasingly as though your friend Lino Rinaldi may have been involved,' he said.

'No!' she said, her voice breaking, 'No! Please don't say it, not Lino –'

'He's gone missing,' the inspector said bluntly. 'He seems to have run off with a young woman called Peggy Whitmore.' He paused, looking at Marionetta for a response. 'I'm sure I don't need to tell you who she is, there was a picture in the paper of her with your husband,' he began, but Marionetta waved her hand for him to stop, a very Italian gesture.

'I know all about Peggy,' she said. 'And you're saying Peggy and Lino have disappeared?'

Tony returned with a glass of brandy for his sister. 'Drink it,' he ordered. She obeyed.

Inspector Davis stood up, wishing the day was over and he could go home to his wife and have a brandy himself. 'It doesn't look good for them,' he said. 'They had both been at the club earlier. There are witnesses.'

'Surely that's just circumstantial?' said Tony, falling effortlessly into his old policeman role for a moment.

The inspector looked at him, his face wry. 'I need hardly tell you, of all people, Tony, that when all you've got is circumstantial evidence, that's where you start. You have no choice.' He stood up. 'You can go now, both of you,' he said, 'if you want. We don't need you here any more. Unless, of course, Mrs Moruzzi, you want to stay here.'

She shuddered and did not reply. 'The house probably belongs to you,' he went on politely, 'so if you wanted to stay –'

'I can think of nothing I want less,' she said very quietly.

The inspector headed for the door. 'You know where I am if you need me,' he said. The door closed quietly behind him.

Tony looked at his sister, concerned. 'Netta,' he said, 'are you all right? You're not going to faint or anything, are you?'

She laughed, tremulous. 'No, I won't faint. I'm just trying to absorb it. Barty's dead. I'm a widow. He's dead.'

Tony gripped her hand, which was holding the brandy glass and shaking. 'Yes, he's dead. Isn't that terrific? You're free, Netta! He's dead!'

She looked at him, anguished. 'I'm free of Barty,' she said, 'but that doesn't free us from the Moruzzis, does it? And Lino, poor Lino ... and Peggy Whitmore – you should see her, Tony, she's just an ordinary girl like me, and now she's hiding from the Moruzzi brothers in fear of her life. Barty's dead, but it's not over yet, is it?'

And at last she began to cry, spilling brandy on to the sofa, clutching at her brother and sobbing, 'When will it end, Tony? When will it end?'

They were about to leave the house half an hour later, Marionetta's face blotched from so many tears, when she remembered something. 'I must go back a moment,' she told her brother. She headed for the kitchen, where she had already said her goodbyes to Mrs McQueen. The housekeeper was adjusting her felt hat in the reflection of the back door as Marionetta appeared.

'Mrs Moruzzi,' she said, flustered. 'I thought you'd gone.'

'I almost had,' said Marionetta, 'But there's one more thing ...'

And she stepped out of the back door into the garden, now looking overgrown and forlorn, with the February damp clinging to the branches of the conifers that lined the end wall, and the drooping heads of dying plants bobbing in the sharp wind.

She called out and waited. There was silence for a moment, then the rustle of leaves in the evergreen. She called again, hope fading. Darkness was beginning to fall. Then suddenly out of the gloom a tiny creature hurtled across the tangled grass towards her. She knelt down and picked it up. 'Nevata!' It was indeed the tiny white cat, now a dishevelled and grimy grey. She could feel its tiny bones through the matted fur. 'Nevata, *povera*!' she murmured, holding the tiny body inside her jacket. Then she heard the growing rumble of a purr. Nevata, forgotten and starving in the past few weeks, would be all right after all. 'You're going to be a café cat,' Marionetta told her, 'you're coming back to Soho with me!' And, carrying the wet creature under one arm, she went back indoors.

Moments later, as neighbours' curtains twitched, Marionetta left the house in Muswell Hill for the last time. Arm-in-arm with her brother, clutching the bedraggled cat, she headed away from the claustrophobic suburban street without a backward glance. She was going back to Soho.

CHAPTER ELEVEN

March 1954

To Marionetta, it was like a dream. She was back behind the counter at the Imperial, shouting orders to Papa, balancing too many plates at once, hot and hurried, deafened by the noise of the wheezing coffee machine, the hiss of the chip fat and Mario's incessant cheerful singing.

Sometimes she would pause for a moment and wonder if it was not everything that had happened in the past few months that was in fact the dream. After all, here she was, simply Marionetta Peretti, as she had always been, Tomasso Peretti's daughter, a waitress. The house in Muswell Hill, the fur coat and, worst of all, Barty Moruzzi need never have existed here in this corner of Soho. But then she would see Nevata sitting in the back yard contentedly washing her luxurious white fur, or, with a sinking heart, she would see the Moruzzis' car slide past the windows, and she would know this was only a brief respite, the calm before the storm: the Moruzzis were not going to leave the Perettis alone for long, that much was certain.

For the moment, however, the Imperial and the Mint returned to a semblance of normality. The café continued to feed the workers of Soho their lunch, and to supply endless cups of tea to exhausted tourists; the Mint was still popular with the fun-seekers and the music lovers who frequented Soho at weekends, and Mario, who sang regularly now, was attracting a following of dreamy-eyed young women, much to Marionetta's amusement. Meanwhile a chastened Antonio now seemed content to be a café worker, and listened solemnly to his father's lectures on how to run the business, working harder than any of them and lightening Marionetta's load a little. Marionetta herself, now stronger and braver than in the past, had made a decision about her future, and one day in the café during a lull she decided to announce the news to her assembled family. She clapped her hands to stop their incessant flow of gabbled half-Italian, half-English conversation, and as they turned to stare at her in surprise, she said the words quickly, before she had time to think too hard. 'I'm going to leave the café,' she told them, 'and train to be a nurse!'

She waited for the explosion from her father. None came. He simply stared at her, open-mouthed, while Mario rushed forward from behind the counter to give her a hug.

'I can't believe it!' he said, delighted.

Marionetta grinned. 'What is it you can't believe? That I've actually enrolled as a student nurse, or that the hospital was mad enough to take me on?'

Tony, clearly pleased as well, laughed. 'Both, I should think! Well done, sis.' He came forward to give her a kiss on the cheek.

She turned to her father, who still had not spoken. 'Papa?'

He wiped his hands on his apron, an action she had seen him perform a hundred times before, and which she knew signalled a pronouncement. His children stood waiting for their father to give his opinion, as they had so many times in the past. Finally he spoke.

'You know what I think about young women going to work away from their families,' he began.

'But Papa, it's what I've always dreamed of –'

He held up his hand for silence. 'This is not the way things are done in Sicily. This is not what your Nonno would have wanted for you.'

Mario and Tony exchanged a look. This did not augur well. Tomasso sighed and sat down at a nearby table. He seemed suddenly older, smaller, more vulnerable. 'I can't stop you,' he said finally. 'It wouldn't be fair, not after everything you've been through this past year.'

Relief flooded through Marionetta's bones. She had done it! She had overcome the biggest hurdle of all – Papa's sense of tradition and Italian family values. She could hardly believe it! Impulsively she went and kissed him. 'I'll make you proud of me, Papa,' she promised.

He looked up at her, his face sad. 'You should be here, working with the family,' he said doggedly.

Tony made a movement, wanting to stop his father from spoiling the moment. He returned to his place behind the counter and picked up the knife he had been using to slice tomatoes. 'Just think,' he said brightly, 'she could be cutting out bits of people's insides soon!' And with a flourish he cut into a ripe tomato, so that the soft pulp in the centre oozed out on to the cutting board, making Mario groan in disgust.

Tomasso rose to his feet with a sigh. The world was beginning to move too quickly for him. 'I wish you luck, *figlia*,' he said finally. 'When do you start?'

'Training starts in two weeks,' she told him.' And, Papa, it's only round the corner, at the Middlesex Hospital. I'll never be far away.'

As her brothers went back to work, hopeful that the moment of crisis was over, her father pulled her back. 'You know there's a condition to all of this, don't you?' he whispered. 'If the Moruzzis say you're not to be a nurse, then you'll have to forget it . . .'

She nodded, silent, and went back to wiping the tables, trying to suppress the feelings of anger and frustration that she was sure were written on her face. Always the cursed Moruzzis controlling their lives!

Two weeks later, feeling strange in her blue uniform and starched hat, Marionetta began her training. From the moment she began, she loved the work. No task, no matter how dirty or futile, was too much for her. This was what she had always dreamed of doing, something useful and important, something that helped people. To her surprise, the Moruzzis had not intervened. As in the past, they had installed a series of large, surly, silent men in the corner of the Imperial who watched the comings and goings of the café without comment, sipping endless cups of tea and intimidating Tomasso when they collected their weekly protection money. For the moment, apart from this resumption of old demands, the Moruzzis seemed content to watch the situation and do nothing.

Sometimes, as she hurried through the dark streets in the early hours on her way home from a night on duty, she would glimpse Micky Angel through the smoky windows of a club, or see Peter Travis emerging from some dark cellar, struggling with his double bass. She would step back into the shadows, afraid to speak to them, afraid of what they might say. Did Micky Angel think she had stopped loving him? Were his friends even now telling him to forget her, that she was just a gangster's moll after all? Did they think she had simply run out on him and gone back to Barty on a whim? It was too painful to contemplate, so she stayed hidden, hoping against hope that she could somehow continue to live in Soho and never be seen by Micky Angel and his friends. It would be safer for all of them.

She had no idea what the Moruzzis would have done if she had stayed with Micky. Perhaps they would not have hurt him. He was, after all, a Moruzzi himself. Perhaps they would not have hurt her. But there was always Mario – bright, talented Mario, with so much ahead of him and so much to lose. Who was to say they would not turn their attentions to the only remaining Peretti untouched by their sordid activities? No, it was better this way, even if it hurt so much that sometimes she felt she would burst, so hard was it not to start weeping, and then weep forever.

Apart from her feelings for Micky, which she refused to confront or think about, Marionetta's life, with its new independence, had improved considerably. The café functioned happily without her, and the Mint was still flourishing, mainly thanks to Mario and his increasing reputation as a crooner. She ignored the speculation in the newspapers about Barty's death, and the announcement of the date of the inquest. She did not want to think about Barty, about her brutalized existence as his wife, about the sheer pleasure she had felt when she had been told he was dead. She worried sometimes about Lino and Peggy, who were still missing and still being sought by the police. But she could not – would not – become embroiled again in the sordid machinations of the Moruzzis and their victims. While she could, she wanted to make a life for herself, a life that gave her some freedom away from their evil stewardship.

One afternoon after a long shift she went into the Imperial for a quick cup of tea, to find her father and brothers in a state of excitement. 'Someone from a record company phoned this morning,' Mario told her, his face pink with anticipation, 'and they're coming round to hear me sing!'

It was Marionetta's turn to be delighted for her brother. 'That's wonderful!' she said. 'When are they coming?'

293

'This evening,' Tony said, 'and Papa says we can close the café early so that Mario and the band can rehearse!'

Marionetta looked at her father in surprise. Closing the café before the appointed hour was tantamount to revolution. He grinned at her sheepishly. 'Well,' he said, 'it's not every day your son gets to sing in front of important people . . .'

At seven o'clock the Imperial was in darkness, and the 'Closed' sign was on the door. Only one man refused to leave, following the Perettis downstairs to the club and installing himself at the back, unsmiling and watchful. They knew he had been sent by the Moruzzis, but they kept silent for Mario's sake, pretending to him that the man was a club regular who just couldn't bear to miss the audition of his favourite singer. Tony was posted at the door of the café to keep a look-out for the men from the Decca recording company, while Marionetta and her father, trying to ignore the presence of the Moruzzi employee, watched Mario rehearse with his band. When the men from the record company arrived – three of them, in sober suits – Mario was ready. He sang, as usual, like an angel, making Marionetta's heart glow as his voice soared to the ceiling of the tiny little club. The men from Decca needed little consultation; they simply nodded at each other, and then one of them approached the stage.

'Nice voice, Mario,' he said, as the Perretti family held their breath. 'It needs a bit of polishing, but you've definitely got talent. We'd like you to come along and make a demo disc at the studios. All right with you?'

It was more than all right. After the men had left, and the musicians were packing away their instruments and clapping Mario on the back, Tomasso opened a bottle of wine, so proud of his youngest son that he was almost beyond speech. It was Tony who held his glass aloft and made a brave toast. 'To the Perettis! May we all live to see Mario at the top of the Hit Parade!' They all cheered and drank. Then the sound of slow hand-clapping made them turn round. Standing at the foot of the stairs, applauding ironically, was Attilio Moruzzi. Behind him stood the man who had been watching the audition. Evidently he had gone quietly upstairs and let his boss into the café while the Perettis were celebrating. Now he discreetly resumed his seat in the corner.

'Congratulations.' Attilio did not move, leaning against the stair rail, a cold smile on his face. 'So nice you have something to celebrate. My family on the other hand,' he was slowly removing his gloves, 'my family is in deep mourning.' His eyes met Marionetta's across the room. She shuddered a little. Those were Micky Angel's eyes fixing her with their dark stare. 'So quickly out of your widow's weeds, Marionetta?' His eyes took in the nurse's uniform, his face expressionless.

She said nothing, afraid of what her anger and hatred might drive her to say if she started. The musicians stood frozen on the stage, unsure of what they were witnessing, but knowing they were in the presence of one of the Moruzzis, and afraid for their lives.

'What do you want, Mr Moruzzi?' Her father's voice was hoarse with fear, his hand unconsciously creeping protectively to Mario's shoulder.

Attilio smoothed the fingers of his leather gloves, his cold eyes watching the family grouped in front of him. 'I was passing,' he said. 'I thought you might like to hear some news.' His eyes were on Marionetta again. 'I've just come from the inquest into my brother's death.'

Marionetta made a sudden movement. 'No,' she said. 'I don't want to hear.'

'Netta!' Her father's tone was tense. 'Let Mr Moruzzi say his piece –'

'All right!' she said, her voice sharp. She could not look at this man. He was the father of Micky Angel, and if she met his gaze she was sure he would know everything. 'Tell us your news, Attilio, and then for God's sake get out!'

He was already mounting the stairs, his body taut with suppressed fury. 'I just thought you'd like to know,' he said, pausing for a moment, his face lit by the gleam of the stair light, 'that my brother wasn't murdered.' He watched with satisfaction as Marionetta slowly raised her head to look at him, an expression of disbelief on her face. 'Don't look so scared,' he said, smiling a little, 'he hasn't risen from the dead like Lazarus, if that's what you were thinking. No,' he went on, his tone conversational, 'apparently he shot himself.' His eyes moved glacier-like to Tony, standing protectively by his father. 'He knew the police were closing in on him. Then he heard you'd come back,' he said to Tony. 'That was the final blow. He knew you'd talk. He killed himself to save the rest of us. He decided to take responsibility for all our –' he hesitated '– our business affairs that had come to the attention of the police, if you understand me.' He was moving slowly up the stairs again, his face now invisible in the gloom. 'I thought you'd like to know that, you being an Italian family, I know you'll understand. Family loyalty, and all that.'

Mario shifted, not understanding. 'What's he talking about?' he asked no one in particular. 'What does he mean?'

'You'll know soon enough,' the disembodied voice said. Attilio had reached the top of the stairs and was talking now from the darkness of the café. 'I just wanted you all to know that they may have got Barty but they won't get the rest of us. There's no evidence. Barty's going to look bad in the papers, which is unfortunate, but the rest of us are clean as a whistle.'

Marionetta crossed to the foot of the stairs, moving too swiftly for her father to stop her. She looked up to where she could see the tall shadow of Attilio still looming in the darkness. 'You've told us,' she said, her voice shaking. 'You've done what you came to do. Now get out!'

'It's not over,' the voice was saying. 'You still owe us.'

'Get out!'

'Marionetta —' Tony had hold of her arm, pulling her back. She heard the quick sound of footsteps above her head. Attilio was moving into the café now, away from the door. There was a loud crash, then another. Before Marionetta could begin to mount the stairs, the man in the corner had stopped her, moving swiftly for such a large man.

'I wouldn't, if I were you,' he said. Marionetta was helpless, imprisoned by Tony's grip on one side and the man's on the other. She struggled for a moment and then stopped, resigned.

The café door slammed. Attilio Moruzzi had gone. The man let go of her arm. Tony ran up the stairs ahead of her, flicking on the lights in the café. She heard him groan.

'Oh, God . . .' he said.

She was behind him, and let out a little gasp at what she saw. The beautiful Gaggia machine had been ripped out of its place on the bench and was lying buckled on the floor, water dripping in a pool on the lino, sparks hissing from the ruins of its mechanism.

'What on earth is going on?' Mario was asking, puzzled. He had followed his sister up the stairs, with his father close on his heels and, a little way behind, the silent man who had been installed in the club by the Moruzzis.

'Good question!' Marionetta said, gazing at her father in despair. Behind them, they heard the bell of the café tinkle. The large man who had sat through Mario's audition was leaving quietly.

'Who *was* he?' Mario asked, confused but persistent.

Tomasso Peretti sighed and patted his younger son on the back. Now was not the time. This was Mario's moment. 'Nothing for you to worry about, son,' he said. 'Come downstairs and sing me "Smoke Gets in Your Eyes" again, will you?'

Tony and Marionetta were left alone, gazing down at the debris of their beloved Gaggia. Finally Tony managed an ironic smile. 'So much for protection,' he said. 'Shall we start clearing up?'

It was going to be a strange day, Marionetta thought. The April skies were full of gusting clouds scudding across the rooftops, and the trees rustled loudly in Soho Square as she emerged from St Patrick's after confession. She hurried down Greek Street, past the Mary and Martha Hospice, waving at the waiters in the little row of restaurants before the turning into Manette Street, her nurse's cape pulled tightly round her shoulders against the wind. She had volunteered to open up the café on her way home from the hospital night shift, and to instruct the couple from the catering agency who were going to run the Imperial for the day. She was still a little bemused by the change in Papa; this was surely the first time in the history of the café that he had allowed strangers to run it while he took a whole day off! But he had insisted that today was a special day, a day they should all be celebrating together, as a family. Lino Rinaldi and Peggy Whitmore were going to be married in St Patrick's. They had returned to Soho after reading in the newspapers that the inquest had delivered a verdict of suicide on Barty Moruzzi. Once again, Lino had been cleared of suspicion of murder. Now he and Peggy were going to be married, and Tomasso Peretti was determined that his entire family should be there to see it.

Marionetta had been more than a little puzzled; Papa had hardly known Lino, and certainly did not know Peggy at all. She supposed that part of his determination to attend was guilt at his tacit involvement in the Moruzzis' attempt to get Lino hanged for a murder he did not commit. Or perhaps – and she was sure this was the more likely explanation – he knew, as she did, that today was also the day of Barty Moruzzi's funeral. His body had finally been released by the coroner for burial. According to the newspapers, the funeral cortège would be passing through the streets of Soho. If the Perettis were all at a wedding, they could hardly be blamed for not putting in an appearance to pay their last respects to Barty Moruzzi, could they?

She sighed. Papa had never been very brave, and the Moruzzis brought out the worst in him. She turned into Old Compton Street and saw with relief a middle-aged couple waiting in the doorway of the Imperial. They seemed capable and pleasant, and were soon installed behind the counter dispensing tea to the early customers, while Marionetta checked downstairs in the Mint that everything was ready. This afternoon Peggy and Lino and the wedding party would be coming here for the reception, and Marionetta and her brothers had spent much of the previous day transforming the club from its usual late-night scruffiness into a flower-filled corner of Italy. The couple from the agency had their instructions: at two o'clock they were to close the café and set the tables upstairs for the food Marionetta had prepared. Downstairs Mario's band would play and there would be dancing. It was Marionetta's wedding gift to Lino, offered with Papa's blessing and received with much gratitude by her friend and his bride-to-be. After the events of the past year, Marionetta felt that this party was the least she could offer Lino. Perhaps with Peggy he could make a new start and forget the fact that he had twice almost been the victim of injustice at the hands of the British system. Perhaps after today some of the bitterness he felt about the country where he had worked so hard to lead a decent, normal life would be dissipated.

She stood at the back door of the café, staring out into the yard. Nevata was curled up asleep in a patch of sunlight on the fire escape. Marionetta rubbed her eyes. She would have to try to get some sleep this morning, just a few hours before the wedding . . .

'Marionetta!' She looked up. It was Mrs Lee Fung, at her usual place at the upstairs kitchen window. She beckoned to Marionetta conspiratorially.

Marionetta climbed the stairs of the fire escape until she drew level with her neighbour. Mrs Lee Fung was busy preparing vegetables at the sink as usual, and she did not stop while she spoke to Marionetta, her tiny fingers expertly slicing spring onions.

'Young man watching you,' she whispered. Behind her, a small child cried out, demanding attention. Mrs Lee Fung murmured something soothing in Chinese and continued chopping in neat, precise movements.

'Where?' Marionetta looked around her, surprised, but the Chinese woman shook her head.

'Not now. Before. And the other day, too. Outside. Doorway of the Three X's.'

'You mean the Triple X Club?' Mrs Lee Fung nodded, and Marionetta's heart sank.

'The Moruzzis again,' she said, half to herself, but Mrs Lee Fung had heard and was shaking her head vigorously.

'No, not them. Young man. Black hair.' Marionetta stared at her. Mrs Lee Fung paused and smiled into her young neighbour's eyes. 'Good-looking boy. I see him in the street, early morning, looking for you always.'

'How do you know he's looking for me?' She could feel her cheeks growing warm.

Mrs Lee Fung leaned out of the window and patted her hand. 'Because if you are in the café, he smiles. If you are not there, and it's your brothers or your father, he goes away, sad.'

'So he never speaks to you?'

Mrs Lee Fung shook her head again. 'I ask him once if he wants to leave a message. He says no, and walks away.'

'Thank you, Mrs Lee Fung. Thank you for telling me.' She descended the stairs slowly. So Micky Angel had not forgotten her.

'Good-looking boy!' Mrs Lee Fung repeated, grinning. 'Like Dirk Bogarde!'

She went back inside the Mint, closing the back door behind her. The place looked fresh and pretty, decorated with garlands and pink bows. Even the little wooden puppet, reinstated behind the bar, had been decorated by Mario with a tiny paper veil made from a napkin and a rosebud bouquet. 'You next, Netta!' he had said, when he showed her his handiwork. She did not have the heart to say that the sight of her namesake depressed her beyond measure. She feigned delight at the tiny figure, as well as at all the other wedding decorations in the club. 'Any bride would be delighted with it!' she announced to her brothers, but privately she thought to herself, it will never be me . . .

The wedding at St Patrick's was an emotional affair. Lino Rinaldi had become something of a folk hero in the Italian community in Soho, and it seemed as if every waiter, every commis chef, every humble café worker had turned out in their Sunday best to see him married. The church was packed, not only with beaming friends from the catering trade, but also with girls from the clubs who had worked with Peggy, all dressed in their smartest 'day' clothes.

301

The Peretti family was given pride of place in a front pew, and Marionetta had to struggle to prevent herself from crying as Peggy Whitmore appeared at the altar, smiling shyly from under her veil, resplendent in her fashionable wedding dress with its tiny waist and its enormous hooped skirt. As Father Joseph intoned the words of the ceremony and Lino and Peggy exchanged their marriage vows, Marionetta gazed at her feet, trying not to think about Micky Angel, and trying to forget that she, too, had once stood where Peggy stood. How different her wedding had been! A nightmare she could only half recall, as if her memory was being kind and casting a veil over the details. She envied Peggy; how strange to be saying 'till death do us part' and not actually wishing the man beside you at the altar would be struck down by a miracle from God, a lightning bolt – anything that would mean freedom from the dreadful tyranny of marriage to a man you hated . . .

Tony, seated next to her, was nudging her. 'Are you all right?' he whispered.

She nodded, and tried to concentrate again on the service. This was not the time to be selfishly regretting her own life, she told herself sternly. Today was a day of celebration! Still, as the congregation knelt to pray, she could not resist a glance at her favourite corner of the church, where the painting of Mary and Martha still hung. Mary and Martha, the meek and the defiant. She smiled a small, wry smile to herself. No matter how hard she tried, it was always Martha who attracted her, Martha, who had not wanted to accept her lot in life . . .

The reception was a huge success. It seemed as if most of Soho had crammed into the tiny café and the basement club, singing along to Mario's renditions of Italian ballads, dancing in a crushed huddle on the tiny dance-floor, somehow managing to eat all the food Marionetta had prepared. By five o'clock the tables upstairs had been cleared and the older people sat in groups drinking, while in the basement Mario and his band were playing louder and faster as the younger Italians danced the jitterbug and practised the new rock and roll.

Marionetta was upstairs dispensing chianti to a group of Lino's friends from Leoni's, when she noticed a sudden change in the atmosphere. She looked up. The noise from the basement was as raucous as ever, and the sound of laughter still floated up the stairs, but in the café people were moving away from the steamed-up windows, murmuring, uncomfortable. She came out from behind the counter, shaking off her father's attempt to stop her.

'No, Netta . . .'

She went to the window and made a small circle in the condensation on the glass so that she could look out into the street. She knew what she would see. Passing, very slowly, was a funeral procession. She could see the hearse, gleaming black and heaped with flowers, and the coffin within. Then the mourners passed. Immediately behind the hearse walked Alfonso Moruzzi, his head bowed, his face grey and sombre. Behind him his two remaining sons, Attilio and Carmelo the Pirate, walked slowly in step together, their heads held high, staring around them defiantly. On Old Compton Street people who knew the Moruzzis turned away, not wanting to acknowledge their presence, even at such a time. Strangers stood polite and immobile, removing their hats, murmuring prayers. A woman in a cheap fur coat crossed herself in the doorway of the Triple X Club. Carmelo nodded briefly at her; she was evidently an employee. As the two brothers passed the Imperial, Attilio turned his head and seemed to look straight at Marionetta. She stared back. This was Micky Angel's father . . .

'Come away, Netta.' It was Tomasso, who had joined her at the window. He put his arm gently round her shoulders and drew her away, back to the party.

Later, as darkness fell outside and the mood of the wedding guests changed to one of slightly inebriated sentimentality and Mario's music became more subdued to match, Marionetta was able to talk to Lino and Peggy for a few moments alone, at a table in a corner of the Mint, under the stairs. She had been passing, busy with a trayload of drinks for the girls from Gennaro's, when Lino had called her over and made her sit down.

'I wish you'd stop working and have a good time.' Lino's voice was reproachful. 'You should be dancing.'

'I like working!' she said, grinning at him. 'Anyway, who should I dance with, now the most eligible man in Soho has been taken away from me?'

Peggy, who had liked Marionetta instantly, laughed. 'You can borrow him for a quick cha-cha, if you like,' she said. 'I shan't mind.'

Marionetta smiled at her. It was difficult not to feel the ghost of Silvia hovering whenever she looked at Lino's new bride, but she liked the look of Peggy, with her pink cheeks and open smile. 'He's yours now,' she said, half-joking, half-serious. 'You should hang on to him now you've got him!'

Lino leaned across the table and touched Marionetta's arm. 'We want to thank you,' he began, 'for everything . . .'

She pushed her chair back and stood up. 'You already have,' she said, 'just by being here.'

'I mean it, Marionetta.' His eyes were grave. She, in turn, became serious, and leaned across the table to give him a warm kiss on the cheek.

'I'm just so glad you and Peggy came back,' she said simply. 'Now you really can start again.'

Before Lino could reply, someone called to Marionetta from the stairs. There seemed to be some problem in the café.

'I'll talk to you later,' she told the couple. 'Now go back to your dancing before Mario sees you slacking in the corner!'

She turned quickly and ran upstairs. A small crowd had gathered round the doorway of the café, and seemed to be preventing someone from entering. Tomasso was shouting in Italian and gesticulating. '*Andatevene*! Get out of my café, *sudiciona*!'

Marionetta pushed through the guests. Propped up against the door post, her head lolling to one side, her eyes glassy, was Suzanne Menlove, drunk and determined. 'Come to pay my respects . . .' she murmured. 'Happy couple . . .'

'Not in my café,' Tomasso began, but Marionetta intervened.

'No, Papa. You must let her in.'

He stared at his daughter, amazed. Had she lost her senses? 'But she's a drunk!' he exploded. '*Un'ubriacona*!'

'I don't care.' Marionetta was firm. Ignoring her father, she took Suzanne Menlove's scrawny arm in hers and guided her to a table. Tony was gaping at her from behind the counter. 'Bring this woman a large drink!' Marionetta commanded. Tony looked at his father and did not move, unsure what to do. Marionetta made a movement of impatience. 'This woman saved my life once,' she told the assembled company, her eyes fixed on her father. 'I wouldn't be here if she hadn't –' She was unable to finish the sentence. Her eyes filled with tears. 'People like her, Papa – they're as much a part of Soho as we are.'

Tomasso looked from his daughter to the grey-haired woman slumped at the table, then back to his daughter again. There was a moment's silence. Then, 'All right, Tony,' he said, his voice gruff, 'get the woman a drink.'

The moment of tension was over. The guests moved away, relieved, and soon the café was buzzing with noise and laughter again. At her table, Suzanne Menlove watched the proceedings with a dignified hauteur from behind her wine glass, her eyelids drooping. She seemed content to sit there, observing rather than participating. Tomasso glowered at her nervously from behind the counter.

'She's all right, Papa,' Tony said, seeing his father's face. 'She never gave us any trouble down at the station whenever we pulled her in.' He turned to his sister. 'Come on, you. You haven't danced with your favourite brother yet.' And he pulled Marionetta down the stairs and on to the dance-floor. The band was playing a waltz, and he whirled his sister round competently, half an eye on an attractive waitress from the Café Bleu who was giggling with her friends by the stage. 'You're looking good, sis,' he told Marionetta. 'Some bloke's going to snap you up one day.'

She smiled wryly up at him. 'What, old Scarface Peretti? I doubt it.'

He shook her a little, reproachful. 'That's not funny.' They circled the edge of the floor, jostled by the other dancers, all crowded into the tiny space. '*Faccia d'angelo*, that's what they call you . . .'

She stopped and stared up at him. 'Who does?'

He moved her back into the crush, his mind still on the Café Bleu waitress. 'Those musicians who used to come to the club and hang around – you know, the bloke with the glasses, played the double bass – his gang . . . they used to call you *faccia d'angelo*,' he repeated.

Her hand flew to her cheek. 'Angelface . . .'

Gently, Tony removed it. 'Don't,' he said. 'You don't need to do that.' And he whirled her away with a flourish, into the pack of sweating dancers, the music ringing in her ears, and Mario's sweet voice singing above the band, seeming to murmur *'Faccia d'angelo, faccia d'angelo . . .'*

It was midnight. Amidst much cheering, Lino and his bride had left in a taxi to catch the last train at Paddington Station, bound for a week's honeymoon in Brighton. Upstairs in the café Suzanne Menlove had fallen asleep, slumped across a table, surrounded by a group of men who shouted politics at each other in the colourful accents of Northern Italy. Downstairs, the more determined and energetic of the dancers were still circling the floor. Marionetta stepped out of the back door for a moment to cool her hot cheeks in the night air. Nevata uncurled herself from the fire escape and came towards her with a soft miaow. 'Mind my dress, little one,' Marionetta murmured, bending to caress the cat. She was wearing a lavender-coloured chiffon dress bought specially for the occasion, and it fell in soft folds around her as she knelt. She was lost in thought, stroking Nevata's soft fur, when her father suddenly appeared behind her, white-faced.

'You'd better come, Netta,' he said abruptly. 'Someone is asking for you.'

She followed Tomasso back into the club. The band had fallen silent, and the dancers were standing around the edge of the dance-floor in nervous groups. Alone in the centre of the floor stood Alfonso Moruzzi, an expensive black coat draped over his shoulders, the black armband still in place on his sleeve. There was absolute silence. The old man, gazing slowly around him, seemed to be enjoying the sensation his entrance had caused. His eyes lit on Marionetta. She walked towards him, somehow unafraid. She had been waiting for this moment. It had been inevitable.

'Marionetta,' he said, unsmiling. 'You are looking very

beautiful tonight. You bring back some powerful memories.' His eye suddenly caught something behind the bar. Slowly, he stepped forward and reached out. He was plucking the wooden puppet from its place on the wall. He held it for a moment, looking at the painted smile, the paper veil, the rosebuds in its wooden fingers.

She turned to the band who stood silent, clutching their instruments. 'Please,' she said, 'please carry on playing.'

Alfonso Moruzzi took a few steps towards the stage, looking at Mario, paralysed behind the microphone. 'Yes,' he said, 'Please continue. I wish to have a private conversation with Signorina Peretti here. I have no desire to spoil the party.' Mario nodded nervously to the band, and the music started again. Ignoring the stares of the guests, Marionetta turned calmly to the old man. 'You had better come with me,' she said.

He followed her out into the back yard, still carrying the puppet, and she closed the door. She could faintly hear the sound of a trumpet blasting out the tune of 'Oh, Mein Papa' inside the club. She was not afraid. This moment had been inevitable. The old man had come to tell her what she must do to keep the Perettis' part of the bargain with his family.

She turned to him, resigned. 'Well,' she said, 'what do you want to say?'

'You're shivering. Shall I lend you my coat?'

She shook her head impatiently. She just wanted him to say what he had to say and then leave. He placed the puppet carefully on the wall beside him, then pulled a cigar from his pocket and lit it, puffing slowly. She watched the smoke rings curling slowly up towards the Lee Fungs' kitchen window. For once, the window was in darkness; the Lee Fungs were at the wedding reception.

'I buried my son today,' Alfonso Moruzzi finally said.

'Your husband.' She said nothing. There seemed to be nothing appropriate. He sucked thoughtfully on his cigar, watching her. 'I know,' he said. 'I know about you and my grandson.'

She felt as if the blood had drained out of her body. She reached out and clutched the cold metal of the fire escape for support. 'How?' she whispered, somehow unable to find her voice.

She could not see his face, only the bulk of his overcoat and the glow of his cigar. 'You remember the day you came to see me?' he asked after a moment. 'The day you asked me to set your family free from the debt incurred by your grandfather?' She nodded, her heart pounding in her throat. 'Shortly after you left that day,' he said, 'I had another visitor. It was Michelangelo, my grandson.' He paused for a second or two, for effect. 'And do you know what he asked me?' Now she could see his eyes gleaming in the darkness. She shook her head. 'He asked me exactly what you had asked me. He asked me to release the Peretti family from its obligation to the Moruzzis.'

He stepped towards her and placed a finger under her chin, gently pulling her face towards his. 'I had not seen Michelangelo face to face for several years,' he went on. 'I knew it must have taken a lot to make him come back and ask me for something. And he did not just ask – he begged.' He held her gaze, his mouth quivering a little. 'I asked myself a question – what on earth would make a stubborn, proud boy like my grandson do such a thing? And then I knew. He was just like I was when I was a boy, so of course I knew.' He was very close to Marionetta now. She could smell the scent of his expensive aftershave. 'He had fallen in love,' the old man said, 'just as I did. He had fallen in love with the granddaughter of my beloved Giulietta, the girl I lost to a Peretti all those years ago in Sicily.'

He stepped away from Marionetta, his breath rasping, seemingly overcome with emotion. Incongruously, Nevata appeared from the shadows and began weaving around his ankles, her purring the only sound in the soft spring night apart from the distant beat of the music inside the Mint. Then the old man spoke again, his voice low. 'I just need to know one thing,' he said. 'Do you feel the same way about him?'

Marionetta nodded, not trusting herself to speak. Alfonso Moruzzi sighed, a small, lonely sound. 'In that case,' he said, 'I have come here to give you a gift. I don't give it happily or with any sense of generosity, because that is not the kind of man I am. I give it because of my grandson, the only person in this world I have ever loved, apart from your grandmother.'

Marionetta was gazing at him, her face full of hope. She would never know how the sight of her, so young and fresh in her lavender dress, wrenched at the old man's heart. 'I'm giving you back your freedom,' he said. 'I have come to tell you that the debt of honour has been fulfilled. You kept your part of the bargain by marrying Barty, and now Barty is dead.' His voice shook with anger. 'Suicide!' He spat out the word. 'He committed a mortal sin, and this will be my family's eternal shame!'

He threw his cigar to the ground in a shower of tiny sparks and then ground it into the earth with his heel. 'My sons are a great disappointment to me,' he said, his voice almost normal again. 'Between them they produced only one son – Michelangelo – and he has rejected the family.' He drew his coat around him and turned towards the entrance. 'I'm going home,' he said, 'back to Sicily, back to my village. I'm closing down my business interests in London. It's time my sons made their own way in the world.'

Marionetta stared at him, too surprised to absorb the full implication of his words. All she could see was a proud, sad old man who had lost everything. 'Marry my grandson,' he said to her, his hand on the door. 'Marry Michelangelo and have lots of sons. Perhaps one day you will visit me in Sicily. My family will not trouble you again.' He thrust something into her hand.

There was a sudden rush of warm air, bright lights and laughter, and then Marionetta was alone in the darkness again. She looked up at the dark sky above Soho. A star was twinkling high in the heavens. Then she looked down at what was in her hand – the little wooden puppet in its paper veil. 'Marry Michelangelo,' he had said. 'Have lots of sons . . .'

She did not know where to find him, but she knew he would be somewhere in Soho, playing his piano in some dingy little club. She ran out into the street, still clutching the puppet, not noticing the cold. She hurried along Old Compton Street, through the crowds of late-night theatregoers, the drinkers and gamblers, the bored-looking prostitutes shivering on street corners. Suddenly she saw a familiar figure hunched in the doorway of the London Casino. It was the little one-legged man who usually stood in the doorway of Madame Valerie's. He was doing the three-card trick for the benefit of a gaggle of bemused German tourists. He waved at Marionetta. 'Funny to think we was at war with these chaps a few years ago,' he said with a grin, 'and now we're taking their money!'

'Do you know where Micky Angel is tonight?' she asked him breathlessly.

'Plays piano in that combo with Peter Travis – that one?'

She nodded. He pointed behind him. 'Meard Street. The Kitten Club. Next to the Gargoyle. At least, that's where they were last week . . .'

She ran on, calling her thanks, but he was already engrossed in his trick again. 'See this lady? The Queen of Hearts? I'm going to put her in the middle of these two other cards here, like this . . .'

When she arrived in Meard Street and saw the sign for the club, she realized she had been here before. Of course. This had been the Black Cat Club, where she had first met Micky Angel. She climbed the stairs, panting slightly, out of breath, still clutching the puppet, her heart hammering. A large man was standing on the grimy first-floor landing, smoking a cigarette and watching her coming up the stairs with interest. She remembered him from her first visit. 'You're Billy the Bear, aren't you?' she asked, her haste making her brave. He inhaled thoughtfully, studying her face. 'And you're the one they call Angelface,' he said. 'He's in there. They're playing the last number.' He indicated the doorway of the club with a jerk of his head.

Breathlessly, Marionetta pushed open the door and stepped inside. At first it was difficult to see in the gloom of the tiny club. A cloud of cigarette smoke hanging in a pall over the dance-floor obscured her view of the musicians, although she could hear the sound of the piano and Vicky singing 'Secret Love' in a husky voice, trying to emulate Doris Day. The dance-floor was crowded with couples, and the tables round the walls all seemed to be full. The atmosphere was somnolent, the kind of sleepy ambiance she recognized from the closing moments of nights in her own club: people were preparing to leave and start their journeys home, warmed by alcohol and love songs. Slowly she moved forward, standing with the puppet clutched to her heart, and watched Micky Angel finish playing the song. As his hands rested on the keys and Vicky's voice faded away, he looked up and saw her, standing in a circle of light on the other side of the dance-floor.

For a moment, as she waited for his response to seeing her there, she thought her heart might stop. But then he suddenly smiled at her, that smile she remembered so well, and he got up, gently closing the lid of the piano. He said something to Peter Travis and Vicky, who looked across at Marionetta and grinned. Then he was next to her, his hand under her arm.

'It's all right,' she heard herself say. 'Your grandfather – it's all right.' He stared down at her, trying to absorb her words.

'Let's get out of here,' he said. He guided her towards the door, grabbing his coat from behind the bar as they went, and propelled her down the stairs, calling good-night to Bill the Bear who watched impassively from the landing.

Out in the narrow, unlit street they both began automatically to walk towards Dean Street and the lights of Soho.

'Tell me what you just said in there,' Micky Angel said. 'Tell me again.'

She did. He stopped then and looked at her, suddenly realizing that she was shivering. He put his coat carefully round her shoulders. They were almost at the junction with Dean Street, where cars were passing, and the shouts of people heading for the underground could be heard. A prostitute strolled past them, yawning. Micky suddenly noticed the puppet still dangling from Marionetta's hand, its strings tangled, its wooden eye staring up vacantly through the little paper veil. Gently, he prised it out of her hand. 'You don't need this any more,' he said. A street sweeper was passing, trundling his dustcart ahead of him, his brooms tied to the cart handles, his work finished for the night. Micky called to him, stepping out into the road, and dropped the puppet into the dark interior of the cart.

Marionetta smiled. It was funny, she had thought it would be difficult to let go of the past, but as she watched the puppet disappear she felt only relief. Perhaps it was going to be easier than she had thought. Micky Angel was beside her again. 'Come back to my flat,' he said. 'We've got a lot of catching up to do.' She hesitated for only a second. After all, she was a woman now, not the plaything of her family or the Moruzzis. She could do what she wanted with her life. She was free.

'All right,' she said.

'Just one thing.' Micky Angel was close to her now, and he put up his hands and held her face gently. She felt his fingers lightly touch the scar on her cheek. 'Before we go . . .' And he kissed her, full on the mouth.

There was a flutter of wings, and a pigeon flew upwards, away from them, towards the rooftops of Leicester Square. As they embraced in the joyful silence of that shadowy side street, further away the pigeon was flying over the neon-lit brightness and bustle of the main streets of Soho, where another Saturday night was in full swing. The prostitutes, the gamblers, the be-boppers and the jazzers, the barboys and the waitresses, the Greeks, the Italians, the West Indians, the Maltese, all carried on with their lives as they had always done in this vibrant corner of London. Laughing, weeping, working, playing, they were oblivious of the story drawing to its close in the kiss of two lovers under the hazy light of a street-lamp in Meard Street. For they all had a story to tell, if only someone would stop for a moment and listen . . .